A Fenced Yard

Penny Harris Smith

A Fenced Yard

Copyright 1999
By Penny Harris Smith

ISBN 0-7394-1995-1

This novel is a work of fiction

The characters, names, incidents, dialogue, and plot are products of the author's imagination or are used fictitiously. Any resemblance to actual persons or events is purely coincidental.

Manufactured in the United States of America

Cover Design by: Dan Shoemaker

Dedication

This novel is dedicated to the most important people in my life, who love me unconditionally.

To Dennis, my husband and my best friend. Thank you for teaching me what real love is all about and for bringing out the best in me.

To our two miracles - our son Shane, my clone and my constant teacher. Thank you for helping me to see myself more clearly. And our daughter Paris, our piece of sunshine. I pray that you will never lose your glow.

And finally to my mother, Dottie Dell Harris who taught me that we hold the key to our happiness. May I be able to leave that legacy to my children.

ACKNOWLEGDEMENT

I humbly acknowledge that I could not have written this book without the divine guidance of my heavenly Father. Thank you God for putting me in a situation that forced me to seek you first. Thank you for the tears and the pain, for without them my life would still be in shambles. Thank you for all the people and things you put in my life, at the right time, to capture my attention. I have finally found your wonderful peace.

I want to thank Gloria Ann Smith, who is one of our human angels. Thank you for always being there for us and for being the trusted keeper of our treasures.

I want to thank Nia Ward for her spiritual guidance and help in studying the Word. Those lunchtime Bible studies were the answer to my prayers, even thought I didn't realize it then.

I want to thank Mrs. Joy Green for providing editorial assistance, spiritual guidance and prayers.

And finally, I want to acknowledge all of our family and friends who have been a constant source of blessings. God continues to bless us with wonderful supportive family members and friends that we hope to keep for a lifetime. It would take another book to name everyone, but you know who you are.

Introduction

Paula had just put her two-year old daughter down for an afternoon nap and prayed that the reverberating noise from the neighbor's lawnmower would not wake her. It was a beautiful summer day in St. Louis with warm, tranquil breezes. The upstairs windows were open to give the breezes an unobstructed path through the house. Paula wondered if opening the windows to air out the house was such a good idea after all. But the gentle breezes and the smell of freshly cut grass had a soothing affect on her. Something she needed dearly in preparation for her afternoon battle of the wills with her four-year old son. They had just finished their daily debate on his need for a nap; a battle that Paula reluctantly realized she was not going to win. Thank goodness she could still demand an hour of quiet time in his room. She really needed time to think and deal with her escalating anxiety and conflicting emotions. The decision had to be made today.

Paula stared out the window of the upstairs office. The hill was slowly transforming from the barren eyesore of last year. The tangerine marigolds were spreading to form lush circles around the two young saplings. The view from the office allowed Paula to see the full effect. She surveyed the landscape admiring how the contrasting yellow blossoms on the sundrops, the red leaves of the sand cherries and the green, ball-shaped hedges complimented the vibrant spheres. The colorful

1

menagerie of plants painted an original work of art against the rich brown canvas of newly spread cedar mulch and the sea-green carpet of recently mowed grass. Paula was pleased with their decision to put sod at the base of the hill to reduce the size of the bed and change the shape. The scalloped grass border had softened the transition to the hill. The hours of planting, weeding and watering were paying off.

When they moved into the house, the "hill" was a huge, rectangular shaped area spanning the rear width of the lot. Between the house and the hill was an expansive yard, surrounding a wooden swing set in a bark-filled area. The yard had been the deciding factor for them selecting the house. It was like a small park and the perfect size for their son and daughter to run and play. Their yard merged with the neighboring yards to form a vast, open area the length of a football field.

The previous owners had given up on trying to grow substantial grass on the hill. So they killed the remaining grass patches and planted a few shrubs at the base and two young trees at the edges of the hill, prior to putting the house on the market. Paula was amazed that the two trees were surviving the continuous assaults by the neighborhood teenagers who used their backyard as a short cut between the sub-divisions. The developers, who planned meticulously for the vehicular traffic flow, failed to plan for the intermingling of the children. Paula was also appalled at the obvious absence of home training. When she was growing up, you never crossed through someone's yard without asking permission. Not only did these rambunctious children fail to ask permission; they had a disturbing lack of respect for private property.

During the winter, when the hill was snow-covered, the teenagers used the young trees as supports to keep their balance. The remainder of the year, bike riders frequently barreled down the hill with little concern for what was in their path. Paula and her husband had talked about installing a fence to protect their property. But they were afraid that a fence would take away from the openness and doubted if the permissible four-foot fence would even deter the teenagers. Despite all the hard work and her frustrations with the teenagers, Paula was determined to turn the hill into a showpiece.

Paula and her two children had spent the early afternoon at the neighborhood pool. They lived in a Swim Community with mandatory membership in the Homeowner's Association. The association had a covenant that governed the neighborhood from the type of fences that could be installed to the time of day that cars could be parked on the street. Additionally, every homeowner also had to pay a substantial annual assessment for the pool, whether they used it or not. Last summer, Paula and her children had gone to the pool only twice. This year, Paula wanted to get their monies worth. Since she had taken a leave of absence to regain control of her life, she had planned to go to the pool at least twice a week. But after today, she wasn't sure if it was worth it.

Paula was still reeling from the encounter, which was making her decision even more difficult. They were usually the only people with a genetic tan at the pool during the day. Although her children loved playing at the pool, Paula was getting tired of the constant stares and snubs. When they arrived at the pool soon after it opened, there were several other children splashing in the toddler pool. Within five minutes of Paula's children getting in, the others were removed. Paula was angry initially but her children seemed to enjoy having exclusive use of the pool.

As her son and daughter ate lunch, Paula carefully took in her surroundings and listened to the laughter and idle chatter of the other mothers. They seemed so content with their role of housewife or stay-at-home mom. Paula was not even sure what the term was these days. All she knew was that as she surveyed these women, she was overcome by the strangest sensation. She wasn't sure if it was panic or frustration. Despite the fact that Paula had functioned in a predominately white environment since the sixth grade, Paula never felt more alienated in her life. But she knew she had no one to blame but herself. They had chosen this environment but could she adapt to the lifestyle.

When her husband took the job in St. Louis, she had become the "trailing spouse". They had talked about her taking a break from the job market prior to the move. But the difference in housing costs between Atlanta and St. Louis seemed to rule that option out. After three moves in five years, they were not sure how long they would stay in St. Louis so finding a house with strong resale potential was a requirement. Their formula for selecting houses that could sell quickly worked well. Their previous two houses had each sold in less than two weeks. But the formula required buying houses located in a predominantly white suburban neighborhood with highly rated schools. For them to live on one income and meet their resale criteria would require moving into a less expensive neighborhood with a potentially different set of problems.

Paula knew from experience that lower middle-income, all white neighborhoods could mean racial trouble. If you knew what to look for, you could sense it immediately. When they looked at homes or drove through potential neighborhoods in the lower price bracket, the homeowners stared or looked away. Paula suspected it was a "blue collar, there goes the neighborhood" mentality because when they looked at homes or surveyed neighborhoods in the higher price bracket, the homeowners were more congenial.

Equally important in the home search effort was Paula's desire to maintain or improve her standard of living. This was going to be their fourth house and Paula was determined not to buy less home or quality. One realtor had accused Paula of having champagne taste on a beer budget.

Finding the right house took time. They temporarily moved to a two-bedroom, furnished apartment after their initial house hunting trip only produced disappointment. After three months of looking every weekend, they finally found the house with the hill. The price solved the dilemma of whether Paula would get a job. She took an Engineering job at a manufacturing plant with the same employer as her husband. The job was not very exciting or challenging. But with two children under three, Paula knew she had enough challenges in her life.

However, Paula and her husband decided it was time to reconsider their decision regarding her job after fifteen months of rushing between daycare and work. Their daughter had just graduated from the security of the infant room to the pandemonium of the toddler room. Paula had reservations about the quality of care her daughter would receive in the new setting. The law only required one provider for every eight children over two and Paula knew how chaotic handling "one" two-year old could be, validating the "terrible two" label. She wondered how two adults could successfully handle sixteen two-year olds, but decided to try the arrangement before passing judgement.

The transitions did not go well for Paula or her daughter. Each morning it got more and more difficult to leave her crying daughter. Paula had to fight back her own tears as she drove to work. Couple the dislike of two-year old daycare with the fact that every major illness or accident inevitably occurred when Daddy was out of town and Paula had an important meeting made the decision to take a short break easier for Paula. So after paying their taxes in April, Paula started a six-month leave from her job. Six months would be just enough time to get her son settled in a pre-kindergarten program and her daughter in the more civilized pre-school program. But after four months at home, she got the call about a promotion if she could return to work immediately. Paula knew the job would require long hours and limited flexibility. But it meant substantially more money and opportunities like it did not come along often.

Before the call, her husband had suggested that the leave become permanent. They both knew it was the best thing for their children, but Paula was leery of its impact on her, wondering if she could lose part of her identify that she had worked so hard to achieve. She was also afraid of giving up her self-sufficiency; if her husband left her, she needed to be able to take care of her children.

Other women made the transition. But Paula was concerned that she did not know too many African-American, professional women who were successful converts. She wondered if it was easier for women of other races?

Paula had made a lot of decisions in her life. Some without enough thought that she would regret the rest of her life and one that almost took her life. She did not want any more regrets. Paula was beginning to doubt if having choices was truly a blessing and wondered if her mother had made different choices would her life have followed a different path.

Paula got up, went into her daughter's room and looked down at her baby sleeping so peacefully beneath her flowered security blanket that was once Paula's robe. She knew she needed to consider the impact of her pending decision on her daughter. From the moment Paula found out she was having a daughter, she prayed that she would be more successful than her mother in protecting her from some of life's harsh lessons.

What would be her legacy to her daughter? Does it really matter? As Paula stood there looking at her precious little girl, she remembered the chapter in her life that taught her the consequences of hasty decisions and the power of love.

"Trust in the Lord with all your heart and lean not on your own understanding;

in all your ways acknowledge him, and he will make your paths straight."

Proverbs 3: 5-6 NIV

Chapter 1

The drive went quickly as Paula maneuvered the streets in autopilot. The excitement of starting her senior year of high school had kept her up late and then she had overslept. As she pulled into the congested student parking lot, she wished she had left home fifteen minutes earlier. The parking lot resurfacing was supposed to be finished but it appeared that the work had just started, reducing the available spaces. The elderly parking lot attendant directed Paula and the other late arrivals to the remote stadium parking lot.

Heat waves were rising off the freshly laid asphalt toward the cloudless blue sky. The fumes from the hot asphalt combining with the unusually high humidity made Paula nauseous as she got out of the two-tone brown, AMC Hornet.

How can it be this hot at eight in the morning?

Paula quickly grabbed her brown leather bag and spiral notebook from the cluttered passenger seat of the car. The vehicle originally had been the family car until her mother acquired a new one, then it became a "rite of passage" on the way to adulthood. As each sibling graduated from high school, the car passed to the next in line. Paula, who was the third recipient, felt sorry for her little brother, Eric who would inherit the car next. There was not much left to rebuild.

9

Paula, the fifth of six children, was a product of divorced parents since the age of six. Although her mother had primary custody, her father had tried to stay a part of his children's lives with temporary custody in the summers. But after Paula turned fifteen, which was old enough to work, she stopped the summer visits and seldom saw her father.

The last four siblings were two years apart in school and should have attended the same high school. However, Paula transferred to Superior High School to avoid the enormous shadow of her sisters. Karen, who was two years ahead of her in school, had been voted football sweetheart, most-spirited and class favorite; which was no small feat for an African-American in a predominately white school. Although they were only nineteen months apart in age, they had totally different personalities and physical attributes. Her sister was extremely outgoing and slightly overweight. Paula was introverted and lanky, as her sister often described her. Their relationship bordered on hatred after Paula experienced a painful lesson in the seventh grade that was skillfully ignited by her sister for fun. It resulted in Paula losing her first boyfriend in a very public display. From that day on, Paula kept anything going on in her life, regardless of how trivial, secret from her siblings for fear it would be used against her.

Superior High School was in an affluent suburban, school district with a predominately white student body. A small percentage of African-Americans attended the school primarily because of a court ordered desegregation plan. However, there was some natural diversity due to sparsely integrated neighborhoods in the district. Paula had started in the school district as part of the natural integration and had become part of the forced program due to an address change. The African-American community where Paula lived bordered the suburb's city limits. It was divided like a pie by a federal court order to help the suburban school district expedite its desegregation.

After struggling with the court system for five years to collect timely child support payments, Clarice knew she would probably have to leave teaching and find a better job to support her large family. At that time, her two older children were entering college. The Internal Revenue Service had initiated an affirmative action program and was actively recruiting African-Americans with accounting backgrounds. Clarice had filled out an application a few years prior and was surprised when she received a letter asking her to come in for an interview. She knew it had to be divine intervention. The interview went well and she accepted the job as an Income Tax Auditor even though it meant moving away from their family and friends.

The move also meant that they could no longer afford Catholic schools. So Clarice selected a location in the city with a strong public school system to make sure that the quality of her children's education did not suffer. They moved into an apartment within the school district initially because the job offer was contingent on Clarice's successful completion of a six-month training course. She did not want to buy a house until she was sure that the move would be long-term. However two year later, when they began to look for a house in the district, the African-American community of Carver Park was one of the few neighborhoods that they could afford on Clarice's single income. Initially, they rented the house, and a few years later bought it.

Soon after the move to Dallas, Paula's mother regretted her decision to join the IRS. Since Clarice was at the forefront of the affirmative action program, she faced racism and discrimination from her peers and the small business owners that she audited. She would come home and tell stories about how she could not even use the restroom at some of the businesses. But she was too proud to admit making a mistake. Over time, the job and trying to raise four teenage children were taking its toll on her and the children.

Clarice worked long hours and often came home emotionally and physically drained. Paula knew her mother was working hard to support them so she tried to help with the housework. Over time, Paula took on more and more of the responsibilities for cooking and cleaning that her siblings refused to accept, but resented that she had to. Clarice knew that she could consistently depended on Paula, who had never given her any trouble.

As Paula reached the sidewalk, beads of sweat were forming on her nose and the curls in her shoulder length hair were starting to fall. She was startled when Rosalyn walked up behind her. Paula's five feet-ten inch frame towered over Rosalyn who was the same height as Clarice at barely five feet-two. Paula and Rosalyn had been close friends in the eight-grade but drifted apart when Paula started spending more time with Taylor. Rosalyn was the kind of friend that most mothers want for their children. She was the ideal daughter who obeyed all the rules.

Their mothers had been in the same bridge club since their move to Dallas but their daughters did not get to know each other very well until Paula transferred to the same junior high school.

Rosalyn lived in an affluent white neighborhood which most of the "bused" girls held against her.

In junior high, Paula and Rosalyn spent the night with each other often. Although, Paula spent more nights at Rosalyn's house because the accommodations were better. Paula had to share her bedroom with her sister whereas Rosalyn had her own room with a private bath. They probably would have been better friends if their backgrounds had been more similar. Rosalyn had the perfect family in Paula's eyes, a doting father, a loving, patient mother and only one brother. She didn't have to worry about working and had a closet full of beautiful clothes. Deep down Paula was both envious and jealous of Rosalyn, which hindered their friendship.

Paula had more in common with Taylor who was much more adventurous and just what Paula needed in a friend. Paula's siblings had labeled her the "goody tissue" of the family because she was the one who always followed the rules. Taylor helped Paula be more daring. Paula had experienced a lot of firsts with Taylor that included getting their first jobs together, skipping school for excursions to the mall, and drinking wine coolers after the football games. She had even lost her virginity to be like her best friend, a disastrous event that Paula did her best to forget.

"Hi Paula."

"Hi Rosalyn. Where did you come from?"

"I forgot my schedule in the car. Ready for our senior year?"

"Not really. I called you last night but no one answered."

"I went to the mall. My mom stopped answering my phone. She says she's tired of taking messages. How was summer school?"

"Maine was absolutely beautiful. Can you believe I climbed a mountain? But something better happened this summer. I'm in love Rosalyn. It's the real thing."

Paula quickly fished in her purse for her keys. The key ring had a picture of her and Shane holding each other outside of a building. She handed the picture to Rosalyn who looked at the photo and smiled.

"Not bad. Does he have a brother?"

"Sorry. He's an only child."

Paula retrieved her keys and quickly looked at the picture that was taken the last day of the conference.

"Where does he go to school?" Rosalyn asked.

They quickly climbed the stairs and entered the air-conditioned building. The smell of freshly applied floor wax filled the air and the halls were full of students greeting each other and comparing schedules.

"Unfortunately, not in this city." Paula said as they walked past the rubble of what used to be the band hall.

"I guess this work is being done by the same company that's doing the parking lot."

"So where does Mr. Right live?" Rosalyn asked over the commotion in the halls.

"His name is Shane Howard and I meet him at the Our Children Conference. He lives in Austin, goes to a military college prep school and is six feet, three inches tall. I finally found someone taller than I am. Rosalyn, he is absolutely wonderful."

Paula put the keys back in her purse.

"Do you think the bookstore has started selling donuts yet? I didn't have time for breakfast and I'm starving."

"I don't know but let's go see. I didn't get breakfast either. Have you talked to Taylor, lately?" Rosalyn asked.

"Yep. She thinks that she has enough credits to skip her senior year. She's talking to the counselor today. She wants to work full-time this year and save up for college."

They walked down the main hall to the Student Council bookstore. The bookstore was crowded with students getting last minute school supplies. Paula stared at the empty counter where the donuts were usually displayed.

"Oh well, it looks like no donuts this morning."

"Let's get out of here."

Paula and Rosalyn stopped abruptly at the door to let a group of giggling females walk past them.

"Obviously sophomores. Do you remember what it was like when we were sophomores?" Paula asked.

"Yes and we didn't look like that. Did you see all that make-up?"

"They look like they are going to be working on a corner after school."

The bell rang just as Paula and Rosalyn turned the corner of the wing with the senior lockers. They simultaneously looked at their watches.

"Rosalyn, we can't be that late."

"No. It looks like the bell is off schedule."

"What a way to start our senior year! What does your schedule look like?"

"It's not bad. I only took the classes I need to graduate."

Rosalyn and Paula exchanged their schedules.

"Why are you taking so many hard classes your senior year?"

"Poor planning. I need them to get into any engineering program. We don't have any classes together. We even have different lunch periods."

"I'm glad that's not my schedule. I intend to have some fun this year. Here's my locker."

Rosalyn handed Paula her schedule and retrieved hers.

"I've gotta go. Will you wait for me outside the auditorium for the assembly?"

"Sure. Where's your first class?"

"The other side of the world. I'll see you second period."

Paula just missed colliding with another student who was running down the hall as she crossed back into traffic to get to her locker.

Paula made it to her first class just before the bell rang and quickly sat down in a desk against the wall, closest to the door. As the teacher took attendance, Paula's eyes darted around the room in a vain search for a familiar brown face, suspecting that would be the trend thanks to poor planning. She did not start researching the college requirements for Engineering schools until after the start of her junior year which forced her to take Chemistry, Physics and advanced Math her senior year. But Paula was still determined to graduate with honors, which was why she was taking this College Study Skills course. Because Paula could learn things quickly; she managed good grades with very little effort. Paula usually studied for tests the period before, if at all, and papers were always finished the night before the deadline. Despite poor studying habits, her grades were always A & B's. But to graduate with honors she needed an

"A" average of ninety or higher. Paula's average of eighty-nine was borderline. She hoped this course would help her.

The teacher wasted no time, distributing handouts and discussing the course syllabus and requirements. Paula opened her spiral notebook, intending to take notes but found her thoughts quickly drifting from the paper in front of her to Shane.

Why does he have to live so far away?... I wonder if he's thinking about me right now? At least I don't have to worry about competition - a military school.

Paula was sure that their relationship was true love and that they were destined to meet. She had almost reversed her decision to attend the conference but was thankful she had not. Going to the conference and meeting Shane was the best thing that had ever happened to her, it was the turning point of her life.

The annual Our Children summer conference was for teenagers aged thirteen to eighteen. Our Children was a national organization started by middle-class, African-American mothers to provide social and cultural interaction for their children. It included children from the age of three until they graduated from high school. This was Paula's final year to participate. Paula was born into Our Children. Despite the fact that the Dallas chapter made her feel like an outsider, Paula participated in most of the activities at the encouragement of her mother. She had enjoyed the activities when they lived in San Antonio. The San Antonio chapter consisted primarily of teacher's children. Most of the mothers had been friends since childhood, so all the children had been raised together attending picnics and birthday parties. But when her mother took the job in Dallas, Paula's view of the organization changed dramatically. The children in the Dallas chapter were the sons and daughters of Dallas' most affluent African-Americans. They were concerned about where you lived, what type of clothes you wore and what your parents did for a living. Although Paula never thought of herself as poor, she knew they were out of her league - her parents were divorced and her mother was struggling to provide the essentials.

Paula registered for the conference at the last minute. The last conference had been a big disappointment and she figured this one would probably be worse. The conferences were different when her sisters were still going. At her mother's insistence, she got to tag along with her older sisters and their friends who always kept things exciting. This year, she was going to be one of the oldest. However the chance to see New Orleans and get away from home while waiting to go to the summer school program in Maine convinced her to go.

The chartered bus left for New Orleans at six in the morning. Clarice dropped her off at the departure site, confident that she would be well chaperoned. Paula waved good-bye to her mother, tossed her garment bag beside the others and boarded the bus. She went to the back of the bus where she knew she would find her roommates.

Thanks to the sibling connection, Paula was going to be rooming with Michelle, Camille and Charlese. Paula and Michelle's older sisters were good friends, so Michelle had invited Paula to room with them. Michelle and Camille were doctor's daughters and Charlese was the daughter of a prominent minister. Her roommates were the only ones in the chapter who didn't treat Paula like an outsider. She sat in the empty seat next to Michelle.

"Good morning."

"Good morning. Ready for some fun?

"I guess."

"Charlese has a fifth of something. I think it's Vodka. It should be a fun conference? Let's go out in style."

Paula wondered what she had gotten herself into.

"I like your hair."

"Thanks. You know it was my sister's idea. She said this was the only way my hair would survive the New Orleans' humidity."

Paula was thankful her sister had talked her into setting her hair on perm rods. With a little luck, Paula's ringlet curls would last the entire weekend.

"I wish I had a sister who could do hair. Have you decided on a college yet?" Michelle asked, as she passed Paula the box of donuts.

"No, not yet. I have applications from several schools including Hilman, which is low on my list since it doesn't have an Engineering program but at the top on my mother's. Maybe she thinks I'll meet a future doctor there."

"You're really going to major in Engineering?"

Paula nodded.

"You don't seem like the Engineering type. What are you doing for the rest of the summer?"

"I'm going to Maine for six weeks for a summer program at the university. I'll take two courses and receive college credits. How about you, any big plans for the summer?"

"No. I might get a job, but I haven't decided yet."

Paula reached for another donut and closed the box as the bus jerked forward.

"Have you decided on a college?"

"No, I haven't decided that yet either. Probably Hilman, if I can get accepted. It's too early. I'm going back to sleep."

Paula finished the donut and closed her eyes but she could not sleep. She thought about what it would be like on her own at college. The summer program in Maine would definitely give her a taste of college life and independence. Paula opened her eyes and looked at the traffic traveling in the other direction; thoughts of her sisters filled her mind. Her two older sisters had gone to college but neither stayed past their first year. Her oldest sister, Sheryl went to Hilman but hated it. Paula still could not understand why her mother wanted her to go to there after Sheryl's experience. Sheryl was taking classes part-time to finish her degree, but marriage and the birth of her son slowed down her efforts. Lisa, the next oldest, went to Northern State University but came home for the summer pregnant with Autumn. Karen had chosen beauty school over college.

I hope that I will be different. ...I'm going to finish college and get my degree. Paula, it is not optional. You have to.

The conference was being held at the Sheridan hotel in downtown New Orleans. The lobby of the hotel was absolutely beautiful with its cherry décor, crystal chandeliers and exquisite floral arrangements. Paula thought it was the nicest hotel she had ever been to. The conferences were always held at one of the finest hotels in the city. As part of the cultural enrichment, the parents wanted to make sure their children knew how to conduct themselves. Although it was very beneficial to the conference participants, the other hotel patrons were less than impressed. During the conference, the main hotel was host to thousands of African-American teenagers and their chaperons.

Paula saw Sharon, who was with the Austin chapter, in the lobby as they waited for their chaperons to complete the hotel registration. She spotted her easily across the large lobby that was overflowing with excited teenagers. They had met at the conference the previous summer and hit it off immediately, joined by the common bond of height and the same copper brown complexions. After their excited greeting, they agreed to go to the dance together that night.

After checking in, the remainder of the day was filled with sessions intended to teach the attendees about parliamentarian procedures and politics. Following the sessions, was the dreaded practice for the chapter talent show. The parents did a great job of making sure the conference participants did not have too much free time on their hands.

Paula was tired by the time they finally finished the required sessions and returned to their hotel room. Their assigned chaperon was Camille's mother, who came to their room to make sure they understood the rules, especially the ones relating to the curfew, members of the opposite sex in the hotel rooms and alcoholic beverages. As soon as she walked in the room, she turned down the volume on the radio.

Michelle and Paula had to hold back smiles, while Camille's mother read them the riot act. They had witnessed first hand their older sisters break every single rule at previous conferences and knew their group planned on doing the same thing. Paula just hoped they would not get caught. Her mother had been watching her ever since her sister came home pregnant and did not want to give her any reasons to justify additional surveillance. After inspecting the room, she told them she would be back five minutes before curfew for a bed check and departed. As soon as Camille's mother left, Michelle turned the radio volume up.

It didn't take Paula long to change clothes. While she waited for Sharon, she sat on the bed and watched Camille comb her hair and expertly apply her makeup. Paula wore very little makeup - only mascara and lip-gloss. Her mother had mandated that she could not wear make-up until she was fifteen. This was one of the two rules that Clarice had kept for all her daughters. Most of Paula's friends had been wearing make-up since they were twelve. After years of protest, Paula had lost the desire to wear much makeup by the time she finally turned fifteen. The same thing happened with the 'no dating until you were sixteen' rule. Paula could count on two hands, her dates since turning sixteen. There seemed to be a shortage of young men that were interested in dating a smart and extremely tall young woman. The one's that did usually wanted one thing and when they did not get it, they moved on to the next prospect.

Paula watched Camille cleaned what appeared to be some oversized tweezers with a funny attachment.

"Camille, what is that thing?"

"It's an eyelash curler." Camille replied without turning from the mirror.

"Paula, do you want a drink?" Charlese asked as she came out of the bathroom with a glass that appeared to be clear soda.

"I might as well. I'm going to the dance with Sharon. Do you want to go with us?"

"We'll be down later, if we can't find anything else to do."

Charlese handed Paula the half-filled glass. She took a sip and frowned.

"Is it too strong for you?" Charlese asked, with a smile.

"This could put hair on your chest. It tastes like something my sister would make."

Paula got up and went into the bathroom to dilute the drink with soda. She wanted to drink socially, not to get drunk and draw attention to herself. She knew the affects of alcohol too well after being the watchdog for her sisters at previous conferences. Claiming to be overly protective of their little sister, they never let Paula drink with them, so she learned to sit back with a soda and observe alcohol's affect on the other late night guests. She decided it was much safer to watch than to drink excessively.

"I don't know why you are putting on all that makeup Camille. There's no one here to impress. Is it my imagination or does everyone seem younger this year? There must be four thirteen year olds for every seventeen year old!" Michelle said as Charlese handed her a drink and sat in the chair at the desk.

"Who said I was trying to impress those babies? I saw some pretty nice brothers in the lobby earlier."

Camille looked in the mirror a final time before going in the bathroom to fix herself a drink. Charlese stood up with her empty glass.

"Anyone ready for a refill?"

"I don't think I can keep up with you." Michelle said.

Charlese came out of the bathroom with a full glass and held it in the air.

"This is our last conference ladies. How about a toast to get it started?"

They all stood up and held their drinks in the air.

"Here's to a wonderful conference. May we break all the rules and party till we drop."

"Here, here." The others said, as they clicked their glasses together and took a big drink.

There was a soft knock on the door. They all held their breath for the split second to see if the next sound would be a key turning in the lock, indicating that it was Camille's mother coming back to check on them. The chain was on the door, so they would have a little time. Charlese quickly went to the bathroom to make sure the evidence was put away. The chaperons made it very clear that anyone found breaking the rules would be sent home on the next commercial bus. Paula looked at the clock on the nightstand and finished her drink

"It's probably Sharon."

"Who is it?" Michelle asked, walking to the door.

"It's Sharon. Is Paula ready?"

"I'll be right there." Paula shouted.

"Try not to drink the whole bottle tonight." Paula whispered to Charlese.

After rinsing her glass and grabbing her purse, Paula joined Sharon in the hallway. She did not think that Sharon drank and the fewer people that knew about the alcohol the better. They walked down the long dark corridor to the elevator.

"Hi, Sharon. How was your day?"

"Fine. How about yours?"

"Okay, but boy am I hungry. I can't believe they only served us beans and rice for dinner. They could have at least given us some meat for what we are paying. I expected the food at this

24

conference to be better. It must be hard to fix appetizing meals in large quantities."

They reached the elevator and Paula pushed the down button. The alcohol was starting to take effect but Paula knew she had not drunk enough for it to be obvious to anyone else.

"I'm hungry, too. If the dance is boring, we can go get something to eat. There's a Burger Barn across the street." Sharon said, as the door opened to a crowded elevator.

Paula looked in the elevator at the other teens, who looked so young, and starting thinking about what she was going to have at Burger Barn.

Paula and Sharon stepped off the elevator and walked towards the grand ballroom, following the muffled sound of the music. When they turned the corner, Paula saw a tall, handsome man talking to someone outside the ballroom door and wondered if it was a mirage caused by the alcohol. But the image did not fade as they got closer. Paula assumed that he worked for the hotel.

"Now there's someone I wouldn't mind meeting."

"Would you like to meet him?" Sharon asked.

"You've got to be kidding."

"I'm serious. He's in my chapter."

"Does he have a girlfriend here?"

"I don't think so."

She did not care if he had a girlfriend back home. But there was no point getting her hopes up if he was already taken at the conference.

Approaching the ballroom door, Paula tried to maintain her composure while absorbing every detail, without blatantly staring at him. He was more handsome up close. He was at least six

25

feet three inches tall, with a light honey complexion and a very even, short Afro. He had on gray dress slacks and a crisp white, long sleeved, cotton oxford shirt with the sleeves folded up just below his elbows. The muscles exposed in his forearms indicated an athletic build. They stopped talking when Paula and Sharon walked up.

"Hi, Sharon. There's not much happening inside."

Paula thought she saw braces, but she was not quite sure. She had never met an African-American male his age with braces. His voice was deep and soothing. Paula looked at him closer, noticing the deep gray color of his eyes.

"Hi. Shane. I want to introduce you to Paula Hayes, Paula this is Shane Howard."

They shook hands.

"It's nice to meet you Paula. Sharon and Paula, this is Steve Jones. He's with the Ft. Worth chapter."

"Hello. It's nice to meet both of you." Steve said with a smile revealing his braces.

"What chapter are you with Paula?" Shane asked softly.

"Dallas."

"You are a long way from home. Are you enjoying the conference so far?"

"It's getting better." Paula said with a smile.

Paula tried to think of something else to say but her mind was blank. Someone this handsome would not be interested in her. Shane did not say anything either. Paula took that as a sign confirming his disinterest. Sharon sensed the long silence.

"Paula, let's go see what's going on inside."

Inside the ballroom, the lights were dimmed and the music was blasting but no one was dancing. Paula motioned Sharon towards the refreshment table and got a cup of punch for her and Sharon; it was very weak. She tasted a potato chip that was a casualty of the New Orleans' humidity. Paula was ready to go to the Burger Barn, but decided to follow Sharon's lead. They found an empty table and started to talk about who was running for regional offices. Paula was startled when Shane sat down beside her.

"Is this seat taken?" he asked.

"It is now." Paula felt a strange **sensation** when he looked at her.

"So Paula, Have you and Sharon known each other long?"

"We met at the conference last year. I don't remember seeing you there."

"I didn't attend. Have you been to many of these conferences?"

"Yep, I have five older brothers and sisters. I came to conferences before I was even old **enough** to participate. My mother used to chaperon."

"Is your mother here?"

"No. I think she's all **conferenced out.** Besides, I'm the good girl of the family. She doesn't have to worry about me. Do you have any brothers or sisters?"

"No. I'm an only child."

"Lucky you."

"I'd love to have a brother or sister."

"That's because you don't have any. Do you and Sharon go to the same school?"

"Not hardly. I go to an all-male, military prep school... Paula are you a senior?"

" Yes, this is my last conference. How about you?" Shane nodded with a smile.

Steve sat down in the chair next to Shane and they started talking. Paula returned to her conversation with Sharon. The deejay played a song that Paula really liked and the dance floor began to fill. She felt like dancing and hoped Shane would ask her. After waiting almost a minute, she knew that she needed to take matters into her own hands or the song would be over.

"Shane, would you like to dance?"

"Sure."

Shane let Paula lead the way to the dance floor. Steve and Sharon followed them. They danced to three consecutive fast songs before the deejay slowed the music down. Paula started to follow Sharon and Steve off the dance floor when Shane reached for her hand.

"Can I have this dance too?"

Paula wondered if Shane had read her mind. She wanted nothing more than to slow dance with him.

"Sure."

Paula rested her hands on Shane 's shoulders as he gently put his hands on her waist. Paula liked how he held her close but not so close that their bodies were actually touching.

He's the perfect height for me.

The scent of his cologne made Paula want to get closer but she decided to stay a respectable distance to avoid giving him the wrong impression.

"Is your girlfriend going to walk in here and start a scene?"

"Probably."

Paula pushed away slightly but Shane tightened his hold, pulling her a little closer. The warmth of his body and his firm hold sent a wonderful feeling deep inside her.

"I'm just kidding. I don't have a girlfriend here."

"Does that mean you have one waiting for you at home?"

Suddenly, it did matter to Paula.

"Nope." Shane looked into Paula's eyes and smiled.

"You expect me to believe you don't have a girlfriend."

"Yes, I told you I go to an all-male military school and I'm majoring in pre-engineering. I don't get out much."

Paula smiled.

"And what's so funny?" Shane asked looking at Paula very seriously.

"I plan to be an Engineer, too. I guess we are just a couple of nerds."

Shane was relieved that Paula did not think he was strange because he wanted to be an Engineer.

"How about you? Is there a boyfriend somewhere I should be worried about."

"No. I'm unattached."

Shane was relieved but surprised. He wondered whether she could be interested in someone like him. Paula wanted the song and the way she felt to last forever. She finally found someone who had it all – handsome, smart and most importantly, tall. She thought it was almost too good to be true and tried to stay realistic. Someone like him would not be interested in her. He probably had girls throwing themselves at him especially here at the conference, where the females outnumbered the males five to one. And from what she could tell, he was the handsomest male at the conference.

The beat changed suddenly to a fast song; Paula reluctantly released her hold and followed Shane to their table. As they walked back to the table, Paula noticed all of the competition looking at Shane. When they reached the table Shane remained standing.

"Paula, would you like another cup of punch?"

"That would be great."

"Sharon, can I get you a refill?"

"Please. "

Sharon handed him the empty cup. Shane said something to Steve, who got up and left with him.

"He's really nice. You two seem to be hitting it off." Sharon said with a smile.

"I don't know. There's a lot of jailbait waiting for their chance with him. "

Paula looked at Shane as he filled the cups and was definitely glad that she had come to the conference.

"Shane 's not like that. I think he really likes you."

"Really. How can you tell?"

"Just take my word for it."

They returned with the punch. Paula and Shane talked and danced for the rest of the party. Sharon was beginning to feel like a third wheel. Paula was frantic when the deejay announced the last song a few minutes before midnight. She wanted more time with Shane.

"Can I walk you ladies to your rooms?" Shane asked.

Paula looked at Sharon to see if she had any objections.

"It's fine with me."

They walked Sharon to her room first. Paula wanted to spend as much time as possible with Shane. Before either of them wanted too, they reached Paula's room. She wanted to invite him in, but it was too close to their curfew. They stood outside the door and Shane stared into her eyes but didn't say anything. Paula felt the tingling sensation travel through her body, again.

"Maybe I'll see you tomorrow." Paula said.

"I'll look for you at lunch. Have a good night, Paula."

"You too."

He waited for Paula to put the key in the door before leaving. Paula watched him walked down the hall before going into the room. The radio was on and her roommates where enjoying a snack of chips and cookies. Paula put her purse down and reached for the cookies. She had temporarily forgotten her hunger.

Five minutes before curfew, there was a knock at the door followed by the key in the lock. Camille's mother walked in the room with another chaperon and went directly to the radio to lower the volume. Everyone knew there was no sign of liquor. Just soda cans, bags of chips and a half-eaten bag of cookies. She talked as she went into the bathroom to inspect.

"I'm glad everyone is in on time. You know the rules. We are right down the hall." "Mother, please." Camille said.

"Don't forget we have an early start in the morning. We'll be checking attendance, so no sleeping in. I'll give you a wake up call at seven."

With that they were gone. The telephone rang as they were walking out the door. Michelle answered it since she was the closest.

"Paula, it's for you. It's a man!" Michelle teased as she handed Paula the phone.

"Hi Paula. It's Shane ...Do you think your roommates would mind if Steve and I came by? We have some wine coolers."

"Wait just a minute and I'll check."

Paula knew her roommates would be all for taking risks, especially if it involved men and alcohol.

"Would you mind if we had some male company? They'll bring some coolers."

"Not at all." Charlese almost shouted.

"It's fine but are you sure that you want to do this?"

"Definitely. I'll see you in about thirty minutes when the halls clear."

"Okay."

Paula hung up the phone smiling.

While they waited, Charlese retrieved the vodka from her stash and fixed everyone a drink. Paula jumped up when they heard a light knock on the door. She opened the door quickly and shut it quietly after Shane and Steve walked in. Shane retrieved four coolers from the pocket of his jacket and Steve produced another two.

"You don't know how many parents we had to slip past."

"Do you think they'll check your room?"

"I doubt it. Our chaperon looked like she couldn't wait to go to bed."

The music was on loud enough to cover their voices but not high enough to be a disturbance. Shane and Steve stayed until two-thirty. Paula reluctantly suggested that they leave after Camille fell asleep, sprawled across the bed.

"Do you want to meet for breakfast?" Paula said as she prepared to open the door.

"Okay. I'll call you in the morning."

Just as she was about to open the door, Shane leaned towards her and kissed her softly on the lips. Paula wanted to jump for joy after she closed the door.

"How did you manage to catch the only good-looking guy at this conference?" Michelle asked, as she quickly changed into her pajamas.

"Just lucky, I guess."

Paula was too excited to sleep.

Shane and Paula were inseparable the rest of the conference. Paula loved having doors opened, chairs being pulled out for her and the envy of her peers. They talked as if they had known each other much longer. The few times that they managed to be alone, they held hands and kissed but it never went any farther. He always treated her like a lady, a different experience for Paula, who was used to being grabbed and groped under the pretense of fondling.

The sound of the first assembly bell startled Paula. She looked at the picture on her key ring and remembered the rainy Sunday morning they left the conference, their arms locked around each other. Despite the smile, Paula remembered that tears were on her cheeks as Camille took the picture.

The tears swelling inside of her as they waited to board the bus caught Paula off guard. The more she tried to stop the tears, the more that came. She still remembered the looks from the chaperons. She and Shane had been so discrete that they looked

33

at her in disbelief. At that point, Paula did not care; life was unfair. She had finally found someone and he lived in another city. She was going to be leaving for Maine, so any hope of seeing Shane again for the summer was gone. But they had managed to grow closer over the summer with phone calls and long, romantic letters.

Paula looked around the classroom to see if anyone had taken notes. The spiral notebook of the student next to her was blank also. Either nothing of substance was said or everyone else was daydreaming too. Paula picked up her purse and spiral notebook. As she walked into the hall flooded with excited seniors, she wondered if Taylor would be at the assembly.

Chapter 2

Rosalyn was talking with friends when Paula reached the auditorium, thoughts of Shane still lingering in her head. After a quick greeting, they went to their section of the auditorium. It didn't matter if it was an assembly, sports event or even classes; the African-American students at Superior sat together. There were a few mavericks who bucked tradition and they were treated like traders.

Since the beginning of junior high school, Paula participated in the practice of segregated seating; initially because she did not want to be ostracized by her peers, despite not understanding why they would want to segregate themselves after all of the struggles to desegregate. But by her senior year, Paula realized that it was not about segregation; it was about camaraderie - they were her friends, the people who shared a common experience.

When Paula lived in San Antonio, she was oblivious to racism. They lived in an integrated neighborhood and attended integrated Catholic school. But when they moved to Dallas, Paula felt the full impact of being treated differently because of the color of her skin. It started the very first day at the new school; her sixth grade teacher put Paula in the remedial group with the other African-Americans despite the fact that Paula was transferring from a Catholic school with exceptional grades. After a week, the teacher moved Paula to the mainstream group, although Paula knew that she belonged in the accelerated group. In addition to the systematic treatment by the school administration, the only students who would associate with Paula outside the classroom were the other African-Americans students. From then on Paula understood that African-Americans and whites lived in separate worlds. They could share the same school but once the bell rang, they went their separate ways.

Just as Paula was taking her seat, the principal's voice came screeching out of the speakers. She looked for Taylor but did not see her.

"Okay, quiet down. I know you're excited about starting your senior year but we've got to get started. Your first responsibility is to elect the senior class officers. The purpose of this assembly is to communicate the responsibilities of each office and the election process. Your student council president will now read the duties of each office and then I'll be back to discuss the election process."

Paula listened carefully to the duties for each of the five offices. Looking around the auditorium, her adrenaline started pumping as she contemplated what she had to do. An internal alarm had been triggered by the large, empty spaces for leadership experience on the college application forms. The fact that she had not held any significant leadership roles would be blatantly obvious, reducing her chances for admission and scholarships. Paula knew that being an officer for a large graduating class would help distinguish her from the pool of applicants.

Paula calculated that her chances of winning a major office were slim since everything in high school was based on popularity. There were thirty-six African-Americans in a class that exceeded eight hundred. Paula had been on the student council her sophomore and junior years but it was less challenging to get elected to the council since each class has fifteen representatives. Because Paula had played basketball and participated in the drama club in junior high, she had enough name recognition to finish in the top fifteen. But she wondered if she could get the most votes in a major election.

"Are you going to run for an office?" Rosalyn asked.

"I was thinking about running for Senior Class Representative. Have you heard who's running yet?"

"No, but I'm sure there will be a lot of candidates. People are beginning to worry about leadership experience for college applications."

"I know. That's why I'm considering running. I've got to get a scholarship. Are you going to run?"

"No, way!" Rosalyn replied with a frown.

"I don't want to run against one of us and split the vote."

Paula jotted down the deadline for turning in the petition to run then surveyed their group trying to gauge who else might run. Rosalyn knew what Paula was doing.

"Lynn will probably run for either President or Vice president. Gail is the only other one of us that might run, but she is already a student council officer. Go ahead and run. I'll be your campaign manager."

Paula picked up a petition form after the assembly. She decided to run for the office that matched her experience - the

Senior Class Representative to the Student Council. Paula knew that her two years on the Student Council would match or exceed any other candidate. By lunchtime, she had the twenty-five signatures required to run. Two days later, her worst fear was realized when they announced the candidates - she was running against a cheerleader.

She called Shane as soon as she got home to tell him the horrible news. He tried to convince Paula that she had just as much chance to win. She felt much better after their conversation, consoled by the fact that they would be together the day of the election; either they would celebrate or he could comfort her. Given the odds against her, Paula decided not to tell anyone in her family about her run for the office. They could find out later, if she won.

They had a one-week campaign schedule that started Monday morning and ended with the candidate speeches and election during a Friday morning assembly. Paula and Rosalyn made posters to hang in the cafeteria, the stairways and the senior hall over the weekend. They were hanging a poster in the hall early Monday morning, when Paula saw the first one. By late afternoon, every cheerleader and drill team member was wearing a professionally printed button for her competitor. Paula was ready to withdraw her name from the ballot, certain that she could not compete. After struggling with her speech the entire week, Paula was beginning to wonder why she had gotten herself into a hopeless situation; cheerleaders always win.

Thursday evening Paula sat on her bed and picked up the phone. She needed to talk to Shane desperately and was relieved to hear his comforting voice.

"Hello."

"Guess who?"

"Hi! I was just thinking about calling you. How are you doing?"

"As well as can be expected for the night before the election. I don't think this was such a good idea. I haven't even finished my speech. I must be crazy to be running against a cheerleader. You should see all the buttons. Everyone's wearing them."

"I doubt that everyone is wearing them."

"Well, every cheerleader, drill team member and athlete."

"What's that, maybe one hundred people? There are over seven hundred in your class so that leaves a lot of votes out there for you. I bet that you have more friends and supporters than she does."

"I don't know. You have to be extremely popular to even become a cheerleader."

"Paula, stop worrying. You are going to do great and tomorrow we will be able to celebrate. I still can't believe we are finally going to be together again. This has been the longest three months of my life."

"I know. Talking on the phone just isn't the same. But I have to be honest. I'm a little nervous about coming."

Paula temporarily forgot about the election and remembered what was really important.

"Why? I won't eat you up."

"I'm nervous about meeting your mother. What if she hates me?"

"I doubt that very much. She is looking forward to meeting you, especially since I talk about you all the time. She will love you as much as I do."

"I don't know about that... And there's something else that's been worrying me. What if I get down there and you decide that you really don't like me after all? It's been so long; you probably don't even remember what I look like."

"How could I forget what you look like? I look at your picture every night before I go to bed. Stop being silly. I love you and can't wait to see you. Sharon said your mother talked to her mother last night."

"Yep, right after she talked to yours. She wanted to make sure that I'm not imposing."

"Are you sure she's not nervous about you coming to see me?"

"I don't think so, especially since we will be sleeping in different houses. There's nothing for her to worry about, if you know what I mean. Besides you're in the social elite and live two hundred miles away. You're my mother's dream come true. Thanks for arranging for me to stay with Sharon."

"I can't take the credit for that. I'd much rather you stay with me. It was my mother's idea. Sometimes she is so old fashioned."

"I'm glad she is otherwise, I might not be coming to see you. Our mothers are from the same school. I don't think they want to tempt us or maybe they just don't trust us."

"They are probably right. I miss you so much. I wish you lived here or I lived there."

"Me too. I worry about you finding someone else."

"You don't have to worry about that. Between school and football, I don't have much time for anything else. Besides, you're the only one who wants a geeky engineer."

"I'm glad you don't know how handsome you are. It might go to your head. I'd better get off the phone before I spend my whole paycheck and I still need to figure out what I'm going to say tomorrow morning. Are you going to pick me up at the airport?"

"No, Sharon is. I won't have the car. Your flight is getting in before my mother gets off work."

"I started to get a later flight but I wanted us to have as much time together as possible."

"It's okay. I'll probably ride to the airport with her."

"I can't wait to see you. Just think, the next time we talk will be in person. I love you."

"I love you, too. Get a good night sleep. Good luck tomorrow. I know you are going to win."

"Thanks. I wish I could believe that. Good night."

Paula was so excited to be finally seeing Shane that she almost ran over an elderly lady trying to get off the plane quickly. They had been apart for so long and she knew he was waiting for her. He would help her forget the humiliating defeat in the election. The walkway from the airplane to the building was hot and so long. She walked and walked, wondering if it would ever end. Finally, the cool, conditioned air greeted her as she walked through the doorway. Her heart was racing. After three months, they were going to be together again. Paula looked around the terminal nervously, unable to find him in the crowd.

There were so many people at the gate. Then Paula saw the back of him. He was talking to someone. She yelled his name and fought through the crowd to get to him. He turned around and she froze.

That can't be him. It's impossible!

Shane smiled when he saw her and started walking toward her. The person walking towards her resembled Shane, only different. The athletic frame she remembered was boney and frail looking. His steel gray eyes budged out of their sockets and when he smiled, the braces looked like railroad tracks. Paula looked frantically for the Shane that she had fallen in love with.

This can't be happening. First the election and now Shane.

Paula cried uncontrollable when he walked up and hugged her. She tried to talk to the stranger holding her but the tears would not stop. Finally, she broke away from his grip and started running through the airport. He was chasing her. She had to get away...

Paula sat up in bed, her heart racing and tears on her cheeks. She looked around her dark room for the clock. It was only one o'clock.

Paula could not get the dream out of her head all morning. She wondered if it was an omen. She was prepared to lose the election but not Shane. The halls were still empty as she put her things in her locker and then went to the bookstore. It was her morning to work. Several students wished her luck as they purchased donuts and supplies. Paula made it to first period just as the final bell rang. Despite trying hard, she could not pay attention to the material being covered. She mentally rehearsed her speech over and over - each time changing the wording just a bit.

The announcement for the candidates to come to the auditorium startled her. She gathered her things and left the class with well wishes from the students and her teacher. As she listened to the candidate's final instructions back stage, Paula felt light-headed. They had a few minutes to wait while the seniors filled the auditorium. Paula looked out at the audience from behind the curtain. She had never spoken to a group this large. She thought again about withdrawing from the election since the outcome was pretty obvious; but something inside of her pushed that thought out of her mind. Paula knew that despite her nervousness, she had come too far to give up. She found a quiet place backstage, clasped her hands together, closed her eyes and prayed. She felt better hoping that the race would be at least close.

The speeches were to be given in reverse order of responsibilities starting with the office of representative and ending with the candidates for class president. Paula was first, based on alphabetical order, which added to the pressure. The assembly started. The Student Council president was at the podium. Paula felt the bile churning in her stomach as she waited off-stage for her name to be announced. Applause came from the right side of the audience when she was introduced.   She walked deliberately to the podium clutching her speech in one hand.   The last thing she wanted to do was trip.

The spotlight shining on her made it difficult to see the audience clearly but she knew they were there.   Her nervousness took control of her body as soon as she reached the podium.   Her hands started to shake and she could feel her left eye begin to twitch.   She propped her speech against the microphone stand and gripped the sides of the podium for support.   She hoped no one could see her twitching eye as she prepared to read her speech.   It seemed like an eternity but only a few seconds had passed.

Take a deep breath.

"Good morning.   I am running for the office of senior class representative . . ."

After reading the first sentence, Paula looked at the audience and stopped reading.

"This is an election that I am taking very seriously.   I have clearly been out spent in the campaign.   But this election should not be about who can spend the most money or who is more popular.   It's about who would be a better representative for our class - the entire class and not just a small group.   I have worked on the Student Council for the past two years and have never missed a meeting.   I have the experience to do a great job but I need your vote.   Please vote for the best candidate and not the most popular.   Thank you."

Paula picked up her crumpled paper and walked off the stage and straight to the water fountain in the hall.   Her opponent had finished her speech when Paula returned.   Now all she had to do was wait until the last period for the results.

Five minutes before the start of the weekend, the election results had still not been announced. Suddenly the chime of the address system brought the school to silence. Paula stared at her notebook on the desk as the sophomore results were announced, her heart raced. She tried to conceal her nervousness, taking a slow, deep breath to calm down after the junior class officers were announced. Paper shuffled in the background followed by a long pause.

"And now for the Senior Class Officers... The Student Council Representative is Paula Hayes..."

Her classmates let out a cheer as she smiled uncontrollably.

The unexpected victory, the flood of congratulations on the way to the parking lot, and the impending reunion with Shane had Paula's adrenaline surging, despite being physically drained from the stress of the day and lack of sleep. Paula could barely contain her excitement as she drove to the mall to pick up her paycheck, thankful to have the weekend off from the job that she worked twelve to sixteen hours a week. Although her sales position at a clothing store was not mentally challenging, standing on her feet for four to eight hours was physically tiring. With Shane in another city, working not only provided much-needed cash; it also kept her busy on the weekends when most of her friends had dates.

After a quick stop at the bank to cash her check, Paula went home to wait for Clarice to take her to the airport. By four-thirty, Paula was getting nervous, wondering if Clarice had forgotten. Her suitcase sat by the front door, carefully packed the night before. Paula looked at the clock again, and was just about to call Taylor to take her to the airport, when Clarice pulled in the driveway. Paula was so worried about missing the plane that she didn't even give her mother time to come inside. Clarice seemed excited when Paula announced that she had been elected to a class office as they drove to the airport.

Clarice dropped Paula off in front of the terminal, confident that her daughter did not need her to go in. The plane was boarding when Paula arrived at the gate. Paula smiled nervously as she sat down in a window seat and looked out the window at the ground crew efficiently working to get the plane back in the air.

Paula, if things keep going like this, you are going to have one unforgettable senior year... A class officer. I still can't believe it. Only one thing could make things perfect. I just wish I had a boyfriend in the same city. Why does Shane have to live so far away?

The memory of the dream rushed back into her head. She took the key ring out of her purse and looked at it.

He is handsome. A picture can't lie. So why did I have that dream? What if his personality is different? Paula, stop being ridiculous! You talk to him on the phone at least once a week. He is the same wonderful person you fell in love with. It's the real thing. I know it. I hope Shane will be at the airport. I can't wait to tell him the news.

The thirty-minute flight went quickly. It took longer for the passengers to deplane. Paula thought about the dream again as she walked down the short jet way.

46

I hope this isn't a dream.

Paula looked for Shane as she struggled to get the strap of her bag comfortably on her shoulder. The weight of the bag forced her to walk leaning to one side. Sharon, who was waiting at the gate alone, sensed Paula's disappointment immediately.

"Hi Sharon."

"Hi Paula. Did you have a good flight?"

"Yes, I did. Thanks for letting me stay with you this weekend. I was beginning to think that Shane and I were never going to see each other again."

"No problem. After all, I did introduce you guys. Shane wanted to come to the airport with me but I was running late. He's so excited."

"I think we both are."

They exited the building and walked across the street to the car. Prepared for a long walk, Paula was surprised that the car was parked so close. Sharon unlocked the passenger doors for Paula, who could tell immediately that the huge, four-door sedan belonged to Sharon's parents. After putting her shoulder bag in the back seat, Paula sank into the soft, black leather seat.

"Is Shane going to meet us at your house?"

"He has to wait until his mother gets off from work. I told him we would call as soon as we got home."

Sharon started the car and merged carefully into the traffic. Looking out the window, Paula tried to hide her disappointment with having to wait longer to see Shane.

"So how is your school year going?"

"Great. I got elected to a senior class office today. I can't wait to tell Shane. I didn't think I had a chance of winning."

"Congratulations."

Sharon thought quickly as she approached the exit for Shane's house. Her mother expected them to come straight home but it should only take a few extra minutes.

"Paula, Shane's house is on the way from the airport. Why don't we stop by for a few minutes? We can't stay long but at least you can see each other."

"Thanks Sharon. That would be great."

After only two turns off the freeway, they were pulling into the driveway of a huge, stately home. Paula was suddenly nervous again. Sharon honked the horn and Shane opened the door. When he saw who it was, he quickly came out the house and down the stairs. Paula got out of the car and watched him approach; all of her fears instantly disappeared. He was more handsome than she remembered with a deep golden tan from the summer sun and a more defined muscular build. Within seconds, they were locked in an embrace that made Paula feel warm and protected, just like she remembered. Sharon was glad she decided to stop. They looked so happy.

"Hello. Was your flight okay?" Shane said as he planted a kiss on Paula's cheek.

"Great. Punctual to the point of feeling like a 'cattle' service. Herd them on and then get them off."

Paula released her grip so that Shane could speak to Sharon.

"Hi, Sharon. Thanks for picking Paula up. I'm so glad you were able to stop by. I don't think I could have waited any longer."

Sharon stepped out of the car and leaned against it, leaving the door open.

"You're welcome. I didn't want to be responsible for keeping you two apart any longer."

Paula looked at Shane ready to burst with happiness.

"Guess what?"

"What?"

"I won the election!"

"I knew you would. Congratulations. I'm so proud of you."

Shane gave Paula another kiss on the cheek and a hug. Sharon felt like a third wheel on a bicycle.

"What do you guys want to do tonight?"

"I thought I'd come over to your house. Maybe we could play some cards." Shane replied, still holding onto Paula, neither of them wanting to let go.

"That's fine...Remember that I have to baby-sit tomorrow night but I've already asked if you could come over after the kids are in bed and it's not a problem."

"I'm going to take Paula on a tour of Austin tomorrow during the day. Would you like to come along?"

"No, thanks. I think you two can manage without a chaperon, besides I have some errands to run tomorrow. Paula, I think we'd better go. I told my mother we would come straight home from the airport."

"Okay."

Sharon got back into the car and closed the door. Shane held Paula's hand as he walked her back to the car and opened the door, wanting desperately for her to stay with him but he knew better. He had to respect his mother's rule of no female company in the house when she was not at home. He thought this was different but did not want to risk encountering his mother's wrath with Paula in town. They would just have to wait.

"Sharon, I'll give you a call after my mom gets home to let you know what time I'll be over."

"Okay."

Shane closed the door for Paula, who opened the window as Sharon started the car. He gave Paula a gentle kiss and whispered in her ear,

"I love you."

Paula felt her heart soar, knowing that it was impossible for her to be happier and wanting desperately to stay with him.

"Bye, I'll see you soon." Paula said.

"Bye, Sharon. Thanks again for stopping by." Shane called as they backed out of his driveway.

"You guys look so happy."

"We are. I love him so much, Sharon. I just wish we lived in the same city."

They approached the end of Shane's street, which intersected with the major access to the highway. Sharon stopped completely at the intersection and looked both ways.

"I hate this street. It's always so busy, especially on Fridays."

They waited as a continuous stream of traffic speed past. Finally, there was a break in the oncoming traffic.

"I think we just got lucky."

There was a clear path across the four lanes, except for a car that was signaling to turn onto Shane's street. They pulled into the intersection but the car did not turn; it came straight at them.

Why now?

The oncoming car crashed into theirs, hitting the rear fender on the driver's side and pushing the car against the curb.

"Sharon, are you okay?"

"I'm fine, how about you?"

"I'm okay."

"I thought he was going to turn. He had on his signal."

"I know. I was sure he was going to turn too."

Paula and Sharon got out of the car and looked at the damage. There was a huge dent in the fender but the car still looked drivable. Paula saw the look of panic on Sharon's face when the other driver stumbled out of his car and walked towards them. Paula and Sharon were both concerned that he was hurt.

"Are you okay?" Sharon asked.

"Yeah. How 'bout y'all?"

"We're okay but I think we should call the police." Sharon said, remembering what her mother had told her.

"That's cool. I'm going over there in some shade."

They could smell the liquor on his breath when he spoke.

Shane watched their car pull out of sight and decided to wait outside for his mother. His heart skipped a beat when he heard the crash. All he could think about was Paula as he sprinted down the street, reaching them just as they were looking around for a place to use the phone.

"Are you guys okay? What happened?"

"I pulled out in front of that car. He had on his turn signal but didn't turn. We're fine but I need to call my mother and the police."

Sharon started walking towards the first open door in the strip shopping center.

"Do you want us to go with you?" Paula asked.

"No. But keep an eye on that guy and make sure he doesn't leave."

"Do you think we should move the cars or leave them in the street?" Paula asked Shane.

"I think we should leave them where they are until the police comes. The traffic can get around them."

Shane put his arm around Paula as they walked over to sit on the curb outside the store that Sharon had entered; keeping a watchful eye on the man who was now lying on the ground beside the tree. Paula was consumed by guilt as she held Shane's hand, knowing that she was responsible for the accident.

"Shane, what if Sharon gets in trouble? I feel terrible. It's my fault. If we had not come by your house first, this would not have happened. Sharon was just helping us."

"It will be okay Paula. Stop worrying."

Sharon returned a few minutes later and she sat on the curb, next to Paula.

"The police said they should have a car here in about ten minutes. I talked to my mom too."

"Is she upset?" Paula asked.

"I don't know… I really thought he was going to turn. I can't believe this happened."

"Do you think he's hurt?" Shane asked.

"I think he's drunk, Shane." Paula whispered.

"Maybe we should go ask him if he needs anything."

"I don't know, but I guess I should go tell him that the police are on the way. Shane, will you go with me?"

"Sure." Shane said, standing up.

Sharon, Shane and Paula were sitting on the curb in the shopping center parking lot when the police car pulled up. After getting the cars moved out of the street, the police officer started gathering information for his report. Shane and Paula stood with Sharon for moral support while she talked to the officer. At first, the officer was congenial but when he went to the back of Sharon's car to write down the license plate, his attitude changed. He returned to Sharon when he saw the license plate, smiling to himself because he was going to enjoy arresting them.

"Whose car is this?" He asked.

"My mother's."

"You expect me to believe that?"

"It is. You can ask her yourself. She should be here soon."

Paula froze, realizing that they would have to face Sharon's mother soon than she had expected. She had assumed that Sharon's mother was waiting for them at home.

"What's your mother's name?"

"Why is he acting like he doesn't believe her?" Paula whispered to Shane, who led her away from the officer.

"Because he probably doesn't. Do you know who Sharon's mother is?"

"No, I haven't meet her yet. Who is she?"

"She's a state legislator. Legislators have exempt license plates. He probably thinks the car is stolen."

Paula was worried now more than ever as she walked to the rear of the car and looked at the black and white license plate with the small words "State Legislator" on top and some larger numbers and letters underneath.

Just as the policeman was beginning to interrogate Sharon, a woman in a small dark car pulled up and rushed over to Sharon and the officer. Paula could see the relief in Sharon's face and knew it had to be her mother. The stately woman walked up and said something to the officer who went to talk to the other driver. Sharon and her mother walked to where Paula and Shane were standing. Paula wanted to crawl under a rock.

"Mom, this is Paula Hayes."

"Well hello."

Sharon's mother said as she gave Paula a motherly hug.

"Are you sure you weren't hurt?"

"Yes ma'am, I'm fine."

Paula tried to appear calm, thinking that if Sharon's mother was upset, she hid it well.

"Shane, how are you doing? Were you in the car with the girls?"

"No ma'am. I heard the crash at my house and came down."

"Thanks for staying with them."

"Mom, I'm so glad you came. He didn't believe me when I told him the car was yours."

"It's okay baby. I'll handle him. Are you sure you're okay?"

"I'm fine, Mom."

"I'm glad you called me. Now tell me what happened so I can go deal with this policeman. I'm sure he doesn't know who he's dealing with."

Paula listened as Sharon retold what had happened.

"You kids go wait over there. I'll handle it."

Shane, Sharon and Paula sat on the curb reviewing what had happened while Sharon's mother and the policemen looked at the cars and the intersection. Paula did not know how to fix the problems she had caused.

"Sharon, I am so sorry."

"Why? It's not your fault, Paula. I was the one driving."

"But you had taken me to see Shane."

"Sharon, do you think you're going to get in trouble?" Shane asked.

"I don't know. We were supposed to come straight home."

They sat there looking at the interchange between Sharon's mother and the policeman. They could tell Sharon's mother was getting upset. Paula felt sick to her stomach. When the policeman went over to talk to the other driver again, her mother returned. They all stood up.

"I can't believe this officer. I had to give him a piece of my mind. He actually thought the car was stolen."

"Mom, I told him it was yours but he didn't believe me."

"Don't worry about it baby. I'm just glad that neither of you was hurt."

When the policeman stopped talking to the other driver, Sharon's mother walked back over to him. After talking with him some more she walked over to Sharon and put her arm around her.

"He doesn't need you any more. I'll stay and finish up the report. You girls take the other car and go home. I'll wait here for the tow truck and get a loaner from the repair shop."

"Mom, are you sure? We can wait with you."

"There's no point in all of us waiting here. I called the shop from home and they're sending a truck. Go ahead home. Paula is probably tired from her trip."

"I'll wait with you, Ms. Davis." Shane announced and then walked Paula and Sharon to the car that her mother had driven.

"I'm so glad you are both okay. I'll give you a call later. Sharon, I'm sorry about this."

"Don't worry about it, Shane."

"Paula, I'll see you later."

"Sharon, I hope your mother isn't too upset." Paula said, as they drove out the parking lot.

"Don't worry."

Sharon didn't sound to convincing.   She was worried too, but not about the accident. She was thinking about how her mother had trusted her with her official car, to go to the airport and come straight home.   If only they had gone straight home or at least called her mother from Shane's house.

"Your mother is really nice. I don't know if I would have called my mother."

"My mother has always told me to call her first when I have a problem."

Paula and Sharon drove the rest of the way in silence not sure what to say to each other.   Paula was also thinking about Sharon's mother too. The fact that Sharon should have come straight home had not been mentioned.

Their house was farther than Paula thought it would be. Sharon's mother had to have exceeded the speed limit to get there so fast. Paula wondered what Clarice's response would have been in a similar incident and tried to remember the last time she had called her mother when she had a problem.

Paula was in the sixth grade at a new school and wondered why she was being called to the principal's office. She had not done anything wrong. A man and a lady were waiting for her when she got there.

"Paula, your little brother came to school without a lunch. Do you have a lunch?"

"No, sir."

"Do you have money to buy a lunch?"

"No, sir."

"Well, you need to go home and get a lunch for you and your brother."

Paula could not believe what she had heard. She and her brother always walked to and from school with a large group of students from their apartment complex.

It is too far to walk alone. What if someone grabs me? What if a dog chases me? Mom will just have to come and bring us a lunch. Besides, there is nothing at home to fix for lunch; that's why we don't have one.

She started to tell the man the reason that they didn't have a lunch but she was too embarrassed.

"Can I please call my mother?"

"We've already tried to call her. She is out of the office."

"Paula, do you have a key to your house?"

"Yes, sir."

"Then you're excused to go home to get a lunch for you and your brother. You need to come to school everyday with either a lunch or the money to buy a lunch. Will you please tell your mother that?"

"Yes, sir."

She had never walked that far by herself. They had only been in the apartment for three months and she still felt uncomfortable in the neighborhood. Paula looked at the united couple, wondering how they could send her home alone and hoping that they would see her fear, but they just waited for her to leave.

She walked as fast as her feet could carry her. Looking over her shoulder, sure that someone was following her.

When she reached the safety of the apartment, Paula dialed her mother's work number.

"Hello, may I please speak to Clarice Hayes."

"I'm sorry, she's out of the office. May I take a message?"

"This is her daughter."

"Your mother is on an audit. Is it an emergency? I can try to reach her for you."

"No ma'am. It's not an emergency. Thank you."

Paula hung up the phone and opened the refrigerator. No lunchmeat. She went to the cabinets. No peanut butter either. Paula knew she had to find something suitable for lunch; her brother's teacher would probably check his lunch. There had to be something. She opened the cabinet again and saw a can of tuna fish in the back. She mixed the tuna with some mayonnaise and made a sandwich for her brother using the last two good pieces of bread. Then she made a sandwich for herself using the ends of the loaf. She carefully wrapped the sandwiches in aluminum foil and put them in brown paper bags.

She looked for something else to include. A lunch needed more than just a sandwich. Paula remembered the chocolate candy bars that her older sister was selling for a fundraiser. Paula broke a bar in half, wrapped the pieces in foil and put them in the bags. Then she took two quarters from the money envelope for milk. It was not much but it was all she could do. Paula walked back to school as fast as she could, delivered her brother's lunch and went back to class.

Paula still remembered the fear that she had walking home that day. Then she remembered the time when she was in the seventh grade and had to stay in the nurse's office at school all day with a broken arm because they could not reach her mother. Paula knew that she and Sharon were different.

Growing up, Paula and her siblings had learned to handle problems for themselves. Initially, their mother usually could not be reached when they had a problem; eventually they stopped trying to reach her. Their mother had enough to worry about.

They got to Sharon's house and waited for her mother, who came home thirty minutes later. She still was not angry with her daughter, but she was furious at how the police officer had treated Sharon. When Sharon's father came home, they retold the story. The only thing her parents stressed was the importance of waiting for a car to start turning before pulling out in front of it. They ate dinner as if nothing had happened. Shane and Sharon's boyfriend came over later that night and they played cards until it was time for them to leave.

Shane picked up Paula early Saturday morning for a tour of the city and the rest of the weekend was perfect.

Chapter 3

At the peak of the holiday season, Paula planned to go out after working the Saturday late shift with her friend Janet to celebrate Paula's birthday that had passed barely noticed by her family. She had initially felt obligated to go out to celebrate finally being eighteen and legally an adult; a fact that her father's lawyer had tarnished by sending a letter stating that she was no longer eligible for child support. But after standing on her feet for eight hours, helping the flood of customers who were searching for the perfect outfit or gift, all she wanted to do was go to bed.

Pulling out of the mall parking lot, Paula intended to go straight home and call Janet to cancel, but since Janet's house was on her way home, she decided to stop by and cancel. It was almost nine-thirty when Paula arrived at Janet's, who was anxiously waiting for her.

"Hi."

"I'm almost ready. Come on back. There's a party at the Windsor Hotel." Janet said as she led Paula to her bedroom.

"Do you know who's giving it?"

"No, but that's where Rosalyn is going?"

"Yep. She told me. I really don't feel like driving all the way downtown. Any parties out this way?" Paula asked as she sat on Janet's bed.

"No."

"I think I'll just call it a night and go home. My feet are killing me."

"Oh, no you don't! Remember that we are supposed to be celebrating your birthday and if you stay home, so do I. Come on. We will have some fun. Do you need to go home to change?" Janet asked continuing to get ready.

"If I go home, there's no way I'll go back out. What I have on will have to do. Besides, who am I going to impress? I already have the love of my life. I just wish he lived a little closer."

Paula stood up and looked in Janet's full-length mirror. Her outfit was conservative for a party - a pleated, knee-length maroon skirt and a crisp, white linen blouse. A maroon and blue plaid vest completed the outfit.

"Okay. Let's go or the party will be over before we even get there."

"Is Shane still coming up for the Toy Dance next weekend?" Janet asked as she put on her coat.

"Yes. I can hardly wait. It's been so long since we've seen each other. I hope this party doesn't cost more than five dollars. I didn't get a chance to cash my check." Paula said as she opened her purse to see how much cash she had.

The latest trend was "pay" parties - the teenage version of traveling nightclubs. Someone realized that they could profit from the boredom of teenagers. They would rent a ballroom, hire a deejay, serve watery punch and charge from three to five dollars per person. The parties were held at some of the nicer hotels that recognized the opportunity to profit from the empty ballrooms when conventions weren't in town. The music was usually good and it was a way to meet teenagers from around the city. Since no alcohol was served, the parties were very peaceful and often well attended.

"Okay, I'm ready." Janet said as she put her lipgloss in her purse.

"Can I use your phone to let my mother know where I'm going?"

"Sure, there's one in the hall."

After calling home, they were on their way. Janet and Paula got to the hotel around ten-thirty. Usually by that time the crowd is at its maximum. Janet and Paula saw Rosalyn standing outside the ballroom and joined her.

"How is it inside?" Paula asked as she tried to look inside the ballroom but the lighting was too low.

"Dead. There's probably less than fifty people." Rosalyn replied.

"Janet, let's just go home and save some money? I'm tired and this doesn't seem worth it." Paula said.

"We're already here. Let's go ahead in. Maybe it will pick up a little later. "

"It's already later. It's not going to get any better."

"Come on Paula. Stay. I've already paid. Besides, the music isn't bad. I'll even pay for you since we are celebrating your birthday." Rosalyn added.

"Okay. But I'm sure that I will regret letting you talk me into this."

After paying, they walked inside the ballroom. The lights in the room were very low. It took a while for Paula's eyes to adjust. When they did, she noticed that despite the blaring music, no one was dancing. They got a cup of punch and sat at a table near the dance floor. Paula was prepared for her ritual of watching everyone else dance because her height intimidated most potential dance partners. The few who did ask her to dance were either someone she knew or someone who bordered on desperation after being turned down by almost everyone else. Paula used to dance with the desperate souls until she realized that they mistook her 'yes' for interest. Then she would spend the rest of the night trying to get rid of them. Janet and Rosalyn danced several times while Paula sat at the table and watched.

By eleven-thirty, Paula found herself thinking about why hotel chairs were so uncomfortable. She wondered if it was a conscious effort to keep people from sitting too long. The deejay changed songs and the dance floor started to fill. Paula felt a tap on her shoulder and turned hoping to see someone she knew.

"Would you like to dance?"

Paula did not know the face staring at her and was about to turn him down. She hesitated for a second. The song was one of her favorites and getting out of the chair was probably a good idea.

"Sure."

Paula stood up and was relieved that he was taller than she was. She led the way onto the dance floor and stopped at a spot in the middle of the crowd. Paula evaluated her dance partner; mentally comparing him to Shane who was her gold standard. He was tall but at least two, maybe three, inches shorter than Shane. He had a smooth, dark chocolate brown complexion with puffy cheeks, long side burns and a well-groomed mustache. Shane was golden with chiseled features and clean-shaven. He appeared to have a stocky build. Paula was not sure if it was fat

64

or just a bulky sweater. Shane was nothing but lean muscle. Paula smiled to herself as she thought that Shane did not have a thing to worry about. *He is not even in the same category.*

"Can I get your name?" He asked as he leaned toward Paula to be heard over the music

"Paula."

"I'm Michael."

"It's nice to meet you Michael." Paula said out of habit.

Feeling uncomfortable with the way he kept staring at her, Paula avoided eye contact and watched how he moved. He was a very cool dancer with smooth, deliberate moves. Shane was much more of a free spirit dancer. Paula was ready for the song to end. The blood in her legs was circulating again and she was ready to return to her perch as observer. The deejay kept mixing songs, which doubled the length. When an obvious break in the music occurred, Michael walked Paula back to the table and pulled out the chair for her. His manners did not go unnoticed.

"Thanks for the dance." Paula said as she sat in her chair.

"Would you mind if I joined you?" Michael asked.

"Actually, we are leaving soon."

Paula wished he would just go away. She hated when this happened and wondered if accepting his invitation to dance was a mistake.

"Just until you are ready to leave?" Michael said with a smile.

" ....Okay." Paula said as she moved her chair closer to Janet so he could slide in a chair from the table behind them. He sat on the side of the chair so that he was facing her.

"You really look nice tonight." He said still staring at her.

"Thank you, although I'm not really dressed for a party. I just came from work." Paula said as she played with the heel of punch in her cup.

"Really. Where do you work?" He asked looking directly at her.

"A clothing store in the mall."

Paula turned towards Janet. Maybe he would get the message and go away. She was just about to ask Janet if she was ready to leave when Janet was asked to dance again.

Michael wanted to keep their conversation going. He had been watching her since she came in and liked what he saw.

"What school do you attend?"

"Superior. How about you?" Paula asked out of politeness.

"Holy Infant."

Paula was impressed. She had not met many males with brown skin that went to Catholic school.

"Oh really. How do you like it?"

"It's okay. But I don't have anything to compare it to. I've gone to Catholic schools all my life. I'm Catholic and my mother wouldn't have it any other way."

"That's a coincidence. I'm Catholic too and a veteran of Catholic schools. I switched to public schools when we moved to Dallas. Are you a senior?"

Paula was surprised that she actually wanted to know more about him.

"Yes, how about you?"

"Yes."

"The crowd is pretty light tonight. I started to leave but then I saw you come in."

"We started to leave after we got here, too."

66

Paula was slightly flattered that he had stayed because of her.

"I'm glad that you didn't. It took me a while to get enough courage to ask you to dance. I was afraid that you were going to turn me down. I guess this is my lucky night. How did you find out about this party?"

"A friend of mine heard about it and we were looking for something to do. This is suppose to be my birthday celebration."

"Is today your birthday?"

"It was a few days ago. I'm officially an adult."

"Happy belated birthday. I turned eighteen in July."

"Really. There are a lot of July birthdays in my family. What day?"

"The twenty-fifth."

"You have the same birthday as my mother."

The lighting in the ballroom was raised, signaling the end of the party. Michael looked at Paula, realizing that he was running out of time.

With the better lighting, Paula got a good look at Michael. He was not drop dead gorgeous but he was not bad. She wondered if the curls in his hair were natural. She still thought he could not compare to Shane as she stood up to leave.

"They're ending early tonight."

"It was nice meeting you, Michael."

"Can I get your phone number?"

Michael knew that he could not let her leave without getting her phone number. He wanted to see a lot more of her.

"I don't have a pen or anything to write on."

Paula lied but she did not want to hurt his feelings with the truth.   Paula walked toward the ballroom door with Michael at her side.

"Please don't leave yet. I'll be right back." Michael said as he quickly disappeared in the direction of the hotel lobby.

"Janet are you ready to go?"

"Aren't you going to wait for him to come back?"

"No, let's go. I've already got a boyfriend."

"Do I need to remind you that he lives two hundred miles away? What he doesn't know won't hurt. You're always saying you wish he lived here so you could go out more."

"I know but he's not my type."

Paula thought for a moment. If she had met him before Shane, she probably would have been happy to give Michael her phone number. They seemed to have a lot in common.

"That's even better. You don't have to worry about getting serious. You can just be friends."

"I don't know."

As the word left her lips, Michael returned and handed her a matchbook and a pen.

"Can I please have your phone number?"

"Okay."

Paula was about to give him the wrong number like she often did but then she thought about her current situation.

I am a senior in high school with a boyfriend two hundred miles away. Maybe Janet is right. What harm could it be to have a friend to go out with every now and then? Michael is a Catholic, college bound and he seems nice.

Paula wrote down her number on the flap of the matchbook and handed it back to him. He torn the flap off and then wrote his name and number on the remaining part of the matchbook and handed it to her. Paula stuck the number in her purse without even looking at it and said goodbye.

The next day started like a typical Sunday. Although Paula was tired from staying out so late after working eight hours, she had gone to early mass with her family and was washing the lunch dishes when she heard the phone ring. Paula was not expecting any calls so she did not bother to answer it. Clarice called Paula to the phone just as she was about to get her books. She had a lot of homework and wanted to get an early start.

"Hello." Paula said hoping it was Shane.

"Hi."

The greeting in return caught her off guard. She did not recognize the male voice.

"This is Michael. We met at the party last night, remember?"

"Oh yea. I didn't expect to hear from you so soon."

He must really be desperate!

"I was wondering if you had any plans for today."

Michael had debated whether to call her so soon. But he could not stop thinking about her. He had to see her again and he did not want to wait until the next weekend.

"I was just about to start my homework." Paula said.

"Would you mind some company this afternoon?" Paula hesitated. She really needed to study.

"I don't think so. I really have a lot of homework and I don't want to be up too late tonight."

Paula did not want to be bothered.

I shouldn't have given him my number.

"I won't stay long. To be honest, I haven't been able to stop thinking about you and want to make sure you're not a figment of my imagination."

Michael held his breath, hoping his risk would pay off.

"You can kick me out whenever you want."

"Let me check to make sure it's okay with my mother."

Paula put the phone down and went to the doorway of the den. Although Paula was eighteen, she still wanted to get permission to have company out of respect for her mother.

"Mom, is it okay if I have company?"

"Who?"

"Someone I met last night at the dance."

"Paula, I thought you had a lot of homework."

Clarice did not like the idea of Paula inviting someone she just met to the house.

"I do. He's not going to stay long."

"That's fine, Paula."

Clarice knew she'd be home all day to keep an eye on them.

Paula returned to the phone.

"It's okay but you really can't stay long."

"Great. Can you give me directions?"

Paula had to ask her mother for assistance with directions. She did not have a clue where he lived. It was at least a thirty-minute drive but he did not seem to mind. After Paula hung up the phone, she felt obligated to tell her mother what she knew about Michael. She knew her mother was enjoying the fact that Shane lived far away. Clarice seemed impressed that Michael was Catholic and attended Holy Infant High School.

Why am I trying to sell him to Mom?

Paula started to have mixed feelings about the impending visit.

What if Shane calls while Michael is here?

Paula decided to take preventative measures and picked up the phone. Shane answered on the first ring.

"Hello."

"How are you doing?"

"Great since you called. I was just thinking about you."

"I hope it was good thoughts."

"Of course. I was going to call you later. My mom's friends live in Carver Park. Do you know where that is?"

"Shane, I can't believe our luck. That's where we live. What street do they live on?"

"Tanner Drive."

"Shane, it is literally right around the corner. That's great!"

"My flight gets in just before six on Friday. That won't be a problem will it?"

Shane had made a reservation on the earliest flight after his mother got off work. He could not wait to see Paula again. They had a wonderful time when she came to Austin despite the horrible start. He loved her so much it scared him.

"Are you crazy? I can't wait until you get here. It's been so long since I've seen you. I don't know if I'm going to let you go home. Don't forget to bring a suit for the Toy dance. My friends can't wait to meet you."

"Okay. Would you mind if I give Steve a call? I'd like to see him while I'm there."

"That's probably a good idea. I need to work a few hours on Saturday. Maybe you could get together with Steve while I'm at work. I'll give you a call Tuesday after I find out my work

71

schedule. I'd better go now before I run up the phone bill. I love you."

"I love you too. Tell your mother I said hello. I'm looking forward to finally meeting her."

"She's looking forward to meeting you, too. I can't wait until Friday."

Paula felt guilty after she hung up the phone. She got her books and sat at the dining room table but she could not concentrate on her homework.

Call Michael and cancel. You have a boyfriend that you love. Shane is handsome, intelligent and from a good family. What more can you ask for?

Paula thought about the words in Shane's last letter, 'I never thought of marriage before until I met you...' He thought of her in future terms of marriage not just whether he could get in her pants. There was no point in misleading Michael. She found his number in her purse and went to the phone in the kitchen.

He'll understand. Just tell him you have too much homework after all - maybe another time.

A little girl answered the phone.

"Hello, Is Michael there?"

"He's not here. May I take a message?"

"No. Thank you."

It was too late. She would just have to let him know that she has a boyfriend and that she is only interested in friendship.

After re-reading the same paragraph several times, her wait was over when the doorbell rang a few minutes before three. Paula opened the door for Michael, who was standing there with a silly looking grin and wearing black slacks and a sweater. She escorted him into the den and introduced him to her mother who was entertaining company also. Michael was polite and well mannered, and although he seemed a little nervous, Paula thought that Clarice was impressed.

Since Paula's mother had company in the den, Paula led Michael into the living room where they were immediately greeted by her niece, demanding to be picked up. Autumn was sixteen months old and full of energy. Paula suspected that the doorbell had interrupted her nap.

"Michael, this is my niece, Autumn."

"Hello Autumn. You are a cutie. Can I hold you?"

Michael held out his hands and Autumn went to him willingly. He had Autumn laughing in seconds as he tickled her. He seemed to be at ease with children.

"Where did you learn to be so good with children?"

"I have two younger sisters. One's six and the other is fourteen."

Michael played with Autumn for almost thirty minutes while they talked, between flips and lifts. It appeared that they were going to be well chaperoned for the evening. Paula planned on giving him another hour before asking him to leave. He was nice but she needed to do her homework. Paula heard cheering from the television in the den.

"Paula, are you a Cowboy fan?"

"No, quite the opposite. I cheer for whichever team they are playing."

"Why?"

"I used to work at the Burger Barn near their training camp. The players would always come in after practice expecting to be treated like royalty. Most of them are so cocky. I think it's good for them to lose. Maybe it will bring them back down to earth."

"Would you mind if I check the score of the game?"

"No, go right ahead."

Paula watched as Michael went to the doorway of the den before walking to the doorway and standing next to him. She liked the smell of his cologne.

"What's the score?" Paula asked.

"The Cowboys just tied it. It's the last quarter."

"Mom, Michael and I are going to finish watching the game in my room. Autumn is with us."

They went into Paula's room with Autumn following close behind. Paula turned on the television and searched the channels for the game. Michael looked around the room, then sat on the chair at the foot of Paula's bed.

"Your father is not going to come in here and shoot me?"

"I doubt it. He lives in another state. My parents have been divorced since I was six."

Paula sat on the bed near Michael so she could have a good view of the game, but had to move when Autumn climbed up on the bed and sat between them.

"My parents are divorced too, but my dad lives here. Do you see your father much?"

"I spent every summer with him until I turned sixteen. Then I started working in the summer. I haven't seen him in over a year." "I see my dad almost every week. Have you decided on a college yet?"

"No. I have four applications that still need to be completed. How about you?"

"I'm thinking about Northern State."

"Have you decided on a major yet?"

"Computer Science. How about you?"

"Engineering"

"I'm impressed. You must be very smart."

Michael knew Paula was different the first time he saw her. The way she carried herself had caught his attention.

"I just like math and science."

"I considered engineering but everyone keeps telling me that the future is in computer programming. I'm taking a class now and I really enjoy it."

Paula was surprised at how easy the conversation flowed between them, even with Autumn trying to get Michael's attention and demanding to be flipped. Paula tried to check him out without actually staring. He was heavier than she remembered. He was actually bordering on chubby. His long side burns stopped just below his earlobes. His hair was cut short on top and slightly longer in the back. It had big, soft looking curls that were definitely natural and not the drippy, wet manmade kind.

He's nice. Maybe we can go out sometimes as friends.

Lisa came home and took Autumn so Paula could entertain her company. Paula welcomed the break because Autumn was at her energy peak. Suddenly, Paula wanted to get to know Michael better. They continued talking for a while about classes, colleges and his family, paying very little attention to the football game. They barely noticed that the game had ended. The sun was setting and the room was getting darker. Paula looked at the clock on her dresser and knew that he needed to leave. Michael kept staring at Paula, as if he were going to say something.

"Michael, I'm glad you came by. I've enjoyed talking to you."

"Does that mean it's time for me to go?"

Come on Michael. You're running out of time. Kiss her!

"Yes, I really do need to start my homework."

Paula knew that even though she was enjoying herself, he needed to leave.

"You know, I tried to call and cancel, but you had already left. A little girl answered the phone."

"Well, I'm glad that I had left. I really wanted to see you again. Thanks for letting me come."

Michael moved from the chair to the bed and leaned over to kiss Paula just as Autumn came barreling back into the room. Lisa quickly retrieved her and took her back to the kitchen.

Paula he's going to kiss you! Don't let him do that! Remember Shane.

Before Paula could get up and put some distance between them, Michael touched Paula's chin with his hand and gently lead her lips to his. His touch was so gentle that she did not resist. His lips were so warm and soft.

What difference can one kiss make?

The kiss was so gentle and inviting. Paula was surprised by her immediate response. It was as if she had known him forever.

Paula! What are you doing? Stop it now!

She could not pull away. A warm glow traveled through her body and it felt like she was floating. As they continued to kiss, she felt her breath being taken away and her pulse was racing; she did not want the kiss to end.

It was as wonderful as Michael thought it would be. Just being in the same room with her had aroused him. He could not understand his strong attraction to her but now he knew that Paula shared his feelings. Her kiss told him everything he needed to know.

Michael, stop it now before you do something that you'll regret.

Michael reluctantly pulled away just as Autumn ran into the room, demanding Michael to pick her up. Paula was relieved that Michael had a distraction. It gave her a chance to regain her composure.

What just happened? How can someone I barely know make me feel this way?... Two hours ago, Shane and I were going to spend the rest of our lives together. ... I didn't even get a chance to tell Michael that I have a boyfriend. Should I tell him now?... Why doesn't Shane's kiss make me feel like this? Maybe they do? NO! If they did, I would remember. Why do I want to kiss him again? Paula are you crazy? How could you do something so wrong?... I am not crazy. Something that felt that wonderful can't be wrong.

Michael looked at her over Autumn's head. He could tell something was on her mind.

"Are you okay?" he asked as Autumn ran off, responding to her mother's call.

"I'm not sure." Paula said.

"I'm sorry, Paula. I have been wanting to kiss you ever since we met."

"You don't need to apologize but maybe I should ... Michael I have a boyfriend, and until this kiss, I thought that we had a perfect relationship."

"I didn't know you were taken. Why isn't he here instead of me?"

"He lives in another city; that's why I didn't want to give you my number. But since he lives so far away and you seemed nice, I thought that maybe you and I could be friends and just go out sometimes. I planned to tell you about him."

"So what do you want to do?" Michael asked.

So she does have a boyfriend.

"I would like to see you again but it's going to be hard to be just friends. I'm sure of that."

"So just call and tell him you found someone else."

"I can't do that. I don't even know you that well. Besides, he's coming to see me next weekend."

"I think you know me well enough. It's obvious to me that we belong together."

"I'm not that sure."

"Look Paula. I'm going to be honest with you. I have never felt like this about anyone else before. I want to keep seeing you but I don't want to share you."

Michael said as he held her hand and looked into her eyes. Just that small touch sent a warm current though her body again. Paula stood up.

"It's getting late. Maybe you should be going. You have a long drive."

Get him out of here Paula so you can think.

"Okay. "

Michael stood up. Paula walked Michael to the door. He stepped into the den and told Clarice good-bye. Paula walked outside the door with him. The cold air felt good. He gave her a soft kiss on the lips and walked to his car.

Paula stood in the cold air for a few more seconds and then went inside, now she had more questions than answers.

What just happened? Why is he having this affect on me? The kiss felt so good. Why did you let him kiss you Paula? Is this what love feels like? This can't be love. I love Shane. It was a very big mistake to have let him come over. You're just over reacting. It was only a kiss. Stop being ridiculous. Shane is a wonderful person. We are perfect for each other. Paula, tomorrow you will just call Michael and tell him you want to be friends.

Paula got herself a snack and settled at the dining room table to study. She opened her book and started reading the chapter. She managed to read the first paragraph before her mind wandered back to Michael's kiss, sending quivers through her body. How was she going to stop thinking about him?

As Paula started the review questions, the phone rang. Not expecting any calls, Paula ignored the ringing. It was probably just some little girl calling for her brother. Paula's mother called her to the phone. Paula picked up the receiver half-expecting Taylor to be on the other end.

"Hello."

"Hi, I just got home and wanted to let you know that I had a wonderful time and I want to see you again."

"I enjoyed your company too... Michael, after you left I did some thinking."

"Oh really. I hope it was about me." Michael teased.

"It was. I don't know how you are going to take this, but I think we should just be friends for a while. After all, we just met."

Paula listened to the silence. Michael smiled. He could not stop thinking about her. A boyfriend in another city would not be any competition. Paula was going to be his.

"If that's what you want, we can just be friends, but I want to see you again."

Why is he being so persistent?

"I really need to go finish my Physics. I'm glad you made it home safely."

Paula was just about to say good-bye when Michael interrupted.

"Are you going to the Toy Dance next weekend?"

"Yes WE are. I have tickets for Shane and me."

"Who's Shane?"

"My boyfriend, who will be in town. I really need to go finish my homework."

"Well maybe, I will see you at the dance. Good luck with your homework. Good night, Paula."

Paula hung up the phone slowly. The thought of Shane and Michael both being at the dance unleashed a wave of panic.

Stop worrying! There are always hundred of people at the Toy Dance. What's the probability that Shane and I will run into Michael?

Chapter 4

Paula rushed home from school knowing that she only had forty-five minutes; his flight was arriving at five-thirty and with Friday's rush hour traffic, it would probably take an hour to get to the airport. When she opened the door to the house, the smell of furniture polish greeted her. Paula called out to see if anyone was home but there was no response. She was glad to have the house to herself. As soon as she put down her purse, she went to the bathroom and plugged in her hair curler. Returning to her room, Paula looked at the outfit hanging on the door. The stiffly ironed jeans hung in front of the mint green sweater. Her polished brown loafers sat on the floor, holding a pair of matching green socks.

After removing her shirt, Paula returned to the bathroom to wash her face and brush her teeth. She looked in the mirror at her hair, trying to decide if she wanted to wear it down or in a ponytail. She curled her bangs, rolled them with a sponge roller and then immediately unplugged the hair curler; a precaution taken ever since Autumn had burned her hand by grabbing the shiny barrel.

Paula changed clothes and looked around her room, amazed by the mess she had created. Although she didn't think that Shane would be in her room, she wanted it to be clean, just in case. The clothes were gathered off the floor and thrown into the

81

basket in her closet. Paula quickly made up her bed and put the pillow and blanket in the storage compartment of her bedroom set, then she walked through the house to make sure that nothing was out of place. She was glad that she had cleaned up the house the night before, in compliance with Clarice's rule about no company unless the house was clean.

Realizing that she was thirsty, Paula stopped in the kitchen to get something to drink. When she passed the phone, she thought about Michael and wondered if he was home from school.

Paula, what is wrong with you? You are about to pick up your boyfriend and you are thinking about someone else. Forget about him. This weekend belongs to Shane.

Paula quickly drank a glass of juice and went to the bathroom for the finishing touches. She combed her hair, deciding to leave it down, and then put on some mascara and lip-gloss. After a final misting of perfume, Paula grabbed her purse and jacket.

This is it, Paula. Please let Shane erase any thoughts of Michael.

It was a cold, gray overcast day; a stark contrast to the beautiful fall day when she had visited Shane. Paula had wanted beautiful weather for his visit. As she turned the key in the ignition, Paula looked at the gas gauge that was too close to empty.

Paula drove to the closest gas station and carefully pumped enough gas to get her through the weekend. She picked up a wipe for her hands and a pack of breath mints when she went inside to pay. Buckling her seat belt, Paula debated the quickest way to the airport, reluctantly deciding to take the highway although she preferred side streets with their slower traffic.

Dear God, please don't let me have a wreck on the way. But if I do, it will be a sign.

Paula let out a sigh of relief after she successfully merged into the fast moving traffic. As she drove, flowing with the traffic, she found her thoughts drifting from the traffic to Michael. He had called three times during the week; each time they talked for over an hour.

Michael is so easy to talk to and we have so much in common. But why do I feel like I am doing something wrong?... You are making too big a deal of this? You are only eighteen. You and Shane are not engaged. Why not date them both? It will be easy. They live in different cities. You and Shane only see each other every two or three months. What he doesn't know won't hurt him. Enjoy your senior year. For so long, you wanted to find that special person and now you have two. First Shane, then the election and now Michael. Everything is going your way. You should be dancing in the streets. All you have to do is get through this weekend. After the dance, you'll be home free. But why did I feel that way during the kiss? You probably just missed Shane so much. And Michael is just more experienced than Shane... I just met Michael but I love Shane. If you love Shane so much why are you thinking about Michael now?... But what will Mom say about me dating them both? She doesn't need to know. After all it's my life. She will probably like Shane more than Michael, but that's okay.

Paula was so distracted by her conversation with herself that she almost missed the exit for the airport, which was a zoo on

Friday evenings. The airport was dominated by one airline that was basically a shuttle service throughout Texas and the neighboring states. All the other major carriers had moved to the new airport outside the city. During the week, the airline catered to business travelers with hourly flights between every major city. But on the weekends, the airline lowered fares to attract leisure travelers. On Fridays, not only were all the business flyers rushing to get home; all the leisure travelers were racing to start their mini- vacations.

Paula wanted to find a parking space in front, so she circled the terminal four times before spotting a car pulling out. After several frustrating attempts, she finally parked the car. Paula put some money in the parking meter, ran inside the terminal and found a flight information screen just inside the door. Shane's flight was on time, which was a relief.

It took Paula ten minutes to walk fifteen gates in a sea of bodies. She wanted to be there when Shane got off the plane, certain that this time with Shane would determine their future. The test had been defined. Could Shane make her feel the same way Michael had? She would have her answer in less than fifteen minutes.

The plane was parking at the gate when Paula arrived, giving her just enough time to pop a breath mint in her mouth before the passengers emerged through the door. She looked nervously at each face wondering if he had missed the plane. Finally she saw him walking towards her with a smile; his trench coat folded over one arm and his bag in the other hand. He looked so handsome and preppy in his signature white, button-down oxford shirt, crisply pressed jeans and loafers.

Paula enjoyed watching a group of young women following Shane with their eyes and their obvious disappointment when he started walking towards her. Paula smiled with pride. Michael could not compare to Shane in physical attributes. Shane sat his bag down and gave her a long affectionate hug and a kiss on the cheek.

"Hello, there." Shane said with a big smile.

"Hi. I was afraid I was going to be late. How was the flight?"

"Great, except I almost missed it."

"You look wonderful."

"Thank you. You don't look so bad yourself."

"I am so glad to finally be here. I've missed you so much."

Shane put on his trench coat and lifted the strap of his bag onto his shoulder. Paula enjoyed the displeasure of his admirers, as she smile at them, knowing that she would be crazy to give him up. Shane put his free arm around Paula's waist, which made her feel very loved and secure.

"Did you check any luggage?" Paula asked as they started walking through the terminal.

"No, I just have this one. Have you eaten?"

"No I haven't. Does that mean you're hungry?"

"To be honest, I'm starving. I haven't had anything since lunch." Shane took Paula's hand as she led the way to her car.

"I'm parked right out front. We can stop at the Taco Fiesta near my house, if that's okay. I told Mom that we would probably eat out tonight, but tomorrow she is making some of her famous Mexican food for you. I hope you don't mind Mexican food two nights in a row."

"Not at all. I could live off Mexican food."

Shane dodged to avoid colliding with a family who decided to suddenly stop in the middle of the aisle, causing him to release his hold on Paula. She saw the policeman writing a ticket for the car next to hers as they walked to the car. She quickly looked at the meter for her space as they waited to cross the street.

"Do you need to call the Johnson's before we leave the airport?"

"I told them I'd call from your house... So this is your car."

Paula opened the hatchback for his bag. He put his bag in and then followed her to the driver's side and opened the door for her. Paula was still impressed with his manners. She could not take her eyes off Shane as he walked around the car to get in. He let the seat all the way back but his knees were still pressed against the dashboard.

"Please excuse the mess. I didn't get a chance to clean it out. It's not much, but it usually gets me where I'm going."

Paula turned to put her books on the back seat. Before she could turn the key in the ignition, Shane leaned and kissed Paula who nervously responded.

Please let this kiss be like Michael's.

Nothing happened as she went through the mechanics until Shane finally pulled away.

"Very nice." Paula said with a smile not wanting Shane to sense her disappointment.

"I was just thinking the same thing."

Paula started the car, quickly turned down the volume on the radio and pulled out of the parking space, effortlessly.

"How come it's always easier to get out of these spaces than to get in?"

"I don't know." Shane said with a smile as he looked at her.

"How are your parents?" Paula asked as they waited for the policemen to give them the right of way to merge into the exit lane.

" My mom is fine but my step-dad isn't getting around very well. Mom had to take him to the doctor today. That's why I almost missed the flight."

Shane was struggled to get out of his coat.

"Is it too warm in here? The heater is the only thing that works really well on this car."

"It's fine. How did you do on that test?"

"I managed to get a B-. I was very lucky. Next time, I'm going to start studying earlier."

"How's your mom doing?" Shane asked as he turned down the radio further.

"Fine. I think she is anxious to finally meet you."

"I'm looking forward to meeting her too. I talked to Steve last night and he doesn't mind keeping me busy while you're at work. I need to call him in the morning to let him know what time to pick me up and give him directions."

"That's great. Now I won't feel so guilty about working while you're here."

"He's coming to the dance tomorrow night, too."

"Good. I'll be able to thank him in person. I hope you like the dress that I'm going to wear."

"You're going to look beautiful."

"I'm not so sure. I should have gone on a diet."

"For what? You're perfect just the way you are."

Paula looked at Shane with a big smile.

"I knew it was some reason why I love you."

"I hope that's not the only reason... How much longer before we get to Taco Fiesta?"

"Be patient. I'm driving as fast as I can."

The sun was setting by the time they pulled into the parking lot of Taco Fiesta, one of Paula's favorite places to eat. You could get a lot of good food for very little money.

"Go ahead and order. It's my treat." Paula whispered when they got to the counter.

"Are you sure? I'm pretty hungry!"

"I'm sure. You are my guest."

Shane ordered what Paula thought was an enormous amount of food and Paula ordered a couple of tacos and a drink. They sat across from each other in a booth by a window. Paula watched Shane eat between bites of her tacos, wondering how so much had changed in one week. Prior to the kiss, she thought they were going to be together forever. Now she wasn't sure of anything except that her feelings for Shane were totally different than those for Michael. Shane touched her hand.

"What's wrong? You were looking pretty serious."

"I'm just a little tired. It's been a long week, waiting for you to get here... You really were hungry." Paula said as she watched him finish his third taco and unwrap the burrito.

"I told you... Paula, instead of calling the Johnsons from your house, would you mind if we drop off my bag on the way? If my suit gets too wrinkled, you'll be ashamed to be seen with me at the dance."

"I could never be ashamed to be seen with you. It's probably the other way around. I don't mind stopping. You probably should call your mother too. I'm sure she's worried about her baby." Paula smiled at him.

"I'm definitely not a baby."

"No one knows that better than me... Shane, I've got a better idea. Why don't I drop you off so you can get settled in and call home? You're only staying five minutes from my house. You can give me a call when you are ready and I'll pick you up. That way you won't feel so rushed and you can visit with the Johnsons before it gets too late."

"You're not trying to get rid of me are you?" Shane asked with a grin that concealed his braces.

"What do you think?"

"I think that I'm lucky to have you." Paula just smiled without comment.

If you knew I kissed someone else last weekend, you'd feel different.

It only took ten minutes to go from the Taco Fiesta to the Johnson's house, a small frame house with a well-manicured lawn. As they pulled into the driveway, Paula saw someone looking out the window.

"Looks like they are expecting you. I didn't ask if they have a daughter." Paula said teasingly.

"Yes they do and I hear she's beautiful."

"Are you trying to make me jealous?"

"I don't know. Is it working?"

"Yes."

"Good. But you don't have anything to be jealous about. Their daughter is thirty-five and married with a couple of children. They're an elderly couple."

"Does that mean I have to have you in early?"

"I hope not. Will you come in to meet them?"

"Sure."

Paula got out of the car and opened the hatchback for Shane to get his bag then followed him to the door. They rang the doorbell and waited. A distinguished looking, elderly gentleman opened the door and greeted Shane with a hug. Shane introduced Paula who thanked them for hosting Shane and then said good-bye. Shane walked her back to the car, holding her hand tightly.

"Hurry up and get settled in. I'll be waiting by the phone for your call." Paula said as Shane gave her a long, firm hug.

"I'm really glad to be here with you." Shane said as he reluctantly released her and opened the car door.

"I'm glad you are here too."

Paula backed out of the driveway and waved good-bye. She wondered why Shane's kiss didn't make her feel the way Michael's had as she pulled into the driveway. As soon as she opened the door, Autumn emerged to greet her with a big hug. Shortly afterwards, Paula's mother came out of her bedroom.

"Where is Shane?"

"I dropped him off at the Johnson's so he could unpack and call his mother. He is going to call when he's ready for me to pick him up."

"Did you get something to eat?"

"Yes, ma'am. We stopped at Taco Fiesta. Did you have to go in the field today?"

"Yes, I had to audit this man who wasn't very happy to find out his auditor was a colored woman."

"Do you want me to cook dinner?"

"That's okay. I think there are enough leftovers for whoever wants to eat."

Paula was relieved. With all the excitement around Shane's visit, she had forgotten to plan anything for dinner. Paula had started cooking weeknight dinners in junior high. Initially, she would just start dinner and Clarice would finish when she got home from work. Eventually, Paula began cooking the entire meal, learning quickly that Clarice was in a much better mood when she came home to a clean house and a hot meal.

Paula picked up Autumn and flipped her over.

"Where is your mother, Pumpkin?"

"She's in the back closed up." Clarice answered.

Paula walked to her room and hung her purse on the door. The door to her sister's room was cracked open. Paula knocked quietly before she and Autumn opened the door and went into the room. The door stopped against Autumn's crib that was rarely used now. Her sister was lying across the bed in the dark room looking at television. Paula could tell she was depressed about something.

"Where's your lover boy?" Her sister teased as Paula deposited Autumn on the bed. The light from Paula's bedroom was providing much needed illumination.

"I dropped him off where he's staying. I'm going to pick him up later."

"Do you have five dollars that I can borrow until payday?"

"You're not going out tonight? You know that I can't keep Autumn."

"I didn't ask you to keep her. She's going to spend the night with her favorite aunt."

Paula went to her room to get her wallet, hoping that the loan would lift her sister's spirit. Paula stood in the doorway while she looked in her wallet.

"I don't have a five dollar bill. It's probably silly of me to ask for change back." Paula said as she handed her sister a ten-dollar bill.

"Sis, you know I am good for it. Don't I always pay you back?"

"Yea, right."

Paula went back to her room, put her wallet back in her purse and turned on the television. A few minutes later, the phone rang, prompting Paula to look at her watch. Her brother answered the phone before she could get it.

"Paula, it's for you. Please don't be long. I'm expecting a call." He yelled from the kitchen.

Paula picked up the hall phone, surprised that Shane called so quickly. It had only been thirty minutes since she dropped him off.

"I got it."

She waited for her brother to hang up the extension.

"Boy that was quick. Are you ready?"

"What was quick?"

The voice on the other end responded. It wasn't Shane.

"...I'm sorry, Michael. I thought you were someone else."

Paula couldn't believe she had made that mistake.

"Obviously. I was just thinking about you and how much I want to see you, so I decided to take a chance and call. I guess your boyfriend arrived safely."

"Yes he did. I'm waiting for him to call."

"So I guess that means, I won't be able to see you tonight."

"Michael, you know that's impossible."

"Have you told him about us, yet?"

"...No."

"Are you going to?"

Why is he pressuring me?

"...I'm not sure there's anything to tell."

"There is and you know it. You feel the same way I do. Would you like for me to tell him tomorrow at the dance?"

"Definitely not. If anyone tells him anything, it's going to be me."

Michael could hear the panic in Paula's voice.

Back off or you'll lose her.

"I'm just kidding, Paula. I'd never do anything to hurt you. Will you call me after he leaves tonight? If I can't be with you, at least let me hear your voice."

"I'll call, if its not too late."

"It won't be too late. I have my own phone."

"Okay. I really need to get off the phone."

"Promise me you'll call after he leaves."

"I promise. "

"I'll be waiting."

Paula hung up the phone.

Paula, are you crazy? How could you promise him that?

She was sitting on her bed wondering what to do, when the phone rang again. Paula answered before her brother could.

"Hello."

"May, I speak to Paula, please?"

93

"It's me. Are you ready?"

"Yep. I'm ready."

"Great, Shane. I'll be there in five minutes."

She thought about her conversation with Michael as she drove the short distance. Shane was waiting for her as she pulled into the driveway. He gave her a kiss as he closed the car door.

"Are you ready to meet my mother?"

"Sure."

"Lisa and Autumn may already be gone. Lisa is going out and Autumn is going to spend the night with her favorite aunt."

"I thought you were her favorite aunt."

"So did I."

"That's okay, I'm sure I'll meet them before I leave."

"What time did you tell the Johnson's you would be back?"

"Around eleven. I hope that's okay with you. They have to let me in and I didn't want to keep them up too late."

"I'll have you back by then. I don't want you to turn into a pumpkin."

It won't be too late to call Michael.

"I thought we'd just watch some TV tonight."

Paula opened the front door and led Shane into the den where Clarice was watching television. Clarice looked at them and waited for the introduction.

"Mom, this is Shane. Shane, my mother."

"Ms. Hayes. It's good to finally meet you."

"It's nice to meet you too Shane. How was your flight?"

"Fine, thank you." Shane said as he took off his coat and handed it to Paula who left the room to hang it up.

"Did you call your parents so they won't be worried?"

"Yes ma'am. They told me to tell you hello."

"Shane make yourself comfortable. Would you like something to eat? " Paula's mother asked as she smoothed her hair down.

"No thank you, Ms. Hayes. I'm still full."

Shane sat on the sofa.

"What about something to drink?" Clarice asked Shane as Paula walked back into the room.

"Mom, I'll get us something a little later."

Paula went to get the television guide off the television.

"Shane, how is school going?"

"Good. We just finished exams."

"Have you decided on a college yet?"

"No ma'am. I'm waiting to see where I am accepted."

"I keep telling Paula that she needs to hurry up and get her applications in. I really want her to go to Hilman. It's such a good school."

Paula tried to hide her frustration. *It's my life, mother!*

"Did Paula tell you that I'm cooking Mexican food for you tomorrow?"

"Yes ma'am. It's my favorite."

"That's good. Well, I'm going to look at television in my room. Shane, let me know if you need anything."

"Thank you. Ms Hayes."

Shane stretched out his legs and leaned back on the sofa after Clarice left the room; Paula sat down beside him. He moved closer and put his arm around her.

"I am really glad to be here."

"Shane, I'm glad you're here, too. What do you want to watch?"

"You!"

Paula felt her heart beating faster but it wasn't the rhythm of excitement; it was fear.

"No, really."

"This is fine. I don't think we will be looking at it very much anyway." Shane said with a mischievous smile.

Paula, calm down.

Shane began to rub his hand up and down Paula's arm. Paula was annoyed by the action but she knew that she needed to hide these new feelings. Shane kissed her cheek and then moved to her neck. Paula knew the big kiss was coming but she wasn't ready. Paula gently pushed away from Shane and kissed him on the cheek.

"I'm thirsty. Can I get you something?"

Paula stood up and waited for his response.

"Sure. I'll take whatever you are having. Do you need any help?"

"No, thanks. I'll be right back."

Paula retreated to the kitchen that adjoined the den. The swinging door closed behind her as she went to the cabinet to get two glasses. She sat the glasses on the counter and leaned against it for support.

Paula, what is wrong with you? You have been looking forward to Shane's visit for two months.

She looked at the phone hanging on the wall and thought about Michael. She wanted him to be in the den waiting for her.

Michael made her feel like she was floating. As she thought of his kiss, her body tingled.

"What am I going to do?"

Paula sighed as she walked to the refrigerator, ignoring the magnetic pull of the phone, opened the door and stared at the pitcher of fruit punch and the cans of soda. She could not return without the drinks that were her excuse to escape. She grabbed the pitcher of punch and took it to the counter. While trying to decide whether or not to get some ice, Paula heard the familiar squeak of the kitchen door as it opened and turned to see Shane walking towards her.

"What's taking so long? I thought you might need help."

"No, I just couldn't decide what to get. Is punch okay?"

"Sure."

Paula turned to the waiting glasses on the counter and began to pour carefully, not wanting to clean red stains from the counter. Just as she finished pouring the first glass, Shane walked up behind her, put his hands on her waist and kissed her on the neck.

"You are going to make me spill this." Paula said as she quickly filled the other glass.

"That's okay. I'm not that thirsty anyway."

Shane gently turned her towards him. Paula was trapped between Shane and the counter. Shane moved in closer so that their bodies pressed together. She could feel his hardness as he looked at her.

"Did I tell you how much I missed you?"

He kissed Paula lightly on the lips. Paula closed her eyes briefly and hoped that his touch could make her feel the same way Michael's did. Shane looked deep into Paula eyes.

"I love you so much. I've never felt this way before."

"I love you too."

The words barely had time to leave her mouth before Shane's lips met hers. He held her tightly as he kissed her with a sense of urgency that revealed his desire. Paula waited but her body would not respond the way it had with Michael. She quickly resorted to the learned technique, hoping to mask her true feelings. Paula knew that Shane had to be the one to end the kiss.

"Paula!"

Clarice's voice, emerging from the other end of the house, was a welcomed interruption. Shane pulled away quickly. Paula gave Shane a smile. He looked like a little boy getting caught with his hand in the cookie jar.

"I'm coming." Paula called.

She wiped her lips with her hand and retreated to Clarice's room.

When Paula returned to the kitchen, Shane and the drinks were gone. She found him sitting on the coach in the den holding their drinks. He handed her the glass after Paula sat down on the middle of the sofa.

"I'm sorry that we were interrupted... Why are you sitting way over there?"

"It's safer! Things were getting a little hot in there and I don't want to start something that we can't finish." Paula said with a smile, hoping Shane would take it as a compliment.

"What did your mother want?"

"She just wanted to remind me not to keep you out too late. Do you want to play some cards?"

Paula hoped to avoid another incident that might reveal her true feelings before she was ready.

"I'd much rather play something else." Shane smiled.

"Okay, I'll behave. Gin rummy or spades?"

"How about gin?"

Paula went into the dining room to retrieve a deck of cards.

"Are we keeping score?" Shane asked when Paula returned.

"Of course. How else will I know how badly I beat you?"

Paula tried to concentrate on the card game but she was trying to decide when to tell Shane about Michael and how.

Paula, wait until Sunday before he gets on the plane. No, Paula. You can't fool him. He probably already knows something is wrong. You need to tell him tonight. He'll understand. You just want to date other people, but don't let him know you've already found someone else to date. Blame it on the distance. He can't expect you to sit at home every weekend between his visits. But what if he finds someone else.

"Gin. I think that makes five hundred points." Shane said with a look of victory.

"You won, but only because I let you." Paula said as she stacked the card.

Paula enjoyed being with Shane and for a brief moment wished that she had never kissed Michael. But it was too late. She had and her relationship with Shane would never be the same. Paula moved closer to Shane and welcomed his arm around her.

"Are you ready to go? It's almost eleven and I'm sure they are waiting for you."

"Not really, but I guess I should. What time are you getting off work tomorrow?"

"Three o'clock. I hope you don't mind but I really need the money for Christmas."

"I understand. Besides, it will be good to see Steve again."

Paula went to tell Clarice that she was taking Shane to the Johnsons and then she got her purse and their coats. Paula decided to broach the subject of dating other people immediately to see how Shane would react.

"Shane, do you really love me?" Paula asked as she backed out of the driveway.

"You know I do. I wouldn't be here if I didn't. Why would you ask that?"

"I don't know, it's just hard to believe sometimes. You live so far away and I know you have to get as lonely as I do. Do you ever think about dating someone else while we are apart?"

"No! Why would I want to date someone else; I have you." *Why is she bringing this up now?*

"Paula, do you want to date someone else?"

Paula saw the hurt in Shane's eyes.

"No!"

Paula, don't do this to him. Wait until he's back home.

"Good. Let's not talk about that anymore."

They pulled into the driveway. Paula wondered how she was ever going to tell Shane about Michael. Shane leaned over and kissed Paula on the cheek.

"What time are you going to pick me up tomorrow?" Shane asked as he got out of the car.

100

"Probably around three-thirty. Let me give you my work number in case you need to reach me."

Paula reached in the back seat for some paper and a pen. She quickly wrote down the number and handed Shane the paper.

"Have fun tomorrow with Steve."

"I will. Drive safely. I love you."

"I love you too, Shane."

Paula knew she meant it, but was their love enough?

She picked up the hall phone on the way to her room and closed the door behind her.

"Hi, did I wake you up?"

"No. I didn't think you were going to call but I'm glad you did. I've been thinking about you all night. Did you tell him about us?"

"No. I started to but I couldn't."

"Why?"

"I didn't know how he was going to take it. After all, he did come here just to see me. I don't think I should tell him."

"I think you should. I want to be with you and I don't want to share."

"Michael, we just met. We don't even know each other. What if I break up with him and you and I don't work out."

"Paula, you and I were meant to be together and you know it. The other night when I kissed you, something happened. I can't explain it."

"I know. I have never felt like that before. But I can't hurt Shane. I really do love him."

"More than you love me."

"Michael, I don't love you. We just meet."

"You do love me. You just won't admit it. I would be happy to tell him tomorrow night at the dance."

"No, I think I should be the one to tell him."

"Paula, I want to be with you at the dance tomorrow."

"But you can't, Michael."

"If I see you, can I at least speak?"

"Sure. But we are just friends."

"Paula, you know that I don't want to be just friends."

"I know... Goodnight Michael."

"Do you know that I've already started dreaming about us?"

"Are they good dreams?"

"Very good. Goodnight Paula. I'll see you tomorrow."

Paula quietly hung up the phone.

Can Michael be right? Do I love him more than Shane?

Chapter 5

Christmas was Paula's favorite time of year. But the holiday spirit eluded her as she tried to understand what was happening to her, spending most of the time between customers wrestling with her emotions. She had been so sure that she loved Shane until she met Michael. Now Paula knew why a long distance relationship was so difficult and she could not deny the chemistry between her and Michael. She could not explain it, but whatever was between them felt too wonderful to be wrong. The ideal situation would be to date Michael and Shane, but that seemed unscrupulous. How could she honestly tell Shane that she loves him and then let someone else make her feel the way Michael did?

Paula bought the toys for the dance and some black pantyhose during her break. The Toy Dance was the major charity event of the year. The admission for the dance was free with a new, unwrapped toy. Last year's dance collected over a thousand toys for under privileged children. Paula picked out a toy truck and a beautiful brown skinned doll. With all the holiday traffic, Paula picked Shane up later than she wanted.

The smell of Mexican food filled the house. Clarice was still preparing dinner when they arrived. Paula and Shane went straight to the kitchen to offer help. The house was full of commotion. Paula introduced Shane to her family and the friends her mother had invited. Shane fit right in and enjoyed himself. With the threat of intimacy removed, Paula realized how much fun it was to be with Shane and by the time she took him to the Johnson's to change for the dance, Paula was convinced that they shared something that she did not want to lose.

The phone rang just as Paula walked out of the bathroom, refreshed from a quick shower and excited about the dance. She decided to answer it since she was so close.

"Hello."

"May I speak to Paula?"

"This is she."

"Hi. I just thought I'd give you a call to see how you are doing."

Paula went in her room and closed the door.

"I'm fine. I was just getting ready for the dance. Are you still going?" Paula asked hoping that he wasn't.

"Of course. I wouldn't pass up an opportunity to see you."

"There will be so many people there that we probably won't even see each other. Are you bringing a date?"

"No, if I can't be with you, I'd rather go alone."

"I'm sure you won't be alone very long."

"Why, are you planning on dumping Shane to be with me?"

"No, I'm not."

"Then I will be alone. Have you told him about us, yet?"

"No."

"You know that we should be going to this dance together but I guess there's nothing that I can do about that now. What time is he leaving tomorrow?"

"Shane's flight is at noon."

"Can I come over after he leaves?"

"I don't know... Can you call me tomorrow? I need to finish dressing."

"I'm looking forward to seeing you tonight. Will you save me a dance?"

"I don't know. I've got to go. Bye."

"Good-bye Paula. I'll see you at the dance."

Paula put the phone down, momentarily dazed and upset with Michael for once more intruding on her happiness. After regaining her composure, Paula finished dressing and was contented with the image reflecting back in the full-length mirror. The black crepe dress that stopped just above her knees had see-through, puffed, short sleeves with bans of colorful satin ribbons. The ribbons gave the conservative black dress the right touch for the holiday. The jet-black stockings and black pumps added to the conservative look. Clarice complimented Paula when she came into the room to deliver her black evening bag.

Shane was anxiously waiting for Paula and opened the door as soon as she rang the bell. Paula looked at him in his suit and remembered the evening that they first met. He looked as debonair as he did then.

"Paula, you look beautiful."

"Why, thank you. You look very nice too. Are you ready to go to the social event of the year?"

"Let's go." Shane said as he held the door open for her.

They both admired the Christmas lights as they drove to the dance. Shane noticed that Paula was unusually quiet. Finally, Shane broke the silence.

"Paula, do you think you'll be able to come visit over the Christmas break?"

"I'm not sure. I know we will be driving through but I don't know what my mother's plans are."

"Maybe I'll be able to drive down and spend a day with you... I thought a lot about what you said last night. I want to see you more often too. How would you feel about us going to the same college?"

"Are you serious?"

"Very."

Shane waited for a response but Paula didn't know what to say, unable to believe the irony of the situation. Two weeks prior, she had wanted to suggest the same thing to Shane but was afraid what his response would be. Now she was the one that didn't want it. She wasn't even sure if she wanted him anymore. Paula knew she had to say something.

"Shane we aren't even applying to the same schools."

"We can. The application deadlines haven't passed."

"You really are serious?"

"Yes, I am."

"Shane, that is a big step that we really need to think about. Here's our exit."

Paula was relieved to be able to change the subject.

The dance was being held downtown at the Wyatt Hotel. As they stepped off the elevator, Paula was thrilled to see the hundreds of well-dressed African-American teens, reminded of the summer conferences.

A table was outside the ballroom door, where parents were collecting the gifts and stamping hands. Paula introduced Shane to the chaperons that she knew; some remembered him from the conference. After exchanging pleasantries and getting a Christmas tree stamp on their hands, they followed the crowd into the ballroom.

Paula looked around in awe as they entered the ballroom; the decorations took her breath away and made her feel like she had stepped into a fairytale. The most magnificent Christmas tree that Paula had ever seen was directly across from the entrance to the ballroom. It was over twenty feet tall and every inch was covered with gold ornaments and thousands of tiny white lights. The spacious dance floor was surrounded by more than a hundred tables, each decorated with a scarlet tablecloth and an evergreen, candled centerpiece. The ambient lighting washed the ballroom in a golden glow. The wall between the ballroom and the lobby was glass, adding to the magical atmosphere. Music was booming in the background. Paula felt Shane take her hand in his and squeeze it tightly.

"Isn't it beautiful, Shane?"

"Yes, it is. Just like you."

"Thank you."

Paula was buoyant as she looked around the room, in search of a familiar face. Rosalyn walked up just as they were about to sit at an empty table.

"Hi, Paula. We have a table over here." Rosalyn said pointing towards a table near the glass wall.

"Hi, Rosalyn. You look great."

"Thanks. So do you.... Well, do I get an introduction?"

"I'm sorry. Where are my manners? This is Shane Howard. Shane, this is Rosalyn Davis. She goes to school with me and has to listen to me talk about you endlessly."

"Shane, it's a pleasure to finally meet you. I've heard so much about you."

"It is very nice to meet you, too."

Paula and Shane followed Rosalyn to the table. Shane helped Paula take off her coat and pulled out the chair for her. Paula watched as he removed his coat, proud to be with him. After hanging his coat on the back of a chair, he sat down next to her. Rosalyn introduced Shane to the others at the table.

"He's better looking in person. " Rosalyn whispered.

"Thanks. Have you seen Taylor?"

"Not yet. Is she suppose to be coming?"

"I'm not sure. I've been so busy that I haven't talked to her."

"Are you sure he doesn't have a brother?" Paula turned to Shane.

"Shane, Rosalyn wants to know if you have a brother?" Shane smiled, blushing slightly.

"Not that I know of."

Shane reached under the table and held Paula's hand. Paula squeezed his hand, enjoying the warmth that flowed between them and then slid her chair closer to Shane's so that they were almost touching. Shane let go of her hand and put his arm around the back of her chair. A song played that Paula loved and she started moving in her chair to the beat.

"Would you like to dance?" Shane asked.

Paula looked out on the dance floor that was filling with enthusiastic dancers.

"Sure."

Shane stood up, pulled Paula's chair out for her and held her hand as he led her to the dance floor. While they danced, Paula looked around the ballroom for Michael, but he was no where to be found.

"I think I'm ready to sit down." Paula whispered in Shane's ear after they danced two songs.

Just as Paula started to leave the dance floor, the music changed to a slow melodious tune. Shane held his hand out for Paula's and led her back to him. Paula placed her hands on Shane's shoulders and he held her securely around the waist. Paula looked up at Shane and felt like she really was in a fairytale; Shane was her prince charming. Paula rested her head on Shane's chest and closed her eyes. The smell of his cologne, the beat of the music and the warmth of his body shrouded Paula in serenity. She felt him hardening as they both tightened their hold. The song ended too soon for Paula who wanted to be held like that forever. She reluctantly let Shane lead her from the dance floor, holding her hand tightly. When they returned to the table, Shane remained standing.

"I'm going to get something to drink. Would you like something?"

"Sure, a glass of punch would be great."

"Rosalyn, can I bring you some punch also?"

"Yes, thank you." Rosalyn said.

"Girl, how did you get so lucky?" Rosalyn asked as soon as Shane left the table.

"I don't know. Sometimes good things happen." Paula said with a smile.

The night was going better than Paula had expected. Being with Shane felt very right, just like at the conference. Paula was listening to Rosalyn's conversation, when someone sat next to her. Paula turned around expecting to see Shane but instead was face to face with Michael.

"Hi. You look beautiful."

"Thank you. But you can't sit here. Shane will be right back." Paula said, resolved not to let Michael interfere.

"I know. I waited for him to leave before I came over. Don't worry, he's talking to someone in the lobby."

"I didn't know I was being watched." Paula said slightly annoyed.

"I promised you that I would not cause any trouble. I just wanted to speak to you and maybe reserve a dance?"

"I don't think so."

Paula was nervous that Shane would see her talking to Michael.

"I'm going to leave. But I'll be back."

Michael left and sat at the table next to theirs. Shane came back with two cups of punch and Steve. He handed Paula and Rosalyn the cups and remained standing.

"Hi, Paula."

"Hi, Steve. I hear you and Shane had a great time today. Thank you for keeping him company while I was at work."

"We had a lot of catching up to do."

"Paula, Steve and I were talking about going to the observation deck in the tower. Would you like to come?"

"No. I'm not a big fan of heights. You go ahead without me."

"Are you sure you won't mind?"

"I'm sure. I'm tired from working. I think I'll just sit here and talk to Rosalyn."

"I won't be gone long."

Shane gave Paula a kiss on the lips and disappeared into the crowd.

"I'd never leave you alone." Michael said as he slid into Shane vacant chair a few minutes later.

Rosalyn looked at Paula with a puzzled look.

"Rosalyn, do you remember Michael? We met him at the party last weekend."

"Oh, yes. Nice to see you again." Rosalyn said politely.

"Where is he going?"

"Up in the tower."

"Then it looks like I may get my dance after all."

"Maybe."

"You really do look beautiful tonight."

"Thank you. You look nice too."

"Do you know that I have been thinking about you all day?"

Paula looked at him and that feeling in her stomach started again. Paula felt angry for letting him affect her like that and was about to ask him to leave when a popular song came on and the dance floor started to fill.

"May I please have this dance? I won't give up until you dance with me."

Paula thought that if she were going to dance with him, it needed to be while Shane was gone.

"...Okay, but just this one and then you need to leave."

Michael reached for her hand but Paula acted like she did not see it. There was no way she was going to risk Shane seeing her holding hands with Michael.

The song was very long and Paula was beginning to wonder if Shane was back yet. The deejay mixed a slow song onto the end of the song they were dancing to. Michael gave Paula a pleading look as he gently put his arms around her and the crowd thinned on the dance floor. Paula tried to resist but once their eyes met and her body was next to his, she couldn't. She rested her hands on his shoulders and struggled to maintain a respectable distance, but his body was like a magnet drawing her closer. Shane had one hand was on her waist while the other hand slowly stroked the center of her back. His touch and the way he looked at her generated feelings that were drastically different from her feelings for Shane. There was no serenity or security, only excitement and the intense memory of a pleasurable experience that she could not forget. Paula could feel the arc between them when he whispered in her ear how much he wanted to kiss her again.

Shane and Steve left the ballroom and walked through the crowded lobby to the escalator. As he rode the escalator up to the main level, Shane looked through the glass window. He saw Paula sitting at their table and smiled as he thought about how happy he was to be with her. Although he was a little concerned that Paula seemed a little distant and preoccupied. He was worried that she was pushing herself too much between school and work.

"Hey man. Why are you looking so serious?" Steve asked as they stepped off the escalator.

"Oh, I was just thinking about Paula. I'm really lucky to have her."

"She's lucky to have you, too. Anything wrong?"

"No, I don't think so. She really looks beautiful tonight."

"Yes, she does."

"So why am I here with you?" Shane said with a smile.

"You were the one that wanted to go to the top of the tower."

"Well, let's hurry up so I can get back to my lady."

They walked to the elevator that went up to the tower. There was a crowd already waiting for the elevator. Shane and Steve had to wait a few minutes. When they got up to the observation deck, they walked to the window.

"It really is turning around?" Shane said with a look of amazement.

"I told you. "

"Look at the lights. It's beautiful. I wish Paula were here to see it with me."

"You guys are pretty serious."

"I think she is the one. I've never felt this way about anyone. I think we could actually get married after college."

"That's serious."

"Have you decided on a college yet?"

"No, but lately I've been thinking about Paula and I going to the same school . . .. We'd better be heading back now. I've left Paula alone long enough."

Shane and Steve worked their way through the crowd and back to the elevator. Shane was in a hurry to see Paula. As they descended the escalator, Shane looked through the glass wall at their table. He saw Rosalyn but Paula was not there. Shane wondered if she had gone to the restroom. Just as they entered the ballroom, Shane heard a slow song start and hoped that Paula would make it back in time for them to dance. He needed to hold her close to him again. Shane was just about to go to the table when he looked out on the dance floor.

Her back was to Shane, so she did not see him but he saw her. Shane felt a knot form in his stomach. At first, Shane wanted to go out on the dance floor but his feet stayed firmly planted. Steve saw Paula on the dance floor a few seconds after Shane.

"He's probably just a friend."

"Yeah, right. Friends don't dance that close. He's rubbing her back!"

"What do you want to do?"

"I don't know. Come on."

"Where are we going?"

"Back to the lobby. I want to see if he's just a friend."

Shane found a crowded spot outside the ballroom where he had a clear view of the dance floor and their table and watched Paula dance with Michael. He knew instinctively that they were more than friends when Michael whispered in Paula's ear and she looked into his eyes. Shane felt like someone had just kicked him in the stomach.

So that's why Paula is acting different. I knew it was too good to be true.

114

After the song ended, Shane watched them walk back to the table and tried to convince himself that he was just overreacting.

If they are just friends, he'll walk her back to the table and leave. Please, let him leave.

When Michael pulled out his chair and sat down next to Paula, all doubts were removed. Steve looked at his friend's pale face and was worried.

"Are you all right, man?"

"I need to get out of here."

"Aren't you going to say anything to her?"

"What can I say? I see you found someone new. No, I need some time to pull myself together. Let's go for a walk outside."

"Man, it's cold out there. You don't even have your coat. How about going back up to the tower?"

"No, I need some fresh air."

Paula looked at her watch and was surprised by Shane's inconsiderate behavior. He had been gone for over an hour. Michael had promised to leave as soon as Paula saw Shane coming. Paula's eyes had been fixed on the escalator for the last thirty minutes, and she was beginning to worry that something had happened to Shane.

"Paula, you know I would never leave you alone like this."

"Shane probably just lost track of time. This is not like him."

"I'm glad he's gone so I can spend some time with you. What time should I come over tomorrow?"

"I don't know… I think you should leave now. He should be coming back soon."

"You don't want to introduce us?"

115

"Very funny. Michael, please leave. I'll talk to you tomorrow."

Michael got up and touched Paula's hand. After he left, Rosalyn turned to Paula.

"Some of us can't even get one boyfriend and you have two."

"Michael is not my boyfriend. He's just a friend."

"You could have fooled me. You two looked pretty serious on the dance floor."

Paula had hoped that her attraction to Michael wasn't that obvious.

"Michael's just someone nice to go out with sometimes."

"Does Shane know about him?"

"No, and he doesn't need to. Speaking of whom. Where is he? He's been gone for over an hour. I guess I'll have to go find him."

Paula picked up her purse and went into the lobby before realizing that she needed to go to the restroom before beginning her search. Just as she was walking in the direction of the restrooms, she saw Steve and Shane coming in the door from outside. Paula was immediately concerned because Shane looked sick.

"Where have you guys been? I was just about to send out the search party. Shane are you okay?"

"I'm fine. We decided to take a walk."

"It's freezing outside."

"Actually it felt better than inside." Shane said coldly then looked directly in Paula's eyes.

"Did you miss me Paula?"

"Of course I did. What time do you want to leave?"

116

"We can leave now."

"Shane it's still early . . .. I was about to go to the restroom but we can leave as soon as I get back."

Shane and Steve went back to the table to wait for Paula.

"Are you going to ask her who he is?"

"I don't think I want to know."

"Hey man, if she wants him then she is not good enough for you."

"Then why does it hurt so much? I wanted to marry her!"

"Hey, talk to her. You guys can work it out."

"I don't know. How can I trust her? She was dancing with him when she came to the dance with me."

"Well you did leave her alone."

"So what happens while I'm at home?"

Steve hated to see his friend in so much pain and didn't want to say.

Paula wondered why they both looked so serious when she returned. Shane helped Paula with her coat and put his on, then they waited for Rosalyn to return from the dance floor.

"Rosalyn, we are getting ready to leave."

"Why so early?"

"Shane is ready to leave."

"Shane, it was a pleasure meeting you."

"It was nice meeting you too, Rosalyn."

"I hope you enjoy the rest of your visit."

"Thank you."

Shane and Paula said good-bye to the rest of the people at their table. Paula glanced quickly at Michael as she walked past his table while Shane repressed the urge to punch him. Steve walked with them to the lobby. They stopped at the door leading to the parking lot. Steve looked at Shane and wondered if he was going to be okay.

"Steve, thanks for everything." Shane said as he shook his hand.

"I'm glad you came to visit. Let me know when you decide on a school. Maybe we can be roommates."

"Steve, thanks for showing Shane around while I was at work."

"Bye, Paula."

Paula reached in her purse for her keys and they walked to the car in silence; Paula wondering what was wrong with Shane and Shane wondering what he was going to do.

Shane opened the door for Paula after she unlocked it then walked around and got in the car. Paula found the parking ticket in her purse and took out some money. In the back of Paula's mind, she knew something was terribly wrong.

"What time did you tell the Johnson's that you would be back?"

"I wasn't sure so they gave me a key."

"Are you hungry? We can stop and get something to eat."

"No, I'm not hungry."

"Shane, are you feeling okay?"

"I'm fine. Why do you ask?"

"I don't know. You look a little pale and you wanted to leave the dance so early."

"I was just ready to leave the dance."

Paula paid for the parking and drove towards the freeway. Shane stared out the window. He had a lot on his mind and the last thing he wanted to do was look at Paula.

I hope she just drops me off. All I want to do is pack my bags and get out of here. How could she do this? I really thought we had something special. At least she could have told me before I wasted the money to come up here. I could have used this money for Christmas. But this explains why she was acting so strange last night. Well once I step on that plane tomorrow, she won't have to worry about me.... Maybe I should just take a taxi to the airport. But if I do that, she'll want to know why. No, the best thing to do is just act like nothing happened. I do not want to hear the words 'let's just be friends'. From now on Shane, you need to focus on your studies and forget about a relationship.

Paula was concerned about the tone in Shane's voice. Something was definitely wrong but what.

Oh my God! He had to have seen me with Michael. But how? I was watching for him - except for when Michael and I were slow dancing. How much did he see?

Paula remembered Rosalyn's comment about her dancing with Michael and suddenly regretted her actions. She came to the dance with Shane, yet the whole time he was gone, she was with Michael.

Steve must have seen it too. That's the only thing that could explain their behavior in the lobby. How could I do this to Shane? He is such a wonderful person. I should be counting my blessing that he feels the way he does about me. So what do I do now? I can't just take him back to the Johnson's. We have to talk . . .. But what do I tell him? I don't want to lose him. What

119

if things don't work out with Michael? Paula, listen to yourself. You want your cake and to eat it too. That is not fair to Shane. Either you breakup with him now or you stop seeing Michael. You cannot have both.

Before she knew it, their exit was coming up and she still had not decided what to do but knew that they needed to talk. There was a little park one street over from where Shane was staying, which was the only option that she could think of.

"Do you mind if we stop by a park and talk for a while?"

"I'd rather not."

"Please, Shane. We need to talk. It's important."

"Okay, Paula." Shane said without looking at her.

The park was on the fringe of the neighborhood and was a popular place for couples to park. One end of the park had a basketball court that was very well lighted; the other end of the park with the playground and picnic table had less lighting. Paula drove until she found an isolated spot to park and turned of the ignition. It was a fairly cold night and she knew that they wouldn't be able to stay too long.

Paula turned the radio down as she contemplated how to begin but she didn't get the chance. Shane took matters into his own hands.

"So who is he?" Shane asked, keeping his eyes fixed on the empty basketball court in the distance.

It was Paula now that had a sick feeling as she gripped the steering wheel and looked straight ahead.

"His name is Michael."

"How long have you been seeing him?" Shane asked continuing to look out the window.

"I just met him last week."

"Is it serious?"

"I don't know."

"Did you tell him about me?"

"Yes."

"Then why didn't you tell me about him, before I flew up here. You could have saved us both some trouble."

Shane's tone frightened Paula who had never seen this side of him.

"Shane, I just didn't know how to tell you. I guess I was hoping that you would come up and everything would be fine."

"But it didn't work out that way, did it. Are you planning to date us both?"

"No, Shane. I know that's not fair to you. You need to find someone else."

"I don't think you'll have to worry about that . . . I'm tired and it's cold. I think we've said about all that needs to be said."

"Shane, I do love you."

"Just not enough."

"Shane, I want us to still be friends."

"Sure, Paula."

Paula reached to touch Shane's hand, but he moved it away quickly. He could not explain the way he felt, but he knew that he never wanted to feel this way again. He hoped that someday Paula would experience the same feeling and wondered what he was going to do with the Christmas present he had already bought for her. He had lost his holiday spirit.

Paula tossed and turned most of the night. She kept thinking about her feelings for Shane and Michael. Her decision had been made for her. When she woke up the next morning, she knew that her relationship with Shane would never be the same.

Chapter 6

Paula rang the Johnson's doorbell at ten o'clock the next morning, apprehensive about seeing Shane. As she waited for someone to open the door, she realized that the cold, gloomy day matched her mood. Mr. Johnson opened the door and invited Paula in. He seemed less friendly and Paula wondered if Shane had told him about her indiscretion. Shane's bag was waiting by the door. He came into the room a minute later, acknowledged Paula's presence then thanked his hosts for their hospitality. A few minutes later, they were driving to the airport.

Despite the gospel music playing on the radio, the silence in the car was overpowering. Paula felt horrible for hurting Shane, who just wanted to get as far away from Paula as possible. They were both relieved to finally get to the airport.

"You can just drop me off at the terminal." Shane said looking out the window, still unable to look at her.

"I can park and come in."

"That's okay. I'd rather you didn't."

Paula parked in the unloading zone in front of the terminal. Before the car had stopped completely, Shane opened the door. Paula got out of the car, but remained by her open door and watched Shane get his bag from the back seat.

"Will you call and let me know you made it home okay?"

"Sure."

Shane reluctantly looked at Paula and his eyes revealed all the pain that he was feeling. Paula looked away briefly, knowing that she was the source of his pain.

"Good-bye, Paula. Thanks for the ride. I hope you and Michael will be very happy."

Shane put his bag on his shoulder and walked away. Paula watched him go through the automatic door hoping he would look back but he didn't. Paula got in the car after he disappeared in the crowd and looked at the clock.

I need to go to church. Maybe if I pray for Shane, I won't feel so bad. Please God let Shane be okay. I didn't mean to hurt him . . . How did things get so complicated?

Paula pulled into the church lot and had to park in the very last row. The noon mass was always crowded and Paula was a few minutes late. When it was time for silent prayers, Paula prayed for Shane's forgiveness and that he would find someone who deserved him. She got up off her knees and reached in her purse for a tissue to wipe away the tears. She still wanted Shane but she could not have them both, only tramps did that. Paula did not know that it was okay to date different people or that there were different types of love. She only knew that she didn't want to be a tramp, the term her mother used repeatedly to describe immoral women.

As she drove home, Paula wondered if Michael had gone to mass. The fact that Michael was Catholic and had the same birthday as Clarice had to be a sign that they were meant to be together.

Why didn't I meet Michael before I met Shane? Then none of this would have happened.

When Paula walked in the house, Clarice told her that Michael had called. Sensing Clarice's disapproval, Paula had mixed feelings about seeing Michael so soon after Shane's departure, the guilt was still too fresh. Paula picked up the phone to return Michael's call but then hung up; she needed some time to decide whether to let him come over.

Paula had just finished making a ham sandwich when the phone rang. She picked up the phone in the kitchen hoping it was Shane.
"Hello."
"Paula?"
"Yes."
"Hi, did your mother tell you I called earlier?"
"Yes, Michael she did. I just walked in from church and was about to eat."
"What time should I come over?"
"Maybe you shouldn't come over today. I really need to study. I have a test tomorrow."
"Paula, I really want to see you. I won't stay long."
Paula paused, remembering the kiss.
"Okay. What time did you have in mind?"
"How about in an hour?"
Paula hesitated. That would barely give her enough time to eat her sandwich and change clothes.
"That's fine."
"Can I bring you anything?"

"No thanks."

"I'll see you in an hour."

Paula sat down at the kitchen table to eat her sandwich despite suddenly losing her appetite. She knew that she needed to eat something, so she took a bite and chewed slowly.

What is Mom going to say about Michael coming over the same day that Shane leaves? You didn't even ask if it was okay . . . Paula, you are an adult now. You should not have to ask permission to have company. Just a little while longer and there will be no more rules.

Clarice walked in the kitchen just as Paula was trying to decide how to ask about Michael's visit.

"Did Shane get off okay?"

"Yes, ma'am."

"He is really a nice person Paula."

"Yes, he is." *That's just perfect Paula! Your mother likes the person you may never see again.*

"I'd like to meet his mother. Maybe we can stop by on our way to home next week. Have you given Shane his gift?"

Stop by to meet his mother!

"No. I haven't." *Change the subject!*

"Where is everyone?"

"Lisa and Autumn are in the back taking a nap. Eric went to a friend's house to look at the game."

"Mom, is it okay if Michael comes over?"

Clarice paused as if something were wrong and Paula got nervous, knowing that Michael was probably already on his way. *Why is she taking so long to answer?*

"Haven't you had enough company this weekend. You just got back from taking Shane to the airport. I know you have some homework."

"I just have a little homework. He's going to be on this side of town for something else and he won't stay long."

"That's fine Paula, as long as you clean up before he comes."

"Okay…"

Something about Michael bothered Clarice, although she couldn't put her finger on it exactly. But she knew that Shane was a nice young man who would amount to something, the type that Paula needed to keep.

Paula picked up the plate with the half-eaten sandwich and took it to the trash after Clarice left the kitchen.

Why did you just tell that lie? Now you'll need to go to confession.

Paula looked at the mess in the kitchen. Everyone had eaten but no one took the time to put the dishes in the dishwasher.

I am getting tired of being the only one who ever does anything around this house. At least they could rinse the food off.

As Paula scraped the plates, she looked at the clock on the wall and wondered how Shane was doing.

He should be home by now.

She picked up the phone and dialed Shane's number. The phone rang three times. Paula was just about to hang up the phone when Shane answered.

"Hello."

He sounded tired.

"Hi, I just wanted to make sure you made it in okay."

"I was going to call you later."

"Sure you were."

"Really. It's nice to know that you still care."

"Shane, I will always care about you. I meant it when I said that I want us to be friends. I just didn't think it would be fair to be going out with someone else and not tell you."

"Paula, I can't even stay angry with you."

"Shane, we just live so far apart. This is our senior year. It's hard to sit at home every weekend."

"I know Paula. I guess it's just easier for me since I go to an all boys' school. There's much less temptation."

"But Shane, you need to find someone to go out with, too."

Paula couldn't believe she had just said that.

"I'm not ready for it to be over."

"It doesn't have to be. If my mother has anything to do with it, you and I will be together forever. After meeting you, she has probably already started the guest list for our wedding."

"I knew I liked your mother for some reason." Shane laughed which made Paula feel much better.

"Will you thank her again for the dinner? She really is a good cook."

"Sure. She enjoyed doing it... Shane, would you mind if we stopped by to drop off your Christmas present when we come through next week?"

" . . .Okay. "

"I'll call you Wednesday to let you know what time."

"Thanks for calling Paula."

" ...Shane, I really do love you. Nothing can change that."

"I love you, too. I'll talk to you Wednesday. Good luck on your test."

"Thanks. I'll need it. Good bye."
"Bye, Paula."

Paula felt much better after she hung up the phone. Maybe it wasn't too late. Paula finished the kitchen and decided to go change into some jeans. She walked into her bedroom and turned on the television out of habit. She flipped through the channels. Nothing worth looking at was on, so she stopped on the football game. They were in the playoffs and she knew that the whole city was probably watching the game. She opened her closet to get a pair of jeans and stared at the basket, spilling over with dirty clothes. With all the commotion of the weekend, she had forgotten that she still needed to wash.

Why did I tell Michael he could come over? Paula, he really can't stay long. Between washing and studying, it is going to be a long night.

She changed clothes quickly then sorted her dirty clothes hoping to have time to start a load. She grabbed the whites, put them in a pillowcase and went to the kitchen. She opened the washing machine and threw her pillowcase down in frustration. Someone had left a load in the wash that needed to be dried. She opened the dryer and found a load that needed to be folded.

I'm so sick of this!

She grabbed the load out of the dryer and took them to her sister's room where she dropped them in the chair. Racing back to the kitchen, Paula transferred the clothes from the washer to the dryer. She was just putting her clothes in the washer when the doorbell rang.

He can wait a minute.

She poured the laundry detergent into the cup; the doorbell rang again.

"Why can't he be patient?"

Paula stopped what she was doing and ran to the door before the bell rang again. The last thing she wanted was for the doorbell to wake Autumn. Clarice was walking to the door when Paula came out of the kitchen.

"It's probably Michael. I'll get it."

Clarice returned to her room. Michael was just about to ring the doorbell again when Paula opened the door.

"Hello. I wasn't sure if the bell worked."

"Hi, it does. Come on in."

Paula led Michael into the den.

"Sorry it took so long for me to answer the door. I was just starting a load of wash and everyone else is napping. Can I take your jacket?"

"Sure. I hope the doorbell didn't wake anyone."

"Only my mother! That's not a good start." Paula whispered.

"I'm sorry."

"Have a seat. I'll be right back."

Michael looked genuinely concerned as he removed his jacket and handed it to Paula. She turned the television to the game, hung Michael's jacket in the closet and returned to the kitchen. After starting the load, Paula went back to her room where she deposited the remaining dirty clothes in the basket before pushing it back into the closet. Finally, she turned off the television in her room and returned to the den, feeling like she had just run a marathon as she sat on the sofa.

"How are you doing?" Michael asked.

"I'm fine, but I forgot that I needed to wash. What's the score?"

"It's tied at seven."

Paula noticed how dark the room looked and got up and opened the curtains. Michael watched her as she walked to the window, admiring how she looked in her jeans.

"The Christmas tree is beautiful." Michael said with a smile.

"Thanks. Autumn and I decorated it the other night."

"Did Shane get off okay?"

"Yes, he did. I think he was very glad to leave."

"I'm glad I got to spend some time with you last night. I wish it could have been longer. Did Shane explain why he left you so long?"

"Yes, he did. He saw me slow dancing with you."

"Was he upset?"

Michael smiled to himself; delighted that things had worked better than he had planned.

"Let's just say he wasn't very happy about it."

"So what did you tell him?"

"The truth. I told him that I met you last weekend and that I thought that we should go out with other people while we are apart. "

"Are you two still together or do I get you all to myself?"

"I'm not sure. He was upset that I didn't tell him before he came up here."

"Why didn't you?"

"Because I wasn't sure what I wanted."

"And now?"

"I'm still not sure. I hope I won't regret this... The last thing he said to me before he left was that he hoped you and I would be very happy."

"He'll get over it. And I promise that you won't have any regrets. I will make you very happy."

Michael moved to the end of the sofa near Paula and before she could object, his lips were on hers. Paula's mind shut down and her body took over, experiencing a more intense pleasure than before. When Michael finally pulled away, it took Paula a few seconds to think clearly again. She was addicted.

"Do you have any regrets now?" Michael asked with a smile.

"No."

A few minutes later, Paula excused herself to go to the bathroom and came back to find Autumn entertaining Michael.

"Autumn, come here. Michael is trying to watch the football game."

"That's okay. She's not bothering me."

Michael continued his conversation with Autumn as Paula watched, thinking he'd make a great father some day. Autumn darted from the room.

"So what do you want for Christmas?" Paula asked

"I think I already have it."

"What's that?"

"You."

"Seriously"

"I'm serious. I want you for Christmas."

"What else do you want for Christmas?"

"A black Porsche would be nice."

"That's a little out of my league. You'd have to be very good to get that."

"I am very good." Michael said with a look that took Paula's breath away.

"Oh really?"

"Really, at least that's what I've been told."

Just as the words left his mouth, Autumn returned with her favorite toy and sat next to Michael. Every now and then Michael would look at the television to see the game but Autumn never noticed that she did not have his undivided attention. When the game ended, Autumn was summoned into the kitchen for dinner.

"Are you hungry?" Michael asked as he turned his attention back to Paula.

"A little."

"Would you like to go get something to eat before I leave?"

"Okay."

"What do you have a taste for?"

"The Burger Barn is fine with me."

"Okay. Let's go." Michael stood up.

"Let me tell my mother that I'm leaving."

Paula went to Clarice's room where she found her still groggy from the nap.

"Mom, Michael and I are going to the Burger Barn. Can we bring you something back?"

"No, thanks. I'm going to heat up some of the leftovers from last night. Did Shane call yet?"

"I talked to him earlier. He asked me to tell you thanks for everything. I won't be gone long."

Paula stopped in her room to get her jacket. Michael was talking to Lisa and Autumn in the dining room when she returned. Paula got Michael's jacket out of the closet and handed it to him.

"I'm ready."

"Lisa, it was nice meeting you. Autumn, don't forget you have to be very good if you want Santa to bring you some toys."

Michael helped Paula put on her jacket before putting on his, then opened the door for Paula. Paula looked at the car parked in front of the house. This was the first time she had seen his car in daylight. It was very big and very brown.

"Do you want me to drive?" Paula asked a little embarrassed to be seen in his car.

"I'll drive but don't laugh at my car. It gets me where I need to go."

Michael walked around and opened the passenger door for Paula. She slid into the oversized car. Michael closed the door for her and walked around to the driver's side. The car was immaculate despite it's well worn interior. There was a Christmas tree air freshener hanging from the rear view mirror. Paula could tell it was a recent addition by the strong smell it emitted. Michael got into the car and put the key in the ignition.

"Are you sure that the Burger Barn is okay?"

"Yes." Paula said, afraid that Taco Fiesta would remind her too much of Shane.

Michael turned the key in the ignition several times before the car started and noticed that Paula was smiling.

"Don't laugh at Betsy. We have been through a lot and she's never let me down."

"You gave your car a name?"

"I had to call her something. So where is the closest Burger Barn?"

Paula gave Michael directions as she tried to remember how much cash she had, in case he expected her to pay for both their meals. Paula decided that she would offer to go Dutch, knowing that she had enough money for her meal. They pulled into the Burger Barn lot and had to park at the rear because it was so crowded. Michael got out and opened the door for Paula.

The lines at the counter were long. Paula took out her wallet when it was time for them to order.

"Put that back in your purse. I invited you."

"Let's at least split the cost."

"Will you please order? There is no way I'm going to let you pay for anything." Michael said.

Paula was thankful that Michael was from the old school. What was the point of having someone to go out with if she was going to have to pay for everything? She ordered a cheeseburger, small fries and a small drink, deciding not to take advantage of Michael's generosity. Michael ordered the double-decker burger, large fries and a large chocolate shake.

He opened his wallet and paid with a twenty. Paula let Michael carry the tray and went in search of an empty table. They found a booth on the side, near the windows, and sat across from each other. Paula starting eating her fries while they were still hot while Michael went straight for his burger with gusto.

"I was afraid you were going to make me pay." Paula said as she watched him eat.

"What kind of person would I be to do something like that?"

"I'd say pretty cheap, and this probably would have been our last date." Paula said jokingly.

"I'm glad I didn't make that mistake." Michael said, pausing to take a drink of his shake.

"Do you mind if I ask you something?"

"No. Shoot."

"Why don't you have a girlfriend or do you?"

"I did but we just broke up."

"It's probably none of my business but can I ask why?"

Paula wanted to know if it was his fault and thought of the possibilities - His girlfriend had caught him with someone else or he had gotten her pregnant and dropped her. She realized that he didn't have to tell her the truth but she hoped he would. Paula took a bite of her hamburger and waited for his answer.

"She found someone else."

"That would have been my last guess. How's that for a twist of fate? What happened to you is the same thing that happened to Shane. How does it feel to be the other person?"

"Maybe Shane will met someone else like I did."

"I hope so. He deserves someone special."

"So do you."

"Do you have anyone in mind?"

"Maybe. We'll have to wait and see."

Paula finished eating her hamburger in silence, thinking about what Michael said.

Would Shane really find someone else?

"I'm still hungry. Do you want something else? I'm going to get another burger."

"You really have a healthy appetite. If you don't mind, my sweet tooth would love a small strawberry shake."

"You got it."

Michael slid out of the seat and disappeared around the corner. He returned with another burger, large fries and a large strawberry shake.

"I thought you might like to share some more fries with me." Michael said as he sat the tray on the table and slid back into the seat.

"If I keep eating like this, I'll have to live on a diet."

"You don't need to diet."

Michael and Paula continued talking while they finished their food. Paula was really enjoying herself when she reluctantly looked at her watch.

"It's getting late. We'd better be going. You have a long drive and I have a math test tomorrow."

"Okay... Are you going to be in town for Christmas?" Michael put the trash on the tray and stood up.

"No, we're going out of town."

"When are you leaving?"

"Saturday morning. Why?"

"I was wondering if I'd get to see you again before Christmas."

"Maybe Friday, I'm not working."

Paula grabbed her purse and followed Michael out the door. When they got in the car, Paula popped a mint into her mouth and then offered one to Michael.

"Are you trying to tell me something?"

"No, I'm not."

They continued to talk about school and what they planned to do over the holiday break. The drive home went quickly. Michael parked, turned off the ignition, and looked at Paula.

"Would you mind if I get a kiss before I walk you in?"

"Not at all."

Paula moved closer to Michael and he put his arm around her, drawing her even closer. The kiss started so gentle that Paula was not prepared for the resulting intensity. She was the one to finally pull away, out of fear that Clarice might look out the window. They were both breathing rapidly.

"We've got to stop doing that?" Paula said.

"Why?"

"Because if we are not careful, we won't be able to stop."

"And what's so wrong with that?"

"You know what's wrong with that. There are certain consequences that I'm not ready for. I love Autumn but that is not going to happen to me."

"Paula, I wouldn't get you pregnant."

Michael got out and opened the door for Paula. They walked to the door in silence and paused outside.

"Thanks for a wonderful time, Paula."

"You are very welcome. Thanks for dinner. Will you call and let me know you made it home okay?"

"Yes, I will."

Michael gave Paula a kiss on the cheek and walked back to his car with a smile. Paula closed the door and listened for his car to drive away. She stopped in the den to tell Clarice that she was home then went to her room. She sat down in the chair and realized that she was extremely wet again. Paula wondered if this was normal.

Chapter 7

Thursday evening, Paula was rushing to finish her Christmas shopping. Everyone on her list was taken care of except Michael and even though their relationship had potential, Paula knew it was too soon to buy him an expensive gift. She wanted to get him something and settled on a token gift; deciding that it would be appropriate at this stage of their relationship, and would not make him feel awkward for not giving her a gift.

Remembering Michael's comment about a black Porsche, Paula went to the toy store and bought him a realistic looking miniature one. That night, she wrapped it and put it in the top of her closet next to the small, narrow box that contained Shane's gift. Paula looked at the box with conflicting emotions about giving Shane an expensive gift after her infidelity. It had taken her weeks to find a thin, gold chain that would look perfect around Shane's neck and had put it in lay-a-way the day that she met Michael, planning to give it to Shane the weekend of his visit. But after the incident at the dance, Paula didn't think that Shane would accept a gift from her. Since their last conversation, Paula knew that Shane deserved the gift now more than ever and hoped that it would show him that she still cared.

Paula had felt obligated to show Shane's gift to her mother before she wrapped it, since she had suggested the stop to give him the gift. Clarice was pleased with the selection and did not inquire about the price, as Paula had expected. Paula had no intentions of showing Clarice Michael's gift as she closed the closet door.

The tension in Paula's house was escalating with the stress of the holidays. Everyone suspected that Lisa was pregnant again, even though she denied it adamantly. Paula prayed that it was not true, knowing that another pregnancy would make it difficult for her to date Michael or anyone else. Clarice's anxiety over Paula getting pregnant would be fueled further.

Making matters worse, Paula's older brother, John, came home to bring and collect Christmas presents. He was eight years older than Paula and had appointed himself the father of the family after her parent's divorce. He did not hesitate to give his opinion even when it was not requested. This time he came home under stress too. He had dropped out of corporate America to succeed without all the politics and was in the process of starting up a business, which was proving to be difficult.

Sometimes, Paula resented the fact that John tried to be the father. But she knew he loved her. He was her protector when she was younger, guarding her from the physical assaults of her siblings and intervening before things got out of hand. And John always remembered her birthday, which was sometimes hard to do because it was sandwiched between Thanksgiving and Christmas. Paula still remembered the time when John was in high school, the year that her birthday fell the Tuesday after Thanksgiving. Paula was so upset because nothing special was being done for her birthday. Just when she had convinced herself that no one cared, off the bus came John with a clown ice cream cone. It had meant so much to Paula that she still remembered it ten years later. Paula was worried about her brother meeting Michael. She did not think that he would even approve of her dating given his protective nature.

Paula had been on an adrenaline rush all week. As she was driving home Friday from school, the hectic pace was beginning to take its toll. She was worried about how she did on the test. A failing grade would make it impossible to get a "B" in the class. She was really looking forward to the two-week Christmas break. Paula realized how tired she was as soon as she walked through the door.

John's car was parked in the driveway but the house was quiet. Paula walked into the den and found him taking a nap, which made Paula want to do the same. She went to her room and set her books and purse on the dresser as she looked at the clock on the wall. It was almost four o'clock. She needed to call Shane and let him know what time they were going to drop off his present. Paula got the hall phone and returned to her room. She propped her pillow in the corner, kicked off her shoes and tried to get comfortable as she dialed the number.

"Hello."

"Hi Shane. It's Paula."

"It hasn't been that long. Do you think I have forgotten your voice already?"

"How are you doing?"

"Good. I survived taking my exams and I think I did well."

"I wish I could say the same. I don't think I did very well on my Physic's test."

"You probably aced it."

"I doubt that very seriously. Anyway, is it still okay if we drop off your present tomorrow morning? "

"Sure. You can get your present, too."

"You mean I still get a present."

"You're lucky. I got it on sale and couldn't take it back." Shane said with a laugh.

"Very funny. You sound like you are in a good mood."

"I told you that I'm glad to have a break from school."

"You know. I haven't told my mother about us. I didn't want to break her heart."

"Don't you think she'll figure it out when what's his name starts hanging around."

"Who said he was going to be hanging around?"

"I haven't said anything to my parents either. I'm still in denial and you never know."

"That's true… Shane, I'm glad that you and I can still talk to each other honestly."

"Me too. Do you remember how to get to my house?"

"I know its right off the freeway but you'd better give me the directions just in case. Wait a second, I need to find some paper."

Paula retrieved her spiral notebook from the dresser and scribbled down the directions.

"We should be there between nine and ten. We won't stay long. My Mom has some sorority function in the afternoon, but she is looking forward to meeting your mother."

"Well, I guess I'll see you tomorrow… Hey, Paula."

"Yes Shane."

"I love you."

"I love you too, Shane. See you tomorrow."

Paula smiled as she hung up the phone and moved it to the floor. She knew that she really did love Shane. Their relationship made her feel secure and he would never hurt her. Paula stretched across the bed and stared at the ceiling. Although she really needed a nap, Paula decided to pack her clothes. Clarice had already announced that they were going to get an early start.

Paula had just finished packing when she heard Clarice come home. Paula looked up at the clock and then went into the dining room where she found Clarice going through the mail.

"Hi, Mom."

"Hi, Paula. Where is everyone?"

"John's in the den taking a nap. I heard Eric come in a few minutes ago. I think he's in his room. Lisa and Autumn aren't home yet. Do you want me to cook something for dinner?"

"No, I'm going out to dinner tonight. There should be enough leftover for whoever wants to eat."

"Is it okay if Michael comes over?"

"Paula, you know I don't allow you to have company when I'm not home."

"Mom, I'm eighteen years old!" Paula said, declaring her independence.

"I'm well aware of how old you are but as long as you live in my house, you'll follow my rules."

"Fine, we'll just go out."

Paula turned to go to her room but stopped when she saw her brother walk into the room, hoping he'd come to her rescue.

"She can have her friend over. I'll stay here until you get home." John announced.

Paula looked at Clarice, who looked irritated. Paula wasn't sure if it was she or her brother that was the source of irritation.

"Mom, is it okay for Michael to come over since John will be here?"

"I guess so, as long as your brother is here. But I don't want Michael here all night. Remember, we are leaving early."

"Thanks, John."

Paula returned to her room, glad that John had intervened but still upset that her mother was treating her like a baby that needed to be watched. Paula knew that if she really wanted to do something, her mother's rules could not stop her.

Lisa came home a few minutes after Clarice in a fowl mood and announced that she was not going with them for Christmas before secluding herself in her room. Eric had stormed out of the house after having an argument with John over the condition of his room. And Karen and Lisa argued when Karen picked up Autumn to take her to have her picture taken with Santa. Clarice had been pushed beyond her limits and Paula was thankful that she was going out to dinner with a friend.

After two hours of screaming and door slamming, Paula found herself in the calm after the storm and decided to wait for Michael in the den. She plugged in the Christmas tree lights, played some Christmas music, turned off the overhead light and cuddled up on the sofa. Christmas had always been her favorite time of year. It was the one time of year that everyone usually tried to get along, but this year everyone in her family seemed so unhappy.

Paula listened to the Christmas music, mesmerized by the colorful flickers of the twinkling lights, and smiled as she looked at the concentration of ornaments on the lower branches. Paula had tried to rearrange the ornaments but Autumn had been adamant that they stay where she had put them and cried every time Paula moved one. The tree had a collection of presents spilling from under its branches, sending Paula's thoughts back to past Christmases when the massive amount of presents around the tree prevented them from walking into the living room on Christmas morning. Then Paula remembered her special Christmas.

Paula was seven years old and had stopped believing in Santa Claus thanks to the information provided by her older sisters. The week before Christmas, Paula found a new pink bike in the utility room. She sat on it just to make sure that it was her size before running to ask Clarice who the bike was for, confident that it had to be for her. Clarice told her that they were keeping the bike for the little girl next door; since she still believed in Santa, her parents did not want her to see it before Christmas. Paula asked Clarice if she could get a bike like it for Christmas and ran from the room crying when her mother told her that they could not afford one this year.

Upset that she had so many brothers and sisters and would never have a beautiful new bike, Paula sulked around the house the entire week; convinced that she was destined for a life of hand-me downs. On Christmas morning, Paula was the last one to go into the living room; if she could not have a new bike, then she did not want anything.

There was so much excitement in the living room that Paula did not see the bike that had been in the utility room sitting by the Christmas tree. John asked Paula if she saw her new bike and

Paula replied that it belonged to the little girl next door. Clarice walked up behind Paula and told her that it really was her bike.

The doorbell summoned Paula back to the present still smiling, remembering how happy she had been. Paula turned on the ceiling light as she went to answer the door. Michael stood before her in black slacks, a burgundy sweater and a black leather jacket. He had a beautifully wrapped small present in his hand.

"Hi, Paula"

"Hello, Michael."

"Can I take your coat?"

"Sure. Merry Christmas, this is for you."

He handed Paula the present and then removed his jacket and handed it to her also. Paula led him into the den, wondering if Michael ever wore jeans.

"You didn't have to get me a present."

"I know, but I wanted to."

"I have a present for you, too. Can I open this now or do I have to wait until Christmas?"

"Open it now. I want to make sure that you like it."

"First, let me hang up your coat. Please have a seat. I'll be right back."

He sat on the sofa. Paula sat the gift near Michael and then went to hang his coat in the closet. She came back, picked up the gift and sat near Michael. She did not want to seem too anxious as she carefully removed the elegant bow.

"Did you wrap this yourself?"

"No, the salesperson at the store did it."

"You really didn't need to get me anything."

"Will you please open it?" Michael said with a smile.

Paula removed the wrapping paper, discovered a jewelry box and looked at Michael, who was still smiling at her. She opened the black box and was shocked to see a beautiful gold, dress watch. She needed a dress watch and had hoped to get one for graduation.

"Michael, I can't accept this. We just met."

"I really want you to have it. I had saved up the money to buy a present for my old girlfriend. I decided to spend the money on you."

"I can't believe that you bought this for me."

"Does that mean you like it?"

"I love it. Thank you."

Paula gave Michael a kiss and then removed the watch from the box to get a better look at it.

"Put it on. I want to see how it looks on you."

"Will you help me?"

Paula removed her well-worn watch and Michael took the new watch and put it on her wrist.

"How does it look?" Paula asked, extending her arm.

"It looks beautiful on you."

"Thanks. I'll be right back. I need to get your present."

Paula left the den to get the present she had bought for Michael but was embarrassed to give it to him now. He had bought her a beautiful watch and she had bought him a toy car. She thought about Shane's present sitting next to Michael's and thought about giving it to Michael. But Paula quickly realized that it was not an option. She had already told Shane that she was bringing him a present and she did not have time to get a replacement. Paula was trying to decide what to do when she bumped into John in the hallway.

"Was that your friend at the door?"

"Yep, look what he gave me for Christmas."

Paula held her hand out.

"Let me get a closer look at this."

John took her hand and looked at the watch under the light.

"Nice. This is an expensive watch."

Paula did not know enough about jewelry to be impressed by the brand name but she knew her brother could tell quality. Clarice had often accused him of having expensive taste.

"I didn't expect him to give me anything. I just met him this month."

"Did you get him anything?"

"I just got him a token gift. He said he wanted a black Porsche. So I got him a toy one. Now I'm embarrassed to give it to him."

"Go ahead and give it to him. I'm going to meet the young man who's buying my sister expensive gifts."

"John, please be nice to him."

Paula hurried to her room to get Michael's gift. She did not want to leave John alone with Michael too long, knowing that John would grill him. Paula opened her closet and stared at the gifts. She was the one who felt awkward and thought about telling Michael that he would get his gift after Christmas. Reasoning that if he really liked her, it would not matter what she gave him. Paula retrieved the gift from her closet and went back to the den, squeezing by John who was standing in the doorway talking to Michael.

"That's a very nice watch you bought my baby sister."

"Thanks. I hope she likes it."

"I love it." Paula said.

"Paula said that you go to Holy Infant. I graduated from Catholic school. You really get a good education in the Catholic school system. Have you attended Catholic schools long?"

"All of my life."

"Are you Catholic?"

"Yes, I am."

"Have you decided on a college yet?"

"I'm thinking about State University or Northern State."

"I went to State. It's a good school. Have you decided on a major yet?"

"I'm thinking about Computer Science."

"Are you two going out tonight?"

"I'm not sure. It's up to Paula."

"No, I think we'll just hang around here. John are you finished giving Michael the third degree?"

"I guess so. I'll leave you two kids alone. It was nice meeting you Michael."

"Same here."

Michael stood up to shake John's hand. After John left the room, Paula sat on the sofa next to Michael. She handed him the wrapped present.

"This is a pretty big package."

"Don't get too excited. Wait until you open it."

"I'll love whatever you bought me."

Paula watched Michael's face as he opened the present. He carefully unwrapped it to reveal the toy car.

"You said that you wanted a Porsche for Christmas. I couldn't afford the real thing."

"Thanks. It's definitely the closest thing to a real Porsche that I'm going to get."

"I feel bad giving you a toy after you bought me this beautiful watch."

"Paula, I didn't give you the watch because I expected a present from you. I just wanted to show you how much you mean to me. I know we just met a few weeks ago. But you are very special. And I wanted you to know that I am very serious about us."

"I'm sure you are just telling me this. You probably say the same thing to every girl you meet."

"And I suppose you think I'd buy a gold watch for everyone I meet also."

"Maybe."

"You know better than that. Do you remember the other gift that I said I wanted?"

"No."

Michael smiled at Paula who felt a tingling sensation travel through her body. He wasn't going to push her.

"So what do you want to do tonight?"

"Do you know how to play Yatchzee?"

"No, but I'm willing to learn. Is your mother home? I'd like to say hello."

"She went out to dinner with a friend. She should be home before you leave."

"Would you like something to drink?"

"Sure."

"Punch or soda?"

"Punch. Do you need any help?"

"No, but you can start reading the directions."

Paula reached under the sofa to retrieve the game and handed it to Michael before going to the kitchen to get their drinks. She opened the cabinet and began searching for two glasses without chipped edges. With all of the people in the house, the good glasses were dirty in the dishwasher. She finally decided to wash two glasses. As Paula was washing the glasses, John walked into the kitchen and leaned against the counter.

"Looks like you found a really nice fellow."

"It seems that way but it's way too early to tell."

"Well, he seems intelligent and has a good head on his shoulders. That's a really nice watch he bought you."

"I know."

"What did he say about his present?"

"He said he liked it, but I felt stupid giving him a toy."

"Don't. You are not suppose to be buying men expensive presents anyway. Let him wine and dine you."

"Do you really think he's okay?"

"Would I let my baby sister go out with someone I didn't think was good enough for her?"

"I doubt it. Thanks. We are going to play Yatchzee."

Paula picked up the drinks and stopped at the kitchen table to get some paper napkins.

"Okay. I'll be in your room watching television."

"Thanks for agreeing to chaperon."

Michael had the game set up when Paula returned to the den. She handed Michael the glass of punch wrapped in a napkin and then sat down on the couch.

"Paula, this is a lot like poker."

"Thanks again, for the beautiful watch, Michael"

Paula kissed Michael on the cheek.

"I'm just glad you like it."

"Now, lady's first." Michael said as he handed Paula the cup with the dice.

"Thank you, sir. Are you ready to get beat?"

"I usually don't lose."

Paula and Michael were still playing the game when Karen and her boyfriend came in carrying Autumn who was sound asleep. They stopped in the den.

"Looks like someone had a great time. Did she enjoy Santa?" Paula asked.

"She wouldn't go anywhere near him but we let her run around the mall to tire her out."

"Michael, this is my sister Karen and her boyfriend Bobby."

"Nice to meet you Michael. Where's her mother?"

"In the back, but she's not talking to anyone."

"Come on Bobby. Let's get her to bed. I'm ready to go home."

Paula looked at the clock after they left.

"Are you ready to quit?" Michael asked.

"One more game. It's only nine o'clock."

Clarice came home around nine-thirty and looked into the den. Michael stood up when he saw her.

"Hello, Ms. Hayes."

"Hello, Michael. How are you doing?"

"Fine. Thank you. Your daughter was just beating me at a game of Yatchzee."

"Paula, is your brother still here?"

"Yes, he's in my room. Karen and Bobby just brought Autumn home. They said she wouldn't go near Santa."

"Michael, it was nice to see you again. Good night. Paula don't forget that we are leaving early."

Clarice left the room and Paula picked up on her mother's disapproval of Michael's presence.

"I think it's time for you to leave."

"When are you coming back?"

"The day after Christmas."

"Can I have the phone number where you are staying? I might want to call you."

"Sure."

Paula tore a sheet of paper off the score pad, wrote down the number and handed it to him. Then she went into the living room to get his coat.

"Paula, I had a wonderful time."

"So did I. Thanks again for the watch."

"I'm glad you like it."

Michael put on his jacket and followed Paula to the door. Stopping under the mistletoe, he wrapped his arms around her waist and gave her a gentle kiss on the lips.

"Merry Christmas, Paula."

"Merry Christmas, Michael. Drive safely."

Paula closed the door behind him, wanting a real kiss but there was too much traffic in the house. She looked at the watch repeatedly as she put up the game and took their glasses to the kitchen before going to her room. She was admiring her new watch when Clarice stood in her doorway.

"Your brother told me that Michael gave you a watch."

"Yes, he did."

Paula reluctantly held out her wrist for her mother to see. She had not planned on telling her about the watch, but she should have known her brother was going to say something.

"I thought you and Michael were just friends."

"We are."

"What kind of friend buys you an expensive watch?"

"I offered to give it back but he refused."

"What did you give him, Paula?"

"A toy car."

"What about you and Shane?"

"What about us?"

"Are you still together?"

"Yes, I talked to him today. He's expecting us to stop by tomorrow so I can give him his present?"

"Does Shane know about Michael?"

"Yes, he does."

"Paula, you know that I didn't raise you to be a tramp."

"Does accepting a gift make me a tramp mother?"

Clarice looked at Paula and then left the room without answering. Paula knew that her mother was not going to be happy about her dating Michael, but she had not expected this. Paula took off the watch and looked at it closely before putting it back in the case. Her mother had managed to steal the joy that she had felt moments earlier. John came and stood in the doorway.

"Hey, I'm going out. I probably won't be up in the morning when you leave. You have a Merry Christmas."

"I wish you hadn't told Mom about the watch."

"Why? I thought you'd be excited about it."

"I was...I don't think Mom likes Michael very much."

"Don't worry about it. Your mother is under a lot of stress."

"Do you think that I should give the watch back?"

"No, I don't. Besides, I don't think he would take it. It's obvious that he really likes you."

"Have a good time tonight. Will you be gone when we get back?"

"Yes. I have to get back to work."

"I thought you were the boss now."

"I am. That's why I have to get back to work."

"Be careful out there tonight. Your present from me is under the tree."

Paula closed the door to her room and changed into her pajamas. She got on her knees to pray; imagining what her life would be like if Lisa were pregnant again and reminding herself that she only had eight months before going at college.

They left before sunrise. Paula was extremely quiet during the drive and as soon as it was light enough, she began to read her romance novel. The only time she spoke to her mother was to give her the directions to Shane's house, where they arrived a little after ten. Shane was genuinely happy to see Paula and they exchanged presents, promising not to open them until Christmas morning. Their mothers talked while Shane and Paula exchanged gifts. It was a short visit but long enough to convince Clarice that they were still a couple. Clarice still didn't like the fact that Paula had accepted the watch from Michael but she seemed more relaxed after the stop. There was a truce between mother and daughter. Paula kept the watch out of her mother's sight. She knew that there was no reason to fuel the fire.

Christmas day brought lots of family and food. Paula's older sister Sheryl had also driven down. Paula helped with the preparations but was still in a solemn mood due to Clarice's tramp comment. The softness of the sweater that Shane gave her comforted Paula and just wearing it made her feel closer to him. But the watch was by far the best present that she received. Each time she looked at the watch, she thought about Michael.

When the phone rang, Paula would listen for her name. Finally, Michael called to wish her a Merry Christmas. They talked for fifteen minutes before Clarice interrupted to remind Paula not to monopolize the phone but then suggested that Paula call Shane after she hung up. Paula could not wait to get back home to be with Michael again and Clarice was not happy to have something else to worry about.

Chapter 8

The pre-Christmas tension turned into a volcanic eruption as soon as they returned home. Although Paula was not the source of the upheaval, she was definitely caught in its destructive path. They came back to the reality that Lisa, who could not hide it any longer, was definitely pregnant. Complicating matters was the fact that Lisa was rapidly approaching her fifth month, which limited her options, and she had not been to a doctor.

Clarice, who was livid, estimated that the baby was due sometime in April. In addition to the public disgrace that another unwed pregnancy would bring to the family, Clarice also had to deal with the possibility that the baby might have health problems. But Clarice failed to realize that pre-natal care would have made the pregnancy a reality and Lisa had been in serious denial. Now, Lisa's denial was replaced with depression and embarrassment and Paula worried about her sister's mental state. Lisa had always been so confident on the surface but now that she faced another major setback, the facade was crumbling.

At school, the workload was mounting and Paula was struggling to maintain her grades. In addition, the senior class officers were meeting regularly to plan and execute all the senior activities. Paula was glad to see January come to an end; she was one month closer to graduation. Paula felt like she was walking a tight rope, trying to keep her focus in the mist of all the chaos. She was trying to be sympathetic, although angry with Lisa for letting it happen again. Because of Lisa's actions, Paula would have to withstand six more months of Clarice's pregnancy lectures. Eventually, sympathy won out over anger once Paula truly saw her sister's pain.

Paula came home from school and heard Lisa crying. She knocked softly on her sister's door and then slowly opened it to find Lisa lying across the bed. Paula could tell she had been crying for some time because her eyes were red and swollen, like her stomach, which now had a pronounced round shape.

"Hi. Where's Autumn?"

"I haven't picked her up yet."

"Do you want me to pick her up?" Paula asked still standing in the doorway.

"No, I'll get her in about an hour."

"Are you okay?"

Her sister wiped the tears from her cheeks. Paula walked into the room and sat down in the chair nestled in the corner.

"Paula, why do I keep screwing up? I was just getting back on my feet and now this."

"It will be okay." Paula tried to sound reassuring.

"Lisa, can I ask you something?"

"What?" Lisa looked up.

"Why didn't you get on the pill after Autumn was born?"

"I tried them but they made me so sick. Paula, I didn't want this to happen again."

"I know. Have you decided what to do about the baby?"

"I can't raise another one. I'm barely managing with Autumn. I'm going to put it up for adoption."

"That's probably a good idea. Have you contacted anyone?"

"I was planning to use the same agency I worked with for Autumn."

Lisa paused wondering if she should tell Paula why she was so upset.

"Aunt Dorothy called me yesterday."

"I guess Mom told her about the baby."

"Yes, she wants me to let her adopt the baby."

"You've got to be kidding! Lisa, she's over fifty. She'll be almost seventy when the baby graduates from high school."

"I know. She talked about how she always wanted children and how she had tried to adopt but the agencies had originally said she needed to be married and now they think she is too old."

"She is."

"Then she went on and on about all that she has done for us and that I should be thankful that someone in the family wants the baby."

"I know she had done a lot for us but you don't owe her your child. Lisa, you've got to do what's best for the baby and you. Did you tell Mom that she called?"

"That's the problem, Paula. Mom doesn't agree. Now they are fighting about it and I'm caught in the middle."

"Lisa, you really need to think about this. How are you going to handle watching someone else raise your child? The baby deserves to be raised in a family with a mother and a father. Look at how hard it was on us growing up without a father in the house. It's up to you but I would put it up for adoption through the agency."

"I know."

"Try not to worry too much. Things will work out. Can I get you anything before I start my homework?"

"No, thanks."

"Let me know if you change your mind about me picking up Autumn."

After closing the door to Lisa's room, Paula grabbed her books and went to the dining room table to study. She opened her Physics book and tried to do her homework but she could not concentrate, wondering what Lisa was going to do. She knew that Lisa would not be able to handle watching someone else raise her child and felt strongly that a closed adoption was the best option for everyone. Paula even wondered if adoption would have been better for Autumn. Everyone had tried to get Lisa to put her up for adoption. All the paperwork had been completed and everything was set, until the day that Autumn was born and Lisa changed her mind after seeing her.

Paula thought of all the nights that she had gotten up to feed and change Autumn while her sister worked the third shift. Autumn still slept with Paula whenever she could. But come August, Paula was going away to college and would not be around to help. Paula stared at the Physics problems for another thirty minutes before deciding to call Michael and confirm their plans to go out.

Michael was Paula's only refuge. She talked to Michael every day usually before Clarice got home. He listened and validated her feelings. But most of all he helped her escape with a few hours of pleasure each week. Despite Clarice's obvious disapproval, Michael was becoming a regular part of Paula's weekend plans. Given the tension in the house, Paula made sure that they kept the physical aspects of their relationship outside the house.

They found a quiet park where they would go to be alone. They would start off talking and end up fogging up the car windows. Although Paula was not technically a virgin, she had a lot to learn and Michael was a willing teacher. Michael skillfully taught her what she needed to know about her body and his. He assured Paula that her body was responding the way it should and that the best was yet to come. Paula and Michael always managed to stop short of going all the way. They both wanted the first time together to be special.

After the movie, Paula wanted to delay going home and suggested that they stopped by their park, even though the night was too cold for parking. Paula slid across the seat so Michael could hold her to keep her warm.

"Michael, I hope Lisa will stick with her decision to give the baby up for adoption. I can't stand the way Mom and Aunt Dorothy are pressuring her. I haven't told you the latest. My aunt is calling Lisa almost daily. I feel sorry for her. I think she might just snap. She was just adjusting to having Autumn and now she has to deal with this."

"She'll be fine. How are you holding up?"

"Okay. I still haven't finished my college applications. I'm having a hard time writing the essays. Have you finished yours yet?"

"Yep. But I'm only applying to two schools."

"Maybe we can both end up at State."

"I don't know. My dad said he'd pay for my college if I go to Northern State. I'll have to get a scholarship to go anywhere else."

"The deadline for all the applications is next week. I always to wait until the last minute. If I keep fooling around, I won't be going anywhere. I know one thing for sure; I need to get a full scholarship because I don't have any offers to pay for my college. That's why it's so important that I graduate with honors. I wish I could count on my father."

"Why don't you apply to Northern State?"

"They don't have an engineering program."

"You could major in computer science. That field is really taking off."

"No, thanks. My father works with computers and it doesn't seem too interesting. Michael, do you ever wonder what it will be like to live on our own? No one to tell us what or when to do anything."

"Yeah, I think about it often."

"I got a small taste of freedom last summer when I went to Maine. With the exception of not having any money and being the only African-American female on the campus, it was wonderful. I decided what I wanted to do and went. And I only had to clean up after myself. I remember being so scared the first few days. I flew there by myself and didn't know anyone. But once I made a few friends, everything worked out."

"I'm looking forward to college and having my own place. Then I won't have to park with my girlfriend."

Michael kissed Paula's cheek.

"Oh, are you planning on going to college and finding someone new?"

"I don't know. It all depends on how you treat me."

"Then, I think you'd better start looking now."

"I found what I'm looking for and I don't intend on letting you go."

Michael smiled and gave Paula a firm hug.

"I'm glad we got together. You're so easy to talk to, not to mention other things."

"Speaking of which, why are we doing all this talking?"

Michael kissed Paula on the neck and Paula turned so that she was facing Michael. He unzipped her jacket but the coldness of the car made Paula shiver.

"It's too cold. Come on. Let's go."

"That's okay Michael. We can stay a little longer."

"No, let's get you home. We need to stop making out in the car anyway."

"Do you have any better suggestions?"

"I'm working on it."

Michael started the car and turned the heater on high. Paula wondered what Michael had in mind. She knew what the next step was in their relationship but wondered if she was ready. Paula grimaced as she thought of the baseball analogy. Michael had been to first, second and third base. He was definitely ready for a home run. She had sent him home on several occasions to take a cold shower. A few times she was the one that needed the shower.

Paula knew that Michael cared about her, but to go all the way was serious. They had a good thing and she wasn't sure if she wanted to risk losing it, keenly aware of how her first serious boyfriend had lost interest after the conquest. Paula wondered if Michael was just after the conquest too. But Paula was haunted by the fear that if she did not take care of Michael's needs; he would find someone else who would. Michael noticed how quiet Paula was as he drove her home but assumed she was just tired.

Paula went to early mass with Clarice so she would have the day to finish her college applications. After mass, Paula decided to wash clothes and clean her room before starting the applications. It was almost one o'clock before Paula retrieved the pile of applications from their resting-place in her room and deposited them on the dining room table beside the electric typewriter. It took Paula about two hours to type the information in the spaces provided on the applications and the transcript request forms. She decided to take a break before working on the essays.

Two of the applications had similar essay questions about why she wanted to attend their university. Paula planned to use the same essay for those. But the last application asked a soul-searching question about what she wanted to do with her life and why? Paula didn't have a clue how to answer that question; she had never really thought about her life in those terms. She wanted to be an engineer because she had done well on the math and mechanical reasoning section of a standardized test in the ninth grade and her counselor recommended engineering. If the counselor had recommended a different career, she may have headed down that path. And after some research indicated that engineers had the highest starting salaries, she was hooked; but not for any noble reason that would benefit society. Beyond getting the Engineering degree, Paula didn't have a clue what she wanted to do with her life.

Searching for a distraction, Paula started to call Michael but remembered that he had to work. She called Taylor who she had not seen in a few weeks between school, work and Michael, but she wasn't home either. Paula took it as a sign that she needed to finish her applications. After finishing two, Paula decided to finish the other one during the week after giving up on the essay.

Paula arrived at school early Monday morning. It was her turn to sale donuts in the bookstore. Mondays were usually the busiest day of the week for donut sales. Gayle was already there when Paula arrived. Gayle and Paula lived in the same neighborhood and had been on the student council together since the tenth grade. They had also been in a drama class together in the ninth grade. But by high school, Paula had no interest in drama and Gayle's interest in drama had escalated.

They had about ten minutes before the bookstore opened. Paula put her books on the shelf behind the counter and looked at the boxes of donuts on the counter.

"Good morning, Gayle."

"Good morning. How was your weekend?"

"Okay. I finally worked on my college applications. Have you finished yours yet?"

"Yep. I finished mine last week but I'm only applying to two schools – Southern Christian University and State."

"Isn't SCU pretty expensive."

"Yes, it is. But they have an outstanding drama department. I'm trying to get a scholarship."

Paula put a stack of napkins on the counter by the donuts and removed the tops of the donut boxes. They looked so appetizing that she decided to buy one before they unlocked the door. She retrieved some money from her purse, gave it to Gayle and then she picked a sour cream cake donut. Gayle put the money in the cash register and arranged the boxes on the counter as Paula ate her donut.

"Don't forget that the nomination forms for 'Favorites' go out today. I put the blank forms over there. We need to make sure an African-American is nominated for every category."

"What are the categories?"

"Senior Class Favorites, Most Talented, Most Congenial, Most Likely to Succeed and Mr. and Miss Superior. I think you should be nominated for Most Congenial."

"What is congenial anyway?"

"Friendly."

"Wrong category for me. That's for the cheerleaders." Paula said with a smile and took another bite.

"Leave it to me. I'll take care of the nominations. Are you going to the Favorites Dance? I helped select the deejay. He's not bad."

"I don't think so. Besides none of us ever win and even with a deejay, the music will still be hard rock."

"Paula, you really should go. After all, this is our senior year and you are a class officer."

"I'll think about it."

Gayle opened the door to let in the waiting students. Paula wiped her mouth, disappointed that she wasn't going to have time for another donut.

The decision whether to go to the dance was made for Paula. Gayle had taken care of the nominations and every category was covered. The elections were held Friday morning. The Student

Body President made the announcement during last period of the three finalists for each category. The finalists would be presented at the dance where the winners would be announced. Much to her surprise, Paula was a finalist for Most Congenial. Paula knew she wasn't going to win since one of the most popular cheerleaders was in the group, but she was still excited about the nomination and was eager to tell Michael.

However the initial excitement of getting nominated was quickly replaced by concern on the drive home from school. The dance was formal and she did not have an appropriate dress or the money to buy one. The formal dresses that she owned were too juvenile. She thought about asking Clarice for the money but quickly dismissed the thought.

As soon as Paula got home, she threw her books on the bed and picked up the phone in the hallway to call Michael with the news. His line was busy so Paula decided to start dinner early since she was baby-sitting later. As she was browning the ground beef, the phone rang. She grabbed the phone in the kitchen, knowing instinctively that it was Michael.

"Hello."

"Hi. Did you try to call?" Michael asked.

"Yes, but the line was busy."

"My sister was on it. I had to threaten her to get her off. Did you have a good day at school?"

"Yes, actually it was pretty interesting. Do you have big plans for next Saturday?"

"Other than seeing you. No, why?"

"I was nominated Most Congenial and the nominees will be presented at the Favorite's Dance on Saturday. Will you go with me? But before you answer, it's formal."

"Sure, I'll go with you. I wanted us to do something special for Valentine's. Do I need to rent a tuxedo?"

"You can, but a dark suit will do."

"What are you going to wear?"

"I don't know yet . . . Michael, thanks. I was afraid you wouldn't want to get dressed up to go to a school dance."

"Paula, you don't have to thank me. I love the opportunity to see you all dressed up. Besides I think we will make this a very special night. Just leave the details to me."

After getting a gold watch for Christmas, Paula didn't know what to expect from Michael for Valentine's Day.

"Hey, I'd better go finish cooking before I burn dinner."

"Are you still baby-sitting tonight?"

"Yes, I'll give you a call after the girls go to bed."

"Okay, think about what you want to do tomorrow."

"Okay. What are you doing tonight?"

"I don't know. Maybe I'll just hang out with the boys."

"Make sure that's all you hang out with." Paula said with a laugh but she was very serious, hoping that Michael was not seeing someone else.

"Is that jealousy I hear?"

"Do I need to be jealous?"

"No, you are the only person I'm interested in."

"I wish I could be sure of that."

"Paula, what do I need to do to convince you how much you mean to me?"

"Michael, I love you."

The words slipped out and she regretted it instantly. Paula bit her lower lip and waited for a response to her declaration knowing that - he's supposed to say it first. It seemed like an eternity to Paula before Michael spoke. The ground beef was starting to dry out.

"I'm sorry, Michael. I didn't mean to put you on the spot."

"You don't need to apologize. I love you too, Paula."

"I'd better finish dinner before I burn something."

"I'll talk to you later." Michael said, happily.

"Bye, Michael."

Paula hung up the phone with a big smile because Michael loved her too. Nothing could ruin her day. Now, she just needed a dress. The thought of borrowing one from her sister popped into her head. Before Sheryl had her son, they were the same size.

She had just poured a can of green beans into a pot when she heard the front door open. She looked at the clock; it was four-thirty. She turned the pot handles towards the back of the stove and waited for Autumn to come running but was surprised when Clarice walked into the kitchen instead.

"Hi Mom, you're home early."

"I finished the audit and decided not to go back to the office." Clarice said as she inspected what Paula was cooking.

"I was going to cook dinner today. I didn't realize you were going to start it so early."

"I'm baby-sitting tonight at six. I just made a hamburger casserole and green beans. We have a can of peaches in the cabinet."

"Are Lisa and Autumn home yet?"

"No, I thought you were them."

"I'm going to change clothes . . . By the way, I'll be gone until Sunday for that training session. If we stay a Saturday night, the ticket is half price and the government is trying to save money." Clarice started to leave the kitchen.

"Mom, there's a school dance next Saturday night."

"Paula, I'd rather you didn't go out since I'm going to be out of town."

"Mom, I need to be there. It's the Favorite's Dance and I was nominated Most Congenial. They are going to present the nominees and the winners at the dance."

"Paula, let me think about it." Clarice said as she left the kitchen.

Paula felt a lump form in her stomach. She threw the spoon in the sink, turned off the burners, and went to her room.

Why is she always treating me like a baby? What is she thinking? Does she think that by making me stay home, I won't get pregnant? If she only knew. I am eighteen now and smart enough to make my own decisions. In six months I'll be on my own at college. If she thinks that I'm going to sit at home next Saturday, she is very much mistaken. I have played by the rules long enough. I make good grades, clean the house, and cook most of the dinners and even work. I'm drawing the line. From now on I'm making my own decisions regardless of what she says.

Deciding to eat dinner with the girls, Paula stayed in her room until it was time to leave. She only spoke to Clarice to tell her that she was going to the Anderson's, the only family that Paula continued to baby-sit for after turning sixteen.

Bruce was a volunteer with Big Brothers and Sisters of America and had been matched with Paula's little brother three years earlier. Paula had been matched with a Big Sister too but after two outings, Paula didn't hear from her again. Bruce was a young doctor, which impressed Paula. He and his wife Adrienne had two daughters who were four and six. The girls were well-behaved and fun to watch. Paula liked being around Bruce and his family. Bruce answered the door for Paula.

"Hi there. Come on in. The girls are in the den coloring. Adrienne's upstairs getting dressed. Go ahead back. I'm on the phone with a parent." Bruce said as he returned to his study.

Paula went to find the girls. A few minutes later Adrienne came downstairs.

"Hi Paula. I have a frozen pizza for the girls. Have you eaten?" Adrienne said as she went to the freezer to get the pizza.

"No, I haven't. Let me do that."

Paula reached for the pizza.

"I like your dress."

"Thanks. I made it today. The cookie sheet is in the oven."

"I took home economics in the ninth grade but that's the extent of my sewing. I wish I could sew that well, especially now. I need a formal dress for next weekend."

"What's happening next weekend?"

"Our Favorite's Dance at school. I'm nominated for Most Congenial."

"That's great Paula. Congratulations." Adrienne said.

"Thanks. I probably won't win since I'm running against two cheerleaders but it's actually exciting to even be nominated."

"Don't count yourself out so soon. Do you know what kind of dress you want? I can help you make it."

"That's okay. I don't have a sewing machine. Besides, you don't have time to do that."

"You can use my machine and if we find a simple pattern, it won't take long. We can go to the fabric store tomorrow, if you'd like."

"Adrienne, that would be great. Thanks so much."
Bruce came into the kitchen tying his tie.

"Bruce, Paula is nominated for Most Congenial at school."

"That's great Paula. Congratulations!"

"Thanks. Your wife is going to help me make a dress. I don't think she knows what she just volunteered for. My sewing skills are extremely limited."

"You guys will do great. Adrienne, are you ready to go? We need to be there in thirty minutes."

"Sure. Paula, the number where we'll be is by the phone. Make sure the girls brush their teeth before bed. We should be home before midnight. Help yourself to anything in the kitchen."

"Have a great time." Paula walked them to the door after they said goodbye to their daughters. She was happy again as she went to check on the girls and the pizza.

Paula got up early Saturday morning to clean the house since she needed to meet Adrienne at the fabric store at ten and she didn't want Clarice to have a reason to stop her. Paula was wiping off the table when Clarice came into the kitchen.

"You're up early... I talked to brother last night. They are coming through Dallas next Friday and are going to stay here until Sunday so you can go to the dance. Do you have something to wear?"

"Adrienne said she'd help me make a dress."

Paula did not look at Clarice, who knew she was upset but did not know why. Her mother left the kitchen. Paula finished cleaning up and then called Michael.

"Hey, would you mind if we don't see each other tonight? I'm tired from baby-sitting and I have to work until nine."

"That's fine. My dad called anyway. He wants me to come over tonight. He has something to talk to me about."

"Sounds serious. What did you do?"

"Nothing that I know about."

"What time will you be home?"

"I'll should be back by the time you get home from work. Give me a call when you get home."

"Okay. Hey, I think I found a solution for a dress. Adrienne is going to help me make one."

"I didn't know you could sew."

"I'm not very good, so who knows what the dress will look like."

"You'll look good in anything."

"I'd better go. We are going to look for a pattern and some material this morning. I love you. Have a good day."

"Love you too. Find something sexy."

"Do you ever think of anything else?"

"No."

Adrienne was waiting for Paula at the store. It didn't take long for them to find a simple pattern and a lightweight, mauve satin crepe. The dress had a halter-top and side slit and Paula knew that Michael would like it the moment she saw it. Since Paula had some time before she needed to be at work, she followed Adrienne home to start the dress. They pinned the

173

pattern pieces to the fabric and Paula carefully cut the fabric, under Adrienne's watchful eye. It took a while for Paula to cut out all the pieces but she enjoyed spending the time with Adrienne. Finishing just in time for Paula to go to work, they made plans for Paula to come back Sunday after mass to work on the dress some more.

As Paula drove to work, she worried about how the dress would turn out and if they would be able to finish it in time.

Chapter 9

When Paula returned after mass, Adrienne had the dress almost finished. The hem was the only thing remaining to do. Paula couldn't believe that they had made a formal dress in two days. As she stood in the dress for Adrienne to pin up the hem, she wondered what Michael was planning for the night of the dance.

The drive from Adrienne's house was refreshing. Paula was thrilled with how the dress turned out and it was a beautiful day. The sunshine warmed the car and Paula's spirits. With the dress almost finished, Paula could focus her efforts on studying.

The quarter exams were starting Tuesday. Paula's grades for the first six weeks had surprised her; she had managed four A's and one B, which encouraged her to set a goal of all A's for the quarter. But that goal was slipping from her reach. She had blown several tests and was barely maintaining a B in English, which surprised her since she had taken honors English her junior year. Senior English should have been an easy A.

The pressure was on. Paula knew that if she didn't have an A-average this quarter, she would not graduate with honors and her chances of getting a full scholarship would be reduced. Paula was taking every final even though seniors had the option to be exempt if they had a B or higher average in the class. Most teachers were encouraging exempt seniors to take their finals.

The exam grade would only be included if it raised their average. Paula had everything to gain and nothing to lose.

Autumn greeted Paula at the door, as soon as she opened it. Paula swept her up into the air, which set off a chain reaction of giggles. Autumn was a happy little girl and appeared unaffected by her mother's solemn moods. Paula bounced Autumn all the way to her room and tossed her on the bed, making sure she landed safely on the pillow. She was happy to see that Lisa's door was open, which was unusual these days and a clear sign that no one else was home. Lisa took her attention off the television when Paula walked into the room with Autumn on her heels. The phone receiver was lying on the floor. Paula picked it up and placed it on the base.

"I assume you're not taking any calls. I'll answer it."

"How's the dress coming?"

"Great. Adrienne had it almost finished by the time I got there. The only thing left is the hem. Where's Mom?"

"At the grocery store. She left about thirty minutes ago. I'm glad you're home. Autumn has just about worn me out."

"Did Michael call?"

"I don't think so. I took the phone off the hook as soon as your mother left. I don't want to talk to anyone."

"Well, I'll keep the little one busy until naptime. Come on little lady. Let's go find Aunt Paula something to eat."

Paula scooped Autumn up and galloped to the kitchen. Settling for some peanut butter and crackers, Paula put Autumn in a chair at the kitchen table with some plain crackers while she fixed their snack and tried to decide what she wanted to do before calling Michael.

He answered the phone on the first ring.

"Hello."

"It's me."

"I tried to call you but the line was busy."

"I know. Lisa had the phone off the hook. I just got home anyway. What do you want to do today? It's beautiful outside."

"My car is on the blink. It wouldn't start last night at my dad's house. He is still trying to fix it. It was too late when I got home to call you back."

"I thought you were out having too much fun. What did he want to talk to you about anyway?"

"You won't believe it. I'm going to have a new sibling."

"You're kidding. When?"

"June."

"You're old enough to be the baby's father."

"Well, you could be its mother."

"That's not very funny. I guess your car trouble means we won't get to see each other today. Maybe that's a sign that I need to be studying."

"Why don't you come over here? I want you to meet my family anyway."

"I don't know. I really do need to study."

"Please, I really want to see you. Besides, my mother wants to meet you. You're invited to dinner."

Paula paused. What if his family didn't like her? But Michael had told her so much about his sisters that she did want to meet them, especially his little sister, who sounded so sweet on the phone.

"Okay, but I need to wait for my mother to get back from the store and get Autumn down for her nap. Is three o'clock okay?"

"That will be great. Let me give you the directions."

Paula got some paper and wrote down the directions.

"I don't know if I'll be able to find it. These directions sound complicated."

"Don't worry. It's easy, but call me before you leave."

"Are you sure you want me to meet your family?"

"Good-bye, Paula."

After finishing their snack, Paula decided to clean the kitchen before Clarice got back. She gave Autumn, who wanted to help, a dry cloth to wipe off the table while she washed the dishes. Autumn was determined to help sweep, which made the task take twice as long.

They were just finishing the kitchen when Clarice came home. Paula, with Autumn on her trail, unloaded the groceries and debated how to tell her mother that she was going to Michael's.

"Paula, thanks for cleaning the kitchen. I really appreciate how you help out around the house."

"That's okay. I don't mind."

"I tried to buy enough groceries to last while I'm gone this week. You might have to go back to the store for some milk and bread. I'll leave you some money."

"Okay. When are you leaving?"

"Tuesday, after work and I'll be back Sunday afternoon. Your uncle will be here Friday, probably around three. How's the dress coming for the dance?"

"Adrienne had it almost finished by the time I got there. It looks great. It just needs to be hemmed . . . Mom, Michael invited me to his house for dinner today. Is it okay?"

"That's fine, Paula. But you need to be back before dark. He lives pretty far out and I don't want you driving that far at night by yourself."

"Okay, I'm going to put Autumn down for her nap before I leave. Come on little one. Let's go lie down."

Their conversation had gone much better than Paula expected. She wondered if her mother was having a change of heart about Michael as she carried Autumn to her room for their naptime ritual, which required Paula to lay down with her.

It was two o'clock before Autumn was finally asleep and Paula was able to slip out of the bed. She looked in the mirror and debated changing clothes, but decided to just brush her hair and teeth. She called Michael to tell him that she was on her way and then stopped in the den, where Clarice was reading.

"Mom, I'll be home before six. I'll call you before I leave Michael's house. I wrote his phone number in the address book under the telephone in the hall."

"Okay, Paula. Be careful driving over there and have a nice time. Tell his mother I said hello."

After driving for twenty minutes, Paula was really impressed that Michael willingly drove so far to see her without complaining. The farther Paula drove, the more nervous she became about meeting his family.

It was just before three o'clock when Paula pulled in the driveway. Michael opened the door immediately with a beautiful little girl standing beside him. Paula could smell the wonderful aromas of dinner as soon as he opened the door.

"Hello, everyone's waiting to meet you. This is Brandy."

"Hello, it's nice to finally met you."

The little girl just smiled. She was chocolate brown like Michael and her waist-length hair that was pulled into two ponytails, was just like Michael's. Paula touched one of her ponytails. It felt like cotton.

"I love your ponytails."

Brandy smiled and ran around the corner.

"Michael, I'm a little nervous about meeting your mother."

"Don't be. She doesn't bite."

Michael led Paula through the den and into the kitchen, where Brandy was already waiting for them. His mother was busy cooking but turned her attention to them. She had a kind smile, which immediately relaxed Paula, and beautiful brown skin just like Michael, but she was shorter than Paula had expected. His mother was almost the same height as Clarice, but appeared to be much younger.

"Mom, this is Paula Hayes. Paula, this is my mother, Ms. Williams."

"It's very nice to meet you, Ms. Williams."

"It's nice to meet you Paula. Do you like fried chicken?"

"I love it. Can I help with anything?"

"No thanks, dinner will be ready in a little while."

His mother turned her attention back to the covered skillet on the burner. Paula followed Michael into the den and sat down on the leather sofa. Brandy ran pass and disappeared down the hall.

"Nia is on the phone, as usual. She'll be in here soon. Did you have any problems finding my house?"

"No, but it sure is a long way."

"There's a shorter way, but I didn't want to get you lost."

Michael's other sister came into the den with Brandy, who ran and jumped on the sofa next to Michael. Paula was amazed at the differences between Nia and the rest of her family. She had a light complexion and although her hair was long, it had a visibly different texture from Michael and Brandy.

"Paula, this is Nia."

"Well, hello. So you're the person my brother can't stop talking about."

"Oh really, what has he been saying?"

"Nothing."

Michael interrupted before Nia could answer.

"Don't you have some homework to do?"

"No." Nia replied with a mischievous smile.

It was apparent that she intended to keep her brother in the hot seat, but Paula could tell that Michael was a good big brother. Just then, Michael's mother stood at the edge of the kitchen.

"Nia, come set the table."

Nia frowned and walked into the kitchen.

"Nia, can I help you set the table?"

"Sure."

Paula stood up and followed Nia into the kitchen.

The dinner was excellent and Paula complimented Michael's mother on the meal several times. Now Paula knew why Michael had such a hardy appetite and the extra cushioning around his waist. Michael's mother was the first to leave the table.

"Paula, there's some pecan pie for dessert." His mother said before going into the den.

"Thank you, Ms. Williams but right now I don't think I could eat another thing. Come on Michael, let's do the dishes."

Paula stood and picked up her plate.

"Nope, it's Nia's week to do the dishes."

"We can't leave her with all these dishes. Come on. It won't take long."

"Okay... Nia, you'd better be glad that Paula's here, otherwise you'd be on your own."

"Thanks, Paula."

Paula knew she had made a friend as she took off her watch and slipped it in her pocket.

After they finished, Paula retrieved her watch from her pocket and looked at the time. Nia noticed the watch as Paula was putting it back on.

"Paula, that's a nice watch. I want one like that."

Paula held out her wrist so Nia could get a good look. Michael tried to get Paula's attention but it was too late.

"Thanks, your brother gave it to me for Christmas."

"OH REALLY."

Nia looked at Michael with a smile and went into the den.

"Mom, you should see the watch Michael gave Paula for Christmas."

Paula looked at Michael, who looked uncomfortable as his mother came into the kitchen to see the watch.

"Paula, that's a very beautiful watch. My son has good taste."

His mother looked at Michael, who had obviously spent more money on Paula's gift than hers.

"Mom, Paula and I are going to watch television in my room."

Michael led Paula through the den to his room.

"Why didn't you tell me your mother didn't know about the watch?" Paula whispered, as soon as they got in his room.

"It's no big deal. It was my money. So what do you think about my room?"

Michael turned on the television that sat on an upside down crate in the corner and then sat down on the bed. Paula sat next to Michael and looked around the extremely small room. It barely had enough space for the twin bed and dresser. Several blacklight posters covered the walls and a fishing net hung from the ceiling. A small stereo sat on the floor under the window. In Paula's opinion, it was definitely a masculine room.

"It's nice."

"What time do you need to leave?"

"I told Mom that I'd be home before dark. She doesn't want me driving at night by myself."

"I agree with your mother. If you leave around five-thirty, you should be on your side of town before dark. Do you want to play some cards?"

"Sure, Spades or Gin?"

"How about Gin?"

Michael stood up and searched in the top drawer of his dresser. Finally, he pulled out a deck of cards and handed them to Paula.

"See if they are all there?"

Paula quickly counted the cards.

"It's only fifty."

"Let me get a deck from my mom."

Michael left and Paula looked around the room again while she waited. Brandy came in the room and jumped on the bed near Paula.

"Your brother went to get some cards. Do you want to watch us play?"

"Sure."

Michael returned with a new box of cards.

"Brandy, will you please get out of here?"

"Paula said I could stay and watch you play cards."

"Oh, she did."

"Yes, I did. She can help me beat you."

Brandy smiled and moved closer to Paula. Michael shuffled the deck of cards and dealt the first hand. Paula attempted to explain the rules of the game to Brandy without giving away her hand. It slowed the game but Paula didn't mind. They were just finishing the first hand when Michael's mother called Brandy and she ran into the den but didn't return.

"I'm glad you came. What do you think of my family?"

"I think they are very nice. Do you think that they like me?"

"I'm sure they do. But even if they didn't, it wouldn't matter. Are you looking forward to the dance?"

"I guess so. How about you?"

"Yep."

"What do you want for Valentine's Day?"

"You know what I want."

"What?"

"You."

"You have me."

"You know what I mean, something that will make this Valentine's Day very special."

"What?"

Michael lowered his voice to just above a whisper.

"I want to take you to a hotel after the dance."

"Michael, I can't stay out all night. My aunt and uncle will be staying at the house."

"Who said anything about all night. We can leave the dance a little early and be home by two. Just tell them we are going out to eat after the dance."

"I don't know Michael."

"Paula you want me as much as I want you. What we have is very special. I want our first time together to be special too. You don't have to decide now, but promise me you will think about it."

"I promise."

"Do you still want to play cards?"

"No, it's about time for me to leave. I really do need to study. Don't you have to study for some tests."

"Nope, I don't have any more tests until the week before spring break. You have to get some pie before you leave. My mom makes the best pecan pie."

"Okay, but just a little piece." Paula said, reluctantly following Michael.

Paula thanked Michael's mother then she called Clarice to let her know that she was on her way home. Michael walked Paula to her car after she said good-bye to his sisters.

"Think about next weekend."

"Okay. I hope you get your car fixed."

185

"I'd better go call my dad and see how it's coming. Call me when you get home." Michael said before he kissed her and closed her door.

It was five-thirty when Paula backed out of Michael's driveway. Her attention was initially on finding the way back to the highway. But when she was safely on the highway, her thoughts quickly went to Michael's request. Paula had been secretly relieved that neither of them wanted to go all the way in a car. But now that barrier was being removed and it panicked her. She had to make the decision soon, but she still wasn't sure if she was ready. Everyday she saw the impact of an unplanned pregnancy and how her sister's life had been forever changed.

Paula knew that she did not long for the ultimate intimacy. She enjoyed the activities leading up to the event much more. Her memory of the only time she had actually had intercourse was not very pleasant. Three years later, she still cringed at the thought. But there was something different about the way her body responded to Michael's touch. She wondered if it would be different with him and she would feel the ecstasy that was the basis for so many songs. Paula was afraid that if she didn't agree to Michael's request, she would lose him, which scared her more than the potential unpleasantness of the experience.

Paula was so absorbed in her thoughts, that she was home sooner than she expected. She sat in the car a few minutes after turning off the ignition. Finally, she took a deep breath and got out of the car. Her mother was in the den watching television when Paula stopped in the doorway.

"Mom, I'm home."

"How was dinner?"

"It was very nice. His mother cooked fried chicken."

"Was his mother nice?"

"Yes, ma'am."

"I'm going to call Michael and let him know that I made it home safely and then I'm going to go study. I have a couple of tests and a paper due this week."

"It sounds to me like you should have stayed home and studied. When will grades be out?"

"Next week. It's pretty quiet. Where is Autumn?"

"Karen picked her up to take her for ice cream. They should be back soon."

Paula picked up the hall phone on the way to her room and closed the door before dialing Michael's number.

"Hi, I made it home okay."

"I'm glad. My mom thinks you're very nice."

"Good, maybe she won't ban you from seeing me."

"I don't think she could."

"Did she say anything about the watch?"

"No. Did you think about next weekend?"

"Yes."

"Well..."

"...Okay."

"Paula, are you sure? I don't want to pressure you."

"I'm sure. Now I'd better go study before Autumn gets back. I'll call you tomorrow"

"Paula, I love you. I'll take care of everything."

"I love you too, Michael."

Paula hung up the phone and stared at the floor, surprised at how quickly she had agreed to Michael's request but doubtful that she really had a choice. Michael was her only source of happiness and she couldn't risk losing him, whatever it took. But there was one limit. Although she was willing to risk some unpleasantness, she wasn't going to sacrifice her future; they needed to take precautions.

After a brief hesitation, Paula opened her book bag and prioritized the work. First, she would do the Physics review problems; she'd write the rough draft of the English paper, and finally, if she were still awake, she'd review her math notes.

The bed turned out to be a poor workspace. Her thoughts kept drifting to Michael and the upcoming event. She decided to move to the dining room for some serious studying. Her Physics took more time than she had expected but Autumn was still not home, so Paula continued to work. She reread the English assignment that counted twenty percent of her grade for the quarter then stared at a blank piece of paper as she chewed on the cap of her pen, waiting for some inspiration. She looked at the clock and squirmed in the chair.

The lack of progress started a chain reaction that escalated to a full-fledge panic attack. Paula jumped up from the table, driven by some internal force, and instinctively went into the kitchen to get a drink. Pacing the kitchen while she sipped her juice, Paula knew that her panic was not solely attributed to her lack of creativity. She had serious doubts about her decision.

Autumn ran into the kitchen before Paula could return to her paper. Knowing that her studying would have to wait until Autumn was asleep, Paula went to the den to look at some television. No one else was in the den, so she stretched out on the sofa. The national anthem was playing on the television when Clarice woke her up.

Paula woke up Friday morning with trepidation, still unsure of the outcome of the weekend. Moving from one test or deadline to the next all week and shouldering the burden of ensuring the house ran smoothly in her mother's absence could not even keep her mind off the event. The stress of finals, her mother's absence, and Michael's weekend plans, left Paula mentally and physically exhausted.

Usually Fridays bought some relief, but this weekend was different. She had talked to Michael daily and each time he bought up their plans for Saturday night, Paula managed to change the subject. Then to make the situation worse, Michael announced that their itinerary would include a stop by his father's before the dance. He wanted to meet her and take pictures.

The decision to comply with Michael's request was now an ominous cloud looming over her spirit, promising to deliver a powerful blow of destruction. Paula thought constantly of reversing her decision but the excitement in Michael's voice when he talked about the weekend reminded her of a child on Christmas Eve. She wondered how they could feel so differently about the same impending event; and felt trapped with no idea how to free herself.

Delivering Valentine carnations in the morning kept Paula's mind temporarily off the next major milepost in her life. The Favorite's election later in the morning also served as a diversion. But after the busy morning, the afternoon dragged by, giving Paula too much opportunity to think. By the time that the final bell rang, Paula was looking forward to the task of cooking dinner for their guests and playing with Autumn to keep her mind off her impending fate.

A delicious aroma coming from the kitchen surprised Paula when she walked in the house. She had rushed home from school to cook dinner but someone else was taking care of that task. Paula walked into the kitchen and hugged her aunt, who was busy at the stove.

"Hi, you didn't have to cook dinner. You're our guests."

"It is no trouble. We stopped by the grocery store on the way in."

"Where's the rest of your family?"

"They went back to the store for a few things I needed. Lisa and Autumn went with them. Your mom called. She says you have a big night tomorrow."

"Yes, I do."

Chapter 10

Paula had slept in later than normal for a Saturday since Clarice was gone and she knew it was going to be a long day. From the moment she opened her eyes, her thoughts focused on Michael's plans for the evening. She had hoped that working would help, but it didn't. The store had been busy and she was glad when three o'clock finally came.

A delicious aroma greeted Paula again when she walked in the house. She went directly to the kitchen and found her aunt frying pork chops.

"Hello, you sure do have it smelling good in here. But you aren't supposed to be cooking every night. You are our guest."

"I enjoy cooking. Will you have time to eat before your date?"

"No, Michael is picking me up early. We're going to his father's house to take some pictures and then we're meeting some friends for dinner before the dance."

"You go ahead and get ready. Don't worry about us."

"Thanks for cooking. It smells delicious. I'm sorry to miss it."

Paula was tempted to sample a chop. She went into her room, dropped her purse on her bed and glanced at the dress, hanging on the door. It was after four when Paula took off her watch, wondering what Michael was going to give her for Valentine's Day. Letting out a sigh, Paula picked up her robe and disappeared into the bathroom.

Taking a final look in the full-length mirror, Paula wished that she had time to lose some weight. The clingy dress outlined every detail of her body. She looked at her purse lying on the bed and then went into Clarice's room to borrow her evening bag. After putting the necessary items in the small purse, Paula went to the den to get another opinion of how she looked. Her aunt and uncle looked up when she walked into the room. Her uncle was the first to comment.

"Paula, you look beautiful and so grown up."

"That dress is nice. Did you really make it?" Her aunt asked.

"Yes, with a lot of help."

Her aunt looked at the revealing dress.

"Do you have a shawl? Your shoulders might get cold."

"I didn't think of that. Mom might have one. I'll go check."

Paula went back to Clarice's room and found an off-white lace shawl. She came back and modeled it for her aunt.

"That looks good with it. Sometimes they keep those ballrooms ice cold. Let me get my camera so I can take some pictures. Your mother will be so sad that she missed this night."

"I probably won't be home until two. The dance ends at twelve-thirty and then we are going to go out for breakfast."

Michael rang the doorbell at exactly five-thirty, wearing a dark double-breasted suit and a tie that matched Paula's dress perfectly. It was the first time that Paula had seen him in a suit and was pleased. She introduced him to her aunt and uncle. Paula's aunt took a picture of them before they left and suggested that Paula wear her coat since it was dressier. After they said their good-byes, Paula walked to Michael's car as if she were going to her last meal. Michael looked at Paula.

"You look beautiful. I love that dress."

"Thanks."

"I talked to my father this morning. He's looking forward to meeting you."

"How long are we going to stay? I told Rosalyn that we'd meet them at the restaurant at seven."

"Not very long, he just wants to meet you, see how we look and probably take some pictures. What time are they going to announce the winners?"

"I'm not sure. Why?"

"I thought that we could leave the dance around ten. That will give us plenty of time."

"Okay."

Paula was quiet on the drive to his father's house, only talking enough to be polite and hide her true feelings. Several times she started to tell him that she wasn't ready but she didn't have the courage. She noticed a sleazy motel off the freeway and could not believe that anyone would stay there.

When they got to his father's house, Paula livened up a little. Michael was a lot like his father in looks and mannerisms. True to his word, they did not stay long. Paula noticed Michael's father handing him some money as they were leaving.

"Do you want to stop and check into the room before we meet at the restaurant?"

"No, we are running late. Let's wait."

They got to the restaurant just as Taylor and Rosalyn were arriving with their dates but food was the last thing on Paula's mind. Her stomach was churning - fueled by her nerves; despite her best attempts, Paula could not relax and enjoy herself. She found herself getting angry every time Michael looked at her. They left the restaurant at eight-thirty, which left them plenty of time to get to the dance. Michael helped Paula with her coat and held her hand as they walked to the car.

"Paula, are you okay?"

"I'm fine."

"You have been very quiet all night."

"I'm just tired. It's been a busy week and I don't think I did too well on my tests." Paula said, wanting to tell Michael what was really wrong.

"I'm sure you did great. Don't worry about it. Just think about you and me finally being together tonight."

That is the last thing I want to think about! Paula, it's now or never. Tell him you're not ready.

"Michael."

"Yes, Paula." Michael looked at her.

"About tonight?"

"What about tonight?"

Paula knew she couldn't tell him the truth. She decided to use a different approach."

"I'm not on the pill and I don't want to take any chances."

"Is that what's worrying you? Don't worry. I told you I would take care of everything. I always keep protection with me."

Paula was angry that her plan wasn't working and decided to try another approach.

"Oh really. Do you find yourself needing protection often?"

"Paula stop being ridiculous. My father told me I should always be prepared. You know that there is no one else but you.

I haven't even called anyone else since I started dating you. Don't you know how much I love you?" Michael asked as he turned the car into the parking garage.

"Yes."

"Then, stop worrying and let's go have a wonderful time. After that, I will show you how much I love you."

Michael picked up Paula's left hand and kissed it gently. Then he got out of the car and walked around to open the car door for her. Paula took Michael's hand as they joined the other couples heading for the ballroom.

The ballroom was decorated with red and white balloons and streamers. Paula's group found an empty table in the middle of the room. The music was playing so loud that they had to shout to be heard. Paula and Michael danced to a few songs while they waited for the presentations. Michael looked at his watch every few minutes. Finally, the lights came on.

The nominees for each category were announced and had to stand in the spotlight while they waited for the winner to be announced. The sophomore class nominees and winners were presented first. Before Paula knew it, it was time for the seniors. Being in the stoplight scared Paula more than losing.

The first senior category was Most Congenial. Paula walked to the center of the dance floor with the other two nominees. Paula smiled nervously as she waited for the announcement. The winner was not a surprise. Paula returned to her table, knowing that she only had one more hurdle to overcome. Michael stood up and gave Paula a hug before she sat down.

"You should have won. You were definitely the most beautiful."

"Thanks."

Paula sat in silence as they announced the other winners, wishing that she had followed Clarice's advice to stay home. What should have been a romantic date had turned into a nightmare. She could only think about what was going to happen after they left and how soon it would be before Michael was ready to leave. It didn't take long. As soon as the presentations were over and the music resumed, he leaned over and whispered in her ear.

"Are you ready to leave? I can't wait to be alone with you."

"Michael, I think we should stay at least until ten-thirty. I don't want people to think I'm a sore loser." She said with a smile, hoping to postpone as long as possible.

Paula pretended to be having a good time so people wouldn't think that she was upset about not winning. She didn't know whether to be angry or flattered when Michael kept looking at his watch. Ten-thirty came much too fast for Paula. Michael looked at her as if pleading. Without saying a word, she reached for her purse and stood up.

"You guys aren't leaving already?" Rosalyn asked.

"Yes, my mother's out of town and I told her I wouldn't be out too late."

Paula was surprised at how easily the lie came out. But there was no way she was going to tell them the truth. Taylor, who knew, looked at Paula and smiled.

Tired of explaining to everyone why they were leaving so early as they made their way through the crowd, Paula was relieved when they were finally in the car.

"So where are we going, Michael?"

"It's a little motel. I wanted somewhere secluded."

"Okay."

Paula leaned her head back on the seat and looked out the window as they started the drive. It looked as if they were headed back to his father's house. She saw a billboard for that sleazy little motel again and looked at the gas gauge on the car when they took the exit for it.

"Michael, do we need to get some gas?"

"No, the motel is off this exit."

Paula looked around hopefully for another motel. She could not believe it when Michael pulled into the parking lot of the hooker motel that looked worse as they got closer. It had a neon sign in the window advertising hourly rates. Paula looked around in fear as Michael parked in front of the office and turned off the ignition.

What is Michael thinking? This motel is for prostitutes. Is this what he thinks of me?

"It's not that nice on the outside but the rooms are clean. Wait here and I'll get us a room."

He went into the office and Paula's nervousness was quickly replaced by outrage.

How does he know the rooms are clean? Not that nice! Michael is being way too generous. The place is a dump. How could he even think of taking me to a place like this? ...How stupid can I be? And I thought he actually loved me. This is all the proof that I need.

Suddenly, Paula thought of the words her mother had said to her two years earlier when she had caught her kissing a boy in the living room and the night Michael had given her the watch - I didn't raise you to be a tramp!

Michael returned to the car triumphantly.

"I got us the nicest room. It's around the back. I didn't want anyone to see us."

"Michael, I don't think we have to worry about that."

Michael didn't even catch the sarcasm in Paula's voice. His attention was on other things.

No one I know would be caught dead in a place like this.

"How much did you have to pay for this place?"

"Fifty-five dollars."

"For this?"

"Paula, I promise you that the rooms are nice."

I can't believe this. Shane would have never brought me to a dump like this. The back seat of a car has more appeal than this place.

The rear of the hotel looked as bad as the front, only darker and the parking lot was full of wrecked cars. Paula's anger was replaced by fear when Michael got out of the car and walked around to open the door.

Why is he bothering to open the door for me now? He obviously doesn't think enough of me to take me to a nicer place.

Paula walked quickly behind him, angry with herself for even getting out of the car. The roar of the cars on the freeway could still be heard as they stepped inside the room. Michael closed the door behind them and turned the lock, but the lock did not help Paula feel secure.

Paula looked around the room and was surprised that it actually smelled clean. The floor was covered in brown shag carpet, which matched the brown bedspread, both from the sixties. The lamp on the table by the bed cast a yellow glow. Michael walked over to Paula smiling and wrapped his arms around her waist. Paula felt sick; she needed to get away from him.

"I need to go to the restroom."

Paula freed herself from his grasp and started to take off her coat. Michael quickly came to her assistance, offering help that she did not want. She tried to smile as she retreated into the bathroom and closed the door. The bathroom was about the size of a closet and the fixtures were very old, but at least they looked clean. Paula looked in the mirror, not sure whom she was angrier with, herself or Michael.

How could he bring me to a place like this?. . . You should have told him to take you home.

Tears began to swell in her eyes. She quickly grabbed some tissue, pressed it into the corners of her eyes to plug the wells and took very slow and deep breaths. Once satisfied that the tears had been halted, she focused on her current dilemma.

You can't stay in the restroom until time to go.

There was a soft knock on the door.

"Paula are you okay?"

"I'm fine. I'll be right out."

Paula looked in the mirror again. This time the image looking back at her had changed. It was a look that she had seen too often before.

You know what you need to do. Just go do it and get it over with. You don't want to lose Michael.

Paula took a deep breath, opened the bathroom door and walked out. Michael was still standing by the door. He had removed his shirt and folded back the bedspread. She wanted to say a prayer to help her get through this challenge like she always did. But even that was not an option since she knew that sex outside of marriage was a sin. Michael hugged her.

"Are you sure you're okay?"

"I'm fine, just a little nervous."

"I thought you told me you weren't a virgin."

"Technically, I'm not. It's just been a very long time. Three years to be exact and it wasn't that great."

"Don't worry, I promise to be very gentle. The last thing I want to do is hurt you."

You have already hurt me more than you will ever know.

Michael's hands moved from her waist to the halter straps of her dress as he kissed her and expertly untied the straps. Without missing a beat, his hands moved down to the zipper. She waited for her body to respond but nothing happened; there was no light-headedness or warmth as her dress fell to the floor. The only thing that she felt was cold. Michael's kisses moved from her lips to her neck. He didn't realized that Paula was cold until he went to kiss her breast and finally noticed that her arms and breasts was covered with chill bumps.

"You're cold. I'm sorry. Let's get under the cover."

Michael sat on the edge of the bed and removed his shoes. Paula quickly removed her shoes and panty hose and got under the cover. When Michael finished undressing, he walked to the table and got something from his wallet. Then he sat on the edge of the bed and quickly put on his protection.

"Now, where were we?"

Michael slipped into the bed and wrapped his arms around Paula, pulling her closer. All she wanted to do was get dressed and leave. Michael kissed her shoulder and turned her towards him. Paula tried to respond, but the touch, which had previously left her body full of desire, now repulsed her. Before she knew it, Michael was maneuvering on top of her. Paula closed her eyes and hoped it wouldn't take too long. She wasn't prepared for what happened next.

Her body would not accept Michael. The wetness, which had always appeared, was absent. Michael tried repeatedly to merge their bodies but finally realized that he was probably hurting her. He raised his head to look at her then quickly rolled off her when he saw the tears. Paula turned her back to Michael, embarrassed by the tears that she had tried to suppress.

"Paula, I'm sorry. I didn't mean to hurt you."

"It's not that."

"Then what's wrong?"

"Michael, I'm not ready for this. I thought I was."

"Paula, we don't have to do anything. The last thing I want to do is rush you. We can wait. I'm getting good at taking cold showers." Michael said with a smile.

"You're not mad?"

"About what? Do you think that this is all I want from you?"

"But you just spent fifty dollars for this room."

"It doesn't matter, though I wish you would have said something sooner."

"Michael, I didn't think that I had a choice. I was afraid that you were losing your patience, and there are plenty of others who would be more than willing."

"Paula, I love you. I want to be with you and only you. Do you think that I'd drive all the way across town every chance I get just to get you in bed? Believe me, this has to be love."

Michael got out of bed and went into the bathroom. Paula wondered what he was doing.

He came back a few minutes later and put on his briefs.

"Now, is it okay if I just hold you for a while? I promise not to attack you."

"Michael, I love you."

Paula slid over to make room for Michael. She knew at that moment that Michael really did love her; it was the best Valentine's present that he could give her.

Chapter 11

Springtime had always been Paula's favorite season and she was happy despite all the drama occurring around her. Graduation was a month away. She was college bound, almost on her own and she had Michael. The night at the motel had actually made their relationship stronger. It had been over two months and Michael had been the perfect gentleman. It became harder and harder for Michael to wait, but he was determined to let Paula decided on the time and place. Paula didn't tell Michael but she had already picked the time for the big event; it was going to be her graduation gift to him.

The tension between Paula and her mother had escalated to new levels. Paula's grades for the second trimester had dropped from four A's and one B to four B's and one A. As soon as Clarice saw her grades, she commented on the drop. Paula knew that Clarice blamed the drop in grades on Michael, but Paula attributed the drop to the difficult course load, all the senior class activities, and the stress associated with Lisa's pregnancy.

To prove something to her mother, Paula quit her job and studied harder than ever. Her performance for the next six weeks would determine whether she was going to graduate with honors. Since so much depended on class rankings, schools could not wait until the end of the year to calculate averages. Although she only had six weeks to raise her average, Paula was ready to get it over with. At least she would be able to relax and enjoy the last six weeks.

Thursday morning, the official graduation list was posted on the wall outside the cafeteria, starting with the honor graduates by class rank followed by the other graduating seniors listed in alphabetical order. Paula held her breath as she approached the list, ready to find out if her hard work had been enough. She started with the list of regular graduates and quickly located the H's; her name wasn't there. Her heart raced as she worried whether she even had enough credits to graduate. She quickly moved to the list of honor graduates and started at the bottom.

Her name was sixth from the bottom. It took a while for it to really sink in. She checked the list several times just to make sure. She had barely made it, but she was going to graduate with honors. Paula was floating on air the entire day and called Michael as soon as she got home.

Paula had been accepted at SCU and State University but she was leaning towards SCU because of the financial aid package and its proximity to Michael, who had been accepted at Northern State. She had to make her final decision soon. SCU had an Engineering intern program that started the first week of June. The interns lived in a dorm for the summer and worked for their sponsoring company. Paula liked the idea of living on campus for the summer, especially since her relationship with Clarice was getting more and more strained.

The overnight visit to SCU was an eagerly awaited event. Not so much because Paula wanted to experience college life, but for the freedom that it offered. She just wanted an escape from her house, which was on the brink of collapsing under the tension. Lisa's baby was due any day and she still hadn't decided what she was going to do. Paula was ready for the drama surrounding Lisa and the baby to end. It was making it difficult for her to find peace at home. But Michael was less thrilled about Paula's overnight visit. He didn't think she needed to spend the night in the dorms to make her decision.

The campus visit started early Saturday morning with tours of the campus and presentations on the freshman program. Paula was having a great time. Her decision was made by dinnertime. When they returned to the dorm from dinner, there was a message waiting for Paula to call home immediately. She wondered if she would ever be able to escape as she reluctantly called home. Clarice answered after the first ring.

"Hi Mom, I got a message to call home."

"Paula, I'm sorry but you need to come home now. Lisa's labor has started. Karen took her to the hospital, but I need to get there soon. I'm not sure how long it will take, so you need to keep Autumn."

"Mom, can't Eric keep her? The program is really good."

"I'm sorry Paula. I've been trying to get in touch with him but he's out. How long will it take for you to get here? I need to get to the hospital soon."

"I'll be home in thirty minutes."

"Thanks, Paula."

Clarice hung up the phone and looked at her watch. She would not let Paula make the same mistake and wondered what to do while she waited for her.

Lisa gave birth to a healthy girl just before ten o'clock that night. Much to Paula's dismay, Lisa had relented to the pressure and agreed to let her aunt adopt the baby. Paula was furious at Lisa for letting other people run her life. She would never let anyone make her that miserable. Even though her visit was cut short, she had seen enough to make her decision. If she heard the lecture about getting pregnant one more time, she was going to scream. She had to move out of the house as soon as possible.

Sunday afternoon, Michael was supposed to come over around three o'clock. They had gotten into a pattern of staying at her house on Sundays. Paula was surprised when Michael called and suggested picking her up instead; but with all the tension in the house, Paula was happy to have an opportunity to leave. Michael was extremely serious when Paula opened the door. He spoke to Clarice but he seemed rather formal and in a hurry to leave. Paula sensed something was definitely wrong.

He did not say anything for almost ten minutes after leaving her house. Paula wondered if he had argued with his mother.

"So where are we going?" Paula said with a smile hoping to lift his spirits.

"I don't know. How about my house?"

"Michael, that's a lot of driving. We could have stayed at my house."

"I'm not welcomed there."

"That's crazy, Michael. What's wrong?"

"I'm not suppose to say anything, but I think you have a right to know. Your mother called my mother."

"About what?"

Paula couldn't believe what she had just heard and the tone in Michael's voice let her know that it wasn't a social call. But she hoped that she was wrong.

"Us. Apparently your mother thinks we are getting too serious. She asked my mother to talk to me."

"What does Mom think? That your mother will order you to stop seeing me. I can't believe this. How dare she interfere like this? I'm eighteen years old and my mother is acting like she can control my life... What did your mother say?"

"She said that I was old enough to make my own decisions. Your mother is concerned that we may do something that will jeopardize your going to college. She also told my mother that since we started dating, you have changed and your grades have dropped. My mom told her that she would talk to me, but the decision was up to me. Of course, Mom reminded me that we need to be responsible, if you know what I mean."

"And what's your decision, Michael?"

Paula held her breath, trying to contain her anger at her mother and her fear about Michael's response. She could not bear losing him.

"Paula, I love you. I am going to keep seeing you until you tell me to stop, regardless of what your mother thinks. If it's up to me, we'll be together forever."

"Thanks, Michael. I would never forgive my mother, if she were responsible for breaking us up. First she blames the drop in my grades on you. Now that I'm graduating with honors, she is still not satisfied . . . Didn't she know that you would tell me?"

"I don't think she realizes how much I love you. What are you going to do?"

"I don't know but I'm sure glad I don't have much longer to live there."

"Don't tell your mother I told you. She didn't want you to know that she called."

"At this point, I don't think you'll have to worry about that. As a matter of fact, I don't think I'll be talking to my mother very much at all. The last time I checked, eighteen is considered a legal adult. I'll be out of her house soon. Then we can do whatever we want."

"I know I won't be coming to your house any more if she's there, so don't even ask."

"I understand completely. I still can't believe she did this."

They spent the day at Michael's house and he reluctantly took her home a little before eight. Paula went straight to her room and closed the door. She had always suspected it. Now, it was clear to both of them – her mother did not approve of Michael. Paula did not come out of her room that night until she was sure that Clarice was asleep, afraid that she would not be able to contain her anger. Paula was relieved that her mother's ploy had not worked, but she did not know what to do about it.

The last weekend in April was beautiful; Paula overheard Clarice saying she was going to be out Sunday afternoon. This was the first opportunity since Paula found out about the call for Michael to come over. She called Michael as soon as she could to tell him that the coast was clear for a visit.

Clarice left with a general announcement about the time of her return. It was a very warm day so, Paula decided to wear a sundress just in case they decided to go to the lake. But everyone was taking advantage of the beautiful Sunday afternoon. Even Lisa who was experiencing extreme post-partum depression had decided to go out. Since they had the house to themselves, Paula and Michael decided to stay there. Paula suggested that they watch television in the den instead of her bedroom. She did not want to tempt fate, especially since Michael was being so patient. Since nothing good was on the television, they ended up playing cards.

"I'm thirsty. Do you want something to drink?"

Paula passed in front of Michael, who admired how the dress draped against her body.

"Sure."

Michael moved the cards to the floor and switched the channel on the television, hoping to find a distraction. Paula came back with two glasses of juice.

"Do you think I can get a kiss?"

"Of course, Michael. You don't have to ask."

Paula sat down next to Michael. She took a sip of her drink and then placed the glasses safely on the floor by the leg of the sofa. He kissed her gently and pulled away; he had promised to wait. Paula moved closer and kissed Michael. This was the first time all week that Paula had felt relaxed.

Within minutes, they were both following their desire. Neither Paula nor Michael wanted to stop. When their bodies could not get comfortable, they managed to slide to the floor. Paula suddenly realized that they needed to stop.

"Michael, I think we need a break."

Michael silenced her with more kisses. Paula's mind went blank. It felt so wonderful that she didn't want to stop. Her body was drawn to his. Michael was breathing rapidly and Paula knew he wanted her desperately. Everything was happening too fast. Paula tried to sit up and push Michael away knowing that she had to stop them.

"Michael, we need to stop."

"Paula, please don't stop. Please!"

He looked at Paula for a brief moment and continued to kiss her in a way that made her wonder why she was trying to stop. She felt herself giving in when she realized they didn't have any protection. She pushed Michael harder.

"Michael, we can't take a chance."

"Please, Paula. I promise we won't. You want me too; I know it…"

Michael knew just what to do and within minutes, he had melted away any ability for Paula to resist. The sundress offered no deterrent to Michael's experienced maneuvers. The next thing Paula knew he was inside of her and unlike their first attempt, their bodies merged effortlessly. The urgency of Michael's movement brought Paula back to reality.

"No, Michael we can't!"

She tried to push him off her, but it was too late. Michael was a runaway train barreling towards its final destination - to satisfy his desire for her. He could not think; his body had taken control. He had waited so long that he felt he was going to explode. It just kept feeling better - just a few more seconds. His head was spinning by the time he exploded in ecstasy and collapsed on top of Paula, oblivious to what he had done.

Paula knew the seriousness of what had just happened and pushed Michael off of her with all her strength. Michael looked at her, surprised by her force. His body was still controlling his mind. She straightened her clothes and sat on the sofa. Michael closed his pants and sat next to her.

"Michael, how could you do that? You promised."

"I don't know what happened. It felt so good that I just couldn't stop. I can't help the way you make me feel."

"What am I going to do now? What if I get pregnant?"

"Paula, you are jumping the gun. You don't know for sure that you're going to get pregnant."

"It's easy for you to say! It's not you that could be pregnant. You can just walk away and forget that this ever happened."

Paula didn't realize that she was screaming. All Paula could think of was Clarice. How many times had she heard her mother's warnings? Michael put his arm around her but she quickly got up, not wanting him to touch her. He was finally starting to feel some remorse.

"You know that I wouldn't do that. We are in this together. I love you."

"I think you'd better leave."

"Paula, I can't leave you like this."

"I'm fine. I just need to take a shower. I'll call you later."

Paula knew that she wouldn't call him but she also knew that he wouldn't leave unless she convinced him she was okay. And she wanted him to leave desperately. She hated Michael at that moment. Not only did she feel used, she also felt cheated. Michael had been completely satisfied; she had not.

"Are you sure you're okay?"

"I'm fine. Now will you please go so I can get cleaned up before someone gets home?"

"Please, don't worry. Everything will be okay, Paula."

"Sure."

Paula tried to smile as she walked him to the door and reluctantly let Michael kiss her on the cheek.

Michael's euphoria began to dissipate as he drove home. He thought about how sexy Paula looked in that sundress, arousing him from the moment he walked in the door. He had honestly thought he would be able to pull out in time. Michael knew he had messed up, but he had no doubts about his love for Paula. If she did get pregnant, they would just get married. An abortion was totally out of the question. They were Catholic and it would be a sin to kill their baby. He was not that concerned since they were probably going to get married anyway. It would just be sooner than planned. He had told Paula that he would wait as long as she needed, but Michael rationalized that Paula must have wanted it just as badly as he did because she didn't resist, very much.

The event kept replaying itself in Michael's mind. Michael was surprised at how quickly he got home. As he got out of the car, he wondered if it felt as good to Paula and made a mental note to ask her when they talked. Michael had a huge smile on his face as he walked toward his house.

Paula had to resist slamming the door after Michael left. She returned to the den, picked up the two drinks that were barely touched, and went to the kitchen. She sat Michael's drink in the sink and took a sip of hers as she stared out the kitchen window. The liquid stuck in her throat as she tried to swallow. Paula poured the juice down the drain slowly. The dirty dishes in the sink reminded her of how dirty she felt. Paula knew she had to take a quick shower before anyone came home. She went to her room and retrieved some clean underwear from her dresser and retreated into the rear bathroom, locking the door behind her. She'd put on the same dress or someone may get suspicious.

Paula turned on the shower and adjusted the water temperature. The droplets from the shower matched the tears that began rolling down her cheeks. Paula sat on the edge of the bathtub as her tears turned to uncontrollable sobs. The shower muzzled the sounds of her crying. After ten minutes, she knew that she had to get in the shower or risk running out of hot water.

The warm water massaging her body helped subdue the crying for a while until Clarice's voice began echoing in her mind - I hope you don't get pregnant like your sister. The tears started again. When the water turned lukewarm, the tears suddenly stopped. Paula knew what she had to do. Even if she were pregnant, Clarice would never know. She was not going to have a baby before she graduated from college and was married. An unplanned pregnancy was not going to ruin her life. Paula turned off the water, grabbed her towel, and began to dry off. She looked in the mirror and looked away quickly.

Paula calculated that she would have until mid July to get an abortion, if necessary. She would be living in the dorms and working by then. Money would not be an issue even though she thought that Michael should pay half since it was his fault too. Paula wrapped her soiled underwear in her towel and felt much better as she came out of the bathroom fully dressed. She got the basket of dirty clothes from her closet, deposited the towel on top and went to the kitchen to wash the clothes. The first load in the washing machine contained her underwear.

She looked at the calendar hanging on the kitchen wall after closing the lid on the washer. Her period had just ended a few days ago. Now she would have to wait three weeks to know if she were pregnant. She almost laughed at the irony of the timing. She would find out if she were pregnant the same week that their graduation activities started.

By the time Clarice came home, Paula was sitting at the dining room table doing some homework. She was still studying two hours later when the phone rang. Paula knew it was Michael, but she wasn't ready to speak to him.

"Paula, it's Michael." Eric called from the den.

"Will you tell him I'm busy? I'll call him back."

"Sure."

Paula listened for the sound of the receiver returning to its base. Paula knew that she was not going to call Michael back and wasn't sure when she would talk to him. She was not going to let him off the hook that easy. He broke his promise. She had trusted him and he had betrayed her.

The distraction of school helped Paula to keep her mind off the possibilities, even though Michael called every day as soon as she walked in the door from school. Paula kept the conversations very short. Clarice assumed that her call was having the desired effect, but Paula just wanted to punish Michael.

After a week, Paula finally agreed to see Michael, who was very remorseful, not about the incident, but because Paula was upset. They decided to go to the lake to talk. It was another beautiful spring day and Paula wanted to be outside. This time she wore jean.

"Any signs?" Michael asked as soon as they were in the car.

"No, I told you it's too soon to tell."

"If you are pregnant, we can get married and you can take a semester off, after the baby is born."

"Michael, are you crazy? I am not going to have a baby now."

"You know that abortion is murder, Paula."

"It's not your life that's being affected."

"How can you say that? You know that we are in this together. I think we should have the baby."

"First of all, WE don't know for sure if I'm pregnant. Secondly, it's not your decision."

"Paula, you are not being fair."

"Let's not talk about being fair. Is it fair that you lied to me? Is it fair that you wouldn't listen to me when I asked you to stop? Whose fault is this anyway? I tried to stop you. Remember."

"Look, I don't want to argue with you. Like you said, you may not even be pregnant. Let's wait and see what happens . . . But you are not going to kill my baby."

"Let's just wait and see if there's a baby."

Michael wondered why Paula was being so unreasonable and she wondered why he was being so irrational. Paula did not have a good feeling after the conversation with Michael. He loved her but it was her life that they were talking about. By the time they left the lake, Paula knew that she would be the only one to know her decision. No one, including Michael, would know if she were pregnant.

Chapter 12

Paula opened her eyes to the yellow glow peaking around the window shade, enjoying the rare occasion to sleep late. She stretched her long body, turned onto her back, and contemplated staying in bed longer, knowing eventually that she needed to get up. Everyone else had gone to church and the house was quiet. Clarice knew that Paula was tired and had not insisted that she go too. Paula threw back the covers and sat on the edge of the bed.

Her body felt like lead and she wondered if it was an early sign of pregnancy. She was tired of constantly monitoring her body for changes and the stress of the uncertainty was taking its toll. Michael was being extra attentive, but she had made her decision. He would never know if she were pregnant. Paula quickly forced her thoughts to the events of the day, since there was no point dwelling on what could be.

The prom dress, which Adrienne had made as a graduation present, was still lying on the other bed. She had been too tired to even hang it up. She still could not believe that their proms were on the same weekend. Paula's was Friday night and Michael's was Saturday. It was a costly weekend for Michael but he didn't complain. Paula wore the ivory, halter dress to both proms. But Michael rented two different tuxedos so that their prom pictures would look different; a gray tuxedo for Paula's prom and a white tuxedo with tails for his. For economic reasons, the all night celebration was reserved for Friday. Their night together had lost most of its significance since Michael had taken his graduation present early. But this time, they took the necessary precautions, just in case Paula had not gotten pregnant the first time. They both agreed that they were not crazy enough to tempt fate twice.

They were home by midnight after Michael's prom. They were exhausted and did not want to fall asleep during his Baccalaureate service, Sunday afternoon. The graduates had to be there early, so Michael was picking Paula up at one. Paula looked at the clock on the wall and was trying to decide whether or not to go to mass when she heard Clarice coming in the house. Paula jumped out of bed. It was almost eleven-thirty and she did not want her to know that she had slept so late. As Paula was getting her clothes, Clarice appeared in the doorway.

"Are you going to mass today?"

"I don't think I'll have time. The service starts at three o'clock and Michael's going to pick me up early so I don't have to drive that long distance by myself."

Paula's mother turned and left without saying another word. Paula did not think about inviting Clarice, since it was clear how she felt about him. Paula got her clothes together and went to the bathroom for a quick shower. As she adjusted the water temperature, she reminded herself that she only had two more weeks. Her housing confirmation came in the mail on Friday. She would be moving into the dorm the Sunday after her graduation.

Michael called just as Paula finished getting dressed.

"Hey, I'm running late."

"Do you want me to drive?"

"No, I want to pick you up so we won't have two cars. Remember that we are coming back to my house afterwards for dinner. Would you mind if I didn't come to the door?"

"Not at all. Just blow the horn. I'll be waiting for you."

"I'll see you in about forty-five minutes. I love you."

Paula was glad to have time to eat. She quickly cleaned her room then went into the kitchen to find something to eat. After a quick check of the refrigerator, Paula decided a bowl of cereal would have to do. She ate in the kitchen then went in the living room to wait for Michael, since her mother was in the den looking at television. A few minutes later, she heard the horn and grabbed her purse, stopping in the doorway of the den on her way out.

"Mom, I'm leaving. We're going over to Michael's after the service for dinner. I won't be out too late."

"Why couldn't Michael come to the door and get you?" Clarice asked.

"Mom, he's running late."

Paula slammed the door as she walked out, wondering if she would ever understand her mother.

"I can't wait to move out." Paula said as she got in the car.

"What's wrong?" Michael asked as he leaned over to give her a kiss.

"Oh nothing new. Just more of the same. Mom asked why you couldn't come to the door."

"Forget about it. This is supposed to be a happy occasion. How are you feeling?"

"Fine. How am I suppose to be feeling?"

"You know what I'm talking about."

"Still no sign, so stop worrying."

Paula enjoyed sitting with Michael's family during the service and had a wonderful time during dinner. She came home at eight-thirty. After announcing her return, Paula went to her room. She was still tired but needed to study for two finals. As she changed into her pajamas, her mind kept drifting to the upcoming events. She had waited so long and now her independence was only two weeks away.

There were only four days of school remaining. Michael was graduating first on Saturday. Paula's Baccalaureate was Sunday followed by her graduation on Tuesday. Finally, but most importantly, she was moving into the dorms the following Sunday. Paula picked up her Physics book and crawled under the covers to study. Finally giving up on studying after dozing off several times, she said her prayers and went to sleep thinking about her future.

The week flew by. She and Michael spent all of Friday together starting at the lake for her senior picnic and ending with ice cream before he dropped her off. Paula got up early Saturday morning to get an early start on cleaning the house. She did not want an argument with Clarice to ruin this important day. They said very little to each other the entire week. Paula could not forget that Clarice had tried to take the one thing that made her happy.

Michael was picking Paula up at four and taking her to his house. He wanted her to ride with his family to the graduation. His father was going to have a party for him after the ceremony and he didn't want her to have to drive.

She finished cleaning up just before two. The house had never been cleaner. Paula mopped every floor, scrubbed every corner of the bathrooms, vacuumed every room, and dusted everything. She was exhausted but thought it was well worth it, especially since it kept the peace. Paula was laying her clothes out on the bed when Clarice came to the door.

"The house looks nice. Thanks for cleaning up. What time does Michael's graduation start?"

"At five."

Her mother left the room. Paula assumed she was just curious about what time she was leaving. Michael called to make sure she would be ready on time. It was almost two-thirty before Paula finally went to take her shower.

Paula finished dressing and went into the den to watch television while she waited for Michael. Clarice came into the den.

"You're dressed early. What time do you think we should leave?"

Clarice's question caught Paula off guard. Did her mother think they were going to Michael's graduation together?

"Michael's coming to pick me up. I didn't know you were planning to go to his graduation."

Paula did not say what she was thinking - *You don't even want me to date him. Why do you want to go to his graduation? To keep an eye on us or to check out his family.*

"The family was invited. Paula, I don't know what is wrong with you these days. Are you ashamed of your family?"

"No, I'm not ashamed of my family. I just didn't think you wanted to go to Michael's graduation."

"Paula, I don't like how you've been acting since you started dating Michael."

The declaration was more than Paula could handle. All the anger she had been holding in since finding out that Clarice had called Michael's mother spewed out.

"And just how have I been acting, MOTHER. I'm the only one who ever cleans up this house; I've worked since I was fifteen and if you failed to notice, I'm graduating with honors . . . It's obvious how you feel about Michael. After all, you did call his mother and try to break us up."

Paula, just leave it alone. Michael will be here soon.

She got up and went to her bedroom to wait for Michael, slamming her door behind her.

Michael, please get here soon. I need to get out of this house.

Clarice came and threw open Paula's door.

"As long as you are living in my house, you will not slam any doors."

"Well, MOTHER, I won't be living in your house much longer."

Paula looked at Clarice, as if challenging her.

"Don't you get smart with me young lady. If you can't go to the graduation with your family, then you can't go at all."

"Fine mother, I just won't go."

Clarice left Paula's room trying to remember if she had taken her blood pressure medicine. Paula was tired of arguing with Clarice and there was no way she was going to the graduation with her. Michael would just have to understand. Paula went to Lisa's room to use the phone in privacy. She needed to catch Michael before he left the house. His sister answered the phone on the second ring.

"Hi, Nia. Let me speak to Michael."

"Paula you just missed him. He left about five minutes ago to pick you up."

"Okay, thanks."

Paula hung up the phone, disappointed that she didn't catch him before he drove all the way out to her house. She went into the bathroom and locked the door, furious with Clarice for ruining what was supposed to be the happiest time of her life. Paula turned on the faucet and cried profusely for five minutes, unable to handle all the stress. When she looked in the mirror, she noticed that her mascara had run, creating the illusion of two black eyes. Paula stopped crying, turned off the faucet and looked at the watch Michael had given her. He would be there in thirty minutes.

Michael loved her and that was all that she needed. Paula took a deep breath and got a wash cloth out of the cabinet. After washing her face, Paula put drops in her eyes to clear the redness. She was not going to give Clarice the satisfaction of knowing that she had made her cry. As she walked out of the bathroom Paula whispered to herself,

"Just one more week!"

Clarice was lying down in her bedroom when Paula returned to the den to wait for Michael. She saw his car pull in front of the house and quickly went outside. She did not want him to come in.

"Hi, Michael." Paula said not sure how to tell him.

"Are you ready to go?"

"Michael . . . I'm not going to your graduation?"

Michael's expression rapidly changed to one of disbelief.

"What do you mean you're not going to my graduation. I just drove all the way across town to pick you up!" Michael yelled. Paula hoped that Clarice could not hear him.

"I tried to call you but you had already left. My mother and I got into an argument. She said if I didn't go to the graduation with her, that I couldn't go."

"Where is your mother? I want to talk to her!"

Michael started towards the house. Paula got in front of him and grabbed his hands to stop him.

"Michael please! It's not going to help for you to get into an argument with her too. Just go to your graduation. I only have another week here. Please… Do this for me."

"I'm not going to my graduation without you, Paula."

"Michael you're being ridiculous. You have to go to your graduation. I'm not going to have your family mad at me too. Please just go!"

Paula reached for his hand but he pulled it away.

"I told you! I'm not going without you."

"Why, Michael? Why can't you just go?"

"Because I love you and I want you to be at the most important event in my life."

"Michael, I can't go. Can't you understand that? I need you to understand."

Paula tried to hug Michael, but he pushed her away.

"I told you, if you're not going, neither am I."

Michael started pacing back and forth on the sidewalk. Then he stopped and threw his keys across the yard. Paula was so surprised by Michael's actions that she didn't see where the keys went. She looked at him in disbelief.

"Michael, why did you do that? Are you crazy?"

Paula began to search the grass for the keys.

"Even if you find them, I'm not leaving without you."

Paula looked at her watch, feeling trapped; it was almost three-thirty. If Michael stayed much longer, he really was going to miss his graduation and his family would blame her. But if she went with him, Clarice would be angry. Paula decided she would rather endure Clarice's anger, doubting that she could get much angrier than she already was.

"Okay, Michael you win. I'll go with you. Now will you please find the keys so we can go? I'll go get my purse and tell my mother."

Paula reluctantly went into the house, wanting so much to keep peace but knowing what she had to do. She peeked into Clarice's room as she went to get her purse and stopped in her mother's doorway on the way out of the house.

"Mom, Michael won't go to his graduation if I don't go. I don't want to be responsible for him missing his graduation. I'm going to ride with him since he's here, if that's okay with you."

"That's fine Paula." Clarice said without even looking up.

When Paula came out of the house, Michael was still looking for his keys and he was beginning to panic.

"Paula, I can't find the keys!"

"Do you have a spare set?"

"Not with me."

Paula's sister and her boyfriend drove up while they were looking for the keys.

"What are you looking for?"

"Michael's car keys and don't ask why. It's a long story. If we don't find them soon, he's going to miss his graduation."

They got out of the car and started looking for the keys too, and ten minutes later they finally found them in some thick grass.

Michael was driving too fast. Paula wanted to ask him to slow down but she knew she was the reason they were so late. They drove in silence for a long time. Michael knew that he needed to stop her mother from interfering with their relationship. He reached over and took Paula's hand in his. Without changing his gaze, Michael finally spoke.

"Paula, I want us to get married even if you're not pregnant."

"Are you serious?"

"I am very serious. I'm tired of your mother trying to keep us apart. If we're married, she won't be able to. We can get married this summer before we go to college. It will be hard the first year, but next year we can transfer to State and live in married student housing."

Paula hesitated for a moment. After the last encounter with Clarice, she was more convinced that Michael was the only one who cared about her. She looked at Michael who was finally relaxing.

"Of course, I'll marry you."

"Now you won't have to worry about me marrying you just because we got pregnant." Michael said with a smile.

Paula looked out the window. Even with the marriage proposal, Paula wasn't sure she was ready to have a baby.

By the time they got to his house, Michael did not have time to walk Paula to the door. He let her out and sped away. Paula prayed he would not have a wreck as she rang the doorbell. Michael's mother came to the door immediately.

"What happened? I was afraid Michael had car trouble."

"I was running a little late."

Paula hoped her answer would be enough. They left fifteen minutes later. Paula was relieved when she saw Michael march into the auditorium. It was the first time she had seen him in his cap and gown. She was so proud of him and happy that he loved her enough to want to marry her. For the next few hours, she pushed her problems with her mother out of her mind. All that mattered was that she and Michael were going to be together forever.

Clarice was already in bed by the time Paula came home, which was a welcomed relief. Paula had a wonderful time with Michael's family and was not ready for another confrontation.

Paula got up early Sunday; she thought that maybe she could make peace with Clarice by going to church with her. Paula heard Clarice in the kitchen.

"Mom, what time do you want to go to mass?"

"I went to the evening service yesterday."

"I'm going to the nine-thirty mass. I need to be at the school by one for the Baccalaureate service. Michael offered to take me so you wouldn't have to go so early.

"That's fine, Paula. Is his family coming?"

"No, ma'am."

Paula walked out of the kitchen. She quickly took her bath, dressed and went to church alone. Her stomach felt queasy during the service; which she knew could be good or bad. Feeling better by the time mass ended, Paula stopped and bought some donuts on the way home. She walked in the house a little before eleven, but Michael wasn't picking her up until twelve-thirty.   Playing with Autumn kept her distracted until it was time to change into a white, lace sundress for the service.

Michael was a few minutes early, but Paula was ready. He waited for Paula at the door, not wanting to come in.   Clarice was getting dressed when Paula walked into her room.

"Mom, I'm leaving. I'll see you at the service."

"Okay, Paula."

Clarice felt bad about the incident with Michael's graduation. Karen had told her about Michael's keys and understood why Paula thought she had to go. She decided to surprise Paula and take everyone out to an early dinner after the service, including Michael.

Paula had a cold sweat while waiting in line to march into the auditorium. She knew all to well what that meant; it was an early sign that her period was about to start. She went to get her purse from Michael, who had already taken a seat inside the auditorium.

"Well, I think I have some good news"

"We could use some good news. What?"

"I don't think we're pregnant."

"How do you know?"

"Because I feel horrible, and I always feel this way before my period."

"Are you going to be okay?"

Michael was relieved that she was not pregnant but was still worried about her. He knew how sick she got with her periods.

"I hope so. This is the first sign. I still have a few hours."

After stopping in the restroom to make sure that she was prepared and returning her purse to Michael, Paula went back to her place in line, hoping it wasn't a mistake to wear a white dress. She could feel the bile building in her stomach while they waited and prayed that she would make it through the service. Finally, it was time for the service to start.

The senior class officers were at the beginning of the procession. Paula kept her focus on the stage as they marched in, thinking that she would be fine if she could just sit down. She tried to remember how long the procession had taken during the rehearsal.

Standing on the front row, Paula hoped that no one could see her shaking. She looked out in the audience and saw her mother sitting towards the back. It took a long time for all the graduates to march to the stage, for the solo to be sung and finally the invocation to be delivered. Paula was ready to collapse by the time they all said Amen.

It's happening too fast this time...Why did I eat those donuts?

Paula was terrified that she was going to get sick on the stage. Usually, she had more time. Paula knew she had to make it through the service. Her stomach churned. She was not sure which end the donuts were going to come out of first. Paula was unable to pay attention to anything that was being said.

Dear God, Recently it seems like I'm praying to you all the time with a problem. Thank you for not letting me be pregnant. I don't care about the pain, which I probably deserve. But please let me make it through this service, just let it wait until I get home. Please God.

The minister kept talking and Paula kept praying, every time she felt like she was losing control. Finally, in answer to her prayers, the benediction was delivered. It took another ten minutes for the graduates to march out of the auditorium.

Paula saw Clarice outside while she was looking for Michael. She had her camera and wanted to take some pictures. She reluctantly obliged and posed with some of her classmates. But she needed to find Michael and get home as soon as possible. After taking several pictures, Clarice saw Rosalyn's mother and went to say hello as Michael finally appeared in the crowd. The heat was oppressive and made Paula feel worse.

"Michael, I've got to get home. I'm going to be very sick."

"Okay, let's go."

"I need to find my mother and tell her I'm leaving."

Paula looked in the direction that Clarice had gone but she didn't see her in the sea of jubilant bodies. Everyone was hugging and talking. Paula and Michael looked for Clarice for another five minutes. Michael was afraid Paula was going to collapse. He had never seen her look so sick and wondered if she might really be pregnant.

"Maybe she already left, Paula. Come on. Let's get you home."

Paula felt bad that she couldn't find Clarice and hoped that Michael was right; Clarice was probably on her way home. They stopped briefly to talk to Taylor, who was looking for her parents, on the way to the parking lot.

Clarice saw Taylor's parents inside the auditorium door and went to speak to them. The cool air-conditioning felt good. After a few minutes, Taylor walked up.

"There you are. I've been looking everywhere for you." Taylor said as she gave her father a hug.

"Well, I'd better find Paula and ask them where they want to go eat."

"Ms. Hayes, I think Paula and Michael have left. I just saw them on the way to the parking lot."

"They are probably looking for me. I'd better go."

Clarice looked through the crowd, which was starting to thin, and decided to go home since the afternoon heat was unbearable.

Michael drove as fast as he could and then helped Paula into the house. As soon as Paula walked inside the door, she ran past Lisa and Autumn to the back bathroom. Michael went into the den to wait. Paula threw up as soon as she lifted the lid to the commode. Before she could brush her teeth, her bowels turned liquid. She barely made it back to the commode in time. Her sister, knocked on the door.

"Paula, are you okay?"

"My period just started. Is Mom here?"

"No, she hasn't come home yet."

"Will you check and see if Michael is still here? If he is, tell him I'll be there in a few minutes."

"Sure. Do you need me to get you anything?"

"No, thanks."

Paula was still on the commode when she heard Clarice's voice, disseminating through the house.

"Is Paula here? I can't believe how ungrateful she is. I'm looking everywhere for her to take them to lunch and find out that she and Michael left."

Paula was too sick to leave the bathroom and defend herself. Lisa came to her defense.

"Mom, Paula's in the bathroom. She's sick."

"What's wrong with her?"

"I think her period started during the service."

"Well, she could have at least told me she was leaving instead of having me make a fool of myself."

Paula listened but did not hear anything else. She should have tried harder to find Clarice. But it was too late now. Twenty minutes later, Paula was finally able to leave the bathroom and passed Clarice on the way to tell Michael good-bye.

"Are you okay?"

"I'm fine. My period just started. I tried to find you to tell you that I needed to leave. I'm going to tell Michael good-bye then I'm going to lay down."

Paula went into the den and Michael stood up when he saw her, looking so pale and weak. He wanted to take care of her.

"Are you okay?"

"I'm fine. Thanks for getting me home so fast."

"Do you need me to get you anything from the store?"

"No, thanks. I'm going to take some medicine and get in bed. I'll call you later."

"Is it your period?"

"Yes. You're off the hook."

"Do you want me to stay?"

"No, I think you'd better go now. Besides, I've caused enough trouble for one day."

"If you need anything, just call me. Okay?"

"Okay."

Paula walked Michael to the door and whispered in his ear.

"Are you disappointed that you won't be a father?"

"I can wait."

"Me too...Michael, I love you."

"I love you, too. Don't forget to call me if you need anything."

Michael paused before leaving.

"You know that I was serious about what I asked you yesterday."

"So was I."

Paula closed the door, knowing that Michael was just as relieved as she was. She stopped in the bathroom to get some pain medicine and the hot water bottle. After a quick trip to the kitchen to take the pills and fill the bottle, Paula retreated to her bedroom for her monthly ritual. She quickly changed clothes and crawled into bed, carefully positioning the hot water bottle snugly against her abdomen. While she waited for relief from the cramping, she thought about how fortunate they were; they would not take a chance like that again. Now that she had her period, she could start taking the birth control pills that Taylor had given her until she could get her own prescription from the clinic.

It was after seven o'clock, when Paula woke up to her sister gently shaking her arm.

"Paula, Michael's on the phone. Do you want to talk to him?"

"Sure, tell him I'll be right there."

Paula looked at the clock, folded back the covers and stood up slowly. She had not planned to sleep so long.

"Hi. How are you feeling?"

"I'm feeling much better, thank you. Usually all it takes is some pain reliever and sleep."

"I don't want to keep you long. I wanted to make sure you were okay, and to see if you have any plans tomorrow for Memorial Day?"

"No, but I was hoping to see you."

"My dad just called. He's having a barbecue at his house. Would it be okay if we went by, for a little while?"

"Sure."

"Great. I'll pick you up at noon. Paula, is your mother still upset?"

"I don't know. I haven't seen her since you left. Is your grandmother still in town?."

"Yep. She cooked a great dinner. You need to get some more rest. I'll see you tomorrow. I love you."

"I love you, too."

After turning on her television, Paula went to the bathroom and then crawled back in bed. The water bottle had lost all of its heat but Paula did not feel like refilling it. She thought about the events of the weekend and was relieved that she wouldn't have to stay around the house for Memorial Day. She was convinced that the fewer interactions she had with her mother, the better for both of them. Clarice did not comment when Paula told her she was spending Memorial Day with Michael.

With so many high schools in the city, the major auditoriums and coliseums had two graduations each day. Paula's graduation was at Southern Christian University's coliseum, which Paula thought was ironic because she would be ending her high school years at the same place that she would be going to college. On the weeknights, one graduation started at five o'clock and the next started at eight. This year, Paula's graduation was scheduled for Tuesday at eight, which relieved her because it would give her family enough time to get there

Paula and Michael ate lunch before he took her to the rehearsal. After the rehearsal, Michael dropped Paula at her house and went home to change clothes, promising to be back on time to take her to graduation.

He rang the door promptly at six, dressed in a dark suit. Clarice still wasn't home from work and Paula worried if she would make it to the graduation on time. Lisa was getting Autumn dressed and even Eric had started getting ready. They had been warned at the rehearsal that the traffic would be heavy between the graduations. Reluctantly, Paula decided that she and Michael needed to leave.

Paula was excited as they drove and ready to celebrate. She was graduating from high school; the biggest event in her life and she wasn't pregnant.

"Do you want to go out to eat afterwards?" Michael asked while they waited in traffic for a parking place.

"Let's check with Mom after the ceremony. She may have something planned."

When they walked into the staging area, Paula felt the excitement in the air. She quickly found her friends and started talking about their plans for the night. After finding out that most of them were going to the school sponsored all-night party, Paula was sorry that she and Michael weren't going.

The coliseum was huge. Paula surveyed the audience, trying to locate her family in the crowd. She immediately found Michael proudly sitting on the first row of the section closest to her. Paula continued searching for her family throughout the ceremony. She couldn't see them, but she heard their applause when she walked across the stage.

It was ten-thirty when the last graduate walked across the stage and the school superintendent presented the graduating class to the audience. Caught up in the wave of excitement, Paula threw her cap into the air and felt ecstatic.

She could not wait to find Michael and her family after the ceremony. There were so many people outside the building. The first person Paula saw was the mother of her first real boyfriend, who gave Paula a big hug and told her how proud she was of her for graduating with honors. Then Paula saw Bruce, Adrienne and their daughters who had hugs for her as well. Finally, Paula found Michael and they looked through the crowd for her mother. They finally saw her oldest sister and her family.

"Hi, Sheryl. Have you seen Mom and them?"

"They left already."

"Are you sure?"

"Yes. They were sitting with us and left right after you walked across the stage."

"Are you going back to the house?" Paula asked Sheryl who was holding her sleeping son.

"No, we've got to get this little guy to bed. I forgot your present in the car. We'll drop it by the house tomorrow."

Paula felt her excitement drain as she gave her sister a hug. Then she and Michael began to work their way through the crowd towards the parking lot, stopping often along the way for hugs and congratulations. Michael could see Paula was disappointed that her family had left. He took Paula's hand.

"Maybe they are waiting for you at home."

"You're probably right. Let's go."

They pulled up to the house. It looked dark and her mother's car was gone. Paula wondered if they were having a surprise party for her. That would explain why they did not stay for the whole ceremony. Paula got her key from her purse and turned it in the lock. The house was quiet when they walked in. Paula turned on the light and looked in the den; no one was there. Then Paula and Michael walked into the living room.

Paula searched the house. No one was home. Paula could not believe this was happening to her. They went to her room where she looked around, not sure what to do.

"Michael this is the most important day of my life and my family doesn't even care."

She sat on her bed and started to cry. Michael sat next to her and put his arm around her shoulder.

"Paula, it's okay. Don't cry. We're going out to celebrate."

"Michael, I can't believe this. No presents, nothing. My mother has made it pretty clear. She won't ever have to worry about me again."

"Come on, Paula. Stop crying and change your clothes so we can leave."

Paula was so upset that she could not find anything to wear. She finally decided on the white jeans and an oversized T-shirt that Bruce and Adrienne had given her for graduation.

Just as they were about to leave, a car pulled into the driveway. Paula watched in disbelief as her family came into the house, laughing and talking loud. It looked like they had a celebration without her.

"I looked for you after the graduation." Paula said to Clarice.

"We left early and went out to dinner. I figured you and Michael probably had plans."

"We are going to the all night party. I'll be home in the morning."

Paula had to fight back the tears; she was not going to give Clarice the satisfaction of knowing how hurt she was. She walked out the door with Michael and cried all the way to his house. Now, she knew without a doubt that Michael was the only one who cared about her. She also knew that the pain she felt at that moment would stay with her forever.

Chapter 13

Paula rolled onto her side and looked around her room, locking the image in her mind. She had been too excited to sleep soundly. This was the last morning that she would wake up in this room. The four days following graduation had passed without any further incidents between her and her mother. Paula was drained of life except for when she was with Michael. She still could not believe that her family had been so cruel. Talking to her friends only made Paula feel worse. Their families were having barbecues and parties to celebrate their graduation. Paula tried hard not to even think about her graduation; just thinking about the evening caused tears to swell up inside.

The house was still quiet. Paula heard her mother in the kitchen but everyone else was still asleep. The two suitcases that were carefully packed the night before sat in front of the closet door. All she needed to do was put her toiletries in her overnight bag. The dorms were opening at one o'clock and Michael was picking her up at noon, so they could get some lunch before checking Paula in. Paula was ready to start life on her own, without help from her family.

She had accepted the full-tuition scholarship to Southern Christian University. She knew that she was fortunate to find out about the scholarship days before the application deadline. The scholarship was designated for minorities entering the

Engineering program, wanting to work while earning their degree. It was just what Paula needed to finance her education. Given the events of the last week, she was sure that her family could not be counted on. The program would take five years to complete. She would have to either work or be in school year round; but she would graduate with two and a half years of work experience in addition to the Engineering degree.

Angela, a friend of Paula's from her high school, received the same scholarship and they were going to room together for the summer. Paula had hoped that she and Angela would work for the same company but it did not work out. After interviewing with three companies, Paula was offered a position at an automobile manufacturing plant. Paula did not have a clue what an automotive plant was like, but the interviewer promised the job would be challenging and it paid the highest salary of the sponsoring companies.

Transportation was the only thing concerning Paula. The automotive plant was thirty miles from the campus and Paula had surrendered her car to Eric. She had inquired about transportation to work after accepting the scholarship and the program director assured her that arrangements would be made once they got on campus.

With her clothes in hand, Paula quietly walked through Lisa's room to the bathroom. She paused before closing the door and looked at Lisa sleeping so peacefully with Autumn snuggled against her. Paula wondered if Lisa was going to be okay. She had been through so much and now Paula wasn't going to be around to help with Autumn as much.

Stop worrying Paula. Autumn is almost two; she'll be good for Lisa. It's hard to be depressed when you have a beautiful, healthy two-year-old who loves you unconditionally.

Paula closed the bathroom door and started the water for a shower then changed her mind. She had plenty of time for a bubble bath, and it would be a long time before she would be able to take another bath; the dorms only had showers. Paula smiled as she took the Sir Bubbles from the cabinet. She had bought the bubble bath for Autumn but Paula thought that she enjoyed the bubble baths more.

After locking the bathroom door, she stepped into the bath, filled to the overflow. The water was so warm that she had to lower her body slowly into it. Paula stretched out in the bathtub, leaned her head back and closed her eyes. She thought about how lucky she was to have Michael, who was always there for her. When she needed something, she knew she could count on him, unlike everyone else in her family. Paula wondered if her life would have been different had her parents stayed together. She had not talked to her father in a long time, and she secretly had hoped that he would come to her graduation, but he could not get off work. He forgot to call or send a present. The more Paula thought about her family life, the sadder she became until she reminded herself that things were about to change.

Paula, what is wrong with you? This is supposed to be the happiest time in your life. I am eighteen and heading off to college with a scholarship and a great job. I don't need my parents any more. I am an adult. I have Michael. This time next year, we'll be married. Married! The thought brought a smile to Paula's face. *Michael and I are really going to be married. But when? I guess that's something we'd better decide soon. I don't even know what's required to get married . . . There you go, worrying again. Just relax . . . Everything is going to be perfect. I have to stop letting my family depress me. They don't need me and I don't need them, anymore.*

A long bath always made Paula feel better. She drifted into a light sleep and was awakened by Lisa knocking on the bathroom door, forcing her to soap quickly. Paula dressed and left the bathroom, ready to move on with her life. She finished packing her overnight bag and sat it near her suitcases that contained her summer clothes, some towels and a set of sheets. Since she would move into a different dorm in the fall, she only took the essentials for the summer.

Michael arrived on time. When Paula and Autumn opened the door, a blast of heat came in with him. He kissed Paula on the cheek as he walked in the door, then picked up Autumn, who let out a string of giggles. Paula smiled.

"Hi. You look very nice."

"Thanks."

"It's going to be a hot day. Are you ready to go?" Michael asked as he flipped Autumn and set her gently on the floor.

"What do you think? Let me get my bags."

"Where are they? I'll put them in the car and we can get going."

"They're in my room. Just get the big suitcases. I'll get my overnight bag."

"Come on, Autumn. Help me get your Aunt Paula's bags."

Paula's mother entered the living room just as Michael and Autumn were going to Paula's room. Paula felt a chill in the air.

"Hello, Michael."

"Hello, Ms. Hayes."

"I told Paula that I could take her. You didn't need to drive all the way over here."

Paula wanted to scream, but she controlled herself. Michael sensed Paula's frustration and wanted to leave as soon as possible.

"I wanted to take her. Paula, I'll get your bags."

"Thanks, Michael."

"Paula, do you want something to eat before you leave?" Clarice asked.

Paula took a deep breath.

Why is she trying to be nice now? It's too late.

"No, thank you. Michael and I are going to stop and eat on the way."

Paula was relieved when Michael returned carrying the two suitcases. She didn't have anything else to say to her mother.

"Are you ready?" Michael asked, looking directly at Paula.

"Let me get my overnight bag and we can go."

"I'll put these in the car and start cooling it off. Goodbye, Ms. Hayes."

Michael bent down to Autumn's level.

"I'll see you later."

Paula could see the tears forming in Autumn's eyes as she followed Michael to the door.

"Thanks, Michael. I'll be right out. Autumn, will you help me get my bag?"

Autumn reluctantly left Michael's side and followed Paula into her room. It was almost nap time but Paula knew that she did not have time to put her to sleep. Paula sat down on her bed and scooped Autumn up into her lap, knowing that she would miss her the most.

"You remember what I told you about Aunt Paula going to school?"

Autumn shook her head, but Paula wasn't sure if she really understood. She was almost two and extremely smart but she never had experienced someone leaving.

"I want you to take good care of my room for me. I'll come back to see you soon." Paula gave Autumn a hug and a kiss.

"Let's go see what your mommy is doing."

Paula hoped that she could leave without any tears. She opened the door to Lisa's room and found her sister lying on the bed looking at the television.

"I think your little one is s-l-e-e-p-y and I'm getting ready to leave."

"Come on little pumpkin. Let's see if we can find some cartoons. Paula, you take care."

Autumn ran and jumped in the bed with her mother, which relieved Paula.

"Thanks. I'll call and give you my phone number as soon as I find out what it is. You still have a babysitter any time you need it. We'll have fun running around the dorm."

Paula closed the door between their rooms as she returned to hers. She quickly grabbed her purse and overnight bag then scanned the room one more time. Even though she dreaded it, Paula knew she needed to say good-bye to Clarice. She stopped and looked in her mother's room but it was empty. She heard the television in the den and went in, pausing in the doorway.

"Mom, I'm leaving."

"Do you need anything?"

"No, the money I got for graduation should last until I get my first paycheck. I'll call and give you the phone number as soon as I find out what it is. Good-bye, Mom."

"Good-bye, Paula. Call if you need anything."

Paula felt a sense of relief as she closed the door behind her. The oppressive heat helped shift her thoughts. It was definitely going to be a hot summer. Michael was relieved to see Paula come out of the house. He was worried that Clarice might say something to upset her.

"I thought I was going to have to come in and get you."

"Sorry. I wanted to get Autumn settled. She looked like she was about to cry when you left . . . Michael, I'm so glad to be leaving that house."

"I know Paula. But hey, you are in charge now so let's see a smile on that beautiful face."

Paula looked out the window; she didn't feel like smiling.

"What do you have a taste for? I'm starving."

"Anything is fine with me?"

"Come on, Paula. You are supposed to be happy."

"I'm sorry. I just have a lot on my mind. How about hamburgers?"

"Will we have time to eat inside or should we get it to go?"

Paula looked at the watch.

"We have time."

Clarice stared at the television and listened for Michael's car to pull away. She had wanted to take Paula to the dorm and help her get settled in. She thought about how Paula had been the perfect daughter, the one that she could always count on and the one that she never expected any trouble from, until Michael. She wondered what she had done wrong.

Paula was quiet as they drove to the restaurant, wondering about her future. She told him what she wanted and found a booth near a window.

Michael sat the tray of food on the table and Paula put a straw in her shake and immediately took a sip to cool off.

"So how does it feel to be free?"

"I'm not sure, yet... So, have you decided what you are going to do for the summer?" Paula asked, staring out the window.

"I'm going to keep the job at the gas station."

Michael opened one of his burgers and took a huge bite.

"I thought you were going to find a job where you could work during the day. I want us to spend our evenings and weekends together. We don't have much time before school starts."

"I can't find another job making the same amount of money. Besides, I talked to the manager and he's going to work with me on my schedule. You are going to see me so much this summer that you might get tired of me."

"I could never get tired of you."

"Are you sure? Because I plan on spending the rest of my life with you."

"I'm sure."

"So, when are you going to become Mrs. Williams?"

"You still want to get married?"

"I wouldn't have asked you if I didn't."

"I am giving you a chance to rescind your proposal."

"Will you please answer my question? When would you like to get married?"

"I don't know. How about at the end of the summer, before school starts?"

"I like that idea."

Michael paused; he needed to get something clear.

"Paula, we won't be able to tell anyone that we are married. No one can know but us. My dad got married young and he wouldn't understand. He's paying for my college tuition and I can't risk having a fight with him. And your mother wouldn't be too happy about it, either. It will be our secret, but you'll be able to stop worrying about going to hell."

"What do you mean?"

"You know what I mean. Good Catholics girls only have sex with their husbands. You'll be able to stop worrying and start enjoying it."

"You're crazy."

"Yep, crazy for you. Do you want some of this? " Michael asked as he started his second burger.

"No, I'm fine. Thanks."

When they finished eating, Michael put the trash on the tray and stood up.

"Let's go start the rest of our lives."

"I'm nervous."

Paula got up and followed Michael who held the door open for her. They opened the windows as soon as they got in the car

247

to cool it off. Michael turned the air conditioning to high immediately after starting the engine.

"So where to?" Michael looked at Paula for directions.

"I don't know the exact location but it's Jefferson Hall. They sent me a campus map with the housing papers."

Paula pulled some papers from the side of her overnight bag and looked for the map. They were familiar with the campus because they had attended several concerts at the auditorium but there were several dorm clusters.

"What time is Angela checking in?"

"I talked to her before you came. She's coming later, probably just before the orientation meeting starts at six."

"Good."

"Here's the map. It looks like the dorm is across from the student center. Why is that good?"

"No particular reason. I just wanted some time alone with you. We haven't been alone since graduation night."

"Michael, we are alone now."

"You know what I mean."

They found a parking spot in front of the dorm. Michael cracked his window before getting out of the car.

"Let's make sure that this is the place before we get the bags."

Paula picked up the papers, grabbed her purse and led the way to the dorm. Beautiful shade trees surrounded the Georgian structure. They entered the building through a heavy, oversized door. Paula stopped inside the doorway, unsure where to go. The cool air conditioning felt wonderful as she glanced around the large lobby that looked more like a hotel than a college dormitory. The traditional furniture was meticulously arranged around beautiful rugs with exquisite patterns in deep, warm colors. There was a baby grand piano in the corner near the fireplace. Everything in the lobby fit into the rich color scheme. Paula smiled when her eyes stopped on the painting above the fireplace; it was perfect for the room.

As they walked farther into the lobby, Paula noticed a television area, adjacent to the door and recessed from the main area. Some students were lounging on the couches, watching the television. Paula was just about to ask them where to check in when she noticed a bearded man coming out of a door behind the counter. She and Michael walked to the counter.

"May I help you?" The man asked with a pleasant smile.

"Is this where I check in for summer housing?"

"It is, if you have your housing form."

Paula handed him her housing form and he looked at it briefly.

"Well Paula, it looks like you are in the right place. I'm Hugh, the dorm director. Let's get you checked in. Are you with the Engineering program?"

"Yes, I am."

Hugh walked over to a box and flipped passed several manila envelopes before pulling one out and handing it to Paula.

"Here's your information package. Your program has two counselors living in this dorm. You will meet them tonight at your orientation meeting. The meeting will be in this lobby. Now, let me get your room keys."

Hugh walked over to another small box and pulled out a card that had two keys.

"You're in room 205. It's on the east wing of the second floor. This is a co-ed dorm. The third floor is male, your floor is female, the first floor is co-ed by wings and the basement is co-ed by suites. Both the second and third floors have community restrooms and showers on each wing. Members of the opposite sex are not allowed on the second and third floors before nine in the morning, any day of the week, and after ten at night on weekdays and midnight on the weekend. Here's the key to your room and this key is for the dorm entrances. The dorm doors are locked after dark, for security. There's a phone outside the main door if you get locked out. It will cost you fifty dollars if you lose your room key and two hundred and fifty dollars if you lose the dorm door key."

"That's pretty expensive for losing a key." Paula said.

"It's so high because the locks will have to be changed and new keys issued."

Hugh pointed to a door that looked like a closet.

"There's the elevator but it's rather old and slow. If you ever get stuck in it just push the alarm button. The stairs at the end of each wing are usually faster. Did you buy a full, meal plan?"

"Yes."

"Service starts with breakfast tomorrow morning. There are several places to eat across the street, but they close early on Sundays. All of this information is in the package but I like to tell everyone also. Any questions?"

"No, I don't think so." Paula said trying to absorb all the information.

"Would you like for me to take you to your room?"

"No, I think we can find it. Thank you."

"Just go through the double doors. The stairs are through the door at the end of the hall. If you need anything, I'll be here all evening. My wife and I are graduate students. We live right here." He pointed to the door behind the counter.

"My schedule is posted on the bulletin board over there. Each floor has a Resident Assistant that can also help you. They'll have a floor meeting to meet everyone and make sure that you understand the system. Welcome to Jefferson Hall, Paula."

Paula started to walk away and remembered something.

"Are phones already in the rooms?"

"No, there's information about phones in the packet. You or your roommate will have to contact the telephone company. There are pay phones in the lobby and one on each floor. There's a five-minute limit, if someone's waiting. Are there any other questions?"

"No, thanks."

"Paula, why don't we go up and see the room first. I'll come back down and get your things."

"Okay...What do you think?" Paula looked around as they walked through the lobby.

"It's nice. I'm finally dating a college woman."

"Very funny."

They passed some students on the stairs as they reached the second floor landing. Room 205 was two doors from the exit. Paula put the key in the door lock and slowly turned. The door opened to reveal her new home. The room was a stark contrast to the warmth and grandeur of the lobby. Paula looked around the room and immediately noticed the absence of any significant

251

color. The floor tile was a pale gray, the walls were painted off-white and the furniture was a natural wood tone. The room had two of everything - beds, dresser chests, closets, sinks and desks with chairs. The beds were in an L-shape, one elevated above one of the desk and dresser and the other bed was in front of the single window, opposite the door. The window had a white mini-blind that was closed. Paula put her purse and the information package on the desk, closest to the door. She walked over to the window and opened the mini-blind, revealing a view of the circular parking lot and a small building in the center.

"Don't you think that it's a little drab?"

"I like it. You just need to fix it up a little."

Michael wrapped his arms around her.

"How about a kiss to christen your new place?"

Paula willingly obliged and they were breathing rapidly by the time Michael pulled away.

"I think I'd better get your bags."

"Thanks, Michael."

As soon as Michael left the room, Paula pulled out the chair and sat at the desk, where she had put her things. She stared at both the beds trying to decide which one to choose. Paula suddenly realized how cold it was in the room. She looked up at the wall vent above the door and then looked for the thermostat, but she couldn't find it. Paula was startled by the sound of the door opening. Michael walked in caring the two suitcases and her overnight bag, sweating as if he been exercising.

"Man, it feels good in here. It must be a hundred degrees already. I hope you didn't have anything in these that could melt. Where do you want them?"

"You can just sit them there. I haven't decided which side of the room to take yet . . . Michael, I can't find the controls for the air conditioner."

"There's probably only one control for the entire floor."

"I can't sleep in a room this cold without a blanket and I didn't bring one."

"Maybe your sister has an old one you can borrow."

"That's okay. I'll buy one. Will you take me to the mall after I unpack?"

"Sure."

"I'm going to really miss having my own transportation."

"Don't worry about it. I'll take you wherever you need to go. When will you find out who you're going to carpool with to work?" Michael asked as he sat down at the other desk.

"I guess at the meeting tonight."

Paula picked up the packet of information and pulled the papers from it. The first page was a welcome letter that Paula read quickly.

"They are going to provide pizza for us tonight and will match us with our rides at the meeting. Will you help me unpack then we can run to the mall?"

"Okay. I need to leave around five. I told my dad I'd stop by today."

"That's fine. I didn't expect you to hang around here. After the meeting, I'll need to get ready for work. I need to be there at seven-thirty."

"What can I do?"

"You can make up the bed. Which one should I take?"

Paula walked over to the bed in front of the window and sat down. The cold air from the vent was blowing directly on the bed.

"Honestly?"

"Yes."

"The one you're sitting on."

"But the vent blows directly on it. I'll freeze."

"But the access is easier. I can't see us both up there."

"Who said you're going to be in my bed? But you have a good point. I'm too tall to be climbing that ladder. I hoped Angela won't mind."

Paula opened the big suitcase and handed Michael the sheets.

"You can make up the bed while I unpack my clothes."

"Okay."

"You do know how to make up a bed?"

"Do you want some help or not?" Michael said with a smile.

Paula put her clothes in the drawers and was thankful to find some hangers in the closet. She had forgot to bring some. In thirty minutes, the bed was made and the suitcases were unpacked and stored in the bottom of the closet.

"Are you ready to go to the mall?"

"What's the hurry?"

"I thought you needed to get to your father's?"

"I need something else more."

Michael locked the door and kissed Paula.

"Michael, what if Angela comes early?"

"You said she wasn't coming until later and this won't take long."

"...Okay, Michael."

Michael took his wallet from his pants pocket and started to open it.

"You won't need that; I'm on the pill."

Michael's smile could have lit up the room.

"Since when?"

"Since my period."

"This is definitely a special day."

Michael quickly undressed Paula. Within seconds Michael was on top of her. Paula was too worried about being interrupted. Although Paula and Michael could not have been physically closer, they were both in very different places mentally. Michael was lost in his pleasure and Paula was being consumed by guilt. She kept thinking of the repeated warnings - sex outside of marriage was a sin.

She tried to assure herself that this was not a sin because she and Michael were going to be married soon. Then a thought entered her mind. If they were married in God's eyes, they would not be sinning. Paula closed her eyes and prayed.

Dear God, I know that sex outside of marriage is a sin. Please forgive us. I don't want to sin but I love Michael and want to make him happy. I'm praying to you to unite us in marriage right now. I take Michael to be my husband from this day forward. Bless our marriage and make it strong. Amen.

Paula didn't feel guilty anymore. They were now married in God's eyes, which was all that mattered. Just as Paula opened her eyes, Michael reached his climax, which Paula thought was a sign that God had heard her pray. She kissed the cheek of her new husband, as he laid exhausted on her. This was truly the start of her new life.

"Come on, Michael. Don't you fall asleep. We need to go."
Paula said softly as she rolled Michael off of her.

"Okay. Are you all right? I don't think you enjoyed it very
much."

"I was just worried that someone was going to walk in on us.
Don't worry. This won't be the last time."

They dressed quickly. Just before they left, Paula smoothed
the sheets and sprayed some perfume in the air. She didn't know
Angela that well and did not want to start on the wrong foot.

It did not take long for them to go to the mall and find a
blanket that could double as a bedspread. Michael dropped Paula
off at the dorm and rushed to his father's. Angela was unpacking
her things when Paula opened the door.

"Hi. I hope you don't mind me taking that bed. I'm a little
too tall for the upper bed."

"I don't mind. I'm actually glad. That bed has too much air
blowing on it for me. Besides it really doesn't matter. I'll
probably be staying home on the weekends anyway."

Paula knew Michael would be glad to hear that.

"Do you need any help unpacking?"

"No, I only brought enough for tonight. I'll get the rest of
my things tomorrow. What time does the meeting start?" Angela
asked as she tossed some sheets on the bed.

"In ten minutes. I hope they start with the pizza."

"I'm not hungry. I just ate."

"Angela, what do you want to do about a telephone?" Paula
asked as she opened the blanket and spread it on the bed.

"I'm not planning to get one, since it's only for the summer. I can use the pay phone."

Paula was disappointed. She had wanted to split the cost of the phone. She could not limit Michael's calls to five minutes.

"I'm going to go ahead and get one. The telephone company will be in the student center tomorrow. I'll stop by after work. Are you ready to go down to the meeting?"

"In just a moment. I need to brush my teeth. You go ahead. I'll be down in a few minutes."

The meeting was starting when Paula walked in and found an empty chair in the back. She recognized several of the others from the interview weekend, but could not remember many names. Angela came through the door just as the counselors were introducing themselves. Both counselors were Engineering students with the same scholarships.

After the introductions, the pizzas were delivered. Paula was hungrier than she thought. She ate three slices of pizza while talking to Angela, and was contemplating a fourth when the counselors suggested that those working for the same companies get together to work out transportation details. It was almost eight o'clock.

Paula walked to the other student that was working with her to find out what time he wanted to leave.

"I hope you don't mind giving me a ride? We probably need to leave around six forty-five. I will help pay for gas. "

"I think that we have a problem. I don't have a car. I thought you did."

"Let's go talk to the counselors. Maybe they can work something out for us."

They walked over to the female counselor who was talking to a small group. When she stopped talking, Paula got her attention.

"Excuse me. We need your help. We don't have a car. Who do we need to talk to about a ride?"

"You're with American Motors, right."

"Yes."

"This is their first year in the program. You are the only two in the program that work there. Hold on, maybe you can ride with the group from Roth. I think that their facility is close to the American Motors plant."

Paula and her co-worker followed her to the other counselor.

"They don't have a ride to work. Can they ride with you?"

"Sorry, I have a car full. Do either of you know anyone in town with a car you can borrow?" The counselor asked.

"I don't know anyone in town. Do the buses run out there from here?" Paula's co-worker asked.

"No, and a taxi would cost about thirty dollars, each way."

"Paula aren't you from here?" The counselor asked.

"I am, but I don't know anyone with a car that I can borrow. I might be able to get us a ride for tomorrow. Let me make a call."

Paula found out what room her co-worker was in and told him she would let him know if she could find them a ride. Then she left to call Michael, hoping that he would be willing to take them to work. She left several messages for him before he finally called her back just before ten.

"Paula, what's wrong? Nia said you called several times."

"Michael, I don't have a way to work tomorrow. The other person who's working there doesn't have a car either. Can you take us to work tomorrow?"

"What time?"

"We need to be there for an orientation at seven-thirty?"

"...Paula, I wish I could, but I have to be at work at eight. There's no way I can take you and make it back in time. Maybe I could pick you up. What time do you get off?"

"Three-thirty. How about you?"

"That's not going to work either. I don't get off until four. With the traffic, it would probably be after five before I could pick you up. What about Lisa? Isn't she still working nights? "

"She doesn't get off work until seven-thirty in the morning and then she has to take Autumn to the babysitter."

Paula started feeling sick.

"Maybe your mother will let you use the car until you can work out something. Eric is not working."

"Michael, I can't ask her. I don't want anything from her, not after graduation."

"Paula, it looks to me like you don't have a choice. Call her. If you can borrow the car, I'll come take you to pick it up."

"Michael, can't you take the day off tomorrow?" Paula sounded desperate.

"Baby, I wish I could, but I need to make as much money as possible this summer. My dad said I have to earn half of my tuition. That's what he wanted to talk to me about today."

"Can you go to work later?"

"I can't change my schedule now. I asked for the early shift so that we could have the evenings free. Besides, it's too late to call the manager."

"Okay, I'll call you back in a few minutes."

"Are you going to call your mother?"

"I don't know. Are you going to be up for a while?"

"I won't go to sleep until I talk to you."

"Thanks."

Paula put the receiver back in the cradle and stared at the phone. Her mother was the last person in the world she wanted to ask for help. She thought for a moment; there had to be someone else she could call. Finally, Paula looked at her watch. It was getting late. If she were going to call, it had to be now. Paula felt foolish. She had been out of her mother's house for less than ten hours and she was already calling home. She slowly lifted up the receiver, deposited a coin and dialed the number. Paula thought about hanging up the phone and just missing work the first day. Just as she was about to hang up the phone, she heard Clarice's voice.

"Hello."

"Hello, Mom. It's Paula... I'm sorry to be calling so late, but I have a problem."

Chapter 14

The smell in the waiting room was horrible. Paula looked at the roomful of destitute individuals and thought about how fortunate she was to have medical insurance to pay for doctors with well-furnished offices. But this visit could not be processed through her mother's insurance - it had to be paid for with cash. She would not understand and probably would try to stop them. They needed to get the blood tests somewhere they could be anonymous; there was no chance of anyone knowing them at this clinic. But now Paula wished that they had picked a clinic in a nicer part of town.

Michael had picked Paula up at the house before Clarice came home. Every Sunday evening, Paula would pick up her mother's car and every Friday she would bring it back home. The arrangement was supposed to be temporary, but Paula could not find alternative transportation to work. Her mother insisted that it was not an inconvenience. After her transfer to the downtown office, she rode the bus to avoid the traffic and the cost of parking. But Paula knew she was making a sacrifice for her. Especially since it was the hottest summer on record, and standing in the heat waiting for a bus was not easy. Paula knew that she owed Clarice.

There was a knot the size of a tennis ball in the pit of Paula's stomach and deep breathing was not helping. She was not sure if her anxiety was due to the atmosphere or fear of having her blood drawn. The agony a few months earlier at the clinic, where she got her birth control prescription, was still fresh in her memory. The nurse started in one arm but after several painful attempts to find a vein, she switched to the other arm. After poking several more times, the nurse mercifully found a vein willing to fill the two glass-tubes.

Several times, Paula thought about telling Michael that she wanted to leave. But the state required a blood test prior to issuing a marriage license and time was running out. They only had a week before Michael left for college. Even though Paula knew they were already married in God's eyes, they still needed to make it official.

Finally, the lady at the desk called their names and directed them down a long hall to the lab. Much to Paula's dismay, they found another smaller waiting area. They checked in at the desk, where the nurse said that she would be right with them and instructed them to take a seat. Paula wished the knot in her stomach would go away and attributed the anxiety to her fear of needles and not what the needles represented. Nothing could be more right than she and Michael getting married. Michael loved her more than anyone and she loved Michael even more. Paula's thoughts drifted to their life after graduating from college. It would be perfect. They would adopt Autumn and then start a family of their own. Paula was summoned back to reality when she heard her name being called.

"What were you just thinking about?" Michael asked as they got up from the hard, plastic chairs.

"What our life will be like after college."

"And what do you think?"

"It's going to be perfect." Paula said with a smile.

They followed the nurse into a small room with a steel-frame chair sitting beside a small table, filled with jars of medical supplies, and a series of cabinets mounted on the wall. The nurse looked young and Paula was certain that she was not experienced enough to draw her blood without excruciating pain.

"So who's going first?" The nurse asked smiling.

Michael looked at Paula.

"I will. " Michael said, after Paula didn't respond.

"Have a seat."

Michael sat down in the chair and positioned his arm on the table. Paula was afraid to watch, but needed to evaluate the nurse's skills. If she hurt Michael, the nurse was not going touch her. Sensing the tension in the air, the nurse tried to lighten the moment as she tied a rubber strip around Michael's arm just above his elbow.

"So when is the big day?"

"In a couple of weeks." Michael replied.

"You have great veins... Are you having a big wedding?" The nurse asked, looking directly at Paula as she tore open an alcohol wipe.

"No. It's going to be very small." Paula replied, wishing to change the subject.

They had not talked about their wedding plans with anyone and Paula felt uncomfortable telling a complete stranger. It was such a small world that this nurse might know someone they knew. Once it became public knowledge, it would be only a matter of time before Clarice found out. The nurse picked up the needle and removed the protective cap. The needle looked huge and Paula knew that there was no way it would fit in her small veins. Panic quickly replaced her anxiety.

"I wish we had done that. We had a huge wedding with all the trimmings. It cost a fortune. Okay Michael, you're going to feel a little stick."

Paula looked at Michael to see if it hurt. She noticed that he flinched a little.

"...We are almost done." The nurse said as she filled the syringe with Michael's blood.

"Does it hurt?" Paula asked Michael.

"Not really."

"Okay, you are all done." The nurse said as she removed the needle and put a cotton ball and bandage over the spot.

"Bend your arm for a minute to stop the bleeding."

Michael stood up, following the nurse's instruction, and Paula reluctantly sat in the chair and put her arm on the table. She was visibly nervous.

"Relax, it won't be that bad." The nurse said as she prepared for Paula.

"I have extremely small veins. The last time I had blood drawn was very painful. They had to try both arms before finally finding a vein that worked."

"Don't worry. I'm pretty good at hitting a vein on the first try. Now, let's take a look at those veins." The nurse said, tying the rubber strip on Paula's arm.

"Okay, make a tight fist for me."

Paula balled her fist as tightly as she could.

"You're right. You do have small veins. Let's take a look at your other arm."

The nurse removed the rubber strip and Paula placed her other arm on the table. The nurse tied the rubber so tight that it almost hurt.

"Now make a fist...This arm is not much better but I think I can get this one to work. But we'd better use a smaller needle on you."

Paula was slightly relieved, but did not like having to stretch her arm across her body. The nurse stood up and got something out of a cabinet then sat back on the stool. She opened an alcohol swab and wiped the area. Paula looked at her arm but didn't see any veins bulging to the surface. She watched as the nurse removed the protective cover off the needle, which did not look much smaller to her.

"Are you ready? Try to relax but keep your fist closed tight. You are just going to feel a little sting when the needle goes in."

Paula took a deep breath and closed her eyes tightly. She flinched when she felt the needle penetrate her skin.

"Did you get it?" Paula asked with her eyes still closed.

"Not yet. It jumped from me."

That was not what Paula wanted to hear. She could not hold her breath any longer, so she exhaled. Paula hoped that the nurse would be able to make this one work. She didn't know how much longer she could last.

"Are we going to have to switch to the other arm?"

"I think I've got it. Now, open and close your fist."

Paula tried to follow the instructions but she had held her fist tightly closed for so long, it took a few seconds to regain control.

"Paula, are you okay?" Michael asked.

"As well as can be expected." Paula replied.

"You are doing great. We're almost done."

Paula took another deep breath and tried to relax. Finally, the nurse removed the needle from her arm.

"You are going to have a small bruise but it should go away in a few days. You need to keep pressure on it for about five minutes."

The nurse disposed of the needles and inspected the tubes.

"You need to go back to the front desk and take care of the paperwork. The results will be ready in three days. You can either pick them up or have them mailed to you. If you chose to pick them up, you both need to come in. We can't give test results to anyone else."

"We'll probably pick them up since we don't have much time. Thanks. Have a good day." Michael said cheerfully.

"Good luck with the wedding." The nurse replied as she walked out of the room.

Michael handed Paula her purse and they walked down the hall in silence. Paula's arm was hurting but at least it was over. They stopped at the administration desk to pay the bill. As they walked out the clinic door into the blistering heat, both Michael and Paula were deep in thought. They strolled slowly to the car because the heat was too oppressive to exert any more energy than necessary. Michael opened the passenger door and the heat came rushing out. The car was so hot that Paula was surprised the seats had not melted. She wondered if this heat wave would ever end. Michael walked around to the other side of the car and opened his door. He waited a few seconds before he carefully reached in and turned the ignition. The air conditioner was still on full blast.

They both knew it would be a few minutes before the car was safe to enter. They had been through this ritual the entire summer. The vinyl in the car needed time to cool down or else it would burn unprotected skin. Michael walked around to the front of the car and joined Paula, who had located a small shady area by a tree.

"How does your arm feel?" Michael asked as they stood hoping for a breeze.

"Okay. It still hurts a little but at least it's over. Does yours hurt?"

"No. I don't even think I need this anymore."

Michael removed the bandage. Paula lifted hers to see if the bleeding had stopped.

"I might as well get rid of mine, too. I don't feel like answering any questions."

"Paula, we have less than two weeks left. I thought we could get married the Friday before classes start and spend the weekend at a hotel for our honeymoon. Since we'll already be living in the dorms, there won't be any questions. I know it's not very romantic but I promise you a real honeymoon one day."

"That's fine Michael. But can I make one request?"

Paula didn't wait for a response.

"Can we stay at a nice hotel? This is a special occasion."

"Of course. You take care of the arrangement with a judge and I'll take care of the hotel. Try to get an appointment after five o'clock so I'll have time to drive down. We should be able to pick up the marriage license next week before I leave.

"Are you going to help me move into my dorm next weekend? Check-in starts Sunday morning."

"I can help you if we do it early. My dad wants to take me up to check in and I told him we could leave around noon."

"That's okay. I'll borrow my mom's car to move my things."

"Are you sure? I don't mind helping you."

"I know. But that's okay. Are you hungry?"

"Now that you mentioned it, I am. What do you have a taste for?"

"Whatever is closer."

"The lab results will be back Wednesday. We can pick them up after work and still have time to get to the marriage license office. Can you be back from work by four?"

"I will be."

Paula and Michael got in the car that was cooling off.

Michael picked Paula up at exactly four o'clock. Paula was waiting outside for Michael so he would not have to park. It was extremely hot and she was exhausted from work. She was working on a project with a senior engineer to fix a problem with leaking windshields. She had been jumping in and out of car bodies all day as they went through the car wash recording the exact location of the leaks. Her body was already aching. All Paula wanted to do was take a shower and a nap, but she barely had time to change into a cooler outfit. She knew that they needed to get the results today. As soon as they got the results and the license, she would have Michael just drop her off.

"Hi baby. How was work today?" Michael asked cheerfully as Paula got in the car.

"Tiring. I spent the entire day riding cars through the car wash."

"That doesn't sound too bad."

"You try to jump in moving cars without seats for eight hours."

"Well, it's over now. Just sit back and relax."

"How was your day?"

"The same as usual. If the traffic isn't too bad, we'll be able to get to the license office today. It should only take about five minutes to pick up the blood test results. Do you want to go to the movies afterwards?"

"Not really. I'm too tired. All I want to do is take a shower and go to sleep. Maybe this weekend?"

Paula leaned her head back and closed her eyes. The cool air blowing from the air conditioner felt wonderful. She was sound asleep by the time they got to the clinic.

"Hey, sleepy head. Wake up! We're at the clinic."

Paula reluctantly picked up her purse and opened the car door. The heat outside only made her feel more drained as she followed Michael through the door to the desk where a nurse was working.

"Excuse me. We are here to pick up some test results. Where do we need to go?"

"I can help you. What's your name?"

"I'm Michael Williams. There should also be some results for a Paula Hayes"

"Wait just a moment and I'll get your information."

"Boy, am I glad we don't have to wait."

The woman returned with a single envelope and handed it to Michael. Paula looked at the envelope and saw Michael's name printed on the label.

"What did you say the other name was?" The lady asked, looking at Paula.

"Paula Hayes."

"Miss Hayes, your results weren't in there. Let me check another place."

The lady went to a set of file folders on a credenza behind her. She pulled out a folder and began looking through the papers. She paused at one paper, read it and then removed it from the folder and walked back to Paula and Michael.

"Paula, you need to talk with someone. Please take a seat and someone will be with you in a few minutes."

Michael found two seats in an unoccupied corner of the waiting room. He opened the envelope and reviewed his results. They both knew that the required tests were for venereal diseases and sickle-celled anemia. His results were all negative.

Paula hoped that they did not need to take some more blood. Her heart began to race at the mere thought of another blood test. All of the test results at the other clinic came back normal, so Paula knew there was nothing wrong with her physically.

"What kind of problem do you think they had?" Michael asked Paula with a worried look.

"I don't know. Maybe they lost my blood sample or dropped it. I hope this doesn't mean that they have to take some more."

"If we don't hurry, the license office will close."

"I know. Maybe someone will be with me soon."

They sat in silence until a woman dressed in white and carrying a clipboard called Paula's name. Paula stood up on shaky legs and was relieved that at least the waiting was over.

"Do you want me to go with you?" Michael asked.

"No, it shouldn't take long. Besides I don't want you to see me cry if they have to take some more blood."

"Okay, I'll wait right here."

Paula tried hard to smile, touched by his concern for her. She thought that he looked more nervous than she did. Paula followed the woman down a long hall to a small office that had a table and two chairs. The woman closed the door behind them and took a seat in the chair on the opposite side of the table. Paula sat down in the other chair and crossed her legs.

"Paula, there was a problem with one of your blood tests. One of the results came back positive. Are you sexually active?"

"What do you mean?"

"Are you having sexual intercourse?"

"Yes." Paula was embarrassed by the question.

"Do you have more than one partner?"

Paula was appalled, wondering why this complete stranger was asking her about her sex life. It was none of her business.

I knew we should have picked a different clinic. This one is used to dealing with prostitutes. I am here to get a blood test to get married. If I had more than one partner, I wouldn't be getting married. Is this lady crazy?

"No! Just my fiancée." Paula said somewhat defensively.

"The result of your syphilis test came back positive."

"I'm sorry. Could you please repeat that?"

"The result of your syphilis test is positive."

"That's impossible. His results were negative."

"It's possible for one partner to test positive."

There is no way I have syphilis. There has to be some mistake. Maybe the nurse got mine and Michael's samples mixed up. Michael's been with several others before me. If anyone has a venereal disease, it has to be him. Could Michael have given me this disease? This can't be happening. Why didn't this show up on the other tests? I remember clearly the doctor at the other clinic telling me that they were taking blood to test for venereal diseases and anemia.

"No. This can't be right. I just had a complete physical at another clinic to get some birth control. They tested for venereal diseases and the results were negative."

"How long ago was that?"

"The month before last."

271

"Well, it is highly unlikely that you'd test negative and then positive two months later unless you changed partners."

"I have only been with my fiancée in the last three years. I swear."

"You may be part of a small percent of people who register a false positive on the primary test that looks for a specific antibody that's usually associated with syphilis. Do you know if that clinic ran two tests?"

"I don't know."

"There is a more accurate test that can be run. It looks specifically for the syphilis virus."

"Will you need to take another blood sample?"

"No, the lab will be able to use the same sample. The results will be back on Friday. Don't worry. It is probably just a false result. You may want to call the clinic Friday morning just to make sure the results are ready."

The counselor felt sorry for Paula, who seemed like a nice girl. She stood up and hoped that it was a mistake. Usually, the primary test was very accurate for their normal patients. But she knew that Paula was not their normal patient; she could tell as soon as she started talking to her. Paula stood up and followed the counselor out of the office before she realized that she had forgotten her purse. She quickly turned and went back to get it. The nurse saw that the news had upset Paula and was a little worried about her.

"Paula, are you going to be okay?" The counselor asked as they walked back to the waiting area.

"I think so."

"You don't need to check in at the desk. I'll take care of the paper work."

"Thank you very much."

Michael was flipping through a magazine when Paula returned to the waiting room. He stood up immediately.

"Is everything okay?"

"I'll tell you in the car. Let's get out of here."

"Do you need to sign anything?"

"No."

Paula walked to the car in silence.

What am I going to tell Michael? Maybe I shouldn't tell him what the problem is, just that they need to run another test. There is no sense in worrying him. I'm sure that I'll worry enough for the both of us.

She could tell that Michael was anxious to know why she had to talk to someone. He opened her door and then hopped in the car, without even waiting for it to cool down. Paula followed his actions and sat on the burning hot vinyl. Michael started the car as they both rolled down the windows to let some of the hot air escape.

"So are you going to tell me what's wrong? Did the nurse give you the paper that we need to get the license?"

"Michael, we can't get the license today."

"Why?"

"I need to come back on Friday. They need to run a different test. One of the results came back positive."

"Which one, Paula?"

Paula did not like Michael's tone.

"The one for syphilis."

Michael put the car in reverse and backed out of the parking spot much too fast.

"Michael, what's wrong?"

"How could you do this to me?"

273

"Do what? What have I done to you?"

"I trusted you."

"Michael, I haven't done anything."

"Obviously, you have. My results were negative, so you must have gotten it from someone else."

"Michael, you must be joking. I can't believe how you are acting."

"Oh really. How am I supposed to act when the person I'm getting ready to marry tells me she has syphilis?"

Paula was fuming. This was not the reaction she expected. Concern, maybe even sympathy, but not anger.

Maybe I don't know Michael as well as I thought I did. He's already tried and convicted me, without all the evidence. Well, if he wants to act that way, let him. Why try to explain to him that it is probably a false result? He probably won't believe me anyway.

He drove Paula back to her dorm without saying another word and pulled the car in front of the entrance, which was her cue that he wasn't coming in. Paula opened the door to get out.

"I'll call you later." Michael said without looking in her direction.

"Don't bother."

Paula slammed his car door and hoped that Angela would be out as she climbed the stairs. She wanted to be alone. Angela was combing her hair when Paula walked into the room.

"I was just going to dinner. Are you coming?"

"No, I'm not hungry. I'm going to take a shower."

"It's only five-thirty."

"I know, but I had a rough day at work and I think this heat is finally getting to me."

"Do you want me to bring you something back?"

"No, thanks. I might get something later."

"Okay."

Angela picked up her purse and left the room. Paula dropped into her chair as soon as the door closed, alone with her thoughts. The bed looked very inviting but she knew if she lay down, she would not feel like getting back up. She was completely drained, physically and emotionally. Paula grabbed the things she needed for her shower and walked solemnly down the hall to the bathroom. She was glad to have the shower area all to herself.

Adjusting the water temperature, Paula thought about Michael and his reaction.

How could he assume that I was sleeping with someone else? With the exception of the weekend in June that I escorted Shane at his cotillion, Michael and I have been inseparable. And even that weekend was harmless since Shane was making his moves on another one of the escorts. Maybe Michael doesn't really love me at all. He should know that I would never be with anyone else but him.

Paula could feel the tears swelling inside. By the time she stepped into the warm shower, the tears were flowing freely down her cheeks. She leaned against the wall and let the warm stream of water flow over her body while she sobbed softly.

What if Michael never calls me again? I can't imagine my life without Michael. He is my husband... Paula, you need to pull yourself together. Everything is going to be okay. Michael just needs some space. When I get the negative results on Friday, we'll be able to go ahead with our plans.

When there were no more tears to cry, Paula soaped herself and rinsed off. She regained her composure before leaving the shower, convinced that everything was going to be okay.

Paula was almost asleep, when she remembered she needed to do something. She clasped her hands together firmly.

"Now I lay me down to sleep, I pray the Lord my soul to keep. If I should die before I wake, I pray the Lord my soul to take. Please God let the test results come back negative. Amen."

Chapter 15

The pre-world war II office was filled with waiting couples of all ages and nationalities. Each couple had the same chocolate brown clipboard with an application form attached. Most of the couples looked happy but some looked extremely nervous. Paula noticed two adolescents sitting between two older couples. The girl was talking to the woman on her left about the information on the clipboard.

I wonder if they are getting married. She looks barely fourteen and he doesn't look much older. Surely they are not here for a marriage license.

Paula's suspicions were confirmed when a woman behind the desk called a name and the girl and boy got the clipboard and walked to the desk. They handed the woman behind the counter the clipboard. She looked at the information and then asked the couple, loud enough for the entire room to hear, if their parents were there. Paula looked at the expression of the parents as they walked to the counter.

That's a shotgun marriage, if I ever saw one. I wonder how long it will last. I am so happy that Michael and I are here because we loved each other and not because we don't want a baby out of wedlock... If God had not been so merciful, we could have been here out of necessity, too.

Paula shuttered at the thought and looked at Michael, who had driven from college that morning so they could get the license. They both had moved into their dorms that Sunday and had spent the first part of the week in orientation sessions. He smiled and kissed her on the cheek still showering her with affection to make up for the two days that he had acted horribly.

Paula was part of that small percent of the population that fooled the primary syphilis test. The nurse tried to explain it to Paula when she picked up the results. It was something about her blood chemistry. But Paula was so excited about the good news that she really wasn't paying attention. She walked out of the clinic relieved but uncertain about her future. The paperwork for the marriage license that was so important three days earlier might be unnecessary now.

Michael had been on pins and needles for two days awaiting the results that would confirm his fate. He had decided after dropping Paula off that he wasn't going to call her ever again. If she had lied about whom she had slept with, he couldn't trust her again. Besides, she had potentially ruined his life. If she had syphilis, it would only be a matter of time before he got it. Some of his friends used to joke about how it caused sterility. If they had not been tested for the marriage license, he might not have found out until it was too late.

But the suspense had gotten the best of him and he missed Paula more than he ever imagined he could. He left two messages with Paula's roommate Friday evening. He didn't know how else to reach her. He even thought about calling Clarice's house.

Paula went home to return Clarice's car after picking up the results and decided to stay a while to help Clarice, who was glad to have Paula around. Her mother had finally decided to quit the job she hated to pursue a more humanitarian career. With part of her retirement money, she leased some commercial space in a small neighborhood shopping center and was converting it into a community center. Clarice was the director.

Paula volunteered to paint a geometrical design on the walls of the building to brighten the atmosphere. It was the least that she could do for Clarice in return for the use of her car all summer. Although Paula still did not feel close to her mother, they could at least hold a conversation about some things; Michael was not a subject that they could share.

Clarice hoped that the separation for college would end the relationship, even though she was still disappointed that Paula had not chosen a college farther from Michael. Clarice did not know exactly how but she knew that Michael was bad for her daughter. She prayed that Paula would be smart enough not to get pregnant like Lisa and ruin her life.

It was after nine when Paula got back to her dorm room. Angela's side of the room was totally empty except for a sheet of paper on her desk. She had already packed her things and returned home, where she had spent every weekend.

Paula looked at the messages written on the paper. Two were from Michael and one was from Angela saying she would see Paula Sunday, when they checked into the freshman dormitory. They were going to be in the same dorm, but were going to have different roommates because Angela had turned in her housing form late. Paula was going to be rooming with Gail.

Michael had called at four-thirty and again at seven. Paula wondered if he had called again after Angela had left. His last message said - Please call as soon as you get in.

Paula knew the reason for the urgency. Michael just needed to know for sure. If he had been worried about her, he would have called Wednesday night. She debated whether to return his call. Instead of supporting her, he had abandoned her. Paula smiled; something she had not done a few days. She thought about letting him stew for another day; it would do him good after the way he treated her, jumping to the wrong conclusion. Paula decided at a minimum, she would make him wait another hour while she took a cool shower.

As soon as she returned from taking her shower, the phone rang. Paula looked at the clock. She knew who it was, so she let it ring a few more times while she put her dirty clothes away and her shower bag on the dresser. Finally, she picked up the phone and sat down on the edge of the bed.

"Hello."

"Why didn't you return my calls?"

Michael sounded angry.

"I was about to, if you would have given me the chance."

Paula smiled.

"Where have you been?"

"Why? Do I need to check in with you?"

"Paula, I didn't call to argue."

"Then why did you call? I haven't heard from you since Wednesday and now I get three calls in one day."

"Did you pick up your results?"

"Yes, I did and then I went to the community center to help my mother, if you must know."

"Are you going to tell me the results?"

"I thought you already knew the results."

"Paula, please."

"The result is negative. I don't have syphilis. Sorry to disappoint you."

"Paula, that's great news. Now we can go ahead with our plans."

"What plans Michael?"

"Paula, you know what plans, getting married."

"I don't know if I still want to now."

"You're kidding."

"No Michael. I'm not. I thought you loved me. Yet, you assumed that I was sleeping with someone else or lied about my previous relationships."

"Paula, what was I supposed to believe?"

"You were supposed to believe me. Was it impossible to believe that maybe the test result was a mistake?"

"Paula, I'm sorry. Please forgive me."

"I don't know if I can. I trusted you Michael and you let me down."

"Paula, please forgive me. I promise I'll never let you down again."

"I need to think about it. I'm tired and I need to move out of the dorm before noon tomorrow. Good night, Michael."

"Good night, Paula. I love you."

Paula hung up the phone. She knew she loved Michael too and in God's eyes they were already married. She didn't have a choice. She would have to forget what happened and move on. She needed to believe that he would not let her down again. Sleep came easy for Paula after the stressful week.

Paula jumped when she heard the knock on the door. She looked at the clock quickly to make sure she had not overslept. The dorm had to be vacated by noon. It was only seven-thirty. Paula wondered if it was her Resident Advisor.

"Who is it?" Paula asked, sitting up in her bed.

"It's me."

Paula catapulted out of bed and ran to the door. Michael was not supposed to be on the floor before nine or unescorted and he knew that. When she opened the door, Michael held out a beautiful bouquet of flowers.

"What are you doing here this early and how did you get on the floor without an escort?"

"Good morning to you, too!" Michael said as he handed Paula the flowers and walked into the room.

"You didn't answer my questions?"

"I came to take you to breakfast and then help you move out, so will you hurry and put some clothes on."

"And how do you know that I want to go to breakfast with you." Paula said holding back a smile.

"You know you love me as much as I love you. Now say that you'll marry me and let's go get some breakfast. I'm hungry."

She was thrilled that he had gone to so much trouble for her, knowing that he was not a morning person. Michael wrapped his arms around her and kissed her on both cheeks.

"You're always hungry. Yes, I'll marry you. Now will you please let me get dressed."

Paula turned her attention back to the marriage license application. When they checked in, the woman at the desk told them it would be about an hour wait, so there was no rush to complete the form. Paula paused at the space for the couple's permanent address. It was one of the required fields. Paula didn't know her new post office box at school. She started to put her home address and then wondered if it would be the address used to mail the license or other information.

"Michael, this space is for our permanent address and I don't know my new address."

"Just leave the space blank."

"I can't. It's required. I'm going to ask what we need to do."

Paula stood up and went to the counter. She waited a few minutes for one of the clerks to finish processing a couple.

"Excuse me. I have a question about the application."

"Yes?"

"We don't know our permanent address yet. Do we have to complete that section?"

"We can't process the application without a permanent address. That's the address where the marriage certificate will be sent. Will you know your permanent address by the time you get married?"

"Yes."

"I suggest that you put your current address for now. It will be typed on the marriage license but you can cross it out and put your permanent address on the license any time before the wedding. The official who marries you will mail the license to this office for processing after the ceremony. We will make the address correction on our records at that time."

"Thank you." Paula said before returning to her seat.

"Well, can we leave it blank?" Michael asked before Paula could even sit down.

"No. It is required. She said to put a current address now and change it on the license before the ceremony. They'll make the change on their records when the license is returned to them."

"Do you want to put my home address?"

"No, that's okay. I'll put mine since it won't matter. I'll have my post office box next week and will change it then."

Paula completed the remainder of the application. They waited for another thirty minutes before their names were finally called and a few more minutes before they walked out of the building with their marriage license in hand. It was almost noon.

"Do you need to drive right back?" Paula asked as they walked down the sidewalk to his car.

"Yes, I do. I missed one orientation session this morning. I have to meet with my counselor this afternoon. Do you want to pick up something to eat?"

"No, I don't want you to be late. Besides, the cafeteria is open until one-thirty. I'll eat at school since it's already paid for. You can just drop me off and drive back."

"Okay...Are we all set for Friday?" Michael asked as he pulled the car away from the curb into a break in the traffic.

"I hope so. The appointment is for five o'clock. Did you take care of the hotel arrangements?"

"I said that I would."

"And where are we staying? Or should I ask?"

"It's going to be a surprise but I promise I'll chose somewhere nice."

Paula wondered if it was nice by her standard or his. He had not traveled as much as she had and she wondered if he had ever stayed in a luxury hotel. Looking out the window, she decided to trust him.

"So how's your roommate?" Paula asked.

"He's pretty cool. He's a computer science major, too. I think we are going to get along okay."

"And what about all the freshman women?"

284

"What women Paula? You know I have what I want. If I wanted someone else, would I be marrying you in two days?"

"I don't know."

"You know just as well as I do that adultery is a sin and I have no intentions of burning in hell."

"So when will I get to see that dorm of yours?"

"When do you want to see it?"

"I don't know. We'll be busy this weekend." Paula said with a smile.

"How about next weekend?"

"Sounds good. Are you going to drive up or will I need to pick you up?"

"I'll see if I can borrow my mother's car and drive up but you know that means I'll have to come back that night."

"Maybe, I should pick you up."

Michael looked over at Paula, happy that she belonged to him or at least would after Friday.

It didn't take long to get from downtown to her dorm. The campus was coming to life, since the upper classmen were starting to move on campus. Michael drove pass Paula's dorm.

"Paula, I still have a few minutes. I'll park and walk you in."

"Michael, you really need to be going. Don't worry about walking me to the dorm. All the parking places are probably taken."

"I'll drive around one more time."

Michael was just about to give up and drop Paula off, when he saw a car pulling out of a space in front of the dorm.

"See, we got lucky. Do you want to keep the marriage license or do you want me to?"

"Why don't you keep it, but don't forget it Friday."

"I won't. I'll lock it in the glove compartment just to make sure."

Paula's dorm was in the center of the freshman quadrangle. It was an all-female dorm. The other dorms were co-ed by floors. As they got out of the car and started walking to the dorm, they both noticed a group of male athletes sitting on the front stairs of the dorm.

"I thought you said your dorm is female."

"It is, but all of the athletes eat in our cafeteria. That's why so many women try to get into this dorm and supposedly, this dorm has the best food on campus."

"Is that why you requested this dorm?"

"Michael, please. This is the only freshman dorm where the students are grouped by majors. Everyone on my wing is either Math or Science majors. I doubt if there will be much partying going on. Don't worry. I'm not interested in jocks. They're not my type."

Michael did not like the fact that Paula would be in such close contact with the athletes. His concern was justified, when some of the athletics whistled at Paula as they walked past. If they would whistle at her when he was around, what would they try when he wasn't?

A few days earlier, Michael had thought about delaying their wedding plans. After moving into the dorms and seeing his schedule, he knew it was going to be difficult for them to see each other every weekend as planned. However this incident convinced Michael that he needed to marry Paula as soon as possible. He could trust Paula once they were married but he wasn't so certain otherwise. What if she met someone in the next two days who could make her change her mind? Michael was silent as they went through the doors to Paula's wing.

"Man on the floor." Paula announced; one of the requirements that her Resident Assistant stressed was very important as a common courtesy.

"Paula, I need to go back there and say something to them."

"And what would that prove. They just did that because you were there. I'm not their type. They prefer women who will throw themselves at athletes. I've never been interested in the athletic type and I'm not about to start now."

Paula opened her door with the key. She was glad that Gail was out. She wanted to say good-bye to Michael in private.

"Are you jealous?" Paula asked as she put her purse down on the bed.

"Should I be?"

"I should be asking you that. I hear that there are five females for every male at Northern State." Paula said as she circled her arms around Michael's waist.

"You know you have nothing to worry about." Michael said holding her so tight it almost hurt.

"Then neither do you. In less that two days, we will be husband and wife."

Paula kissed Michael on the cheek.

"Do you think you can stay out of trouble until then?" Michael asked with a smile as he looked deep into Paula's eyes.

"I don't know. It will be hard but I guess I'll try."

Paula could feel Michael hardening against her.

"Speaking of hard, I think you'd better be leaving before we start something we won't be able to finish."

"Don't forget, I'll only be an hour drive away. I can show up here at any time."

"Is that a threat or a promise?" Paula removed her arms from his waist and held his hands.

"What are your plans for the rest of the day?" Michael asked as he slowly walked to the door.

"I thought I might hang out with those hunks out front."

"That's not very funny, Paula."

"Sorry. I have an Engineering orientation and then we have a mandatory floor meeting. Are you going to call?"

"Of course. You don't need to walk me all the way out. Just to the lobby." Michael said with a smile and Paula knew why.

The two days passed quickly as Paula and Michael participated in more orientation sessions and learned the challenges of the registration system. Paula knew that there had to be a better system than waiting in long lines and hoping the classes were not filled by the time you reached the table.

They both had problems sleeping the eve of their wedding day. Paula woke up early but did not get out of bed immediately. She stayed in bed thinking about what her life would be like as Michael's official wife even if no one else would know. They had not talked about rings but Paula hoped Michael had picked something simple that would look more like an engagement ring than a wedding ring. Since Michael had not mentioned a ring, Paula assumed he wanted it to be a surprise.

Paula regretted that she would not have a wedding like her sister, initially. But after graduation, they would do it right. So they decided to forgo most of the wedding traditions and agreed to dress casual, but Paula still wanted to wear something white. She decided to wear an off-white sundress with large pastel flowers and narrow shoulder straps. The dress was made of imported cotton gauze that flowed when she walked. She thought the dress was elegant but casual and perfect for the occasion.

Paula ate lunch late to miss the long lines associated with the athletes and their female groupies. After lunch, she took another long shower and dressed. She looked in the mirror as she put on her pearl earrings and the gold watch Michael had given her just eight months earlier.

Finally, Paula picked up the opal ring that Sheryl had just given her and started to put it on her left ring finger, but remembered that she needed to leave that finger empty for her wedding ring. She put the ring on her right hand, where it complimented the dress perfectly with the purple and green highlights on the creamy-white background. She had been so excited when Sheryl had given her the ring. It was her first expensive ring and now she was going to have two. She felt a surge of excitement.

I wonder what my wedding ring is going to look like. Michael has set the standard. Look at this beautiful watch he gave me after only two weeks. I can hardly imagine what he's going to give me for our wedding day.

Paula packed a small suitcase with the things that she would need for the weekend, carefully laying the new nightgown on top. She sat down on her bed and looked at the suitcase.

I wish we were going to have a real honeymoon. At least, we are going to be able to spend the entire weekend together. I hope Michael keeps his promise and picks a nice hotel. It would be so romantic if he got us a room at the hotel where we met. I should have suggested it... Maybe he'll think about it on his own. It's expensive, but you only have one honeymoon. I'll offer to help Michael pay for the hotel, even though my funds are tight. I still can't believe that housing and books cost so much. At least, I didn't have to ask Mom for any money.

Paula remembered that she had forgotten one very important detail.

What if Mom tries to call me this weekend?

Paula had already told Gail that she was going to spend the weekend at home. It would blow her cover, if Clarice called. She decided to be proactive and dialed the number.

"Hi, Mom."

"Hi, Paula. How did registration go? Did you get all the classes you needed?"

"Yes, but I ended up with a late afternoon Physics lab."

"The painter finished the walls. When do you think you'll be able to start work on the design?"

"Mom, this weekend is going to be pretty busy with orientation. I thought I could start Monday afternoon. I'll be finished with my classes by noon, if you can pick me up then."

"Okay. What are you doing tonight? I was thinking about cooking some Mexican food."

"I'm waiting for Michael to pick me up. He's coming home for the weekend."

"Why don't you both come home for dinner?"

"Mom, I think he already has something planned. I'll give you a call Monday when I get out of class. Have a good weekend, Mom."

"Bye, Paula. Tell Michael I said hello."

Clarice wondered how long it would be before Michael found someone else and hoped it would be soon. Paula would be hurt but in the long run it would be much better for her. Michael was not right for Paula, but there was nothing left for her to do. Her conversation with his mother didn't help. But the separation of college, even if he was only one hour away, may be enough to break them up.

Michael wanted to get to the judge's office before the Friday traffic got too heavy. He left his dorm right after eating lunch. Since he was early, he decided to stop by the motel and check in before he picked Paula up. He was relieved that he was able to get a room in the back and hoped that Paula would like the room. It was the best he could do, without a credit card.

When he went to put his bag in the room, he felt better. The room was much larger and nicer than the other motel. It had two double beds and a big television with cable. It was a little closer to Clarice's house than he desired, but the rooms on the backside were pretty discrete.

The phone rang at three-thirty. Michael was in the lobby waiting. Paula's heart raced. She had been waiting for thirty minutes, checking herself in the mirror every five minutes. When she saw him in the lobby, she was glad that he belonged to her. He had decided to wear his suit after all but had left his jacket in the car. Michael thought Paula looked beautiful and knew he was making the right decision.

The traffic was heavy traveling to the judge's office but they arrived fifteen minutes early. Michael had thought about telling Paula in the car but he didn't know how. He knew he needed to tell her soon; he was running out of time.

The judge's office was a white, colonial building surrounded by huge shade trees and ample parking. Paula felt like she was walking into a southern plantation. They went inside and were greeted by an older lady with cotton white hair.

"Well, hello there. Don't you two look very nice."

"Thank you. We have a five o'clock appointment with Judge White." Michael said with a nervous smile.

"Of course. Are you waiting for someone else to join you."

"No ma'am."

"What a shame! This happy day should be shared. The judge is finishing another wedding. You can wait in his study and he'll be right with you."

The lady led Michael and Paula through a large door into a room that looked like a library. There were two wingback chairs in front of a large mahogany desk. Built-in bookshelves covered the wall behind the desk.

"Do you have your marriage license and the rings?"

"Here's our marriage license."

Michael handed the lady the folded paper. She unfolded it and inspected the front and back.

"You changed the address. Is this the address you want your marriage certificate mailed?"

"Yes, ma'am. They told us it was okay to change it on the certificate once we knew our permanent address." Paula said.

"That's fine honey. I'll just go get things ready. It won't be long."

The lady left the room and closed the door behind her. She shook her head, after the door was closed.

I hate to see weddings like this. The poor girl must be in a family way and hasn't told her parents. Teenagers are always so anxious to grow up. At least, she's not showing yet and they are trying to do the right thing.

Paula and Michael sat down in the wing-backed chairs as soon as the door closed. Michael knew he could not wait any longer. He didn't want her to find out in front of the judge. Michael took a deep breath and looked at her.

"Paula, I didn't have enough money to buy you a ring." He thought he saw a glimpse of hurt in her eyes, but it passed quickly.

"Michael, why didn't you tell me? I could have given you some money for it."

Paula could not believe it. She had accepted the fact that they were not going to have a traditional wedding, but now she was also going to be deprived of a wedding ring.

"Paula, I thought I'd be able to work out something but my share of my tuition and housing was more than I expected. I promise I'll get you a ring. It's just going to take some time."

"That's okay, Michael. But what are we suppose to use for the ceremony?" Paula asked, looking at the floor.

"I have my senior class ring."

Paula winced and slowly slid the opal ring off her finger then handed it to Michael.

"We can use this. It's not a diamond but I think it will do."

Paula stood up and walked to the window.

Well that destroys any hope of a romantic honeymoon. I just hope that we are not going back to that same dump.

The door opened and an elderly, white man came into the study with a warm smile. Paula turned from the window and quickly joined Michael as he stood to greet him.

"So here's the happy couple. I'm Judge Blackwell and you must be Michael and Paula."

Paula looked pass the judge, through the open door at the wedding party that was leaving. It was a large, happy group. The bride was showing off her ring while the groom hugged an older man. Paula felt empty.

"Can I see the rings before we get started?"

"We just have a ring for Paula." Michael said handing the judge the ring

"It's very pretty."

The judge knew immediately that it was not a wedding ring and thought it was probably the best they could do, given the circumstances.

"Now before we get started, I give all the couples the same speech. Marriage is a very serious endeavor. It is not an institution that should be entered into lightly. Are you sure that you understand this and still want to proceed?"

Michael and Paula looked at each other.

"Yes, we are sure." Michael said.

"Miss Hayes, are you sure you want to marry Mr. Williams?"

"Yes, I'm sure."

"Okay, follow me and we will get you two married."

Paula thought it was too late to be asking that question. She and Michael were already married; this was just a formality.

The judge led the way out of his office to a small room with a podium in the front. Paula looked around the room and noticed that there were no chairs, just the podium. The walls had dark cherry paneling and except for the filtered sunlight coming through the windows, the room was very solemn. Paula knew that this was not the kind of wedding she wanted. Instead of the elation that she was expecting, she just wanted the whole thing to be over. The ceremony took less than five minutes. After paying the judge and the congratulations, they left to start their honeymoon.

Paula was quiet in the car, which worried Michael. He hoped that she didn't already regret marrying him.

"Paula, I'm sorry about the ring."

"That's okay. It's probably better anyway since we aren't going to tell anyone."

Paula continued looking out the car window, wanting to hide how she really felt. As they drove, she wondered where they were going to be spending their honeymoon but was afraid to even ask. The last remaining hope of the romantic honeymoon at the hotel where they met faded as they drove away from downtown, in the direction of her house.

They were both afraid to say anything and were deep in their own thoughts about the future. Paula was startled back to reality when they got off the freeway at the exit prior to the one for her house. Paula tried to think of what hotels were off the exit and then as they circled back under the freeway she saw the sign. They turned into the parking lot below the big Hacienda Motel sign. Michael drove to the back of the building and parked.

"I've already checked us in . . . Let's go Ms. Williams."

Michael hopped out of the car and walked around to open the door for Paula. Even though nothing was working out as she planned, she did not want to ruin the weekend for Michael and forced a smile. He put his arm around Paula's waist as they walked up the stairs to the room.

"Anything you say, Mr. Williams."

"Paula, I promise you that we will have a beautiful wedding and a real honeymoon as soon as we get out of school."

He kissed her on the cheek and seemed so sincere that Paula felt better and decided to make the best of the situation. She was surprised, that despite being a motel, the room was nice.

As soon as he locked the door, Michael wrapped his arms tightly around her and kissed her so affectionately that it started a passion in them that could finally be satisfied, guiltlessly.

"I don't have the energy to go out for dinner. Would you mind if I just pick up a pizza for us?" Michael asked, as they lay in each other's arms completely satisfied.

"Not at all, but hurry. I'm starving."

Paula smiled at the thought of a gourmet dinner of pizza on her honeymoon and the new nightgown that had not been used. She reached for the television remote control as Michael dressed.

Chapter 16

The piercing pain that had started in her hand, traveled quickly down her arm. She tried to ease the pain by loosening her grip on the paintbrush but a firm grip was the only way to keep the paint within the lines. When the pain got unbearable, Paula rested the paintbrush across the top of the can and slowly massaged her arm. She took a few steps back to assess her progress.

It was going to take longer than she had expected. This was just the first color of the three-color geometric design. The pattern was going to run the full length of the wall on both sides of the huge, rectangular-shaped space. The community center, that had been the focus of Clarice's every waking hour since she quit her job, was finally taking shape. The contractors were working at a hectic pace to finish their work before the grand opening. There was a big event planned with several community leaders and the press. Initial community support for the center was high but there were a few vocal skeptics who Clarice wanted to prove wrong.

Paula was glad to see the change in her mother's disposition. Since Clarice resigned, she was much more energetic as she coordinated the pre-opening activities. Her mother had to be reminded to go get some lunch, and Paula volunteered to supervise the contractors while Clarice went home to eat and check the mail. Her mother was expecting her lump sum pension check, which was funding the work on the building.

She had been painting since Clarice picked her up at noon and wanted to finish as much as she could before Michael came. He was picking her up at the community center and then they were headed back to the motel for more honeymooning. Michael planned on going home after they checked out of the motel but they were going to be together most of the weekend, even if it was just painting the walls.

When the pain in Paula's arm finally subsided, she picked up the brush and resumed her painting. Despite the fact that both air conditioning units were working as hard as they could, the room was still hot from the sunshine through the wall of plate-glass windows and the constant traffic through the door. The summer heat wave still had not eased up. She looked up at the clock. It was almost four o'clock. She was surprised that her mother had been gone so long. But Paula knew that she needed some time away from the center.

Clarice checked the mailbox before going into the house, but it was empty. She had hoped that the mailman would run early today. The check needed to be deposited before three, in order to cover the checks that she had already written. Clarice hoped that by the time she finished her lunch, the mail would be there. Then she could stop by the bank before going back to the center. She knew that Paula could take care of things while she was gone, so there was no need to rush. Now that Paula and Michael were separated by a little distance, Clarice was sure that Paula would return to her former self soon.

Clarice paused in the living room and looked at the sofa that Paula and Sheryl had bought for her birthday. Yes, Paula was going to make her very proud. Clarice made a mental note to call and find out what information she needed for the Debutante presentation. Paula was going to make a beautiful Deb. Clarice smiled, as she thought about Paula in a long white dress being escorted by Shane on the dance floor. She wondered if Sheryl had kept her dress as she went into the kitchen to heat some leftovers.

Clarice was just coming out of the kitchen when she heard the familiar clank of the mailbox closing. The timing was perfect. She would be able to make it to the bank. The heat rushed in as she opened the door and reached into the mailbox for its contents. The envelope on top of the pile was the check she had been waiting for; relief washed over her. She returned to the dining room to get her purse. If she rushed, she could make it to the bank and miss the school traffic. She took the top envelope off the stack of mail and started to put the rest of the mail on the table when the next envelope caught her attention. She looked at it closely.

"It can't be! Not again. God, I can't take this too."

Clarice grabbed the chair for support as she felt herself become weak. Quickly looking at the clock on the wall, she knew that she had to get to the bank. She put the envelope in her purse, not sure what she was going to do.

Paula was trying to access how much more she could get done before Michael arrived when she heard the familiar clicking of her mother's heels on the tile floor approaching.

"Paula, I'm back." Her mother paused.

"It looks nice, but you still have a lot of work. Will you need some help to finish? I don't want this to interfere with your school work."

Paula stopped working and looked briefly at Clarice who was holding an envelope and looking worried. Paula assumed Clarice was concerned whether she would be able to finish it in time for the opening.

"Don't worry, Mom. I will finish it before the opening. The first color is the hardest. The rest should go quicker. I plan to work on it most of tomorrow afternoon. Michael said he'd help if we need him. He's coming home this weekend."

Paula did not notice Clarice's grimace. Her mother hesitated for a minute as if she were going to say something. Paula was just about to start painting again when she spoke softly.

"Paula, are you and Michael married?"

The question caught Paula totally by surprise. They had only been married for a week and they had not told a soul. Paula wondered how she could know already. Paula tried to stay calm and hide the panic she felt inside. She knew that she could not tell her the truth. She had to find out how her mother knew and convince her otherwise.

"What makes you think that?"

Paula tried to act like her surprise was because she asked the question and not because she had found out.

"This came for you in the mail today."

Clarice handed her the envelope and Paula looked at the mailing address on the envelope. It was addressed to Mr. and Mrs. Michael Williams at her home address but the return address was a business name that she did not recognize. Paula quickly opened the envelope and removed the letter that it contained. It was from a furniture store congratulating them on their marriage and inviting them to visit the store for their new home furnishing. Paula knew instantly what she needed to do. She handed the letter back to her mother.

"Mom, this is nothing. Michael and I entered a contest at the mall a few weeks ago for a new car. It was for recently married couples only, so we entered as if we were married."

"Are you sure?"

"Yes, Mom."

"Paula that's a relief. I wouldn't want you to ruin your life. You and Michael are too young to be married with children. How long are you going to be here tonight?"

"Not much longer. Michael's picking me up soon. We're going out tonight and then he'll take me back to the dorm."

She smiled and hoped that her mother believed her and that God would forgive her. She felt she had no alternative but to lie. Michael needed his father to pay his tuition and if her mother found out, she would surely tell his mother.

Clarice was relieved. The thought of watching another daughter ruin her life was more than she could bear. If they had gotten married, a baby must be on the way. Why else would they get married?

Paula put down the paintbrush and pretended to be assessing her work, unable to look her mother in the face any longer. She was relieved when a contractor called Clarice to look at something.

Picking up the paintbrush, Paula returned to her work. She could not let her mother see how shaken she was by their conversation. Paula tried to determine how the furniture store accessed their information. It had to have come from the marriage license office, although she had changed the address.

Paula wondered if they gave the information to businesses. If the furniture store had the information, others must have it, too.

The paintbrush moved from the paint can to the wall repeatedly, under the directions of Paula's subconscious. She thought over and over about her mother's comment.

How can marrying someone you love and who loves you ruin your life? Michael and I have so much in common. We were meant to be together and now we will be, forever. Mom just doesn't understand and probably never will. Just because her marriage failed doesn't mean mine will. Michael is nothing like my dad and I'm not like my mother. We were right not to tell anyone about getting married. I will prove her wrong about ruining my life. We are going to finish college, get good jobs, buy a nice house and then have some kids.

Michael startled Paula when he walked up beside her with a big smile. Paula looked around for her mother and spotted her at a table in the back talking with the air conditioning contractor. Her back was to them, so Clarice had not seen Michael, yet. Paula was relieved that she would have a chance to tell Michael what was going on.

"Well, hello. How's my favorite person today?"

"Am I glad to see you! We've got a small problem but I may have taken care of it." Paula smiled and acted like she and Michael were just talking casually.

"What's wrong?"

"Just keep smiling and act like nothing's wrong. A letter came to our house addressed to Mr. and Mrs. Michael Williams, She brought the letter to me here and asked if we were married."

Paula immediately saw the panic in Michael's eyes. Paula picked up the paint can and lid and walked away from Clarice. Their backs were to Clarice when Michael followed. She folded up the plastic sheet that was protecting the floor and started arranging her painting supplies along the wall.

"Don't worry yet. I think I handled it, but I had to lie. The letter was just from a furniture store. I told my mother that we entered a contest at the mall that was for married couples, trying to win a new car."

"Do you think she believed you?"

"I think so."

"Okay, but here comes your mother."

"Let me do the talking."

"That's fine with me. It's your mother."

"Hello, Michael."

"Hello, Ms. Hayes. Paula is doing a great job on the walls. I told her I'd be happy to help with the painting or anything else."

Paula was happy that Michael was making an effort to get along with her mother.

"Mom, I was just telling Michael about our mail. The contest must have been just a gimmick to get newlyweds on a mailing list."

"I hope we didn't worry you Ms. Hayes. We were just trying to win Paula a car."

Michael gave Clarice the smile that Paula had fallen in love with.

"Mom, you will probably get a lot of junk mail now. You can just throw it away. I'm going to stop painting for today. I need to go back to the dorm and change. I don't want us to get caught in the rush hour traffic but I'll be back tomorrow after lunch. Michael, I'm going to go wash my hands, if you want to go start the car." Paula said, afraid to leave Michael and her mother alone.

"Okay."

Michael started walking to the door and Clarice followed him.

"Michael, how is school going?"

Paula did not hear Michael's answer as she rushed to wash the paint from her hands. When she rubbed her hands together under the water, her heart skipped a beat. She had forgot about the tiny gold band on her wedding ring finger that she had worn all week to remind her of Michael. She found the ring, which she had bought her sophomore year out of a catalog, in the bottom of her jewelry box the night Michael dropped her off from their honeymoon and had not removed it since. She wondered if her mother had noticed it, as she slipped it off and put it in her pocket. They were going to have to be more careful.

The arid air greeted Paula when she walked out the door. Michael was waiting for her in the car and he did not look happy.

"Michael, I'm sorry. I didn't know they would give the information out. I thought it was confidential."

"Do you think she will call my mother?"

"I don't know. Do you want to cancel our plans? You can drop me at the dorm and go home."

Michael paused for a moment, then he backed the car out of the parking space.

"No. If she does call my mother, it's probably better if I'm not there. My mother will definitely need some time to calm down. Do you want to go to the motel first or to the dorm?"

"Can we pick up my things first. I want to take a shower at the motel."

"Sounds like a good idea. Can I join you?" Michael said with a mischievous grin.

"Of course. Are you okay?"

"I'm fine. Look, we're married now. It will be simpler if no one finds out until we can support ourselves. But if they find out, they'll just have to accept it. Besides, both of my parents like you. It will be a shock at first but they will eventually accept it. We were planning to transfer universities next year anyway. Now, they won't challenge our decision."

"Michael, I love you."

"I love you too, and I'm glad that you are my wife. Now let's forget about our parents for now. Do you want to stop and get something to eat first or pick up a pizza on the way back?"

The weekend passed quickly and Paula was up late Sunday night finishing her Calculus and Physics assignments. By Monday morning, she had stopped worrying about their parents finding out about them being married. Michael had called home Friday evening, after calling his roommate to make sure that his mother had not called looking for him. His mother seemed normal. They were both relieved that Clarice had believed their story. Otherwise, she would have called his mother, once more, to voice her concerns. Paula did not need that distraction. She was already struggling to keep up with her assignments as the intensity of the course load continued to increase.

Although she was initially disappointed, Paula was relieved when Michael called late Thursday to say that he wasn't coming home for the weekend. He was having problems with a computer program that was due Monday and he wasn't going to be able to work on it until after his classes on Friday. Paula assured him that she understood and had enough to keep her busy with two tests the following week and the painting for her mother.

Before classes had started, they planned on seeing each other every weekend. But as the realities of college life set in, they both secretly wondered if it would be possible.

Saturday morning Paula woke up early and went to the library after eating breakfast, giving Michael a wake-up call and calling Clarice to arrange a pickup time. Her mother mentioned that she had saved some mail for her. Paula knew it was probably more junk mail and didn't give it another thought.

She studied until it was almost time for Clarice to pick her up only taking a short break for lunch. As she walked back to her dorm, Paula decided to spend the night at home since she planned on painting Sunday too. She put her dirty clothes in a pillowcase, packed her overnight bag and threw several books into her backpack. Her mother drove up just as Paula was walking out of the dorm.

"Hi, Mom. I hope you don't mind me doing a couple of loads of wash."

"No, but there's a load still in the washer that you will need to dry. You look tired. How's school going?"

"Fine. It's just a lot of work. But I knew engineering wouldn't be easy. How are things going at the center? Did all the contractors finish?"

"Yes, but they needed to replace two of the air conditioning units which I hadn't planned for. I had to get a small business loan from the bank this week. Are you sure you are going to have enough time to do the painting? If you need to be studying, I'll understand. Lisa and your brother can probably finish it."

"I'm fine, Mom. I've been studying all day. Painting will give my brain a break. I brought my books. I'll study some more tonight."

"Are you hungry? We can stop and pick up something."

"I ate a late lunch. Maybe we can get something later or I can cook dinner. Dorm food just doesn't taste as good as home cooked."

"Why don't you drop me at the center and you can go home to start your washing and maybe take a nap?"

"That sounds like a good idea."

Paula opened the door to a quiet house. After putting her backpack and overnight bag in her room, she went to the kitchen and deposited her dirty clothes by the washer. She decided to start a load, so she would have something clean to sleep in. After moving the clothes from the washer to the dryer, Paula started her load of whites. She looked at her watch to determine how much time she had for a nap.

On the way to the bedroom, Paula noticed a large stack of mail on the dining room table and decided to separate her mail that was probably mixed in with the stack. To Paula's surprise, every envelope in the stack was addressed to Mr. and Mrs. Michael Williams. Paula was furious, wondering how many businesses had their information. She panicked when she realized how many people must know. It was bound to get back to Michael's parents. She took the stack of mail to the den and sat down on the couch to open their mail; her plan to take a nap was totally forgotten. The mail was from newspapers, insurance firms, hospitals and even baby stores.

After opening the last piece of mail, Paula was solaced by the fact that it had all come from businesses and nothing official. But then she realized that she had not received their marriage certificate. If it were mailed home, her mother would definitely know the truth. She needed to call the marriage license office to confirm the address where the certificate would be sent. But the call would have to wait until Monday since the office was closed on Saturday.

Before leaving on Sunday, Paula asked her mother to throw away any more mail that came addressed to Mrs. Michael Williams.

As soon as she could Monday morning, Paula called the marriage license office. It took almost thirty minutes before she talked to someone at the county office that could help her. And another five minutes to find out that the license had been sent to her school address but returned by the school because the post office box was not registered to a "Mr. and Mrs. Michael Williams". Paula asked the clerk to hold the certificate and arranged to pick it up, not wanting to take another chance with something so important.

Before hanging up, Paula asked the clerk about all the mail she was receiving. The clerk informed Paula that marriage license information is public record, accessible by anyone. Paula wondered if her mother knew this. The clerk checked her record and confirmed that it still had her home address, which could only be changed in person. Paula knew that she needed to get the record changed as soon as possible.

Tuesday night, Paula studied in the library later than usual. She had not been able to study as much as she needed to over the weekend and she was beginning to worry about her Physics test in the morning. Even thought she had Physics in high school and the material was basically the same, she failed both of the practice tests she had for review.

In college, Physics tests were multiple choice to expedite grading. But with multiple choice, the answer was either right or wrong; there was no partial credit. Paula made a lot of little mistakes, like misplacing a decimal point or forgetting to change a number from negative to positive that resulted in the wrong answer.

Walking back to the dorm, Paula thought it was going to take a miracle for her to pass the test and knew that it was going to be a late night cramming. But she needed a snack to replenish her brainpower before she resumed studying. A few minutes after Paula returned to her room, Gail walked in from taking a shower.

"Your mother called while you were at the library. She wants you to call her back as soon as you can."

Paula decided to call her mother while she ate a snack. She sat down at her desk with a pack of vanilla cream sandwich cookies and called home. Her mother answered on the first ring forcing Paula to quickly swallow the bite of cookie.

"Hi, Mom. Gail said you called while I was at the library and wanted me to call you back."

"Paula, you got a letter from the social security office today addressed to Mrs. Michael Williams. I was getting ready to throw it away and decided to make sure it wasn't important."

Paula felt the energy drain from her body. She put her head down on her desk. As if reading Paula's mind, Gail whispered to her that she was going down the hall to study. Paula did not know what to say to Clarice so she said nothing.

"It had a form for you to change your name . . . PAULA, are you and Michael married? AND DON'T LIE TO ME!"

"Yes ma'am, we are."

Before Paula could say anything else, Clarice hung up.

Paula quickly redialed her mother's number. She had to stop her. The line was busy. Paula wondered if she was talking to Michael's mother and started to panic. She had to talk to her mother and beg her not to tell Michael's parents. Paula dialed home again and got another busy signal. Knowing that she couldn't wait, Paula dialed Lisa's number. After three rings, Lisa answered the phone.

"Lisa, I need to talk to Mom. It's important."

"Paula, she doesn't want to talk to you."

"She has to. Please go get her."

"Paula, this is a shock to her. I think she needs some time. Try calling back tomorrow. I don't know why you and Michael got married but it's your life and he is a nice fellow. Don't worry what other people think. Remember that."

"Thanks. Bye."

Paula knew that tomorrow would be too late, if it wasn't already. She didn't know what else to do. Reluctantly, she picked up the phone and dialed Michael's number. He needed to be prepared when his mother called him.

The ringing startled Michael, who had fallen asleep while waiting to go back to the computer center.

"Hell-o."

Paula started crying into the phone; just hearing his voice opened the floodgate. She needed to be with him but she knew that it was too late.

"Michael, I'm sorry... I thought... you'd... still be up?"

The sobbing was blurring her words. It took Michael a few minutes to recognize her voice through the crying and when he did, he woke up completely.

"Paula, what's wrong. Are you okay?"

"Michael, I'm...so... sorry."

"Paula, calm down and tell me what's wrong."

Paula took several deep breaths to calm down and looked around the room for some tissues. Michael was sitting straight up in bed now, his heart racing. He knew something was very wrong and prayed that she was not hurt. After blowing her nose, Paula was able to calm down enough to be understood.

"Michael, Mom knows."

"How did she find out Paula?"

"I got a letter from the social security office addressed to Mrs. Michael Williams with a name change form . . . Michael, when she asked me if we were married, I couldn't lie again."

"Did she say that she was going to call my mother?"

"She didn't say anything. She just hung up the phone as soon as I said yes and when I called back, she wouldn't talk to me. Michael, I don't know what to do."

There was a long silence. Michael did not know what to do either, but he knew that Paula needed him.

"Paula, I'll be there as soon as I can. We'll go over and talk to her. It's going to be okay baby. Don't worry. We have each other and that's all that matters. We love each other and we just need to get her to understand that."

Paula felt better as soon as she hung up the phone. She went to the sink to wash her face. She didn't want Gail to return and see that she had been crying. The cool water on her face helped calm her. After washing her face, Paula looked in the mirror. Her eyes were still red, but that could be caused by too much studying.

The phone rang just as Paula was hanging up her washcloth. She wondered if it was her mother and hoped that Michael had not changed his mind about coming.

"Hi, Paula. I just got off the phone with our mother."

"Hello, Sheryl. I guess she told you Michael and I are married."

"Yes, she did but she didn't know when the baby is due."

"What baby?"

"Aren't you pregnant?"

"No! I am not pregnant. I have some sense. I've been on the pill for months."

"Then why did you two get married?"

"Because we love each other."

"Paula, that's no reason to get married. How long have you been married? Maybe it can be annulled."

"I don't want my marriage annulled. I love Michael and want to be his wife."

"Well, I'm glad you're not pregnant. Let me go call Mom and let her know you're not having a baby and dropping out of school. I'll call you tomorrow so we can talk."

"Thanks."

Paula hung up the phone.

So that's why Mom was so upset.

Michael called from the lobby. Paula was surprised he had gotten there so fast and knew that he must have sped. She grabbed her purse and left a note for Gail saying that she would be back later. Michael was waiting for Paula in the lounge that was dark except for the fuzzy glow radiating from the television.

He gave Paula a big hug as soon as he saw her and they walked out the dorm with their arms locked tightly around each other's waist. Neither said anything until they were in the privacy of the car that Michael had left double-parked.

"Michael, I know why Mom was so upset. She thought I was pregnant. Sheryl called after I talked to you to find out when the baby was due. She said she'd call Mom and tell her that there's no baby."

Michael started the car and then looked at Paula.

"Then maybe it won't be so bad. Now you're sure there's no baby."

"I'm positive."

"Then don't worry. Remember, we are in this together."

"Michael, Sheryl didn't understand why we got married if I wasn't pregnant. Do you think Mom will?"

"We'll make her understand. Look Paula, I married you because I love you and couldn't imagine my life without you. What would they rather us do? Sleep together without being married. Paula, we did the right thing. Our parents will just have to understand."

Paula was concerned about something else that Sheryl had said.

"Michael, do you think they'll make us get the marriage annulled?"

"Do you want our marriage annulled, Paula?"

"No."

"And neither do I. We are adults. They can't make us do anything."

The traffic was extremely light so they were at her house quickly. Paula looked at the watch that had started it all; it was almost eleven o'clock.

"Michael, maybe it's too late. Let's just wait."

"Look, Paula. I drove all the way down here. You're upset and it's not going to get better until we talk to her. I know she is still awake. Do you still have your house key?"

"Yes. What are you going to say?"

"I'm not sure."

Michael gave Paula a kiss and got out of the car. Paula took a deep breath before getting out of the car and opening the door with her key. Michael followed Paula in. The television was on in the den. They walked in expecting to find Clarice. Her brother, Eric, was stretched out on the couch watching television. He sat up when he saw Michael with Paula.

"Hey, I hear congratulations are in order."

"Thanks. Where's Mom?"

"I think she's in her room looking at television. Do you want me to get her for you?"

"Yes, please."

Eric left the room. Michael held Paula's hand tightly.

"Paula, everything is going to be alright. I promise you. Just trust me."

"Michael, I have trusted you with my life."

"I know and I will not let you down."

They stood in the den and waited.

"Tell them they can leave. I don't have anything to say to them."

Clarice's voice permeated the house. Paula looked at Michael and tears started to roll down her cheek.

"Paula, don't let her make you cry."

"Come on, Michael. Let's just leave. It's no use."

"No, she is going to talk to us!"

Michael released her hand and walked into the living room.

"Ms. Hayes, I would appreciate it if you would give us a chance to explain."

Her mother came to the doorway in her robe.

"What's there to explain? How Paula has thrown her life away?"

"Mother, I have not thrown my life away. I'm not pregnant and we both are in college. Please explain to me how that is throwing my life away."

Paula was so upset that she didn't even realize she was screaming. Her mother did not respond. Michael walked over and put his arms around Paula and held her for a brief minute.

"Baby, calm down."

Clarice could not stand the sight of him touching her daughter. She went into the kitchen.

"Michael, it's no use. Let's just go."

Michael led Paula to a chair at the dining room table and pulled it out for her.

"Sit here for a minute. I'm going to talk to her, but I need you to stop crying. Okay?"

Paula nodded like a little girl and dried her tears on her sleeve. Michael kissed Paula's cheek and walked into the kitchen. Paula looked at the letter on the table in front of her. It was the letter from the social security office with a name change form attached.   Paula stopped crying so she could hear the conversation in the kitchen.

"Ms. Hayes, I wish you would give us a chance to explain."

"Michael, there is nothing to explain. She made her decision, now she's going to have to live with it."

"Ms. Hayes. Paula and I love each other very much. I'd never do anything to hurt her."

"The next thing you know, she'll be pregnant and dropping out of school, just like her sister."

"Ms. Hayes. Paula is on the pill. We are not going to have any children until we are ready. And I am personally going to make sure that Paula finishes college. We both know the importance of a college degree. Next year, we are going to transfer to the University and move into married student housing. Ms. Hayes, you have a very smart daughter. She is not throwing her life away. We just wanted to do what was right."

"Was it right for you to sneak off and get married?"

"Ms. Hayes we thought it was our decision. We are adults. And you already made it clear that you didn't even want us dating. I told Paula about your call. I thought she had a right to know."

"I wanted so much more for her. Now she can't be a debutante or have a big wedding."

Paula had tried to stay out of the conversation but when she heard this she went into the kitchen and stood next to Michael.

"And what about what I want or do you even care? I never wanted to be a debutante or to have a big wedding. Michael is the only person who has ever cared about what I want. That was pretty clear when I came home to an empty house after graduation.   You should be happy that I found someone to love me. Come on Michael, let's go. I have a test in the morning."

"Okay, Paula. Ms. Hayes, I love your daughter very much. I hope you'll accept our marriage. It will mean a lot to both of us."

He started to walk out of the kitchen and then stopped in the doorway and turned to face Clarice.

"My parents don't know about our marriage and I'd appreciate it if you didn't tell them. We would still like to keep this secret for a while so we don't hurt anyone else."

"It's not my place to tell your parents."

"Thank you, Ms Hayes. Good night."

"Do you think she'll call your mother?" Paula asked as they walked to the car, concerned for Michael.

"I don't know."

"Michael, she didn't even say good-bye. If she wants to be like that, I don't care if I ever talk to her again."

"You don't mean that. Paula, don't stoop to that level. Will you do something for me?"

"You know I'll do anything for you."

"I want you to finish painting the walls for your mother and then keep calling her as usual. It's just going to take her some time to accept our marriage. I don't want to be responsible for coming between the two of you. Can you do that for me?"

"Yes ... I love you, Michael. Thanks for coming home."

"I love you, too."

Michael looked at his watch.

"Are you going to be okay, if I just drop you off? I need to get back and finish that program. It's due in the morning."

"As long as I have you, I'll be fine. I'm sorry I drug you down here so late for my problem."

"It's our problem. Remember, we are in this together, until death due us part."

Chapter 17

Michael rolled over and was awakened by the touch of Paula's warm body. For a brief moment, he had to think about where he was. As he slowly looked around the room, he felt remorseful. This was not what he wanted for them, but it was all that they had for now. Michael was confident that one day they would share the life that they had talked about so often. He propped his head on his elbow so he could watch her. She was sleeping so peacefully and looked so vulnerable curled up on her side like a baby. It was his responsibility now to protect her from any more pain. He was thankful that a major source of her pain had finally been eliminated.

Clarice had met Paula half way. It had taken a month, but Paula had finished the wall and called her mother every few days to see how she was doing. Initially, she was cold and had very little to say, which hurt Paula deeply. She would call Michael crying after each call. But one day Clarice talked to her and even told her about a friend who was willing to hire Paula and Michael part-time on the weekends so they could earn some money and still be together. He had never seen Paula happier than when she told him the news.

Just watching her and thinking about how much he loved her started a wave of desire but he did not want to disturb her. He was thinking about going to take a shower, when Paula opened her eyes and smiled up at him.

"Good morning."

"Good morning to you too, sleepy head. I was wondering if you were ever going to wake up." Michael said as he gently touched her face.

"Have you been awake long?"

Paula stretched her long body and turned over to look at the clock on the dresser. It was almost seven-thirty. They still had plenty of time to make it to church.

"No, not long. I was thinking about whether to jump your bones or to go take a cold shower."

"Michael, will you ever get enough?"

"Of you, never. That's why I married you."

"Well, I don't want to be accused of sending my husband to a cold shower. Let me go brush my teeth."

Michael grabbed her arm and pulled her back into bed just as her feet were about to touch the floor.

"Oh, no you don't. If I have morning breath, so will you."

Paula let out a giggle as she retreated back into his arms under the cover. Within a few minutes, their bodies were free of clothing and the rest of the world was forgotten. Michael rolled on top of Paula, thrusting to his own internal rhythm, which Paula had learned. As each movement became more intense, Paula knew it would not be long, so she listened carefully for the cherished sounds of his pleasure.

Suddenly the bedroom door flew open. Paula looked towards the door terrified that it was her niece. Her body froze as she looked into her mother's eyes. Both mother and daughter stared in disbelief. Paula quickly pushed Michael, who had not heard the door open, off of her. He was just about to protest when he saw her standing in the doorway.

"I'm sorry." Clarice said and slowly closed the door.

Paula and Michael laid in silence while Clarice sat at the dining room table. She was just trying to wake them up so they could go to church before work. It had not crossed her mind that they would be...

Paula could not believe that her mother had walked in the room without knocking. It was her house, but knocking on a closed door was a common courtesy. Finally, Michael spoke.

"Paula, did she knock?"

"No."

Paula continued to stare blankly at the ceiling.

"Paula, we're married. We were not doing anything wrong. She was wrong to walk in without knocking."

"I know, but why does it feel like we are the ones who were wrong. How can I look at her again without being embarrassed?"

"Paula, she had to know when she offered us a place to stay on the weekends that we'd be sleeping together as husband and wife. She is not going to hold it against you. She did apologize."

"Michael, I can't go out there and face her."

"Paula, it's embarrassing but it will be okay."

"That's easy for you to say. It wasn't your mother."

"You are making too much of this. Think of it this way, I bet she won't open that door again without knocking." Michael grinned.

"You're crazy."

"I know; that's why you love me. Now where were we before being so rudely interrupted."

"You're crazy. I recommend that you go take that shower now."

While Paula was taking her shower, she re-lived the moment over and over again. She felt sick. Her mother had gone out of her way to help them and this was how they repaid her. It was Clarice's house and she would respect it. By the time she got dressed, Paula knew what she must do, but wasn't sure she'd be able to convince Michael of it. She rehearsed the speech several times in her head. She would just apologize to her mother and promise her it would never happen again. She and Michael would just have to satisfy their sexual needs elsewhere. Clarice's house was off limits.

Paula went into the kitchen and saw her mother refilling her coffee cup. She took a deep breath.

"Mom, I'm sorry. I'll understand if you don't want us to stay here anymore."

"Paula, I offered you a room here because it didn't make since for you to be wasting your money staying in motels. I'm the one who should apologize. I thought you both were asleep and I didn't want you to miss mass. You and Michael deserve your privacy. It will not happen again."

"Thanks, Mom." Paula walked over and hugged her mother.

"Where's Michael?"

"He's taking a shower."

"Paula, I know it's none of my business but has Michael told his parents about the marriage?"

"No."

"What's he waiting for?"

"He's afraid if his father finds out, he won't pay his tuition."

"Paula, if Michael really loved you, he wouldn't keep your marriage a secret. He's acting as if he's ashamed of you. You don't even have a ring. Paula, you deserve more than this."

"Mom, I'll have a wedding ring one day, when we can afford it. Michael does love me. We just can't take the chance that his father won't understand. Michael didn't get a full scholarship, like I did. He can't tell his parents until after his spring tuition has been paid. Next year, we will be able to qualify as independents for financial aid. If they cut him off, it won't matter. Mom, it would be too hard to catch up if Michael had to sit out a semester. And if he didn't graduate, he'd never forgive me. I can't ask him to risk his future."

"I don't think Michael is giving his parents enough credit. They may be willing to help you, too."

Paula didn't say anything. What could she say?

"Paula, the holidays are coming soon and his family is going to expect him to spend it at home. He should tell them, so you can be together."

"I'll talk to him about it Mom, but I won't mind us being separated for the holidays. There'll be other holidays."

Michael was concerned about Paula being so quiet as they drove to work. She had only said a few words since they left the house. He hoped that she wasn't still upset about Clarice walking in on them. One day they would probably both laugh about it. Usually he could make her laugh but not today.

"Paula, don't worry about the incident this morning with your mother."

"I'm not worried about that. Mom and I talked about it and everything is fine."

"Then what's bothering you. You were fine until this morning. Are you worried about school?"

"I probably should be but that's not it."

"Then what's bothering you? I'm your husband and have a right to know. Are you pregnant."

"Will you stop asking me that? No, I'm not pregnant. If you really must know, I was just thinking about something my mother said."

Michael frowned. He knew it was too good to be true. Her mother was still determined to break them up. She had just pretended to accept their marriage until she could find a way to end it. He was glad to pull into the parking lot and put an end to their conversation.

The parking lot was empty. Michael looked at his watch. They were thirty minutes early since they came straight from church. Usually only a few people worked on Sundays. The one's that did were either college students like Michael and Paula or held full-time jobs doing the week somewhere else. The company was a job shop that repaired defective circuit boards. The work was not challenging, but the pay was good and the hours were perfect for their schedule. They only worked on Saturday and Sunday, removing faulty chips and soldering on new ones.

Michael was trapped. He was going to have to continue the conversation, at least until someone came and unlocked the building.

"And what did your mother say that has you so deep in thought?"

"She said that if you really loved me, you would not want to keep our marriage a secret."

"Paula, we've been through this before. You know I love you but I can't tell them yet. Do you want me to miss a semester until I can get a new financial aid package?"

"Michael, you know I don't but maybe you aren't giving your parents enough credit. Look how my mother is handling it. Initially, she was upset but now she is doing everything she can to help us. She found us these jobs and even rearranged the house so we could have a place to stay on the weekends. Your parents seem like they would understand that we love each other. They were young when they got married."

"And look how it ended. That's why I don't think my dad will understand. They got married right out of high school because they had too. Paula, please don't make me have to choose between you and my education."

"I'm not asking you to do that. I'm sorry I brought it up. You do what you think is best. I won't mention it again."

Paula looked out the car window, wondering if her mother was right about Michael being ashamed of her. A chill traveled down her spine at the thought, which she quickly dismissed. Michael loved her. She just needed to trust that he knew what was best. After all, they were his parents.

The weekend supervisor and his wife parked their car next to Michael's car. Paula and Michael got out of the car without saying another word.

The weeks passed quickly, following the same pattern. Michael would pick Paula up on Friday and they would go to her house. They would study Friday night, work eight hours on Saturday and four hours on Sunday. As soon as their shift ended on Sunday, Michael would drop Paula off at the dorm and head back to school.

Paula was looking forward to the Thanksgiving break. They had decided not to work and enjoy the four days off. Both of them were concerned about their grades. Paula was worried that she was going to fail Physics and Calculus. She had a D average in both classes. They had been so concerned about Michael's college finances that Paula had not given thought to hers. But her academic advisor kindly pointed out that her scholarship was contingent on her maintaining at least a 2.75 grade point average. Paula knew that without the scholarship, she could not finance her education.

Michael picked Paula up the Wednesday before Thanksgiving, after her last class. This time he was only going to drop her off at home. Paula was concerned because Michael did not seem very happy to see her. She wondered if he had done poorly on his test. But she knew that whatever it was, she could help him forget about it. He carried her bag to the car and opened the door for her. She did not bring much with her. Everything she needed was already at home.

Michael was concerned, too. He didn't know how to tell her. She seemed so happy and he didn't want to upset her. Paula waited in vain for Michael to speak first but he just drove in silence.

"Did your grandmother get in okay?"

"Yes, she did."

"I told you that Thanksgiving dinner is at my sister's house. Do you want to meet us there?"

"Paula, my mother wants me to eat Thanksgiving dinner at home since my grandmother is here."

"Oh."

"She also wants me to spend some time with my family."

"...I thought I was part of your family or have you forgotten?"

"You are my family but my mother doesn't know that."

"Well, maybe she should." Paula whispered under her voice, continuing to look out the window.

"What did you say?"

Paula looked at Michael.

"I said, maybe your mother should know that I'm part of your family too."

"Paula, please."

"Please, what? Am I suppose to be happy that I can't have Thanksgiving dinner with my husband?"

"Paula, I didn't say we couldn't have dinner together. We just need to eat with my family."

"No thanks, Michael. I don't want to intrude."

"Paula, don't be silly. You wouldn't be intruding."

"Does your mother know I'll be coming for dinner?"

"No, but I'll ask her when I get home. She won't mind."

"Forget it, Michael. You eat dinner with your family and I'll eat dinner with mine. It's probably better that way anyhow."

"Paula, please don't be like this. I want us to be together on Thanksgiving. I love you."

"Well, apparently not enough."

Paula knew her words hurt Michael but she wanted him to hurt as much as she did. Her mother was right. As long as his family didn't know, they couldn't be together for the holidays.

They drove the rest of the way to her house in silence. Michael parked the car in front of the house and started to get out.

"Don't bother."

Paula got out the car and retrieved her overnight bag and backpack from the back seat.

"Paula, at least let me walk you in."

"You'd better go. Your family is probably waiting for you."

Paula slammed the door. Michael got out of the car and stood by the door, knowing that he had hurt her.

"I'll call you tonight."

Paula didn't even turn around to acknowledge him. Michael got back in the car and drove off. He knew that he would have to make this up to Paula. He just was not sure how.

Clarice was sitting in the den watching television when Paula came in. Even though Paula was feeling anti-social, she knew it would be rude not to speak. She walked into the den, stopping inside the doorway.

"Hi, Mom. I'm home."

"Hi, Paula. Is Michael with you?"

"No ma'am. He needed to get home. His grandmother's in town."

Clarice knew that Michael would not be spending the night this weekend. She also knew that the separation was going to be hard for her daughter.

"Is he coming to dinner tomorrow?"

"No, ma'am. He's eating dinner with HIS family."

Clarice could tell by her tone that this was a painful subject and decided not to push it further.

"If you're hungry, there are some leftovers in the refrigerator. I'm not going to cook until your Aunt Dorothy gets here."

"Since Michael isn't staying here, they can have our room. I'll sleep on the couch. I'm going to go lay down for a little while."

"Paula, are you okay?"

"I'm fine, Mom. I'm just tired from being in classes all day. If Michael calls, will you tell him that I'll call him later."

Paula felt strange being at home without Michael and she already missed him. She walked into their room and before she could even put down her things, tears blurred her eyes. She quickly shut the door and fell across their bed, crying softly. She tried desperately to suppress the sobs so her mother would not hear her. The last thing she wanted to hear was – I told you so. Paula cried herself to sleep.

Clarice heard her crying when she walked past the door and wanted to comfort her, but she didn't know how.

The commotion of her aunt arriving interrupted Paula's slumber. Darkness had filled the room, which matched her mood. Paula closed the blinds and turned on the light. It was almost eight o'clock. Thoughts of Michael rushed into her mind as she sat on their bed. She wondered if he had called as she stood up and removed the sheets.

Autumn was screaming is the background, so Paula decided to go check on her. She was concerned about how Lisa was going to react to seeing the baby that she had given away. This was going to be the first time that she saw her, since the birth seven months earlier. Paula emerged from their room with the sheets bundled in her arms and went into the living room. Lisa was sitting on the couch, holding the daughter that she had given away, and Autumn was screaming because she wanted to hold the baby too. Paula went into the kitchen to put the sheets in the washing machine. Her mother and aunt were inspecting the turkey. Paula spoke to her aunt and then proceeded to start the wash.

"Paula, Michael called. I told him you were sleep. He wants you to call him."

"Thanks, Mom."

"Paula, how's school going?" Her aunt asked.

"It's fine."

Paula was polite but she was still upset with her aunt for pressuring Lisa into the adoption.

"Mom, I'll put some clean sheets on the bed after I call Michael."

Paula walked through her old room, which now belonged to Eric, to use Lisa's phone in private. She picked up the phone and sat down on the bean bag chair in the center of the room. Michael answered on the first ring.

"Hello."

"Hi. Mom said you wanted me to call."

"Are you speaking to me now?"

"I didn't know I wasn't."

"When your mother said you were sleep, I thought you just didn't want to talk."

"I really was sleep and just woke up. It's been a stressful day. How's your family?"

"I don't know. You tell me. How are you?"

"You know what I mean; your REAL family. Was your grandmother happy to see you?"

"Yes, and she asked about you. Paula, I'm sorry. I didn't want to hurt you."

Paula didn't say anything. All she could do was stare at the brown carpeting on the floor.

"Are you still there?"

"Yes, I'm still here. Michael, I didn't think it would hurt this much. It's different during the week. We both have our classes and homework to keep us busy, but this is a holiday. Holidays are suppose to be spent with the ones you love. I miss you already."

"I know Paula. I miss you, too."

"What are we going to do?"

Paula could feel the tears starting to form again but this time she wasn't going to let herself cry.

"I don't know...What time is your family eating dinner?"

"Probably around three."

"Would you mind if I came over as soon as we finish dinner?"

"I don't mind but what about your mother?"

"Leave that to me. Do you realize that next week is our anniversary?"

Paula thought Michael was referring to their wedding anniversary.

"Are we going to start celebrating every month?"

"I was talking about the anniversary of when we met. It was one year ago, next week. Do you remember the party? You were out celebrating your eighteenth birthday and I knew I wanted to meet you the minute I saw you."

331

"What a difference a year can make? You've got a good memory. Are you sorry that you asked me to dance?"

"No. I'd do it all over again. I was just thinking about what to get you for our anniversary and your birthday. What do you want?"

"YOU."

"You already have me, but I do have a present in mind that I think you will like... I'm going to tell my parents about us."

"Michael, are you serious? Don't just do this for me."

Paula wanted to jump up and dance.

"I'm very serious. I don't want us to have to spend Christmas apart. Wherever we spend it, we will be together."

"When are you going to tell them?"

"I want to wait until after Thanksgiving since I know that they won't be too happy. Maybe I'll tell them next weekend. But I promise you that we will spend Christmas together. Now, am I forgiven?"

"For what?" Paula had a big smile on her face.

"I'm really looking forward to tomorrow. I get to eat two dinners."

"You're really coming to dinner?"

"Of course. You must not know me very well."

Chapter 18

Friday afternoon, the walk back from class had been invigorating. It was a beautiful winter day with a crisp blue sky and golden sunshine. Paula sat at her desk and gazed out the window while she waited for Michael's call to let her know what time he was coming. He had been struggling all week with a computer program and didn't know what time he would be able to leave.

She was looking forward to seeing Michael after their first full week of classes following the Christmas break. After thirty minutes of day dreaming, Paula decided to study while she waited - something she needed to do much more of this semester. Her first semester grade point average was barely within the requirement for her scholarship, but now that Michael's mother knew about them, Paula was confident that things would get easier.

Michael kept his promise and told his mother about their marriage the weekend after Thanksgiving. As expected, she was not pleased and agreed with Michael that it was indeed a secret to be kept from his father. Although she didn't welcome Paula into their family with open arms, she allowed them to spend Christmas together at their house. Paula smiled at the thought of them trying to share Michael's little bed in his cramped bedroom. Michael had finally been relegated to the floor halfway through the night.

Finally the phone rang.

"Hello."

"Hi, baby. How are you doing?"

"Great. I was trying to do some studying before you got here. What time are you coming?"

"That's why I'm calling. Would you be too disappointed if I didn't come home this weekend?"

"Yes, but I guess I can survive. Are you still having problems with that program?"

"Yes, and there's a fraternity rush party that I want to attend."

"I thought you were going to wait and pledge next fall. That way, we'd be pledging at the same time."

"Honey, I just want to get some information. I was talking to some of the brothers and they said it's better to pledge in the spring."

"I was looking forward to seeing you but I guess I'll survive. Don't you fool around with any of those fraternity sweethearts."

Michael smiled. There was certainly an abundance of beautiful women on campus and he had already turned down some very tempting offers, but he had what he wanted.

"I'm a married man."

"Make sure you don't forget that. Hell is pretty hot."

"Don't you get any ideas about those jocks either. Are you going home or staying at the dorm?"

"I think I'll stay here tonight and go home in the morning. It's no fun being at home without you, but I need a car to go to work."

"You're going to work without me?"

"I need the money. After buying my books, I'm totally broke and I still have one more book to buy."

"Will you tell them that I won't be working any this weekend?"

"Sure. I'd better call Mom, so she won't be expecting us."

"Give me a call later. I love you."

"I love you, too."

Paula looked out the window again, disappointed that she wouldn't be able to see Michael. Suddenly, the day didn't seem so beautiful as she debated whether to call her mother before or after a nap.

"Hi, Mom."

"Hello, Paula. I was just about to go back to the center. Aerobics starts in fifteen minutes. What time will you and Michael get here?"

"Michael's not coming home this weekend. He needs to spend some extra time in the computer center. Do you think Eric will be using the car this weekend? I need a way to get to work?"

"I don't think so. It's been parked all week because he doesn't have any money for gas and I refuse to give him another penny. He needs to get a job but he says a job will interfere with his workout schedule. Do you need me to come and pick you up tonight?"

"No thanks, I'm going to study at the library tonight. Can I give you a call in the morning? I may be able to get a ride home with Angela."

"Okay. I need to open the building early in the morning. If you can't get me here, call the center."

"Thanks, Mom."

Paula looked at her Calculus homework and the half-written English assignment waiting for her attention. She set her alarm clock for five-thirty, closed the blinds and crawled into bed.

Breathing rapidly and perspiring, Paula sat up in bed and looked at the clock, confused by the darkness of the room. Her brief slumber had been interrupted by a dream about her and Michael that seemed so realistic it forced her to consciousness. They were at an amusement park having a wonderful time and decided to go in the fun house attraction. But the fun house changed into a haunted house and they became separated by the crowd. Monsters were chasing Paula as she ran searching for Michael. She kept screaming his name but could not find him. Paula was thankful that it was just a dream. The buzzing of her alarm startled her.

The week was passing quickly for Paula. After two weeks apart, she was really looking forward to seeing Michael. They had talked very little during the week. He was always at or on his way to the computer center every time Paula called.

Paula had spent all day Thursday in the library getting her assignments done, so she could have the weekend free. She had just walked in from dinner when the phone rang.

"Hello."

"Hi, Paula . . . Did I catch you at a bad time?"

"No, your timing is perfect. I just walked in the door from dinner. How's your day been?"

"Okay, but I'm beginning to feel like I live in the computer center."

"Are you still working on that program?"

"Yes."

Paula thought that Michael sounded tense.

"That's what you get for majoring in computer science. You should switch to engineering."

"I like my major. It just takes so much time trying to find all the problems in a program."

"You're still coming home this weekend, aren't you?"

"...Paula, that's why I'm calling . . . I'm not coming."

"Come on Michael, not again. We haven't seen each other in two weeks."

"I know but I think I should stay here."

Paula sat down on the edge of her bed and felt guilty for being upset. Knowing that she needed to be a supportive wife, Paula had an idea that she thought would solve both of their problems.

"Michael, it's okay if you can't come home this weekend. I can come there. I haven't been there in a while and I can't stand not seeing you another weekend. I'll even put up with a male dorm to see you. Mom will probably let me borrow her car."

"Paula, that's probably not a good idea . . . I don't know how to tell you this . . . I thought about driving down . . . Paula, I think we should get a divorce."

"Come on, Michael. You shouldn't even joke about that. If you need to stay there and study, I'll understand."

"Paula, I'm not joking. I think we made a mistake getting married and I'd like a divorce."

The coldness in Michael's voice unnerved her. All she could do was stare at the cheap gold ring on her finger.

"Michael, you can't be serious!"

"Paula, I am very serious. I thought about it all week."

He's found someone else. It is the only explanation that makes sense. Even if it hurts more, you have to know the truth.

"Is there someone else, Michael?"

"No, Paula. I swear that there's no one else."

"Then why, Michael? Why?"

Paula moved from the bed to the chair at her desk, unable to believe what she was hearing. Her vision started to blur as tears formed.

"Paula, it just isn't working. I can't do what I want to do and I'm always rushing between here and there. My mother is right. We're too young. I should be enjoying my college years."

So that was it. His mother was behind this sudden quest for freedom. Why didn't he at least have the decency to tell me in person?

"Oh, I didn't realize I was such a burden. I wish you had said something before we got married."

"I didn't think it would be like this."

"Like what Michael? Are you that unhappy? I thought marriage was supposed to be forever. Not something you get out of because it's not what you expected. Didn't our wedding vows mean anything to you? What about till death do us part?"

"Paula, I just think that if we don't end it now, things are going to get worse. My grades last semester were bad. My father said that if my grades don't improve this semester, he's not going to pay for any more tuition. I'm going to start pledging next week and between that and classes, we're not going to be able to see each other very much."

"So now I rank third in your life or is it fourth behind your real family? Well, thanks for letting me know where I stand. Your mother wasn't the only one who was right. My mother was right too . . . How could I have been so stupid?"

"Paula, don't be like this. I still love you very much. I just don't want to be married right now."

"How am I suppose to act? I'm sorry but your little announcement caught me by surprise. Next you'll be saying you still want to be friends."

Paula was crying uncontrollably now as the reality of what was happening came into clear view.

"Michael, I trusted you... This marriage was your idea in the first place. I did not force you to marry me. Look, I've got to go or do you have any more surprises for me?"

"Paula, are you going to be okay? Do you want me to come down?"

"Oh, now you are ready to come down. For what? You've made it very clear how you feel or don't feel. Michael, right now, you are the last person in the world I want to see."

Paula slammed the receiver down.

Michael was concerned. He knew it would have been better to tell her in person, but he was afraid he wouldn't be able to do it face to face. He didn't want to hurt her but there was no other way. His father had been very clear about his expectations and the consequences, and he wanted to pledge. But their love was strong enough to withstand this. He didn't want to lose Paula but they could not have a real marriage now. He knew she would be hurt, but eventually she would realize that he was right.

"Oh God, what am I going to do now?"

The stack of books on the corner of the desk flew effortlessly across the room, fueled by her anger. Next, Paula took the cheap gold ring off her finger and hurled it and looked around for something else to throw - anything to make her feel better. She stood up and paced around the room.

Paula, this does not make sense. Just two weeks ago, we were happy. His feelings could not have changed that quickly. Why is he doing this? He really doesn't mean this. He's going to call back. There is no way he wants a divorce. He loves you as much as you love him. Maybe his mother is pressuring him. . . But what if he really means it?

The oversized pillow cushioned her fall onto the bed. Paula curled up in a ball, hugging the pillow tightly while she cried. The meal she had just eaten churned in her stomach, threatening to come back up. Her head was spinning and the more she cried, the sicker she felt. Paula knew that she needed to pull herself together. She strained to see the clock on her desk through the tears. She sat up on the bed, picked up the oversized blue pillow and hurled it as hard as she could at the door.

It took her remaining strength, to stand up, gather the books that were sprawled across the floor and assemble the things she needed for a shower. She didn't want Gail to walk in and see her like this. A shower would give her time to cry it all out of her system and then she would be able to think clearly.

Paula stayed in the shower for almost an hour, allowing her tears to be washed away by the warm water as she propped herself against the wall, crying until no more tears would flow. Returning to the room, she read the note from Gail lying on her desk; she was spending the night at her boyfriend's apartment. Paula was thankful for some time alone to pull herself together. She put on some warm sweats and propped herself against her oversized pillow at the foot of her bed. Her mind was fuzzy and she felt like she was in a trance.

Paula, maybe this is just a bad dream. If you are dreaming, you won't feel any pain.

She pinched herself hard and flinched.

Dear God, please let Michael call and say it was a mistake. He can't really mean it.

Paula stared at the phone, willing it to ring. Several times, she picked up the phone and started to dial his number. But pride stopped her from calling him and begging him to reconsider.

The phone rang. Paula took a deep breath. The last thing she wanted him to know was that she had been crying ever since they had talked.

I knew he really didn't mean it.

"Hello."

"Hi, Paula. How are you doing?"

It was the last person she wanted to talk to at the moment.

"I'm fine, Mom but I'm busy right now. Can I call you back tomorrow?"

"I was sitting on the couch watching television when I had the strangest sensation to call you. Is everything okay?"

"Yes."

"Is Michael coming home this weekend?"

The question was more than Paula could bear, sending a fresh wave of tears down her cheeks. A lump formed in her throat.

"Paula, are you still there?"

"Yes, ma'am. I'm sorry but I really need to call you back later."

Paula tried unsuccessfully to hide the quivering in her voice.

"Paula, I knew something was wrong. I could feel it. Are you okay?"

"I'm fine, Mom."

"Then what is it? Is it Michael?"

"Mom, he just called and said he wants a divorce."

There was silence at both ends. Clarice closed her eyes, knowing all too well what her daughter was going through. She had felt the same pain of realizing that someone you loved didn't love you.

"Paula, are you going to be okay. I can come pick you up. You really shouldn't be alone."

"No, Mom. I'll be fine. Tomorrow's my heavy class day. I can't afford to get behind this semester. I just barely made the minimum grade requirement last semester. Now more than ever, I can't risk my scholarship. I'll be okay. It was just a shock. I thought everything would be okay since his mother knew."

"Do you think he's found someone else?"

"NO, MOM! At least, that's what he said. He just doesn't think he can keep his grades up, pledge and be married at the same time."

Paula cringed and braced herself for the- I told you so speech.

"Paula, I'm so sorry."

"That's okay. I guess you were right about me throwing my life away on him."

"Paula, you haven't thrown your life away. You're still young, not like I was. I had six children when your father told me he wanted a divorce. Are you sure you don't want me to pick you up?"

"I'm sure, besides I have the room to myself. Gail is spending the night with a friend."

"I'm worried about you being alone."

"Mom, don't worry. I was just about to study to keep my mind occupied."

"Okay, baby. You call if you need anything."

"Okay, Mom. Thanks."

Paula knew she wouldn't be able to concentrate on anything but she didn't want her mother worrying about her. Feeling a little better after talking to her mother, Paula sat at her desk and looked at the pictures of her and Michael that covered her bulletin board. Snapshots, taken at school events, surrounded their prom pictures and the cards he had sent her. She looked at the pictures, waiting for them to explain what had gone wrong. A faint hope that their relationship really wasn't over kept her from taking it all down and burning them.

Not yet!

The phone interrupted Paula's thoughts. This time it had to be Michael. Her mother would not call her back so soon, even though she did expect another call from her before the end of the night. Paula slowly got up from the desk and collapsed across the bed before picking up the phone that was sitting on the floor.

"Hello."

"Hello there. I just got off the phone with Mother."

"Hi, Sheryl. I guess she told you."

"Yes. She's worried that you'll do something stupid. I told her not to worry; you are too smart for that."

"What does Mom do? Call you every time I have a problem."

"Probably. So how are you really?"

"Okay. I guess I'm still in denial, hoping he'll call back and say it was a mistake."

"Do you think that will happen?"

"I guess not but it's all I have to hold on to for now. Did Mom tell you that he is pledging?"

"Yes! If he's so worried about his grades, that's the last thing he should do."

"I know but pledging is important and obviously I'm not."

"Well it's his loss. I didn't think that he was good enough for you anyway. Paula, you are beautiful and smart. You can do much better than him. But I bet he'll come crawling back. I just hope you'll tell him where he can go."

"I'll keep that in mind. Now will you please go tell our mother that I am not going to kill myself."

Paula could hear her nephew crying in the background.

"Okay. I'd better go see what's wrong. Call me if you need anything? Do you want to go to lunch tomorrow? I'll pick you up?"

"No, that's okay. I was thinking about going home for the weekend. I need to work."

"Okay, but if you change your mind, give me a call at work. I'm always looking for an excuse to get away from the office and lunch will be a lot cheaper than shopping."

"You'd better go call Mom. I'm sure she's waiting by the phone. Honestly, I'll be okay. I'll talk to you later."

Paula hung up the phone and looked at the clock on her desk. It was almost nine o'clock. She rolled over on her back and looked up at the white ceiling tiles. Tears formed puddles in the corner of her eyes until they overflowed and raced down her cheeks to her ears. She rolled onto her side and put her pillow over her head and tried to cry the pain away. She was dry heaving when the phone rang again and had to take several deep breaths to calm down.

344

"Dear God, please let this be Michael. Please let it be Michael."

"Hello."

"Hello, there."

It took Paula a second to recognize the voice. It was a man, but it was not Michael.

"Hi, Bruce."

"I just got off the phone with your mother and..."

Paula was angry and didn't even let Bruce finish his sentence.

"What is she doing? Calling everyone she knows to spread the good news."

"Paula, she is just worried about you and thought I might be able to help."

"Bruce, I really do appreciate the call but I don't think anyone can help. I made a mistake and now I'm paying the price. It's my problem and I can handle it."

"Sometimes, talking about your feelings can help."

"Maybe later. I think that I have talked about this enough for tonight. I don't think he really means it anyway. He's just under a lot of pressure at school. Bruce, I'm sorry that Mom bothered you with this."

"Paula, it's not a bother. You have a lot of people that care about you. If you need to talk to someone, just call. I'm usually up late, you won't disturb me and Adrienne is here, if you'd prefer to talk to her."

"Thanks Bruce but I'll be fine. Good night."

The only person that she thought really cared about her, had just informed her that he didn't. Paula turned on the television for a distraction, knowing that it would be impossible for her to concentrate on any of her work. Still hoping that he would call and tell her how much he still loved her, Paula climbed in bed under the covers with her clothes on.

For a brief second before she fell asleep, she thought it would have been better if Michael were dead.

Death would have been easier to deal with. Maybe.

Chapter 19

*D*ear Michael,
I'm sitting at my desk looking at our prom pictures. We seemed so happy then. It's hard to believe that the pictures were taken less than a year ago. It's been over a month since you called and asked for the divorce. I've waited for another call saying it was a mistake but now realize that it's just wishful thinking on my part. As hard as it is to accept, I know that you are serious. I found this valentine card in the bookstore and thought it says exactly how I feel. By now, you probably have someone else to celebrate Valentine's Day with. Michael, I loved you so much, it feels like a piece of me is missing. Everyone says that in time the pain will go away but it's hard for me to believe. You were the most important part of my life, but I know I can't force you to love me. You can have the freedom you want. I hope you will always remember how much I loved you.

Happy Valentine's Day
Your wife, Paula.

Paula carefully folded the letter and placed it inside the Valentine's card with two large interlocking hearts. She looked at the trash can sitting next to the desk.

Do I really want to send this to him? Maybe I should just forget about it. He doesn't care about me. He probably won't even open it. If he cared he would have sent me some flowers or at least a card... I need to do this. He needs to know.

All week, floral arrangements were sitting on the dorm director's counter, waiting for their recipients. Each day Paula anxiously checked her door hoping to find a note indicating that she had a delivery, just like she checked her mailbox. But by Friday, Paula accepted the fact that there would be no flowers or cards or reconciliation.

Paula put the bulging card in the envelope, slowly licked the flap and pressed it down. She laid the envelope on top of her backpack that was sitting on her bed and looked at the pictures on the bulletin board, knowing that it was finally time. She carefully removed the pushpins from the corners of her prom picture and laid it face down on her desk. It only took a minute to empty the bulletin board and get the scissors from the pencil can. The big pictures would be last.

She started with the snapshot that Michael's mother had taken at his graduation, the day that he had proposed. They had huge smiles that masked the pain of the incident at her house earlier. A deluge of tears flowed down her cheeks and dropped on the picture. Paula watched as the salty water blurred the color.

With two cuts of the scissors, the half with Paula fell to the desk. Paula repositioned the remaining part of the picture in her hand and carefully lined the scissors up with Michael's smile and cut. She purposefully cut until Michael's picture was a pile of shreds on the desk.

She was crying so hard that her chest and abdomen started to hurt. The expected relief eluded her. The pain just wouldn't stop. If anything, it intensified. Without the strength to cut anymore, she opened the lap drawer of her desk and slid in the remaining pictures, wondering if Michael had any idea what he had done to her life.

Functioning in a robotic state since the call, Paula managed to go to all of her classes but daydreamed through most of them. Now she was so behind that she would never catch up. Her dream of graduating from college was slipping away and what had started as a passing thought to get back at Michael now seemed like her only option to end the pain. Resolved in her decision, Paula washed her face and then dialed the number.

"Hello."

"Mom, I've changed my mind. I want to come home this weekend."

"What time do you want me to pick you up?"

"Is three too early? I don't want you to get stuck in the traffic."

"That's fine. I'm glad you're coming home."

"Me too, Mom. I'll see you later."

Paula picked up her jacket and the card and walked out the door. She passed Gail in the hall as she turned the corner but neither of them spoke. Everyone she had trusted had let her down. As she walked past the cafeteria, Paula remembered that she had not eaten all day. She stood in the doorway and looked around the cafeteria. There were very few people still eating. Paula decided that it was probably safe to go in. Her fragile state could not survive another barrage of stares, whispers and the resulting laughter. It had gone unnoticed before. But now she was tuned in.

She replayed the incident of her enlightenment over in her mind as she sat down at an empty table in the corner. It had happened a few weeks earlier.

Angela had invited Paula to study together in her room for their engineering test the week after Michael's big announcement. Paula thought that studying with someone else would help her concentrate, but it didn't. Angela picked up on Paula's distracted state and knew she needed someone to talk to.

"Paula are you okay?"

"I'm fine. I just need to do much better this semester."

"How did you do last semester?"

"Not very well. I just barely got the minimum GPA to keep our scholarship."

"Don't worry you'll probably do much better this semester."

"I don't know about that. My entire world is falling apart and there's not a lot that I can do about it."

Paula felt the tears welling up. She wanted to talk to someone other than a family member about what was going on in her life. She had thought about calling Rosalyn several times but was too embarrassed and she knew Taylor well enough to know her reaction to the news of her marriage and right now she did not want to hear it.

"Angela, I really need someone to talk to or I will probably go crazy. Michael and I got married at the end of the summer."

Paula looked through her tears at Angela and waited for a shocked reaction that never came.

"I know."

"You know! But how?"

"Gail told me and probably everyone else in the dorm."

Paula felt like a fool and now everyone else knew. She had trusted Gail to keep her secret. They had told her to explain why Paula was gone every weekend.

"When?"

"Early last semester. I thought you knew."

"Why didn't you say anything?"

"Because I thought if you wanted me to know, you would tell me yourself. But if I were you, I'd be very careful what you tell Gail in the future. She's not very discrete."

Paula closed her book and buried her head into her knees and cried. Angela walked over and sat on the bed next to her.

"Paula, it will be okay. So what if everyone knows you're married. It not any of their business."

"I wish that were my only problem. Michael called last week and said that he wants a divorce. I don't know what to do. I hurt so much that I can't concentrate on anything. If I lose this scholarship, I don't know what I'm going to do."

"Paula, I'm sorry... It hurts now but you'll make it through this. You just have to keep your faith and pray about it."

"I think God must be punishing me."

"Paula, God doesn't punish people. He helps them."

"I hope you are right because I need all the help I can get to survive this."

"You're going to survive. I'm here if you need someone to talk to."

Angela had been in the room when Gail was gossiping about Paula and Michael and speculating about trouble in paradise. Now she wished that she had spoken up and told them to mind their own business.

Paula looked down at her plate of half eaten food. There wasn't even comfort in food anymore; her dessert went untouched. She thought about Angela's words again but it was too late. No one could help her now. She knew what the gossip in the dorm was going to be Monday but she didn't care, hoping that some of them would feel guilty for contributing to it.

The lifeless person that walked towards the car sent a chill down Clarice's spine. She had never seen her daughter looking like this. The forlorn expression on her face was frightening. At that moment, Clarice wanted to strangle Michael for what he had done to her baby. She wondered if he even cared. If he did, he would have called to see how Paula was doing. She knew exactly what she would say to him now, if he dared to call her house. She decided at that moment that whatever it took, Michael was never going to get back into her daughter's life. Attempts to cheer her daughter up on the ride home were unsuccessful, but she had the entire weekend.

Paula went straight to her room, turned on the television and sat on the twin bed that she had slept on since she was ten. The same bed where Michael had kissed her and started them down this path. Eric did not waste any time moving back into his room since Paula and Michael no longer needed it. Paula sat on her bed and debated whether to do it tonight or tomorrow, finally deciding that Saturday night will be better! It would give her time to clean the house. Her mother would have enough to deal with. A clean house might make things a little easier. She decided to start with her room.

It took most of the night to clean her closet and organize her things, throwing out papers and items that were not important and boxing up the things that her mother might want.

As she looked through her photo album, she stopped at the picture of her and Shane and thought again about the kiss that had sealed the fate of that relationship.

I should have stayed with Shane. But it's too late now. I wondered if this is how Shane felt when I told him about Michael. Is this my punishment for the callous treatment that I gave Shane? How many times has Mom told me that you reap what you sow? I am definitely reaping what I sowed! I have been blaming Michael, but maybe the only person to blame is myself.

The album was closed quickly and placed in the box. Her life had been reduced to the contents of two boxes, neatly placed on the top shelf of her closet.

The cleaning resumed at a hastened pace to block the thoughts that were racing through her head. After putting clean sheets on her bed, Paula decided to clean the back bathroom so she could take a hot bath before bed. Autumn was spending the night with Karen and Lisa had gone out with friends. Paula had the back of the house to herself, so she turned on the stereo for company. Their station was playing a marathon of love songs; there was no escape.

As she cleaned the sink, the reflection in the mirror startled her. Wondering when the transformation had occurred, she stopped to study the stranger in the mirror. The eyes engulfed in dark circles, the ashy complexion, the chapped lips and the dirty hair, pulled back in a ponytail. Her exterior now matched her interior. Paula laid the rag on the edge of the sink and washed the cleanser from her hands. In the cabinet, behind the mirror was the answer to her problems.

A month earlier, while looking for some pain medicine, Paula saw Lisa's prescription of tranquilizers and had counted the pills out of curiosity, to see how many Lisa had taken. Paula had thought about those twenty-five tiny pills all week. A peaceful, everlasting sleep. Her heart raced as she opened the medicine cabinet. There it was! But when she picked up the bottle this time, it was empty.

How could Lisa do this to me! I needed those pills.

Paula panicked as she closed the cabinet door and sat down on the commode to weigh her options.

Electrocution in the bathtub will be too painful. Slitting my wrists is too messy, besides I'm afraid of needles. There are no guns in the house. Maybe a plastic bag tied over my head. No, I need some pills so that I can float away in my sleep. I don't want to be conscious of dying. Maybe one of Mom's prescriptions will work.

With renewed hope, Paula finished cleaning the rear bathroom and went to the front bathroom. She closed the door and turned on the faucet, for background noise. The cabinet door opened with a squeak. Starting with the bottom self, Paula read the label of each medicine bottle. Several were out of date, by several years. The cabinet was full of iron supplements, vitamins, laxatives and other over-the-counter drugs. The only pills that Paula thought could serve her purpose were her mother's hypertension medicine but there were only twelve pills in the bottle.

Will this be enough? If I take them all, what will Mom do? She will definitely need her medicine after finding my body. The instructions say to take one tablet a day. These pills have to be strong. Mom is always talking about how dangerously high her blood pressure is. If one can lower her blood pressure for an entire day, eight should be enough to stop mine.

As she sat in the bathtub and thought about how little time was left, the pain seemed bearable. She contemplated her eternal destiny.

Is there a heaven and a hell? I wonder where I will end up, if there is. Taking my life is a sin but maybe God will forgive me. If He is truly merciful, He can't want me to live with so much pain.

The warm bath, clean linen and stress of the day allowed Paula to fall asleep quickly but dreams about Michael interrupted her sleep. Each dream involved Michael with someone else, his cruel treatment of Paula escalating with each dream. Paula was more depressed than ever when she finally got out of bed at Autumn's insistence. Karen had dropped her off on her way to work and Clarice had left early to open the community center. After a bowl of cereal, Paula and Autumn began their cleaning.

As she cleaned, Paula thought about the activities that would occur the next day. After they took her body away, her mother's friends would probably come by to comfort her. The house had to be immaculate. Having a daughter that committed suicide was understandable but having a filthy house was not. Paula decided that if Michael would just call her, everything would be okay and the pain would go away. Every time the phone rang, Paula held her breath before answering, hoping it was Michael who controlled her destiny.

It was almost ten o'clock when Paula finished the kitchen. She had taken a final break to give Autumn a bath and put her to sleep. Paula regretted that she would not be around to see Autumn grow up, but she had enough aunts and uncles to help out.   The dirty dishwater swirling down the drain reminded Paula of her life.

Mom had been right after all. I did ruin my life because of Michael. All I need to do now is to empty the dirty water.

The house was spotless. Paula was glad that she was able to spare her mother any additional embarrassment. She took a final walk through each room, making sure she had not overlooked anything and picking up Autumn's trail of toys. Without the distraction of cleaning, Paula's thoughts returned to Michael and the pain.

She stopped in the bathroom, closing the door behind her. Clarice had taken her medicine for the day and wouldn't be opening the bottle again.   This time Paula flushed the toilet to hide the sound of the cabinet opening. She counted out eight pills into her hand, wrapped them in some toilet tissue and put the bundle in her jean pocket. Paula returned to the kitchen, poured herself a glass of juice and sat at the kitchen table by the telephone. Time was running out.

Paula, Michael didn't even care enough to call you on Valentine's Day - the day to celebrate love. I wonder who he's celebrating with.   Given his behavior, I doubt if he will even wait for a divorce before moving on to the next victim.

Paula waited for tears to come, but they did not. The pain was so deep that she just felt numb. She closed her eyes and saw his face with the smile that had brightened so many of her days.

Burning in hell will at least keep my mind off Michael and just maybe my death will haunt him the rest of his life - cause him the kind of pain that he has caused me.

Her mother walked into the kitchen just as Paula was reaching in her pocket for the pills. Her hand quickly returned to the coolness of the glass.

"Paula, the house really looks nice but you shouldn't be spending your time cleaning. You should be studying."

"I didn't have much work this weekend."

"Are you going to be up much longer?"

"No, I'm tired. I was just going to take a shower and go to bed."

"Do you want to go to church with me in the morning? I can drop you back at the dorm afterward."

"Sure, Mom. I love you."

"I love you too, Paula."

Paula picked up the glass of juice and stood up. She walked over, kissed her mother on the cheek and then went to her room, closing the door behind her. The pills went down smoothly with the sweet chaser. Paula wasn't sure how long they would take to enter her bloodstream so she decided on a quick shower. Fifteen minutes later, she was in bed wearing her best pair of pajamas. She felt herself starting to float as she remembered to pray.

"Now I lay me down to sleep, I pray the Lord my soul to keep. If I should die before I wake, I pray the Lord my soul to take. God, my life is in your hands now. Please forgive me... What have I done!"

Michael walked in his room just before eleven o'clock. He had been running around all day, doing things for the big brothers' girlfriends - delivering flowers and washing their cars. Then the pledge meeting had been long and difficult but he wasn't going to quit. He sat down at his desk exhausted. The picture of Paula caught his attention as he looked at his unfinished homework. He missed her so much but this was the only way. He wondered how she was doing. Call her. Call her. It was a nagging feeling. Maybe he would just call and make sure she was okay; after all it was Valentine's Day.

It had been over a month since he talked to her. The divorce had been his mother's idea but now he wasn't so sure it was really the best thing. He looked at his watch and then picked up the phone. He dialed her dorm number and let the phone ring for a long time but no one answered. Michael wondered if Paula had gone home for the weekend. He started dialing the number but then hung up.

It's too late. She is probably asleep and wouldn't want to talk to me anyway. When I'm finished pledging, I will make it up to her.

Michael remembered that he had not checked his mailbox as he opened his book to study.

The smell of bacon quickly filled the house as Clarice scurried around the kitchen to prepare an old-fashioned Sunday breakfast. She knew that if Paula could survive this weekend, everything was going to be okay. The only way she could help was to feed her. Clarice had been so worried about Paula since she had picked her up. The pain was draining Paula of all her energy and life. But Clarice thought that Saturday had been a good day. Paula stayed busy all day cleaning the house and seemed more like herself before she went to bed.

Clarice yawned as she stirred the pancake batter. She was tired from staying up so late, but she wanted to make sure that Paula went to sleep first. She had even peeked in on Paula to make sure she was asleep before finally going to bed. It was a relief to see her sleeping so peacefully. Clarice's own sleep was elusive at first. The feeling that something was wrong kept nagging her. Thoughts of each of her children floated in and out of her dreams. Someone was in trouble, she could feel it. At least Paula was safe at home where she could keep an eye on her. Clarice woke up with the desire to cook breakfast like she used to when the kids were little. She put the last piece of fried bacon on the plate and sat it on the table. When she turned around, Autumn was standing in the doorway looking around still half-asleep. Clarice picked up her granddaughter.

"Good morning. Is your Mommy awake yet?"

Autumn shook her head.

"Well, how about we go wake up your Aunt Paula so she can eat breakfast with us."

She put Autumn down on the floor and walked towards Paula's room with Autumn following close behind. The door was open from Autumn's trek through. Clarice looked down at her daughter as she went to open the curtains and raise the shade. It was a bright day and when the shade retracted, golden sunlight filled the room.

The sunlight penetrated Paula's sleep. Then she felt something brush against her cheek. She was afraid to open her eyes until her mother's voice and the smell of bacon registered in her senses.

"Good morning. I thought you might want to get up early and study. Breakfast is almost ready. I'm making pancakes, bacon and scrambled eggs."

Paula slowly moved over to make room for Autumn who was trying to climb up on the bed. She was extremely weak but glad to be alive and very hungry.

She closed her eyes and thought three words.

Thank you, God.

"But he said to me, "My grace is sufficient for you, for my power is made perfect in weakness..." 2 Corinthians 12:9. NIV

Chapter 20

The week after Valentine's Day, Paula convinced her Resident Advisor to let her switch rooms with another person on her floor who was also having roommate problems. Paula and her new roommate had little in common, but at least her personal affairs would not be broadcasted in the dorm. This was the first step for Paula who was determined to put her life back together. With Angela's support, she was managing to catch up in her classes. They studied together almost every night and Paula had even started going to church with Angela, searching for answers.

God had spared her life for a reason and she wanted to find out why. After Paula visited Angela's church for the first time, she felt right at home. She left the church with a strong sense of peace and the inner strength that she so desperately needed. Paula was surprised that the beliefs of their religions were so similar and most of the prayers during the service were even the same. But what converted Paula was the fellowship of the congregation. All her life, she had gone to church regularly but never felt a part of the church. Now she did. She had taken the first step across the abyss that almost had destroyed her, finding an unexpected stepping stone to help her across.

Her newly styled hair blew in the warm spring breezes as she walked back to her dorm. Karen had convinced Paula that a new style would lift her spirits and Paula loved the way it had turned out. The blunt cut just above her shoulder with full bangs, combed slightly to one side gave Paula a fresh, carefree look. Karen had even put a brown rinse in to add highlights. Paula felt like a new person when she left the beauty shop, starting to reclaim what Michael had taken.

The pain was still there, but it lessened with each day. Some days were better than others. But slowly, Paula was regaining control of her life, accepting the fact that Michael was out of her life and expecting to find divorce papers in the mail each day. Earlier in the week, she had even accepted an invitation to go to the lake with one of the athletes who ate in her dorm. She was honest with him when he asked her to go but he already knew about her marriage and said that she looked like she could use a friend. Paula enjoyed the setting and the attention.

Spring break was just a few days away. Paula only had two exams left and had just returned from studying in Angela's room. All she wanted to do was take a quick shower and go to bed. The phone rang just as she was walking out the door. Thinking that it might be Angela, Paula answered it.

"Hello."

"Hi, Paula. How are you?"

It can't be!

"Michael…"

"Yeah. It's been a while. Gail gave me this number. Can I come see you tonight?"

Paula paused not quite sure what to do.

"Uh…. I don't know Michael. It's late and I'm tired."

"Paula, it's very important. Please."

". . . Okay. When will you be here?"

"In about ten minutes. I'm already in town. I'll see you soon."

Click.

Ten minutes! Paula tossed her shower things on the bed, sat down at her desk and conversed with herself.

Why are you being so stupid? He has not called you in over two month and now out of the blue, he has to see you. You should have told him where to go. But what if…What if he realizes what a mistake he made? He did say it was important. He's coming to apologize for the way he's treated you. This is what you've been waiting for. Things do work out for the best.

Paula smiled and got up. She changed her shirt quickly, sprayed on some perfume, brushed her teeth and combed her hair. She wondered if Michael would like her new hair cut, as she looked at the clock on the desk. Curfew was at eleven. Michael only had twenty minutes before the doors were locked.

The phone rang. Her heart was pounding so hard that she could see her shirt moving.

"Hello."

"Hi, I'm in the lobby." Click.

Paula took a deep breath, trying to slow her pulse, but it didn't work. She stopped at the water fountain in the hall and took a drink.

That's better. Now Paula, you have to calm down.

She walked through the double doors and stared in disbelief. He was standing there unshaven and in a soiled tee-shirt and jeans. When Paula got closer, she noticed a strong, offensive smell.

"Hi, thanks for letting me come."

"You said it was important."

Paula did not announce his presence as they went through the doors. She walked quickly, hoping that no one on her floor would see or smell him. He hesitated at the door of her old room.

"I changed rooms." Paula said quietly.

"Why?"

"I'll tell you later."

Paula wanted to get him off the floor as soon as possible, quickly opening her door and closing it behind him. Michael sat in the chair at her desk and Paula sat on the edge of her bed farthest away from him. His smell was starting to make her sick.

"I liked your other room better. How have you been?"

"Fine. So what's so important."

"Paula, I had to get off campus. The big brothers are going crazy. I appreciate you letting me come here."

"Michael, why didn't you go to your house?"

This was what was so important! He needed a place to hide.

"One of the big brothers knows where I live. I had to come where no one could find me. Paula they are trying to kill us..."

Paula sat there in disbelief while Michael went on and on about the abuse he had taken while pledging.

I can't believe he has the audacity to expect me to help him. How could I have fallen in love with someone so self-absorbed?

I tried to kill myself and he seems totally oblivious to what he's put me through. And now he shows up because he needs something. What about what I needed? He didn't even notice my hair cut. I have heard enough!

"Michael, correct me if I'm wrong. But didn't YOU choose to pledge."

The coldness of the statement was unnoticed by Michael.

"Yeah but I didn't think it would be like this." Michael sat in the chair rubbing his hands together nervously.

"Then why don't you just quit?"

"Paula, I can't quit now. I'm almost done. You won't understand until you pledge."

"You're right Michael, I don't understand."

"Paula, can I stay here tonight? I can't go back until the morning."

"Michael, I think you'd better go to your house."

"Paula, it's too late. I don't want to wake up my mother or let her see me like this. I know that I smell a little foul but I couldn't risk going back to my dorm to change. I'll sleep on the floor."

His words turned the knife in Paula's heart, reviving the pain that she had fought so hard to overcome, pulling her back towards the abyss.

This is the last time he'll use you Paula.

Her roommate was spending the night with her boyfriend and the doors were already locked. Paula decided to let him stay but knew that she would not be able to take the stench much longer. Paula got a washcloth and towel from her cabinet and an oversized T-shirt from her dresser. She sat the items on the corner of the desk with a bar of soap.

"Here. You can clean up. But Michael, you need to leave early, before anyone else is up."

"Thanks, Paula. I knew that I could count on you."

He gave her the smile that used to melt her heart but now it just hardened it a little more. Paula watched him as he took off his pledge shirt and began to wash off. For the first time she saw him without the filtering of love and his faults came into plain view, he was not going to pull her back. She got her things for her shower and a pair of sweats.

"I'm going to take my shower. Please don't answer the phone."

When Paula came back, fully dressed in her sweats, Michael had returned to his spot at her desk and the air in the room smelled better. While she was gone, he had noticed that all the pictures of them were gone. The urge to ask about them was beat out by common sense. She obviously didn't want any reminders of him. He had been so caught up in his pledging it never occurred to him that she might not want to see him. It finally registered that he should have gone somewhere else.

"Paula, I'm sorry about showing up like this."

Paula put away her things and went to the mirror to comb her hair.

"I like your new hair style. Did your sister cut it?"

"Yes."

"Paula, how are you doing, really?"

"I'm surprised you even care. But for the record, I am fine Michael. At first, I hurt a lot but I've learned how to deal with it."

"Paula, I'm really sorry. As soon as I get off line, I want us to sit down and talk about this."

"There's nothing to talk about Michael. You wanted your freedom and I can accept that. I can see now that we should not have gotten married in the first place. You go ahead and file for the divorce. I'll sign whatever papers are necessary."

After setting the alarm clock for five, Paula picked up her oversize pillow and comforter and handed them to Michael. Then she turned off the lights, climbed into bed under the blanket with her back towards him, hoping to make it clear that he was definitely sleeping on the floor. Tears rolled down her cheeks into her pillow as she promised herself that they were the last tears that she would cry for him.

Michael's visit had been just what Paula needed to close the door on her life with him. She was surer than ever that they no longer had a future together and was thankful that Michael's spring break was a week after hers. Long afternoons at the lake during her break, gave Paula time to think about her life - why things had gone so wrong and what she needed to do about it.

For the first time, she understood Clarice's opposition to Michael. Her mother saw Michael for what he was - wrong for her daughter, who was unprepared for the type of relationship he wanted. Paula could not see past the physical attraction between them; letting her body fool her, mistaking a strong physical attraction for the love and security that she so desperately needed, putting him before her family and her friends.

A lingering pain remained but it was not for Michael, it was the pain of regret and embarrassment. She felt like she had been his prostitute; used to satisfy his needs under the façade of a marriage, and she had willingly obliged. But now the price, marriage, was more than he wanted to pay; leaving Paula feeling like used merchandise that would have to be either offered at a discount to anyone willing to accept her or remain on the shelf.

Paula returned to campus, refocused towards her goal of graduating from college, her key to self-sufficiency; confident that she would never again give her body just to be loved, preferring to remain on the shelf than to be used again.

Her grades were not what she had expected them to be when the school year had started but given the circumstances, Paula was proud of her rebound. She could barely contain her elation while waiting for Angela to call so they could go to dinner. The B+ on the math exam proudly displayed on her desk. She was so excited to share the news with Angela, who had helped her study that she picked up the phone on the first ring.

"HELLO."

"Hi. You sound pretty happy today."

"Oh, hello Michael."

Why is he calling? What does he need this time?

"Don't seem so excited to talk to me."

"I was expecting another call."

"Paula, I went over. I am officially Greek."

"Congratulations."

"I'm going to be home all week for spring break. I wanted us to get together. I know you still have classes but maybe we can go to the lake tomorrow afternoon."

"I don't think so Michael. I have a busy week."

"Come on, Paula. We really need to talk."

"Let me think about it. Can I give you a call tomorrow?"

"What do you mean you need to think about it?"

"Just what I said. You were the one that called me asking for a divorce. Now that you've finished pledging, you want me to drop everything so we can talk."

"Paula, this doesn't sound like you. What's the matter?"

What's the matter?

Paula felt the venom surging and wanted to end the conversation, before it escalated into an argument that would ruin her good mood.

"Look, I'm expecting another call. I'll call you tomorrow when I get out of class. Good bye."

"Paula, please."

"Good bye, Michael."

Click.

Paula replayed the conversation for Angela over dinner.

"He's got a lot of nerve after what he put you through."

"I know. He probably just wants to keep me on the side as a sure thing when he has time. I was a fool once but not anymore. The sooner he files for the divorce, the better . . . I wonder if that's what he wants to talk about."

"You two probably should talk but I wouldn't go to the lake with him. Spring is in the air." Angela said with a mischievous smile.

"You have a point."

Paula called Michael when she got back to her room. She had made up her mind.

"Michael, we do need to talk but I don't want to go to the lake. Why don't you come by the dorm around two tomorrow."

"That's great, Paula. I'm really looking forward to seeing you."

"I'll see you tomorrow."

Paula was furious with herself for letting Michael control her life again. That night, she couldn't concentrate on her work and sleep evaded her. All she could think about was their upcoming meeting. The questions racing in her mind would not stop.

What will he say?... What will I say?... Will I be strong enough to resist any advances? Maybe meeting in my room isn't such a good idea. Maybe the lobby? But we need some privacy. Should I just call him and talk it out over the phone. How long will the divorce take? Should I offer to pay half? No, the marriage and divorce was his idea. Let him pay for it. His mother has probably already offered to pay.

Paula woke up irritable from a lack of sleep, but she knew that the sooner they talked, the sooner she would be able to put her relationship with Michael behind her. Time dragged while she tried to study. Her only class for the day had ended at eleven o'clock.

Finally, the phone rang at one-thirty announcing his early arrival. Paula looked in the mirror again before going to the lobby, wanting to look her best so he would know what he had thrown away.

Michael was standing in the lounge doorway looking at the television when Paula walked through the doors. She immediately noticed his T-shirt with the large Greek letters, which were more important than she was. Several of the football players that were in the lounge watching the sports channel spoke to Paula when she walked up, which seemed to irritate Michael. Paula smiled to herself, enjoying his discomfort.

"Hello, Michael."

"Paula."

"So which one of them are you dating."

"They're just friends, Michael."

They walked through the doors towards her room in silence. After the door was closed, Michael walked over to Paula and tried to hug her but she moved away quickly and sat in the chair at her desk. Michael sat on the edge of her bed. Paula stared at him, purposefully not mentioning his shirt.

"So, what do you want to talk about?"

"Us . . . Paula, I know the way I asked for the divorce wasn't right, but I didn't know any other way."

"The truth is that you were too chicken to tell me in person."

"Paula, I don't want to argue with you."

"Neither do I, Michael. Have you already filed for the divorce? I'm ready to put this behind me and move on with my life."

"No, I haven't filed for a divorce yet. And what do you mean move on? Paula, I still want us to be together. I just don't want to be married, at least not until we can do it right."

Paula struggled not to laugh, and wondered if she had heard him correctly.

"Michael, let me get this straight. You don't want to be married to me but you want to stay together?"

"Yes. Paula, I love you but we're just not ready for marriage."

"Michael, what you really want is to be able to sleep around without worrying about going to hell. Sounds to me like you want your cake and to eat it too. I'm sorry Michael, I'm not into sharing."

"What does that mean?"

"It means that I want to end it cleanly. After the divorce is final, I don't think we should see each other again."

"NO!"

"No?"

"Paula, we are not finished. I love you and you love me."

"I LOVED you Michael. I don't anymore. I can't love someone that I can't trust. You could call next week and say you don't want to be together at all. Every night, I'd be wondering whom you were with. I can't do that, Michael."

"Paula, who says I'd be with anyone else."

"Have you already?"

"Paula, that's not the point."

"Michael, have - you – already – slept - with - someone – else?"

"Yes, but it didn't mean anything."

"Neither did our marriage, obviously. Michael, please leave."

"No, I'm not leaving. Not until you hear me out."

"If you won't leave, I will."

Paula got up, walked over to the door and held it open. She didn't even want to be in the same room with him. He didn't even have the decency to wait until the divorce. Michael jumped up and kicked the door closed. The sudden movement and the sound of his foot hitting the door and it slamming scared Paula. She remembered his outburst the night of his graduation and wondered if he would hurt her. She had to calm him down but he had to leave.

"Look, Michael. This isn't getting us anywhere. I think we both need some time to think about things."

"Paula, I don't need to think about us. I love you and I want us to stay together. I know I made a mistake but it won't happen again."

A voice inside her screamed - Get him out of here now!

"Okay, Michael.... Look, I'm supposed to meet Angela to study for a test. Can we get together Friday, after I've had some time to think? You don't know how much pain I've been going through since you called asking for the divorce. You've had pledging to keep you busy. I didn't have anything." Paula said calmly.

"Paula, I'm not leaving until you promise me that we are still together."

He seemed a little more rational.

"Michael, I can't promise you that. You just admitted to sleeping with someone else."

"Paula, please. I love you"

"Michael, if you really love me, you will give me some time."

" . . . Okay Paula. I'll go but can we go to the lake Friday for a picnic?"

"Sure Michael, if you will just leave."

Paula walked Michael to the door and then returned to her room and sat at her desk, wishing that she really were meeting Angela.

You were right, Paula. He has been unfaithful. I will never trust him again. It's over. I will let him know that Friday. A picnic at the lake will be good. The lake is calming.

Michael drove to his house, exceeding the speed limit and thinking about Paula. He hadn't planned on telling her about his little indiscretion, but he couldn't lie to her when she asked. He had gotten so drunk at the party after they went over. He thought a little harmless flirting wouldn't hurt but she looked so good in those tight pants and it had been so long. Once she had gotten him excited, he couldn't stop. But it didn't mean anything to him, just a way to release some energy. He thought that Paula should be able to understand. He would not accept that they were finished, rationalizing that she belonged to him.

Paula had serious reservations about seeing Michael again, after having several dreams where she and Michael were together and she woke up terrified that something terrible was going to happen. Paula was so shaken by the dreams that she told Angela about them. Angela tried to talk her out of seeing Michael alone and even offered to go along but Paula thought her presence would be hard to explain.

Paula decided that she would just have to be very careful what she said, so she would not upset him. It was reassuring that Angela knew her itinerary. But she was the only one who knew that she and Michael were meeting. Paula knew to keep the meeting from Clarice. Why worry her over nothing? Soon Michael would be out of their lives.

Michael was in good spirits when he picked Paula up just before noon. They picked up some burgers on the way to the lake. It was a warm, cloudless day and they sat on a blanket under a tree to eat. It was still too early in the day for the lake to be busy. There was no one else in eyesight as they ate in silence. After Paula finished her food, she could not delay any longer.

"Angela told me to tell you hi."

"How's she doing?"

"Good. She's been a good friend. We have been leaning on each other to get through our engineering courses."

"That's good. Paula, have you had a chance to think?"

"That's all I've been doing since you left."

"And... Are you willing to give us another chance?"

"Michael, I do still love you. But not the way I did. We can't just get a divorce and continue as if nothing happened. If we stayed together, in my eyes, you'd still be my husband. And I can't have a husband who I can't trust."

"Paula, you can trust me. It won't happen again."

"How do you know that, Michael? If it happened once, it can happen again."

"Paula, I was drunk. It didn't mean anything."

"Maybe it didn't to you, but it probably did to her. Michael, we should just end it while we are still friends."

"Then let's just forget about the divorce. I don't want to lose you, Paula. We can stay married."

"Michael, you don't know how hard I prayed that you would say that, but it's too late now. Too much has happened. Michael, I tried to kill myself because I didn't think I could live without you. I'm so thankful that God didn't let me succeed."

" . . . Paula, I'm sorry. I didn't know."

"I know Michael, but now can you understand why I can't go through that again. You just think you want to stay married. If you wanted to stay married, you would have never asked for the divorce or slept with someone else, regardless of being drunk."

"Paula, please . . . I love you. We just need some time. My cousin asked me to ride down to Louisiana with him at the end of the semester, so he won't have to drive by himself. He's going to drop me off at my grandmother's. We're just staying for a week. Come with us. The time together will be good for us. Let me show you how much I still love you."

"Michael, I don't think that's a good idea. I'm going to start my internship as soon as possible. I really need the money."

"Paula, work can wait a week. Besides, you'll need to rest after finals before starting to work. We'll have a wonderful time and you know my grandmother's a great cook. She has plenty of space. You can even have your own room."

Paula had already planned on taking a week off before starting work but she needed an excuse. She didn't know if she was strong enough to be alone with him for a week.

"No Michael, I can't go."

"Why Paula? Don't you think you owe me a week."

"Michael, I don't think I owe you anything. It's getting late. Will you take me back to the dorm?"

Paula held her breath expecting opposition.

"Sure, Paula. Let's go."

Michael got up and folded the blanket then walked to the car and opened the door for her. Paula got in the car with a sense of relief and hoped that Michael would accept that it was over between them. Eventually, they might be able to be friends but she knew that would take some time.

Paula noticed that Michael was driving fast on the highway that ran along the lake and checked her seat belt to sure it was tight. Michael liked to drive fast, but this was faster than normal and they kept gaining speed. Paula looked at the speedometer - 70...75...80...85...

"Michael, I think you should slow down."

Michael looked straight ahead.

"What's wrong Paula? You said we are finished. We might as well die together."

"Michael, this is not funny. PLEASE SLOW DOWN."

"Does it look like I'm playing, Paula?"

Paula looked at the speedometer...95, and panicked. She hoped that a police would pull them over.

"Michael, PLEASE stop this car and let me out. I'll walk back to the dorm."

"I'm not going to slow down until you promise to go to Louisiana with me."

...100...

"Okay, Michael. Just please stop this car."

"Okay, what?"

"Okay, I'll go with you to Louisiana."

"Do you promise?"

"I promise. Now please stop the car."

95...90...80...70...55...

"Paula, you just don't understand how much I love you. The trip will be good for us."

"Michael, will you please stop at the next gas station so I can get out?"

"Paula, come on. I'll take you back. I swear I won't speed. Everything is okay, now."

He smiled and Paula wanted to hit him. But right now she needed to get out of his car and as far away from him as possible. She moved close to the door and held onto the handle. If he tried it again, she would just jump out of the car.

"Paula, relax."

"How can I relax? You just tried to kill us."

"Paula, I just needed to get your attention and let you know how serious I am. I don't want to live without you."

"That's very comforting. I'm suppose to travel across the country with someone who just tried to kill me."

They drove the rest of the way to her dorm in silence. When Michael pulled outside the dorm, Paula grabbed her purse and started to get out but he gently held her arm.

"Paula, I'm sorry. I didn't mean to upset you and I'm not going to force you to go. Please, just give me a week alone with you. After the week, if you still feel the same way, I'll file for the divorce and never bother you again. I swear."

"Michael, how can I trust you?"

"PLEASE, just this one week. You'll have your own room. My cousin will be with us on the road and then we'll be at my grandmother's house. I promise I will never do anything like this again. And I will leave you alone, if that's what you still want."

"Okay, Michael. You have your one week."

Paula got out of the car and did not look back.

How am I going to explain this to Mom?

Chapter 21

Paula carefully parallel-parked her new car and rushed across the street, congested with motorist heading out of downtown for the Friday rush hour. The letter firmly held in her hand specifying what she needed to do and containing the plastic, American flag lapel pin. When she first read the letter, the request to wear the pin sounded like something from a cheap detective movie. But the man that she was meeting was a stranger and they did need some way of identifying each other. She looked down at her watch again as the cool air conditioning on the other side of the revolving door engulfed her. It was a warm day in May and she could feel the perspiration challenging her antiperspirant. She was thirty minutes early, but she had waited more than a year for this day and had no intention of being late. If she missed this appointment, the divorce would be delayed another month. Summer school started the following week and Paula did not want to carry the distraction into another semester.

The lobby of the Federal building was massive. Paula had never been to the courthouse but it was near the Records building where they had gotten the marriage license. As she stood in the stately lobby, she wished Angela were with her. But that was impossible with her work schedule.

The traffic through the lobby was heavy as the federal employees departed for the weekend. Paula found a spot by a column outside her assigned courtroom to wait and unfolded the letter to reread the instructions. The stationary had the same logo as the advertisement in the television guide. The ad had caught her attention with its claim of 'uncontested divorces' for one hundred and fifty dollars. Tired of waiting for Michael to initiate the divorce, Paula decided to take matters into her own hands. The price was within her range and despite some initial concerns, the divorce process up to this point had been handled professionally.

Michael signed a notarized affidavit stating he did not contest the divorce and that was the extent of his involvement. Paula took care of everything else including the lawyer's fee. But she had never met her lawyer or even visited his office. All the correspondence had been via the mail, except for a phone call from the lawyer's assistant confirming the information.

The trip to Louisiana had been good for Paula and Michael. As expected, Clarice tried to talk her daughter out of going up to the day she left, fearing that Paula and Michael would reconcile. But knowing that it was the only way to be sure of her feelings for Michael, Paula went. Either they would come back as a happy couple or in agreement that their marriage and physical relationship was over; the only two possible options for Paula. Michael's desire to end the marriage but keep Paula was never going to happen; Paula was certain of that, just as Michael had been certain that he could win back Paula's trust.

The trip was like a mini-vacation. They visited all the tourist attractions and even had a picnic along the riverbank, where the mighty Mississippi River merged with the Gulf of Mexico. The scenery was breathtaking and their conversations heart-felt and honest.

By the third day of the trip, Michael and Paula were both convinced that it was over. Their feelings for each other had changed and they could not go backwards. On the way home, Paula thought it was ironic that the trip they should have had as a honeymoon, turned out to be their final time together as a couple. Michael kept his promise and they did not see each other again until the day they had his affidavit notarized.

Paula looked at the clock above the courtroom door.

Five minutes to go. It's time to put on the pin.

The pin was removed from the letter and attached to the left side of her dress as instructed, right over her heart. More people started to fill the lobby, which struck Paula as odd for five o'clock on a Friday. Paula surveyed the crowd trying to locate her lawyer with the matching American flag pin. She spotted a lady with the same pin on the other side of the lobby but she looked just as confused. Paula wondered if she was the assistant who had called her and walked towards the lady. Before she reached her, Paula saw another person with the pin and then another. Looking closely, she noticed that the majority of the people in the lobby had on the same American flag pin.

What's going on?

She opened the letter again. It said nothing about a group, only that her lawyer would meet her outside the courtroom. Paula looked up from the letter and her heart stopped.

Please let this just be a dream. Wake up! This can't be happening.

A television reporter and cameraman had set up in the lobby and were starting to film the rapidly growing crowd. The last thing Paula wanted was to have her face splashed on the evening news. Her heart raced faster and faster, as she realized that she could not go through it alone. Paula decided to just leave and call the lawyer's office on Monday and tell him that an emergency had come up. She was trying to figure out how to leave the lobby without being filmed when a young woman with a stack of papers in her arms rushed to the center of the crowd.

Too late!

"Would all of the people that are being represented by Swindler and Associates, please gather around."

More than fifty people, most wearing the same flag pin, formed a large circle around the lady. The cameraman focused the camera on the center of the crowd. Paula stayed in the back, out of camera range.

"I'm Betty Howard. I've talked with most of you on the phone. Mr. Swindler is meeting with the judge now to finalize the process and will be joining us in the courtroom. Some of you are probably wondering what's going on and why the press coverage. The judge has agreed to a special session for a trial procedure, one massive divorce hearing, almost like a fast food service. All of you are being represented by the same lawyer and have uncontested divorces, which makes this an ideal test. If successful, the court system will be able to process uncontested divorces in a fraction of the time. When we go into the courtroom, we will sit together as a group. After the judge comes in, you will be sworn in and given instructions as a group. Then each of you will be called before the judge, where Mr. Swindler will present your individual case and the judge will make any immediate judgments. If your petition for divorce is granted, and it should be unless there are some last minute changes, the judge will sign your petition and instruct you to go to the clerk. The clerk will take your paperwork for the final processing. You are free to leave after your case is heard, however we ask that you leave the courtroom as quietly as possible since other cases will still be in the process. Are there any questions?"

Paula looked around the group. No one said anything.

"Great. The doors should be opening any moment and we can go in. One more thing, I've asked the press not to film individuals without their permission. However, this is a public hearing so they cannot be barred from the courtroom."

Paula felt her chest tightening as she waited for the doors to open and kept a close eye on the activities of the cameraman. Fighting back the urge to cry, Paula was angry once again with Michael.

He should be the one standing in the courtroom being humiliated, not me. It's okay, Paula. This is the final time he'll let you down. Keep it together a just little longer and it will all be over.

Everyone else had someone with them. Paula took several deep breaths and knew that she had made a big mistake coming alone. Her mother had offered to come with her, but Paula had politely turned her down saying it was just a simple divorce hearing that should only take a few minutes. Paula thought that if she was grown enough to get married without her mother's presence, she was grown enough to get a divorce without her mother. But she never expected the myriad of emotions forming inside her or the press coverage. The humiliation of a public divorce and the fear of what was going to happen inside the courtroom caused Paula to break out in a cold sweat. Her insides started to churn.

Don't get sick!

The doors finally opened. Paula felt weak as she followed the crowd, each step more labor intensive.

I'll never even make it inside the courtroom... Paula don't you dare pass out. The press will definitely cover that. It will be the lead story - Paula Hayes collapses outside courtroom under stress of divorce. Don't you dare, Paula...

As Paula approached the courtroom door, she instinctively looked towards the exit and saw her mother rushing through the heavy doors. Clarice was out of breath when she reached her.

"I'm glad I got here before you went in. Since I was already downtown, I decided to come over. If you don't want me to go in with you, I can wait out here, in case you need something."

Clarice looked nervous. She did not want to interfere, but she was so worried about her baby that she just couldn't stay away.

"Mom, I'm glad you came. You can come in but I'm not sure how long its going to take though. They are trying something new."

Paula filled her mother in on the process while they waited for the judge. Then they sat side by side in the courtroom waiting patiently for Paula's name to be called. Clarice was relieved that the marriage was finally ending, but sorry for her daughter's pain. She knew first hand the pain of a failed marriage and wondered if she could have done something differently that would have prevented her daughter from walking the same path. But it was too late to change the past. All she could do now was support Paula.   It took over an hour for Paula's case to be heard and the divorce granted.

After they left the courtroom, Clarice offered to take the bus home but Paula insisted on driving her home. Both women rode in silence, trying to deal with their pain the best way they knew how and Clarice didn't argue with Paula when she didn't come in the house, understanding her need to be alone. As soon as Paula's car turned the corner off her mother's street, the tears that she had held back all afternoon flowed freely.

Saturday morning, Paula woke up early and finished unpacking her things. She had moved out of Sheryl's house, where she had lived for the semester while working, and back on campus for summer school. She had registered for twelve semester hours, which was a full course load for the summer and was a little concerned whether her course load was too heavy since she was also going to be a Resident Advisor.

It had been a week since the divorce hearing and Paula did not give it another thought. The news coverage had been brief and she was no where in sight. Paula had a new car, a healthy bank account, greatly improved grades and a new church home. There had been no romance in her life for over a year, but Paula had accepted the fact that she would probably not find anyone worthwhile who would want to get involved with a divorcee.

Paula put away her suitcases and rushed down to the lobby to work her shift, checking in students.

Her shift was almost over, when a handsome young man walked up to the desk. Paula didn't recognize him.

He's probably looking for someone.
"Hello. Can I help you?"
"Is this where I check in?"
"For summer housing?"
"Yes."
"I'm Paula Hayes, a Resident Advisor for the dorm. You've come to the right place. Do you have your housing form?"
He handed Paula the folded paper that was in his hand and rested his hands on the desk. Now she knew his name. Paula tried not to stare.
He has beautiful brown eyes.
"I'm a transfer student." He said looking directly into her eyes.
"Really. What year?"
"I'm starting my junior year."
"So am I. What's your major?"
"Electrical engineering. How about you?"
"Mechanical engineering. What a coincident?"

The memory of meeting her husband brought a smile to Paula's face, thankful to have been given a second chance at love. God definitely did work in mysterious ways, bringing her soul mate into her life when she least expected it. She walked back into her daughter's room who was still curled in a ball. She didn't want her daughter to walk her same path.

Circumstances beyond her control had forced her to grow up too fast and without the foundation needed for healthy relationships, disillusioned into thinking that she could handle her own problems and searching desperately for love and someone to take care of her. Clarice had been the best mother she could, but life had dealt her a hard blow. Raising six children on her own was a major feat. Paula was barely managing two, with the help of a loving, supportive husband.

Paula thought about the impact of her career on her family before she took the leave. Rushing to drop her children at daycare by seven and picking them up by five-thirty. Barely having three hours a day with them during the week and during that time she was often tired and irritable. After taking care of her children's needs, she had nothing left to give to her husband or herself.

Her marriage needed nurturing to, or she might end up like her mother, having to raise her children on her own. Her physical appearance had already been sacrificed. The size eight her husband had married had blossomed to a thirteen. And sleep was more important than intimacy, which had been the source of several arguments prior to the leave, creating a strain and threatening irreparable damage. She and her husband had become strangers.

Finally Paula thought about her own emotional state, the reason for the leave in the first place. In trying to do it all, she felt like she was constantly failing at everything; mother, wife, manager, person. She had everything but happiness and she knew that the new opportunity would only make the situation worse. She had to get her priorities straight. Life was not supposed to be so difficult.

Their yard needed a fence to define the boundaries and protect the fragile landscape, even if the fence was only four feet high. Her family needed protection too.

She would be there to guide her children's growth in the safety of boundaries, ensuring that they felt loved and secure and building their foundation on principles and values. And when it is time for them to leave, she would watch them go through the gate, confident in their abilities to make the right decisions.

Her marriage needed a fence, where they could nurture a beautiful, passionate relationship that would grow stronger each year and be impervious to trespassers with little regard for the property of others. The grass needed to be greener on their side of the fence, so there would be no temptation to wonder.

Paula needed the definition and security of the fence also. She needed to be able to clearly see what she was responsible for and to be able to control what was allowed into their yard. God had entrusted her with much and she needed to be a good and faithful servant. No position in the world was more important.

Maybe in the future, she would find a career that would compliment and not compete with her life, allowing her to become a Proverbs 31 woman.

Proverbs 31:10-31 (NIV)
Epilogue: The Wife of Noble Character

"A wife of noble character who can find?
　　She is worth far more than rubies.
Her husband has full confidence in her and lacks nothing of
　　value.
She brings him good, not harm, all the days of her life.
She selects wool and flax and works with eager hands.
She is like the merchant ships, bringing her food from afar.
She gets up while it is still dark; she provides food for her family
　　and portions for her servant girls.
She considers a field and buys it; out of her earnings she plants a
　　vineyard.
She sets about her work vigorously; her arms are strong for her
　　tasks.
She sees that her trading is profitable, and her lamp does not go
　　out at night.
In her hand she holds the distaff and grasps the spindle with her
　　fingers.
She opens her arms to the poor and extends her hands to the
　　needy.
When it snows, she has no fear for her household; for all of them
　　are clothed in scarlet.
She makes coverings for her bed; she is clothed in fine linen and
　　purple.
Her husband is respected at the city gate, where he takes his seat
　　among the elders of the land.
She makes linen garments and sells them, and supplies the
　　merchants with sashes.

She is clothed with strength and dignity; she can laugh at the days to come.

She speaks with wisdom, and faithful instruction is on her tongue.

She watches over the affairs of her household and does not eat the bread of idleness.

Her children arise and call her blessed; her husband also, and he praises her:

"Many women do noble things, but you surpass them all."

Charm is deceptive, and beauty is fleeting; but a woman who fears the Lord is to be praised.

Give her the reward she has earned, and let her works bring her praise at the city gate."

About the Author

Penny Harris Smith lives is the Midwest with her husband and two children. She earned a degree in Mechanical Engineering from Southern Methodist University in 1985 and completed graduate work in Business Administration at the University of North Carolina, Chapel Hill. She worked fourteen years for major corporations before putting her trust in a higher source and deciding to pursue a career in her life long passion – novels.

She and her husband own Legacy Desktop Publishing. This is their debut novel.